Running
for
Yellow

CHRISTINA VARRASSO

Cover art by Tom Wilson

Second edition edit by Kelly Dowd

Permission to use lyrics from "Home by The Sea" by Banks, Collins and Rutherford granted by Imagem Music

Permission to use SPREZZATURA by Peter D'Epiro and Mary Desmond Pinkowish granted by Random House

ISBN-10: 0615715842

EAN-13: 9780615715841

For my mother, Catherine,
and Isolina and Sunny
with all my love

Chapter 1

At night Chiara would lie awake in bed with the window open and listen to the dance, how when the breeze picked up in Papà's sunflower garden, the flowers swayed back and forth in the distance, sounding like the rustle of ball gowns. She'd listen to their leaves whispering with delight—their heads bobbing casually in repose, so sure and content with their place in the world—and long to feel once again as they seemed to feel.

Every morning she saw them reaching their heads to the sky, growing a little taller, a little more yellow, as if they held the answers to life's questions in their fertile flower heads.

Papà sowed the first sunflower garden in the spring of 1984, the year Chiara turned twelve. Looking back now, she had reason to believe it was no small coincidence the family tradition began that spring. Sometimes, the blessing is in the falling.

May 6, 1984, Chiara lay in bed waiting for Papà to wake up after a long night at work so they could plant the sunflower garden, thinking of what he had said sunflowers meant to him. "God uses patterns in sunflowers as a sign to guide his flock, *cara*," he'd said.

Papà was tall and slender, with calloused hands and green eyes that always looked a little greener on him than they would on someone else because of his dark Mediterranean skin. When he was happy, they shone like spotlights and made him look super-handsome in spite of his daily receding hairline and train-track grooves across his forehead. He said he got the worry lines from problems he faced building his restaurant chain after he moved the family to America. Once he'd made his fortune, he built Mamma's dream home with a matching stable for his horse-loving daughters on a one-hundred-acre property. He named it *Girasole* after his favorite flower, to thank God not only for everything he'd been blessed with, but for always leading him in the right direction in life. Papà never had an education; he built his businesses with hard work and a belief in the American dream. Even now, sometimes he still arrived home from one of the restaurants just as Chiara and her sisters were getting up for school. Since Chiara could remember, Papà had been drilling her and her sisters about the importance of getting an education, which would someday ensure them good jobs that offered great pay and the luxury of a good night's sleep.

God uses patterns in sunflowers as a sign to guide his flock. Papà was full of sayings and stories, especially Italian ones. You never knew which one of them was true, but there was something about his personality that always made everybody want to listen to them anyway. Mamma called it *charisma*. Chiara didn't know what the sunflower saying meant, or why he believed it; he said he'd explain today.

Chiara heard Papà knock on her sisters' bedroom doors down the hall, telling them to wake up and meet him in the kitchen. Chiara's room was in the back of the house and had a view of the stable, so she was always called last. She placed a bookmark in Jane Austen's *Sense and Sensibility*, got dressed, and followed her sisters down the spiral staircase, marveling at how wide they were. Her family had only moved into Girasole a month ago. It still smelled like cleaning products and fresh paint.

Papà was in the kitchen sipping a strong espresso and smoking a Marlboro cigarette. "*Ragazze*," he said to them. "Today, we will plant our first sunflower garden, eh?" The excitement of Christmas morning was in his voice. He was dressed in jeans and a T-shirt, which looked odd to Chiara. These days her father always wore dress pants and a dress shirt when he made his rounds to the restaurants. Even on Sundays.

Mamma strode past Papà to the refrigerator, giving him a soft side-ways look. "*Aie*, you and your sunflowers, Gian Carlo."

Mamma was beautiful. At thirty-four, she was petite, with eyes like Sophia Loren, long black hair she always kept in a neat chignon until nighttime, skin like vanilla ice cream, high cheekbones, and hopes to match. Chiara and her sisters had inherited her dark, abundant hair and cheekbones. Fortunately, they had inherited their height from Papà's side of the family.

He grabbed Mamma's hand, spun her around, and dipped her.

Mamma whooped, and Chiara and her sisters giggled.

He held her close, looking at her like she was the most spectacular woman he had ever seen. "Isabella," he said. "*Io sono il girasole, e tu il sole. Finche il girasole gira intorno al sole, Io giraró intorno a te.*"

Papà had recited the Italian poem to Mamma for the first time when he asked her to marry him. Something about him being the sunflower, and Mamma the sun, and as long as the sunflower turned to follow the sun, he would follow her. Chiara was unsure if he had made it up or read it somewhere. She'd heard him recite it at least a thousand times over the years. And not always to Mamma or Chiara and her sisters. Sometimes, Chiara thought he just recited it for the sheer sound of it rolling off his tongue. She'd gotten pretty good at tuning him out when she didn't feel like hearing it.

Mamma righted herself, straightened her coral sundress, and poured two glasses of orange juice for Chiara and her older sister, Valerie. She poured a glass of milk for Sylvia. "I keep telling you that I'm the sun-flower in the poem, Carlo," she said and smiled. "*I* followed *you* to America."

They'd met in a small Italian community in Melbourne, Australia in 1965. In those days it was common for Italians to immigrate to Australia. Her family had moved there when she was a little girl, in order to wait for green cards to move to the United States, therefore her English was excellent. Papà was already eighteen when he reluctantly left Italy after his father died. They met at the grocery store where mamma worked while she helped him find the coffee section. His English was so bad he asked her if she spoke Italian. When she said she *was* Italian, and she spoke to him *in* Italian, handing him the coffee can, Papà wanted to get to know her. It didn't take long before they fell in love. They were married within the year, and within a mere five more years they owned two restaurants in Pittsburgh and had Chiara and her sisters.

Papà took Mamma's hand. In his other hand he held a large bag of sunflower seeds. He motioned toward the kitchen door. "Ready, girls?"

They went out the kitchen door and skipped down the terrace steps. The sky was sea blue and devoid of a single cloud for miles, the grass in the backyard lush and in need of its first cut. Chiara and her sisters raced through the tall grass. Their long ponytails swayed across their backs like metronomes as they ran toward the stable to visit with their horses. Valerie led, and Chiara and Sylvia trailed behind, all three kicking up newly spread gravel with every step as they crossed the yard onto the driveway near the stable entrance. From inside the stable, Julio, the stable manager, called out, "No running in the stable!"

Papà called after them too. "*Aie!* Not yet. This way, girls."

They slowed and turned towards him, and Papà held up and shook the bag of sunflower seeds.

"We must plant the seeds first, girls," he reminded them.

Valerie's shoulders slumped; Chiara and Sylvia rolled their eyes, but the three of them shifted direction and followed Papà to the middle of a twenty-acre cleared field behind the stable.

Opening the bag, he said "What do you *t'ink*, girls, we plant them here?"

Chiara smiled to herself. Papà could never pronounce any word with the '*th*' sound, which is nonexistent in Italian, even after he took two years of English classes. Any word with a '*th*' in it always came out of his mouth sounding like a 't.'

Earlier, it had rained just enough that the tilled soil was soft and moist, perfect for planting. Chiara looked down at the soil and saw an earthworm. She had dissected one in her science class last week. It amazed her how much you could learn about life from plain old dirt.

She knelt down and rubbed a little soil between her fingers. "Papà?"

Papà had his arm around Mamma, admiring the limestone house in the distance. "*Si, cara?*"

"I learned in science class that the deeper the soil color is, the more nutrients it has in it."

"This is true, Chiara."

Papà loved that she shared his passion for science. He told her so all the time. Once Papà wanted to become a doctor, just as she knew she wanted to be someday. He loved to read as much as Chiara did. He especially liked to read about the topics he loved best: math, science, and God. He taught Chiara and her sisters that there was no line between God and science, and he somehow believed that sunflowers were the missing link between the two. He said God made them yellow because yellow is the color of intellect, and people who believed in God were *enlightened.* Chiara thought perhaps this was one of his stories too.

The other passion Chiara and Papà shared was horses. Before they moved into Girasole, Chiara would wait for him to come home from work so they could spend time together. Occasionally they watched *Bonanza* reruns. Chiara didn't particularly like westerns, but it was the only place she could see horses regularly and spend time with Papà as well. On those nights, after he helped her with her school assignments, he'd tell her stories about the horses his family owned in Italy before World War Two began. And he indulged her during those talks, promising her that when he built Girasole, he would also build a grand stable on the property and fill it with horses for her and her sisters. Preparing for that day, she perused horse books every night, studying breeds, colors, and different riding disciplines. She decided she liked dressage, a type of ballet on horseback, best. Each night she fell asleep fantasizing about riding outfits and how she would ride the most beautiful, shimmering white horse into the show ring for a win.

After she turned eleven and started noticing boys, the fantasy changed. And although the seasons in her fantasy varied from night to night, the characters and their mounts were always the same. Chiara was always a medieval princess from a long-forgotten fairy tale, dressed in a sky-blue gown with a train so long that it blanketed the horse's back, cantering Shadowfax—Gandalf's horse in *The Lord of the Rings*—through a lush wooded forest. A dark-haired prince would then appear from behind a coppice on a black stallion and chase her until he caught her. When they dismounted, he would run his strong hands through her long dark hair and kiss her a thousand times while begging her to marry him. She accepted every time. Chiara would play this fantasy over and over again in her mind until she fell asleep, smiling.

Papà winked at Chiara, squeezed Mamma a little tighter, and kissed her. Chiara loved when they looked at each other that way. Chiara wondered if she would ever be loved like that. She was still unsure if she was even pretty. Occasionally, people told her she was "such a pretty girl," but often what followed was that her nose was so Italian looking. Chiara always interpreted that to mean *big*. And it didn't help that Papà said she and her sisters had to wait to tweeze their eyebrows until they turned sixteen. This didn't pose a problem for Valerie or Sylvia, but for Chiara, it was a major issue. Her eyebrows were dark and bushy and formed a unibrow across her forehead. The boys at Saint Ursula School teased her about it ceaselessly. They'd walk by her and pretend to smack her head, telling her they were trying to kill the centipede scrambling on her forehead. She purely resented that. She had pretty brown eyes though, with long eyelashes. Mamma called them doe eyes. And she said that once Chiara was allowed to tweeze her brows boys would notice and fall head over heels for her. Until then, Chiara should ignore that Valerie and Sylvia were getting all the stares from the boys. Chiara was all right with that for now and content just reading about love in books. Where she'd left off in her novel, Willoughby and Marianne seemed to be headed for marriage. It sounded so romantic.

Papà finally released Mamma. He reached in the bag and grasped a handful of sunflower seeds as if he were handling the most valuable gold coins in the world. Then, as if he were King Midas himself, he tossed the seeds into the air, spreading their light across the field. Seeds flew everywhere, coming down on Chiara and her sisters like spring rain.

The girls tried to catch some.

Mamma laughed and slapped her hands on her sundress. "You're crazy Gian Carlo," she said.

Papà reached into the bag, pulled out another fistful of seeds, and held them on his outstretched palm. "Girls," he said, "when these flowers grow, they will be taller than Papà." He looked up at the morning sky as if beseeching the heavens for grace. "They will stretch toward the sky to God. We are planting these flowers, girls, to thank God for always being there for us, for always leading us in the right direction in *la vita.*"

Valerie and Sylvia smiled, and Chiara nodded, even though she had no idea what he meant by this.

"Now, let us plant our first garden, eh? This year it will be small."
He held up his pointing finger as he always did when he wanted to
stress a point. "But next year it will be *enorme, un paradiso* of sunflowers." He pointed toward the back of the house, white and imposing in
the distance. "There, I will plant another garden, reminiscent of the
one I had in *Italia* when I was a little boy, with fountains and statues of
Romani—"

Mamma gave him an annoyed look. "Get on with it, Carlo."

"*Va bene.*" He dropped a pile of seeds for Chiara and her sisters.
They knelt down on the ground and began poking holes in the dirt with
their fingers, dropping three seeds at a time in each one. Sylvia seemed
more interested in soiling her jeans and hands than planting. When
Valerie wasn't looking, Sylvia grabbed a big mud ball and threw it at
her. Sylvia had a strong arm and the mud splattered hard right between
Valerie's eyes.

Valerie wiped the mud off her face with long deliberate strokes,
wincing at Sylvia as if she wanted to kill her. "You little shrimp," she
said.

And just like that, Valerie and Sylvia were pelting mud balls at
each other, soiling their clothes and faces, slapping mud in each other's
hair. Chiara got in on the action too, throwing mud at both of them.
Mamma and Papà laughed and laughed, but before any of them were
allowed back in the house, they would have to wash off with a hose in
the driveway.

When they got back to planting, Chiara stopped to crack open a
seed. She examined the shell for a moment before she popped the seed
into her mouth. Papà knelt down beside her.

"Has Father Bob taught you about the Fibonacci numbers yet, *cara?*"

Father Bob was Chiara's favorite middle school teacher. In fact,
everybody loved Father Bob at Saint Ursula's. The teachers liked him
because he was funny. Chiara and her classmates liked him because he
made science and math class fun. He always offered her extra help after
school since she struggled with reading. Sometimes she truly wished the
alphabet was devoid of Ms and Ws, Ds and Bs—and Ps, too.

"Not yet, Papà," Chiara said.

"Perhaps you will next year, in the eighth grade, when you begin to
learn a little about geometry."

Chiara gave him a curious look. "What are they, Papà?"

Papà cracked open a seed and held it out for her to study. "Sunflower seeds, *cara*, are created in a circle of cells in the center of *il girasole*. As they grow, the circle expands outward into a concentric circle to make the most efficient use of space on the flower head. This expanding pattern follows a mathematical equation called the Fibonacci sequence. It creates the rotation and angle in the flower head that approaches a very important ratio called the *divina proporzione*, the golden ratio."

"I learned ratios last year and Father Bob didn't say anything about the Fibonacci numbers or the golden ratio," Chiara said.

Valerie, fifteen now, looked over from her little plot of earth. "I learned about the golden ratio this year in art history, Papà." She stopped poking holes. "It's the number of balance. The geometry of the ratio was used to build the ancient pyramids and the Parthenon. Famous Renaissance artists used it to make their subjects proportional and more pleasing to the eye." She gave Papà a surprised look. "I didn't know it was in flowers too."

Papà gave Valerie an approving nod. "Very good, Valerie," he said. "Answer me this, girls. If the angle of the circle of cells did not rotate, you would end up with a straight line of seeds, and that would be what for the *girasole*?"

Chiara smiled as she mocked his Italian accent. "*T* least efficient use of space."

Papà laughed. "Exactly. You see, girls, the ratio 1.61803398875 is miraculously present in many things in the world, animate and inanimate, as a sign that God is with us."

Chiara was sincerely impressed that he knew such a long string of numbers by heart. "Really Papà? Where else can you see the numbers?"

Papà smiled at her. "You can see them everywhere, *cara*. In other flowers, pinecones, the horns of certain goats, snail shells. But it is only the yellow *girasole* that grows seven feet tall and turns to face God at the first sign of day."

"Like they're acting as examples for us to follow?" Valerie asked.

Papà smiled widely, proud of Valerie. "Exactly."

"Ah," Chiara said. "So that's what you mean when you say God uses sunflowers as a sign to guide his flock."

"Yes. And did you know, *ragazze,* that the Fibonacci numbers were named after Leonardo Fibonacci, the most talented mathematician of the middle ages, who was also—"

Chiara giggled. "Let me guess, *un italiano?*" she teased. Papà was proud to be an American citizen. Still, he was a little prouder to be Italian.

Papà opened his arms and shrugged his shoulders as if it were a given. "Of course." Then, he smiled. "Papà will teach you the equation when we go inside. Quick, let us plant."

Chiara cracked open another seed and popped it in her mouth. "Papà, do you really think I'll be able to become a doctor with..." She looked down at her pile of seeds on the ground. "You know, my problem?"

Papà pinched her cheek a little too hard, and Chiara winced.

"Do you know who else had dyslexia, *tesoro?*"

"Who Papà?"

One of the greatest, most *intelligente* men that ever lived. And guess what else?"

She shook her head at him. "He was Italian, right?"

Papà let out a boisterous laugh. "Exactly. Leonardo da Vinci. The greatest *architetto* of the Renaissance Period, *il pittore* of La Mona Lisa, sculptor—"

Chiara tipped her head at him, giving him a look like she had heard enough about Italians. "I got it, Papà."

"If you want to become a doctor, you have to be tough, aggressive, persistent, work hard like Papà, and not let anything get in your way of reaching your goals." Papà dropped a few seeds into a hole. "I painted your rooms yellow," he said to Chiara and her sisters, "because it will help you study. It is the color of *intelligenza,* girls, of mental stimulation and higher understanding."

"And unfortunately, it's the color of almost every room in the new house, thanks to Papà and the painter's little secret," Mamma said and everybody laughed. Mamma grabbed another pile of seeds from the bag and dropped them on the ground for her and Sylvia to plant. "If I weren't a practicing Catholic, I'd swear you were a *cantastoria* in a previous life, Carlo," she said.

Sylvia looked at Mamma. Her face was still covered in mud. "What's a *cantastoria* Mamma?"

"A sort of wandering Italian minstrel in really old times, *cara,*" Mamma told her.

Papà grabbed another handful of seeds and dropped a few into a hole. "*Forza, cara,*" he told Chiara. If you want to become *una dottoressa* someday, you have to have faith in yourself."

Papà turned to Chiara's sisters. "*Ragazze,* are you listening?"

"Yes, Papà," Valerie said. "You tell us all the time."

"I love you, Papà," Chiara said.

Papà tapped his hand over his heart and winked at her again. "I love you too, *cara.*"

Mamma rewrapped Sylvia's ponytail which had headed east of her head during the mud fight, while Papà sat back on his heels and motioned for everyone to gather around him. He grew serious, and Chiara knew he was about to say something important.

"Girls," he said. "Mamma and Papà work very hard for you. You wanted horses and a stable, and I promised you one day I would get them for you. He motioned with his head toward the stable. "There they stand." He looked at the three of them, expecting their undivided attention. "Now you girls must promise *me* something."

They nodded as if nothing was too much to ask.

"You must promise me, girls, that no matter what, you will finish *universitá.* I want each one of you to have an active *professione* when you grow up."

Chiara and her sisters kept nodding like little wind-up toys. Chiara could tell Mamma was fighting the urge to laugh.

"I do not ever want you girls to struggle like Mamma and Papà have," he said. "Yes, things have turned out well, but I do not want you girls working in *i ristoranti,* as Mamma and Papà do, for the rest of your lives. I want you to have professional careers." He grew stern. "Promise me you will."

"I promise," Sylvia said.

"I promise, Papà," Valerie said.

Chiara wanted to be a doctor more than anything. Papà knew that, but she promised again anyway.

"Promise me you will not let anything get in the way of this. No laziness in your studies; your studies must come first…" he said, holding up his finger.

They nodded respectfully.

"Your homework must come before *everything*," he insisted.

That was easy for Chiara.

"You must keep away from classmates who are trouble, spend time only with good people."

"We will," Valerie said.

"Someday, you girls will want to date boys," he continued. "You, sooner than your sisters, Valerie," Papà said.

I don't know about that, Chiara thought.

"I know that, and it is fine," Papà said. "But you must promise me you will not marry until you are graduated in your professions."

Valerie and Sylvia agreed.

Chiara stopped nodding and furrowed her bushy eyebrows. "Why Papà? What's wrong with getting married?"

"Nothing is wrong with getting married, *cara*. But marriage can cause many distractions when you are in school. If you want to become *una dottoressa*—" He focused his gaze on Chiara, then on her sisters, "— and you girls want to become whatever you decide to become, then we must avoid what, girls?"

"Distractions," they repeated like little soldiers.

Papà smiled. "Exactly," he said. "So, promise me."

Valerie and Sylvia promised.

Chiara sat weighing the proposition, thinking how beautiful things were between Mamma and Papà, between Willoughby and Marianne so far, knowing there had to be people in medical school who were married. Papà always told her she was *la romantica* of his three girls, and that in English and *italiano*, this spelled trouble.

"Promise me, Chiara," he repeated.

She hesitated a moment, thinking about her studies, her prince charming whom she hadn't met yet, and her new horse in the stable she had dreamed about since she was five. "I promise, Papà."

That September after Chiara had spent the summer watching the sunflower garden spread across the field and looking for some sort of sign from God, the only thing she found was that God was a hoax. It was a Friday afternoon. She'd gone to Father Bob's classroom after school to get some help with her science homework. Father Bob, as usual, was sitting behind his desk, dressed in his black clerical clothes, grading papers. When he saw Chiara, he put his pen down and drew a pretend heart over his heart with his finger.

"Hi, Chiara, you need some help?"

Chiara nodded, placed her notebook on his desk and rolled her eyes at him, embarrassed. He was young for a priest, and it always made her feel a little funny when he did that. But she knew she was his favorite student. She'd been getting the highest marks in his classes for the past two years.

"Come on," he said, motioning her to take a seat behind his desk.

She sat down, straightening her uniform skirt over her thighs. She liked to sit behind his desk. Chiara smiled to herself, thinking someday she would have her own office desk with a name tag on it. *Chiara Lazzaro, MD.*

"What's giving you trouble?" he said.

"The double helix."

He turned toward the chalkboard and drew the helix faster than she could have even spelled the word. Seeing the helix rise up the chalkboard so fast was enough to make anyone dizzy. Chiara noticed Father Bob had a lot of chalk on his pants. She figured he must have drawn the helix a lot that day.

"The double helix," he said, turning back to her. "To understand it, Chiara, you have to understand the purpose it serves."

He knelt down beside her chair and reached for her notebook. Even on his knees he was tall. Chiara noticed sweat sweeping though his shirt, forming little dots around his shirt sleeve.

"Deoxyribonucleic acid is a nucleic acid containing the genetic instructions used in the development and functioning of all living organisms," he said. "The DNA segments containing the genetic information are called genes."

She listened intently, hoping to go home and share something about biology with Papà that he might not already know. Father Bob leaned in closer to her, and when she felt like she was breathing his air, she scooted her chair over a bit, getting some space between them.

"I understand that part, Father," she said. "I just can't seem to understand the role of the letters A, G, T, and C when I'm drawing the helix."

He adjusted his clerical collar. "Nucleobases provide the skeleton for the complementary DNA strands, Chiara. Take your time when you read the complementing letters to place them where they're supposed to go, right side up. You draw one."

She did, and he said it was correct.

"I get it," she said. "They're the bones in the whole operation."

"That's right."

"Thank you, Father."

He winked at her. "No problem."

She closed her notebook, got up to leave.

He stood up. "Chiara, would you mind helping me hang the amoeba pictures for the contest on Monday?"

She looked at her watch. "Sure, Father, I have time."

Father Bob grabbed a handful of drawings from his desk and numbered them with a marker. He handed Chiara half of them with some tape.

"We'll be able to keep them all together if we hang them along the window side of the room," he said.

Chiara went to the first of a long row of windows and began taping the drawings to the window, taking in the turning colors of leaves in the woods outside. She heard the classroom door close softly over the carpet with a *click*. Father Bob came to stand behind her. He taped a picture above the ones she was taping. Chiara felt a wave of uneasiness rise and fall inside her, and she stepped aside, away from him. When she went to tape the next picture, there he was again, standing right behind her, taping a picture above the one she was taping. She stepped away again, more deliberate. When she did, he turned around and sat on the window sill beside her, watching her hang a few more pictures, stroking his mustache as if he was contemplating something important.

After what felt like forever, he said, "Chiara, if I tell you something, would you promise to keep it a secret?"

Chiara looked at him, wondering what on earth he wanted to confide in her about. "Of course, Father."

He looked her over once, and his expression changed. She'd never seen him look at her that way. She'd never seen anybody look at her that way.

"Now, you know it would be a sin if you broke your promise, don't you?"

"I know, Father."

"He took her hand and pulled her towards him. "Chiara, I have very special feelings for you," he said, his eyes on her budding breasts.

In an instant, a chill ran through her entire body and she shivered. She pulled away but he pulled her back so that she was standing between his thighs, face to face. Confused, she pushed him away, but he pulled her back, wrapping his arm around her like she was a little rag doll he could flop this way and that.

"Father Bob, don't. You're scaring me."

"Don't fight, Chiara," he said as if she were overreacting. "There's nothing to be afraid of."

"Let me go," she said, trying to break free of his hold, wanting to run for the door.

He twirled her around and sandwiched her between him and an old iron radiator beneath the window sill.

"Father Bob—"

He covered her mouth with his hand. "Shhh," he said.

"I've helped you, Chiara," he said. "Now you have to help me. You have to keep our secret. If you don't, I won't help you with your homework anymore."

He grabbed her wrists and wrapped her arms across her chest, pressing his body against hers, his mouth against her cheek. His black mustache felt like tiny burrs scratching her face, embedding themselves in her skin.

She thrashed, trying to break free, but he was too strong. "Father Bob! No! What are you doing?"

"Shhh, shhh," he whispered. The warmth of his breath filled her ear and his tongue softly licked its folds. He kissed her cheek, her neck. "Relax, Chiara. Father Bob says this is okay. It's okay for people to touch when they are fond of each other."

Her heart raced. "No, Father Bob! Stop it! I'm not fond of you anymore."

"Chiara," he whispered. He bent her over and pressed her body into his. "Oh, Chiara, sweet, sweet Chiara. It's all right. Relax, my—"

"Father Bob, you're hurting me," she cried. Exhausted, she stopped struggling.

"There there, now," he said in a soothing voice, releasing her arms, but not her body. "That's a good girl."

He lowered his hands toward the radiator and lifted her uniform skirt, stroking the insides of her thighs, between them and over her white panties. Next thing she knew, her panties were down and his maleness was sliding between her legs. Panic soared from her voice and she shrieked.

"No!" The piercing sound caught him off guard and his hold on her softened. She turned around, kneed him between the legs with all her strength, and bolted for the door.

"Chiara, stop," he shouted. But she was already out the door, running down an empty hall toward the illuminated exit sign. She never saw Father Bob again after the incident. Still, every time she saw a man in a cassock from that day forward, she saw him.

On Sunday morning when Mamma came into her room and asked her if she was ready to go to church, Chiara told her she had a stomach ache. When she didn't want to go to school the next day, Papà and Mamma came home early from the restaurant and made her tell them why.

Later that night, Papà came home with swollen and bloody fists. Chiara was sitting at the kitchen table, doing homework. When she asked him what happened, he said he'd hurt them repairing one of the commercial mixers.

That was a lie. Papà didn't repair the mixers anymore.

Mamma grabbed ice from the refrigerator and made a cold compress at the kitchen island. She placed it on one of his hands, but he pulled away.

"Gian Carlo, please."

Papà punched the countertop so hard the crystal fruit bowl vibrated and sent a tiny clinking sound across the room.

Chiara sat there with her eyes on her books, self-conscious and ashamed. Mamma reached for him "Carlo, that's enough, *amore*."

Avoiding her glance, he nodded, reaching into his pocket for a pack of cigarettes. After he lit one, he went and sat down next to Chiara. Mamma poured him a cup of espresso and sat down next to Chiara too.

"Chiara, everything is going to be fine, *cara*," he said as if it were a sure thing. "Father Bob is in a lot of trouble."

Chiara was already in tears. "I don't want anybody to find out. It's embarrassing. Please, just leave it alone."

"No," Papà said.

Chiara couldn't stop folding and unfolding her hands at the table. It was as if they had a mind of their own. "Everybody at school loves Father Bob. They're going to think I made it up."

"No, Chiara. That's not true," Mamma said, squeezing Chiara's hand.

Papà's hand was shaking, and he set his cigarette in the ashtray. He cleared his throat, thick with rage.

"Chiara," he said. "Do you know the story of Saint Maria Goretti?"

Papà was able to finish few prayers in church, but if you asked him to name an Italian saint, he could rattle off a hundred of them in alphabetical order.

"Papà, I don't want to hear any stories right now."

"Listen to Papà," he said.

He took a pensive sip of his coffee. "Maria Goretti was a little girl whose family became so poor that by the time she was six, they were forced to give up her beloved family farm and work for other farmers. They moved into another small *casa* they had to share with another *famiglia* which included Giovanni Serenelli and his son, Alessandro."

Papà picked up his cigarette and took a drag. He blew the smoke away from Mamma and Chiara. He seemed a bit calmer now.

"By the time Maria was nine, her Papà died," he said. "Her *famiglia* was close, like ours, and so while her brother and sisters worked in the fields, Maria helped by staying at home to cook and clean *la casa*."

He looked at Chiara like he wanted to see if she was paying attention. Chiara nodded. She couldn't imagine losing Girasole and Shadowfax.

"*Un giorno*," Papà said, "Alessandro, then eighteen, intending to rape her…" Papà paused and flinched, obviously uncomfortable using the word in front of Chiara. He cleared his throat again. "Alessandro came in and threatened to kill her if she did not do as he said. But Maria…" Papà said, raising his voice as loud as a preacher praising the word of God from the pulpit. "Maria would not submit. She screamed over and over again, 'It is a sin. God does not want it.' When she insisted she would rather die than to submit to him, he stabbed her fourteen times."

Chiara winced.

Papà held up his pointing finger again. "Maria was so tough, *cara*, so strong, that not only did she not submit to Alessandro, but, on her deathbed, she forgave him."

Chiara's eyes widened. "She forgave him? How could she do that?"

"Chiara, I do not know," he said with a soothing tone. "That is why she is a saint. The point Papà is trying to make is this: You were tough, like Maria. You must continue to be tough. You must not allow this incident to scar you. You did nothing wrong."

"Not one thing," Mamma said squeezing Chiara's hand again.

"*Forza, cara.* Be strong. I did not raise you to break. You must stay focused. No skipping school. Remember, you made me a promise, eh?"

Chiara nodded. "All right, Papà."

On the following cool Sunday afternoon, when Chiara went for a trail ride through Girasole with Valerie, Papà and Julio, they rode past the edge of the sunflower garden that gave way to the woods. The sunflowers were seven feet tall now. Shadowfax reached his head into the leafy abyss and pulled out a mouthful of leaves. When he did this, a few sunflower heads bobbed and smiled at Chiara as if they were her best friends. She didn't smile back. There was no God working through them. There was no God at all. God would've helped little Maria. God would've helped her.

Chapter 2

September 1995

Chiara roosted behind her turn-of-the-century writing desk gazing through a floor-to-ceiling window at her stable. It was situated behind Papà's Renaissance-inspired garden on the far side of the property. A medical text, *Human Anatomy: A Clinically-Oriented Approach*, lay open in front of her.

She read a few more pages of the text, stopping every now and then to look at her horses in the field. She hadn't been outside all day, but she could tell that the late Thursday afternoon was cool and breezy by the weathervane above the stable cupola, a copper stallion that had oxidized over the years to a Statue-of-Liberty green, swinging left and right.

She smelled the subtle aroma of sautéing olive oil, garlic, oregano, and sweet onions rising up to the second floor, letting her know Mamma was home from Papà's newest addition to his restaurant chain. He was so proud of this one that he named it after himself. Gian Carlo's.

Chiara's stomach rumbled, reminding her she hadn't eaten all day. She placed a bookmark in the text and closed it, planning on getting right back to her studies after she ate. She wished she could be outside riding one of her horses with the love of her life, Adrian, instead of spending the day locked away like Rapunzel, studying anatomy. But there would be a lot of time for that after she was graduated from medical school.

She looked around the peach-colored room that had once been yellow. In fact, most of the rooms at Girasole were still painted various shades of yellow: saffron, jasmine, ivory yellow, pale yellow, lemon yellow, and sunflower yellow. A massive antique four-poster bed was situated in the center of the room. Striped silk draperies trickled down from it like a gentle stream onto the dark walnut floors. On the far end of the capacious room, a white-painted fireplace she never used was sandwiched between floor-to-ceiling bookshelves filled with *Vogue* and *Town & Country* magazines, science texts, her favorite classic and romance novels, and photos of her family and horses.

When she was a teenager, it had been so easy to promise Papà that she would not get married until she was graduated from medical school. She had loved to please him and Mamma. But that was long before she met Adrian—dark-haired, sapphire-blue-eyed, six-foot-one pitcher for the Pittsburgh Pirates. Adrian. There was nothing she looked forward to more after her long day of classes and studying than an hour with him, when her heart throbbed and her breath was heavy and she was full of life and carefree. And he wanted to marry her. Chiara had no idea why. He could have anyone he wanted.

Papà didn't like him; he would like him less when he heard the news. Chiara was sure Papà was afraid that Adrian would get in the way of medical school. But Adrian would never do that; he wanted her to graduate. Besides, he made her happy; he made her feel like the twenty-three-year-old adult she was, as if she knew what she was doing with her life.

She had decided months ago not to sacrifice her newfound happiness with Adrian, no matter what Papà's well-intentioned dogma for her life was. He had outlined her entire life schemata on paper before she hit puberty. Life called for erasers.

After "the incident," as everyone in the family referred to it, Papà was different, more serious. And he watched over Chiara and her sisters like a guard dog, controlling where they could go and what they could do. Chiara knew he was afraid of anything ever happening to her or her sisters again, guilty he'd failed to see Father Bob as the predator he was. Chiara tried to ease Papà's regret by doing things she thought would please him. She attended a prestigious private college-prep school for girls even though she wanted to go to the local public high school. She audited endless summer science and math classes at the local community college so she would be ahead of her classmates the following year when all she really wanted to do was ride Shadowfax and enjoy her summer vacation. Along with her sisters, Chiara took piano and violin lessons she never wanted to take because Papà thought understanding music was important for a cultured young lady; her teachers were always frustrated with her because she never practiced.

And of course there were the annual sunflower-planting parties at Girasole for a sunflower garden she didn't want to sow anymore because she had traded in her faith in the Creator and the Bible for more concrete things like Darwin's *On the Origin of Species*. Aside from riding her horses, studying math and science was where she found peace now.

But Chiara did it all; she always hoped that if she did, Papà would eventually allow her the freedom to do things she was interested in too, like sleepovers with her friends, proms, high school football games at the local high school, and concerts. Occasionally he did, but it was rare. Mamma argued with him all the time. "Give them a little freedom," she'd say. "You're being too strict with them." But he had never led the family wrong, so she usually gave in to him. And so, aside from endless summer horse shows, there had been very few liberties—for Chiara and Valerie, anyway. Sylvia was an amazing athlete and Papà treated her like the son he never had. She got away with so much more. Chiara thoroughly resented that.

Still, when Papà grew unbearable, instead of fighting with him, she did things to annoy him. In her college years she found that flirting with men he didn't approve of was particularly effective. So, on Saturday afternoons after she was done riding, Chiara and some of her rider friends would go to JR's Pub, a local watering hole for construction workers and landscapers trying to escape a long week of the elements. Bethany liked to walk in ahead of Chiara wearing snug blouses to show off her size D-cup breasts. It was never long before men were offering to buy them a drink, one eye on their faces and the other scanning their fitted riding breeches and breasts. Chiara always got such satisfaction walking in for a Coke, knowing that if Papà found her there his rage would send him into a frenzy. She only occasionally accepted a date and even more rarely made it to her date's car, since Papà would usually be waiting in the foyer at Girasole to stop her from leaving. But she always headed back up to her room struggling not to laugh.

Sometimes she thought it would've been better for her if she'd gone away to medical school, but she could never leave Adrian or the horses. She felt a pang of sadness, knowing how upset Papà would be at her announcement. She pushed away from the desk. In her walk-in closet, she slipped out of her sweatpants and into a pair of slim-fitting jeans and a pale pink rugby shirt that was hanging with all her other barn shirts. *I'll just run down to the kitchen, eat something, and check on the horses*, she thought. *Then I'll come back and hit the books again.*

She quickly ran a soft-bristle brush through her waist-long hair at the dresser, examining her eyebrows. She'd have to tweeze them later. It had become a weekly ritual since she was a teenager.

She ran her hand over a picture of Adrian in his Pittsburgh Pirate uniform on the dresser, and her heart thumped against her ribs. Even though she had just talked to him a few hours ago, she called him again. He picked up on the first ring.

"Hi, *amor*," he said. "I was hoping it was you."

Chiara sighed. *Amor. Amor, amor, amor.* She loved when he called her that. Adrian was half Mexican and often used Spanish endearments. "I'm going to study all night, so I can go to the game tomorrow night," she told him.

"Can you come over here for a bit?" he asked.

"No, because then I won't leave. And I have to study. You should *not* have gotten an apartment so close to my house. It's so tempting to run over there any chance I get."

"I don't ever want to be far away from you, Chiara," he said.

"Me, neither," she said.

"Are you gonna talk to your dad tonight about us getting married?"

Chiara let out a nervous sigh. "Yes, yes I am."

"It's gonna be okay, Chiara."

"I know." A wave of anxiety rose from the pit of her stomach, and she changed the subject. "Who's pitching tonight?"

"Wilson."

"I'll watch the game on TV while I'm studying. Sit near the cameras so I can see you."

Adrian laughed. "You're silly, Chiara."

"Silly in love," she said. "I'll call you tonight after I talk to Papà."

Just as they hung up, there was a quick knock on her bedroom door and Sylvia, now a whole head taller than Chiara, breezed into the bedroom. She was slim and beautiful in her jeans and black T-shirt and walked with a long athletic stride.

"Hey, I have to go to the mall to buy a new pair of running shoes. Do you want to go with me?"

"I can't. I have to study."

"Did you tell Papà your news yet?"

Chiara looked away. "Not yet."

Sylvia sat down at Chiara's desk and pushed her long ebony hair behind her ears. "Chiara...you said you were going to last night."

"I haven't had a chance. We keep missing each other with our schedules."

"You're avoiding him."

"Sylvia, I'm telling him tonight. You haven't come clean with Mamma about your little secret yet, either."

"I did with Papà. And I'm surprised how well he took it, actually. Ma would have a heart attack if I told her I'm questioning my sexual orientation." She flipped through one of Chiara's medical texts. "Besides, I think she has her suspicions. She keeps asking me why I'm not dating anymore." She looked at Chiara. "Anyway, everybody except Papà knows your secret."

"Sylv, I've wanted to tell him for a while, but I know he's going to take it badly. He's been telling me for years not get serious with anybody until I finish *scuola di medicina*."

"The bottom line is everyone at Gian Carlo's knows you guys are talking marriage. It's only a matter of time before somebody slips. Papà is going to be so pissed if he hears it from someone else."

Chiara inhaled deeply. "I know. I'm definitely doing it tonight. I promise."

Sylvia leaned back against the bed. "Look, Chiara. I know Papà has been harder on you and Valerie than me. A lot harder. He wants you to become the doctor he wanted to be. But just finish school and he'll back off. He did with Valerie."

"I know that, Sylv. Believe it or not, I want my degree more than he does. I've been working toward it my whole life; I don't want to spend the rest of my life hostessing at the restaurant. I want to do something that makes a difference."

"Then why not wait?"

"The Pirates are talking about trading him to another team." She lowered her head. "And I don't want to lose him. I love him. He makes me feel good about myself. So if he wants to get married sooner than later, I'm okay with that. I'll still make Papà proud."

Chiara pulled her hair back into a ponytail, thinking how radically her life had changed since she met Adrian. To her it was as epic as the start of Christianity. Not that she was trying to compare her relationship with Adrian or anything about her small existence with Jesus and the magnitude of Christianity; she had lost faith in God a long time ago. But in terms of life occurrences, it seemed as if Adrian came as a savior to rescue her from her mundane, controlled life. Before Adrian—or BA, as she sometimes joked with her sisters—her life had consisted of boring biochemistry and calculus homework and exams, an occasional movie with her sisters or friends, or a rare but boring date with guys she met while working as a hostess at Gian Carlo's. That summed it up. Adrian was exciting, spontaneous. She could never afford the luxury of spontaneity with her commitment to her studies, and she was okay with that. But she loved seeing it in Adrian, and she could never get enough of him. As sure as the atomic number of iron was twenty-six, Chiara believed that a life with Adrian would bring her something that had been taken away from her long ago.

Sylvia shook her head. "You're a hopeless romantic, Chiara. I don't think I ever want to fall in love if it makes me as sappy as you are over Adrian."

"When you do, at least your education won't pose a problem. You have your degree."

"True, but I'll have very different problems with Mamma." Sylvia hopped onto Chiara's bed, patting the cotton duvet embroidered with butterflies, inviting Chiara to hop up, too. "Hang out a bit."

Chiara climbed onto the bed and, one by one, unfastened the draperies that were tied with silk ties to the bed posts; each drape swooped to the floor like a closing curtain at the end of a musical performance, enveloping them in a colorful cocoon. Before she met Adrian, she had always felt protected from all her troubles when she drew them closed. Lately, she felt more like a caged bird, and Papà was the bird keeper who controlled the cage doors; only he could allow her to step out and stretch her wings.

Chiara looked reminiscent. "Remember when we were kids and I would pull the drapes closed just like this and the three of us would stay up all night talking?" She leaned back against a billowy mound of pillows.

"Yeah," Sylvia said. She drew a pack of cigarettes out of her back pocket and tossed them on to the nightstand before she lay back, too. "All Valerie wanted to talk about was how she was going to marry Jon Bon Jovi as soon as she got out of law school. And God forbid we told her he wasn't going to wait for her, she'd tickle us until we almost peed our pants."

Chiara laughed. "All I wanted to do was show Shadowfax and become the youngest Grand Prix dressage rider to ever go to the Olympics before I went off to medical school. Boy, was I delusional."

Sylvia smiled, and a faint thin scar on her face, earned in a motocross competition, disappeared into her laugh line. "No, just naïve and maybe overly optimistic."

"*You* should've gone to New York when that big modeling agency came to town and wanted to sign you. They loved your exotic look. You could be living in New York or LA right now."

"I like what I do. Think of all the accounting fees I save Mamma and Papà every year. Any other firm would charge them three times what I charge them."

Sylvia unlaced her boots, parted the drapes, and dropped them at the foot of the bed. "Besides, I could never model. It's stupid. You strut down a runway half-naked trying to look sexy while hundreds of tawdry men stare at your tits, legs, and ass, wishing they were having sex with you. No thanks. I'm doing just fine with my little accounting firm."

She flipped over onto her side to face Chiara, her wide, angular face showing a hint of sympathy. "Is med school really hard?"

"Yes," Chiara said without hesitation. "I'm only a few weeks in, Sylv, and I'm already stressing. I think my human genetics class is going to be tough. It's really interesting though. I always think about Valerie when I'm studying it, looking for possible explanations for her infertility, things I can relay back to her."

"That's cool that you're so into it." She paused. "What do you think you would've done for a career if you hadn't been accepted?"

"Oh, I don't know," she said, staring up at the ceiling. "All I know is that I've always wanted to help people. Medicine felt right. Maybe I would've pursued the arts." A soft veil of contentment descended over her face. "Not acting or anything—I never liked being center of attention. And I was never particularly good at drawing, either. Maybe I would've become an English professor, teaching kids literature, instead of working to deliver them." There was a nostalgic tone in her voice. She flipped onto her tummy and perched on her elbows. "When my ninth-grade teacher instructed my class to read *Jane Eyre*, and I learned about symbolism, irony, theme, artistic unity, and epiphanies, I thought I'd died and gone to heaven, really. I never knew a story could contain so much stuff. By the time we finished studying that book, I wanted to read every classic that was ever written."

"I think you have by now. You're so brainy," Sylvia said.

"No, I'm not Sylv. My classmates absorb all the material so much faster than I do."

Sylvia squeezed Chiara's arm and smiled. "You are, Chiara. Belmont was a great college prep school. I liked it there. I'm glad Papà sent us there after he pulled us out of Saint Ursula's."

"I am too, now." Chiara picked at was left of her nail polish. "I thoroughly hated Saint Ursula's and all their religious self-righteous bull. Some of the teachers and students looked at me as if what happened was my fault. As if I had lied. As if I had come on to *him*."

"I remember."

Chiara smiled with satisfaction. "I wonder what wicked Sister Agnes would say if she knew that I'm on the pill, and you're gay. Valerie told me she found out about her in vitro fertilization treatments and was aghast."

"Frankly, I don't care. I never let them get under my skin or into my head the way you did. They're not God."

"I know," Chiara said. *Is anyone?*

Sylvia shook her head. "Mamma said she and Valerie get disapproving looks from the clergy every time they go to mass now. I wonder who told them about Valerie." A rueful expression spread across Sylvia's face. "I wonder sometimes how Mamma and Papà can still go to that church after," her expression softened, "you know."

"He was transferred to another parish. I guess that was enough for them. At least they never asked me to go back. They knew I never would. I think what I grew to love most about the Belmont School for Girls was that there was no religion practiced there. No priests, no nuns."

"If you get married, won't you have to do it in a church?"

"I would to keep Mamma and Papà happy. It would be a small sacrifice in exchange for Adrian."

"If you really wanted to keep them happy, you'd wait, Chiara."

Chiara rubbed her eyes, her forehead. "Everybody except Adrian," she said. "I can graduate and be married, Sylvia. Lots of people get married in medical school and graduate. Papà knows that. I can do it too. I'll prove it to him."

"I know you can do it, Chiara. But he's always been so adamant about us waiting."

"I don't think Adrian will wait for me if I don't."

"Did he say that?"

"Not exactly, but I can't see how it would work if he were living in one city and me in another for another three years."

Sylvia shook her head, drew back the bed curtains and turned on the TV in the far corner of the room. On the five o'clock news, a sketch of O. J. Simpson at his trial filled the screen.

"Papà is going to want to kill Adrian. I hope you know what you're doing, Chiara." She pointed at the TV. "Or we're going to end up watching our family saga unfurl on national TV like Mr. Hertz Rental Car over there."

Valerie's voice burst up from the foyer below, shouting for Chiara. Chiara jumped out of bed and ran to the staircase landing. "What? What happened?"

Sylvia followed close behind, carrying her boots.

"It's Hemingway," Valerie shouted. She was already starting back toward the front door.

Chiara and Sylvia shot down the staircase, taking two steps at a time, and bolted toward the stable with Valerie. "Liam and I went down to ride da Vinci and Shadowfax," Valerie explained, catching her breath as they cut through the garden. "When we got there, Hemi was down in his stall groaning."

"Where's Julio?" Chiara said, surprised he hadn't noticed it. He lived in an apartment above the stable with his wife Bibi. They'd trained Chiara in dressage for years and never missed a thing when it came to the horses.

"He's there now," Valerie said. "He was schooling my horse in the outdoor ring when we came in. It must've come on all of a sudden."

When they got to the stable, Valerie's husband, Liam, was hand-walking Hemingway just outside the stable doors. Julio, a tall, dark-haired man, stood in the aisle with a phone tucked between his shoulder and ear. He covered the receiver. "Veterinarian," he said and motioned for the girls to calm down. He handed Chiara a bottle of Jack Daniels whiskey to give to the gelding. Chiara knew then: Hemingway had colic.

She grabbed a large syringe from the tack room, poured some whiskey into it, taking in the alcohol's pungent odor. She wondered how Adrian could drink it straight up. Then she walked over to Hemingway and placed the syringe in the corner of his mouth, administering the whiskey. Normally high-spirited, Hemingway was too sick to protest. She ran her hand tenderly through his abundant black mane, wanting him to know she was going to make everything all right. The early evening sun cast Hemi's massive shadow against the stable doors, and his black coat shimmered midnight blue. His eyes looked weary as she petted him, reassured him. The colic was her fault. Between studying, helping at the restaurant on the weekends and finding time to be with Adrian, she had not been riding him every day as she usually did.

"He's going to be fine, Chiara," Julio said. "But the vet will be here in an hour to double-check on him."

Chiara avoided Julio's gaze. She kept stroking Hemingway's mane.

"Are you sure, Julio?" Valerie said. She fidgeted with a chunky gold bracelet that looked like a small dog collar. "What about the show next month? You two have been working toward that test all summer."

Liam looked at Valerie, his eyes calm and sure. "Relax, honey. If Julio thinks he's going to be okay, he's going to be okay." Liam never seemed to get upset over anything, in spite of his stressful career as a litigation attorney. Chiara liked that about him.

Julio waved, dismissing her concern. "Yes, yes, Valerie. Hemingway will be fine. But Chiara, you have to get focused again."

Chiara knew that, but she didn't say anything.

"You have a competition next month. You know horses need a routine, especially that hothead."

"I know. My mind has been on my classes."

"And on wanting to get married," Valerie quipped.

Chiara looked away from her too.

Sylvia sighed. "Hemi is going to be fine. It's over."

"Enough," Julio said. "This has been a lesson."

Late that night, after she had memorized everything she could possibly absorb about the integumental system, Chiara went down to the stable, wanting to keep an eye on Hemingway herself in case he got sick again. Not bothering to turn on any lights, she took an old fleece blanket and a folding green chaise out of the tack room and carried them down the long bricked aisle to Hemingway's stall. It had grown cool for a September night. A nippy breeze blew through the aisle and the horses' half-open Dutch doors, reminding Chiara that meteorologists were forecasting a bitterly cold winter. For now, though, it was a bright early-autumn night. The full moon stood guard like a sprite outside Hemingway's stall door, casting brilliant lunar rays through the stable. The scene and the smell of the horses, musty and warm, filled Chiara with serenity, trumping her angst about her impending conversation with Papà.

She stepped into Hemingway's stall and gave him a pat. "If you need me, buddy, I'll be right here." She wrapped both her arms around his blue-black crested neck, taking in his freshly shampooed scent. Hemingway nudged her and nickered softly. She pulled a gingersnap cookie out of her pocket and offered it to him. He crunched on it as if he hadn't eaten in days.

"Looks like you're feeling better after all." She shook pine shavings from her pajama pant legs and retired to the chaise.

The moon's glow slanted through the horses' stall doors, creating skewed shadows throughout the stable. Chiara felt embraced by a sense of complete presence in the moment. Everything around her looked surreal, yet vivid and clear. *Why don't I ever feel like this on the inside?* she thought, letting her hair out of its ponytail and covering herself with the blanket, indulging in the moment.

In the night's clear light, the sounds around her grew crisp and lyrical like a symphony. A wind chime hanging on a lamppost outside softly tickled its own pipes with the help of the breeze, its music sounding much closer than it was. The cicadas in Papà's garden sang their *zzzZZZZzzzz* song, a series of crescendo and diminuendo bars in their part of the night lullaby, and the soft, rhythmic sound of a stable full of horses chewing their night hay offered percussion.

This is heaven, she thought. *Real. Attainable. Nothing like that fairytale place those crooked priests in junior high tried to make me believe exists.*

As she closed her eyes to try and get some sleep, she heard Papà's footsteps approaching on the tar-and-chip drive north of the stable, his Italian dress shoes compressing the stones with a repeating and ever loudening *crunch* as he got closer.

When he poked his head into Hemingway's Dutch door, he blocked part of the moon. His shadowed face looked full of concern. He was still wearing a tie. He must have come straight from Gian Carlo's.

Chiara sat up. "Hi, Papà."

"Hi, *tesoro.* I knew you would be here. Like when we thought Shadowfax was going to need surgery. It turned out to be an abscess, eh?"

Chiara smiled. "Yeah, we've been pretty lucky so far with all of them. Julio's the best."

Papà reached in and petted Hemingway. "Hello, big boy. How are you, eh?"

"He's going to be fine, Papà. Dr. Jay said to give him a week off from any strenuous work. I'm going to hand-walk him forty-five minutes a day over the next week when I get back from my classes."

"Valerie found him, no?" Papà stroked Hemingway's forelock. "She always looks after you and Sylvia."

"Yes, she does, Papà. Valerie always looks after everything and everybody."

"How are your studies progressing?"

Papà had been asking her the same question since she was twelve. Sometimes hearing it made her cringe. But even in the opaque light, Chiara could see his eyes beam with pride. That look from him always disarmed her and filled her with confidence, knowing she was getting that much closer to becoming a physician, knowing she was being a good daughter, knowing he loved her as much as she loved him. But tonight, it didn't disarm her. When he asked her, she shifted uncomfortably in the chaise. *Progressing?* She wanted to say that the classes were hard as hell, and that she could better concentrate on them as soon as she told him she was madly in love and getting married. But she didn't. How could she worry him? Instead, she said that her classes were difficult but that her studies were progressing quite well, thank you.

"*Forza*, Chiara. Be tough. Put as much time into your studies as you can. Do not give up." He began his litany about how poor he was when he was her age, and how his lack of education and poor English made the prospect of succeeding in the States a daunting one. But with determination, hard work, and some English classes between running back and forth between restaurants, he eventually became fluent in English, albeit never losing his accent. "And," he went on, "if you want something badly enough, you will have to work as hard as me and Mamma do every day."

"Papà, please!" she said, losing her patience. Hemingway instinctively spooked. "How many times are you going to tell me that story? I study as hard as I can. I study until the words do flips and cartwheels on and off the page and I'm forced to stop."

Papà looked away for a moment. His voice softened. "I know you do, *cara*. Mamma told me today you decided you can only help at *il ristorante* on your breaks now, that you need to dedicate more time to your studies. I know you like to help *la famiglia*, but I am glad you know what you need to do."

Chiara couldn't hold back any longer; she owed it to Papà to tell him about her plans. She took a deep breath. "Papà, there's something I have to tell you that I know is going to disappoint you."

He cocked his head against the moonlight, "*Bah, cara*, you never disappoint me."

A tension she'd been quietly carrying around with her since Adrian first mentioned he wanted to get married grew in intensity inside her. She sat on her hands to avoid gnawing on her fingertips. In an instant, droplets of sweat collected under her arms, seeping through her pajama shirt.

"What is it, *cara*?"

"Papà, Adrian and I want to get married." *Whew*. She'd said it.

For a moment there was an ominous silence in the dark space between them. Even the cicadas had stopped playing mid-bar.

"What about your promise, Chiara, eh?" He said this like he wasn't totally shocked by the news, which surprised Chiara.

"Papà, you made me promise when I was a little girl," she said, feeling a little intimidated. "I'm in med school now and I want to get married. I'm old enough to decide if I can handle both."

When Papà spoke again, his voice was deliberate. "Are you going to sleep here?"

"Yes," she said almost under her breath. She pretended to examine a blister on her finger from a new set of reins she'd ridden Shadowfax with the day before.

Papà slowly stepped back from Hemingway's stall and the moon shone bright on her face. She wondered if he could see the fear in her face: fear of disappointing him, fear of losing Adrian, fear of not graduating if she backed out on her promise. Papà was now only a dark silhouette in front of the honey-ripe moon, his expression indistinguishable. When he spoke again, his stern voice sent a chill down Chiara's spine just the same.

"Chiara," he said. "He is not for you."

Chiara tried to lighten the mood. "Oh Papà, you didn't like Liam either when you first met him. Now you love him."

"Chiara, I will not accept this," he said. Without another word he turned and marched back toward the house.

On one level, she was devastated for upsetting him. His advice to her had always been sound. But on another level she shook with a sense of exhilaration. Her secret was out, setting in motion a destiny with new possibilities. She felt like a dolphin shooting up and out of the sun-soaked sea, soaring high into a beaming baby-blue sky, gasping for air after being trapped underwater in a sailor's net for years. She stood up and paced the aisle, trying to calm her breathing. There was no way she would sleep tonight. She wanted to run to the phone and call Adrian, but his mother was in town visiting, and it was late. So instead, she waited.

Chapter 3

Gian Carlo marched past the garden toward the house, so reminiscent of his childhood home in *Italia*. When he reached the terrace steps, he looked up at his bedroom window. The lights were on. Isabella was already in bed, reading. He wanted to go to her and vent his frustrations about Chiara, but Isabella was always exhausted by this time.

Why? he thought. *Why do lovers always feel more in love when they are battling their genitori?* He lit a cigarette, staring for moment at the flame of his lighter, so bright in the night, hoping it would help him illuminate a way to get through to Chiara. Then he flipped the lighter shut, took a long, deliberate hit of his cigarette and walked back to the garden.

He strolled down the flagstone path, gazing at moonlit statues of lovers peeking through the pink camellias. Cement moss-covered nymphs bathed in red rose bushes, bearded irises, and Asiatic lilies of white and yellow. When he reached the formidable three-tiered fountain in the center of the garden, he sat down on a bench across from it. Purple love grass surrounded the fountain like hovering clouds. It was just what he and Isabella had dreamed of before they moved to America. Behind the fountain, on the far side of the garden near where the girls' outdoor arena was now situated, a small patch of gargantuan sunflowers that he and Isabella had planted in the spring had reached their maximum height, the flower heads bowed, sleeping under the endless indigo sky.

Years ago, that area was the front row of three acres of sunflowers. But Chiara didn't want the sunflower garden anymore. She said it attracted too many bees around the stable. But he knew that was untrue. It had nothing to do with bees. It was what they represented. And *Dio* was nowhere in sight when that *figlio di putana* hurt her. Neither was he. He looked down at the ugly scar on his hand that bore his mark of revenge. It was made in vain; the damage had been done.

Did Chiara believe he did not want her to be in love? He wanted her to love and to be loved, but few romances began and ended like fairy tales. Did she believe all he cared about was her education? He cared about every aspect of all three of his girls' lives. Did she believe he had never been a young man in love? Isabella was the love of his life, but he had loved someone before her.

He recalled the hot spring afternoon when he saw his first love and he felt a sting in his chest, as if the old memory was a fresh and tender wound. It was 1956 and he was eighteen, still living in his home town of Sulmona, in the Abruzzo region of *Italia*. Every day, after he was finished working for his father, he headed to his favorite espresso bar. There he drank double cappuccinos and chatted with his friends, usually about World War Two, soccer, and the upcoming winter Olympics being held in Italy.

"Hey, Gian Carlo, doesn't she make you want to go back to school?" Fabrezio said.

Gian Carlo looked across the piazza. Two high-school-age girls dressed in blue school uniforms were walking down the cobblestone road. One was a heavy-set, awkward looking teenage girl who seemed to be hanging on every word of her friend. The one who was talking was a dark, full-figured girl with deep black eyes. Her stride was smooth and sensual. It intoxicated him. As she walked along the cobblestone path, cradling her books, locks of black hair bobbed and pranced about her tapered waist.

Gian Carlo took off his pageboy cap and held it to his chest. "*Madonna,*" he gasped. "Who is she?"

Fabrezio waved a hand as if swatting a fly. "Elena Zambrano. She's the new town doctor's daughter. They moved here from Sicily a few months ago."

Fabrezio had barely finished his sentence when Gian Carlo leaped out of his chair and ran down the narrowing winding street. When he reached Elena, he was out of breath. It was not because he had run too far or too fast but because she was even more beautiful face to face, like a painting. Looking away to catch his breath, he noticed an old woman sitting on a balcony above them dressed in black from head to toe. She was embroidering a sheet, apparently anticipating an opportunity to entertain herself by eavesdropping. Gian Carlo ignored her at first.

"*Ciao, Signorina* Elena. My name is Gian Carlo Lazzaro."

The girl stopped and smiled. "I know who you are," she said. "All the girls know who you are."

For a moment Gian Carlo felt ten feet tall. His hungry green eyes snapped a picture of Elena, memorizing every curve of her heart-shaped face so he could dream about her later.

"This is my friend, Claudia," she added, but he barely looked at the other girl.

"Would it be all right if I call on you tomorrow?" He stared at her plump tan lips, her dark skin, shifting his weight, waiting for an answer.

Elena smiled, and then looked down at the books pressed firmly against her voluptuous chest. "Perhaps. My parents are very strict; you'll have to ask them."

Gian Carlo peered up at the old woman. She had leaned forward over the balcony, presumably to get a better read on the conversation beneath her. When she saw Gian Carlo looking up, she pulled back and tucked a few silver tresses neatly under a black scarf. Gian Carlo looked at the girls and signaled for them to move on. When they were out of the old woman's earshot, he continued. "I would love to take you *per un gelato* and a walk through my family's flower garden sometime."

"I've heard people say it's the most beautiful private garden in the region. Your family must really love flowers," Elena said.

He smiled at her and his large thumbprint dimples puckered into his cheeks. He felt exhilarated that she had heard of him and his family's house. "Yes, we do. The garden started out as a small vegetable patch my mother planted on our property before I was born. She was a biologist and loved learning about plants and flowers as a pastime."

Claudia curled her lip into a sarcastic grin. "Why don't you go to school anymore?"

Gian Carlo ignored her. "By the time I was five, she had converted it almost entirely to a flower garden. The more she read about flower varieties, the bigger and more opulent the garden grew."

Elena laughed. "Sounds like she is going to run out of land pretty soon."

"No, she passed away a few years ago. Now that she's gone, my father and I keep it up for her. I guess it sort of keeps her alive to us in some way."

"I didn't know that, I'm sorry," Elena said. "That's beautiful. Claudia told me that your house is an eighty-room mansion that used to be a monastery in the fourteenth century. Is it true?"

"It's true."

"Let's go, Elena," Claudia said.

"In a minute," Elena said.

Elena was showing interest in him; Gian Carlo was ecstatic. The idea of spending time with her made his throat tighten. He would tell her ghost stories about the town—how it dated back to the third century, and about his home and how his family came to own it. He would boast of the many famous people who were born in Abruzzo, people like Ovid, the great writer of *Metamorphoses.*

"But I still think you would love the garden best," he said. "It takes up over ten acres of land. We have all kinds of flowers and plants— daffodils, Asiatic lilies of every color, bearded irises, hostas, peonies, African azaleas, begonias, more than ten different kinds of orchids, and enough rose plants to satisfy every lover in Italy. The lemon, tangerine, cypress, chestnut, and fig trees offer shade and the statues of lovers tell stories that will make you cry. I keep telling my father there is only one flower in the whole garden that is missing."

Elena's dark eyes grew curious and playful. "Which one might that be?" She was openly flirting with him.

He stared at her, wondering if heaven itself had sent him such a beautiful woman to admire. He said, "The sunflower."

"Sunflowers?" Elena said, looking disappointed. "They're so common."

"Very," Claudia added.

Gian Carlo smiled. "Ah, *Helianthus annus*. Their name is derived from Greek. *Helios* for the sun, and *anthos* for flower. It comes from the plant's ability to turn its flower head so that it follows the sun."

"Everybody knows that," Elena said.

Gian Carlo's confidence sank to his toes, but he didn't let her know. "I've studied everything there is to know about the sunflower; that is not all that makes it special."

"Really?" She seemed to be intrigued by his excitement over botany. "What else makes it special?"

He regained his composure, stood a little taller. "Have you studied Leonardo Fibonacci in math class?"

"No, who is he?"

Gian Carlo could not stop staring at her, talking to her. He could have kept her there talking for the rest of his life, sharing his passion for math and science.

"Well?" Elena asked.

"I read about Fibonacci this spring," he said. "He was a mathematician who discovered a unique progression of numbers. He theorized about the rate of multiplication of breeding pairs of rabbits, beginning with one pair where each number after the first two was the sum of the preceding numbers."

Elena looked down at the cobblestone walk beneath her. "I don't understand."

"Neither do I," Claudia admitted.

He had embarrassed Elena and was losing her interest. "It sounds complicated, but it's not." Gian Carlo motioned for her notebook and pencil and jotted down the Fibonacci numbers in mathematical terms— $F_n = F_{n-1} + F_{n-2}$—and some numbers: 0, 1, 1, 2, 3, 5, 8, 13, 21 (3 + 5 = 8, 5 + 8 = 13, 8 + 13 = 21). Then he slowly read the numbers aloud. "See how eight, thirteen and twenty one are the sum of the preceding two numbers, eh?"

"Yes, yes," Elena said, looking more encouraged. "But what does that have to do with the sunflower?"

"This series of numbers that Fibonacci discovered is visible in some very beautiful patterning in the world." He handed her back the pencil and paper. "When you look at the head of a sunflower, you can see that the seeds are arranged in two sets of spirals, one set running clockwise, the other counterclockwise. If you count the number of spirals going in one direction and the number going in the other, you will see that these are always two numbers that are next to each other in the Fibonacci series. A lot of other things follow the same pattern in the world."

"Like what?" Claudia said.

"Pinecones, snail shell spirals, some animal horns." Gian Carlo put his cap back on and placed his hands in his pant pockets as they continued strolling down the lane. He could feel the holes in each pocket, but refused to let it faze him. "Even the golden ratio that many architects and artists like Leonardo da Vinci use in their work is related to the Fibonacci patterns. They use it because it is pleasing to the eye."

Elena seemed impressed. "I don't know what that is either, the golden ratio. You must be very smart."

"Well, when I take you out for *gelato* I will explain it to you."

She smiled again. "I would like that."

"I believe that the Fibonacci series of numbers is no coincidence in the sunflower. I've read that it's a pattern that could only come from God's design. Proof of the amalgam between God and science."

Elena raised her perfectly arched eyebrows. "I think you might be right."

Claudia grabbed Elena by the arm and picked up the pace. At Elena's front door, she stopped and said, "I heard the war ruined your family and that you dropped out of school because you were too embarrassed to keep wearing the same clothes to class every day. You're not fooling me with your fancy talk about numbers and science and God, Gian Carlo. You're a nobody."

Gian Carlo felt a burning wave of embarrassment mixed with anger drown him.

Elena looked mortified. "Go home, Claudia. I'll talk to you about this tomorrow."

"I'm sorry, Gian Carlo," she said when Claudia had gone.

They stood face to face in front of Elena's home.

"Elena," Gian Carlo stuttered, "my family did go through a hard time after the war, but things are better now."

"Gian Carlo, you don't have to explain anything. Everyone did. Claudia is bitter with boys right now because they tease her about her weight. She had no right to say that. I'm sorry."

She climbed a set of age-worn limestone steps. "I live here."

The front door swung open. Elena's mother stood glaring at them. She was a red-haired woman with pale skin and a pointy nose. He thought Elena must take after her father.

"Good afternoon, *Signora* Zambrano," Gian Carlo said. "My name is Gian Carlo Lazzaro. I met Elena today in the piazza and I walked her home. I was hoping I could stop by later and ask Dr. Zambrano if I may take Elena for *gelato* on Saturday."

The woman gave him an uneasy stare. "Do you know Elena from school?"

"No, *Signora.*"

"Are you in school?" she said

"No, *Signora.*"

"Ah," she said. "Elena has to study on Saturday."

"Well, Sunday, then," he insisted.

"We go to church on Sunday."

"I do, too. May I take her after mass?"

"Gian Carlo, Dr. Zambrano and I are very particular about who Elena spends time with. You seem like a very nice boy, but you must understand, we have great plans for Elena. She will be attending university next year and meeting educated people," she said with a tight smile. "We do not want her getting close to any of the town boys. Come inside, Elena."

Elena's mother stepped back into the hallway.

"Could you go back to school?"

Her mother called, "Elena!" so sharply from behind the stone walls that Gian Carlo felt like he had been slapped in the face through the door.

Elena waited for him to say something. When he didn't answer, looking forlorn, she slowly closed the door.

Gian Carlo walked back toward the piazza with his hands in his pants pockets. *I would go back for you Elena,* he thought, *if I did not have to go back into the eighth grade.*

That summer they dated in spite of Elena's parents, and when it came time for her to leave for university, she did not want to go. But Gian Carlo insisted she go because he wanted more for her. He did it for her. Although Elena ended the relationship after she started university, he never regretted knowing her or her mother. Elena had taught him what love was. Elena's mother had taught him something too. Drive. Her constant disapproval of him and his summer love with Elena sparked in him a desire to prove he wasn't a bum, to fulfill growing dreams he kept nestled in a secret place inside himself. Someday he would have children too, and no one would ever, ever say they were dropouts.

And almost every one of those dreams had come to fruition. He owned a chain of successful restaurants. He had worked hard and proved himself worthy of Isabella's trust and love. He had built a beautiful home and recreated his family garden. He had brought pride back to his family name. Sylvia was an accountant and Valerie a lawyer. All that was left was for Chiara to finish medical school. He was not going to let a selfish boy get in the way, as he was sure he would.

Chapter 4

At seven o'clock the next morning, Chiara got dressed for class, grabbed her backpack and headed to the kitchen for a quick espresso. When she and Papà crossed paths in the foyer, Chiara stopped and offered him a fragile smile. "*Buon giorno*, Papà."

"*Buon giorno*," he said. But he didn't look at her. He kept his eyes fixed on the marble floor as he passed her.

She tucked her hands in her jean pockets. "Will you have time to quiz me tonight on some medical terminology?" she asked. Chiara hadn't needed his help studying in years, but she knew it made him feel like he was a part of her journey, so she still asked him for help now and then.

"Not today, Chiara," he said with indifference as he moved toward the front door.

She hated being at odds with him, and her disappointment showed in her voice. "Okay, maybe tomorrow then?"

Her father didn't answer.

In her peripheral vision, she saw him stop to adjust his tie in one of the two towering rococo mirrors. She wanted to tell him everything was going to be fine. That she'd graduate. That he would grow to love

Adrian. When she took a step toward him, he turned and walked out the front door, slamming it behind him.

She dropped her head and turned the corner into the kitchen. Valerie was there, standing at the kitchen island dressed for work in a slim dark suit and white blouse, two cups of steaming espresso on the counter in front of her.

"Hey," Valerie said.

"Why aren't you at work?"

Valerie was a partner at Liam's law firm and rarely went in late. "I have a ten o'clock appointment with my gynecologist. I thought I'd stop by and have an espresso with you before you left for class."

"Great. I don't have much time, though. My first class starts at eight thirty. Are you and Liam trying again?"

"Uh-huh." She looked worried.

Chiara took in Valerie's solemn expression. "That's wonderful, Valerie. I'm so happy for you. Why aren't you excited?"

"I'm excited for me, worried for you. I just talked to Papà before you came downstairs. He's livid with you, Chiara. Are you going ahead with it?"

"No, not yet. I just told him that we want to get married. I want Adrian to talk to him about it first. Reassure Papà he's going to be supportive through my studies."

Valerie slid a cup towards Chiara. When she spoke, her voice was calm and unhurried. "Chiara, Papà plans on having it out with you tonight. He said he has no intention of budging on this issue. Especially since he's not exactly crazy about Adrian."

Chiara was not one to feel sorry for herself. What she did feel sorry for was the turn of events that made her break her promise to Papà. She had tried to keep her heart closed to Adrian. But every time she saw him, every time he smiled at her, every time he held her hand, every time he touched her, every time he took his baseball cap off at the games and tapped it against his heart as he looked up at her in the stands, her heart throbbed. And now, to feel like this, to be so engulfed in love with him, was worth the sacrifices she would have to make. Worth the promise she would have to break.

Chiara fixed her gaze on the coffee cup. "Papà wasn't exactly crazy about Liam either Valerie, but you were able to convince him Liam was a good person."

"The only thing Papà disliked about Liam was that he wasn't *Italian*, Chiara."

"Adrian has never been anything but nice to Papà. He has no reason not to like him."

"I know. Papà thinks he drinks too much."

"Valerie, he likes to have a few drinks after the games. It doesn't make him a bad person. A lot of the ballplayers drink."

Valerie ran her hands through her black shoulder length hair. "I know, Chiara," she said. "Papà seems to think all baseball players are womanizers and alcoholics."

"He's stereotyping."

"I know," Valerie said. "I like Adrian, but he does drink a lot. Do you want me to be here tonight when you and Papà talk?"

Chiara gave her an appreciative smile. "There's nothing you can do."

"I can be a five-foot-six human shield."

Chiara gave her a weary smile as she pulled her hair back into a ponytail. "I'll be fine." She reached for the sugar bowl.

"I already put it in for you."

"Thanks. I get so frustrated with him lately, Valerie. I don't need to be pushed anymore. I'm in, I'm studying, and I'm working hard."

"I know you are. And so does he. I don't think he can help himself."

When Chiara finished her coffee, she placed the cup in the kitchen sink. She stared at Mamma's cream porcelain spice jars, each labeled in Italian, just to the right of a large bay window: *Origano, aglio, rosmarino, timo*, and *prezzemolo*. She remembered how during high school, Papà used to drop tiny wrapped gifts in them for her and her sisters when they did particularly well in their classes.

What was Papà going to say to her tonight? Chiara looked out the window past the garden and riding arena to the twenty-acre field beyond it. The five-acre sunflower garden that used to grow there every summer was gone. The small bright yellow patch that stood there now looked lost in the massive field. She thought of how tense things had become with Papà since she met Adrian.

"I have to go to class. Will you meet me for dinner at Gian Carlo's later and tell me what the doctor said? We could go to the game afterwards. I'm only going to stay for a couple of innings. I have to get back to study."

"I can't go to the game, but I'll meet you for a bite to eat after work."

After lunchtime, when the hospital cafeteria was quiet, Chiara met with her PBL group at their usual corner spot to go over their findings. PBL was short for problem-based learning. Medical students were assigned to groups and presented with a fictitious patient with an unknown disease. The group's task was to work together to identify the disease using differential diagnosis, a sort of educated process of elimination.

"I think it's Morgellons disease," Josh said as he bit into a chicken leg. Josh was tall and blond and was always the first to offer a diagnosis.

Chiara flipped through her notes. She'd slept poorly the night before. When the letters in her notebook deceived their words, she focused more intently. When warm thoughts of Adrian breezed past her heart, she focused again, thinking, thinking, always thinking how her pretend patient needed her to be sharp. When she thought of how she was breaking her promise to Papà, she thought if she could pray for his forgiveness, she would. Then she focused again.

"No, it can't be," Chiara said. "Patients with Morgellons complain of a creepy crawly sensation on their bodies. Our patient hasn't complained of that." Chiara rubbed her eyes and read on in her notes. "Besides, his skin is shedding super fast, and there's hair on his fishlike scales."

"I agree with Chiara," Li said. Li was a petite Asian student. Chiara thought she was the smartest student in her class.

"I think it's harlequin ichthyosis," Chiara said.

Li smiled. "It was one of my top two choices. You're good at this, Chiara."

Chiara blushed. "No Li, I'm just a good listener, usually."

Later, before clinical rounds, Chiara stopped in the neonatal unit where she volunteered a few hours per week. Lendina, one of the neonatal nurses, looked up from an incubator where she'd been adjusting a baby's oxygen tube.

"Here comes baby lovin' Chiara again, guys," she called out loud enough for the other nurses to hear. "Ain't this the third day in a row you been in here?"

Lendina had a chocolate face so full and creamy it made Chiara want to pinch her cheeks every time she saw her.

Chiara rolled her eyes at her and smiled. "No, it's only my second day in a row."

After washing her hands, she picked up a little girl bundled in a pink blanket in bed five. Chiara looked at her name tag and gently shook her tiny hand. "Hello, Sarah. It's nice to meet you, little one." She leaned over and smelled her head, taking in the scent of new beginnings only a newborn possesses. Hopefully, someday soon Chiara would be an aunt. And not too far after that, after she reached her lifelong goal, she too would be a mother.

It was after five o'clock when Chiara left clinical. She had enjoyed following her superiors around, visiting patients. Although she was only permitted to observe, someday she would be treating patients, delivering babies, and helping people. What could be more rewarding? She walked into the restaurant just a little taller thinking about it. Papà was standin behind the bar, his shirt sleeves rolled up, rinsing glasses at the sink. Chiara surmised one of the evening bartenders had called off last minute.

"Hi, Papà," she said, acting as if nothing was wrong.

He peeked over his bifocals. His expression had softened since this morning.

"Hi, *cara*," he said.

"Please, will you quiz me later?"

"Yes, Chiara, Papà will help you. But afterward we will have our discussion, eh?"

Papà was always in a great mood after their study sessions together. When he listened to Chiara rattle off anything scientific, pride practically poured out of every pore in his body. She thought having their discussion about Adrian right after Papà quizzed her might keep Papà's anger in check.

"I love you, Papà," she said, leaving her first medical school test on the counter for him.

He looked at the score—ninety-seven percent—and the side of his mouth turned up into a slight smile.

Papà tapped his hand over his heart. "*Forza, cara.*"

Chiara found Mamma, not surprisingly, in the kitchen, the only simple part of the restaurant—a stark difference to the crystal chandelier and Italian marble-decorated dining room. This room was filled with stainless steel everything: ovens, fryers, tables, pots, and pans. Chefs dressed in white jackets and baseball caps embroidered with Gian

Carlo's in cursive script scrambled from station to station preparing for the dinner rush.

"Hi, Mamma."

"Hi, *cara*," Mamma said, offering her cheek.

Mamma was basting chicken breasts at one of the stations, wearing a white apron around her waist to shield her simple dress from the lemon cream sauce. Enzo, the head chef, a potbellied Italian man with a goatee, stood beside her, slicing chicken wing after chicken wing from large breasts, barking orders to the staff. When Chiara leaned over to kiss Mamma, Enzo cracked open another case of chickens and blood spattered on Chiara's cream blouse.

"Oh, God." She rushed to a sink and dabbed at the spot with a mixture of soapy water and bleach.

Mamma gave her a disapproving look. "Don't take the Lord's name in vain."

Valerie, a vegetarian, walked in just in time to witness this. She looked away, disgusted. "Serves you right for getting so close to him when he's mutilating helpless animals."

"They were dead when they got here," Enzo said with casual sarcasm.

"Very funny," Valerie said.

Enzo smiled at Mamma.

Mamma smiled back at him while she continued to paint a lemon glaze on the breasts with a thick basting brush. Even now, in her late forties, her cheekbones still sat high on her face, accentuated by the way she still wore her hair pulled back in a tight chignon. "How was class, *cara*?" she asked.

"Good. Had four hours of lecture, PBL, and a couple hours of clinical."

Mamma gave her a wide smile. "I'm so proud of you. Papà was telling everybody after church on Sunday how well you're doing."

Chiara's face turned red. "Oh, Ma, stop. I just saw him. He doesn't look as angry as he did this morning."

Mamma sighed and dropped the brush. "Well, he is. Come, girls, let's sit down. I'm hungry."

They sat at a table with a view overlooking the city's bridges, its three rivers, and Three Rivers Stadium. Chiara looked down at the stadium and wondered if Adrian was already dressed in his Pirates uniform, practicing on the field. When Papà walked by on the other side of the restaurant, inspecting table settings, greeting customers, asking how their meals tasted, and thanking them for coming, he glanced over at Chiara and a look of disappointment fell over his face again. That truly got under her integumental system.

"Chiara," Mamma said, "I'm going to get right to the point. Papà and I talked for a long time last night about what you said in the stable."

Chiara stared out the window. "And what did he say?"

"I think you know. Look, *cara*, we all know how Papà is, but he does mean well. He always has." Mamma motioned for one of the waitresses. "I know Papà and I sound like a broken record, but you girls don't know what it's like to be poor, wondering how you will feed your three young daughters. Papà and I never want you girls to have to go through that. It is so important to him that you finish your education before you get married, Chiara. He doesn't want you to be distracted in any way."

"I wish he'd have a little more faith in me, Ma."

Valerie unfolded a linen napkin and placed it on her lap. "Chiara, he felt the same way about me getting married before I finished law school. The difference is that I agreed with him. Honestly, I don't see what the big hurry is. You're only twenty-three."

"Adrian seems so understanding," Mamma said. "Can't you ask him to wait until you graduate? With Adrian traveling and you in school, it will be hard on your marriage if you get married next year."

"He won't wait four years," Chiara said.

Mamma offered a sympathetic smile. "He loves you. He'll wait."

A waitress dressed in black and white came and took their order, spaghetti bolognese for Mamma and Chiara, plain spaghetti in a marinara sauce for Valerie.

"Ma, lots of people have spouses who travel for a living. Adrian doesn't work at all from October through the middle of February, when he starts spring training."

"Valerie and I talked earlier—"

"I'm sure you did," Chiara said. "God knows nobody has any privacy in this family."

Valerie gave her a sly smile. "Of course not. We're Italian."

"We have a plan," Mamma said. "We will try our best to help Papà accept and get along with Adrian. Maybe we can even help you to get him to agree to getting engaged and married in your fourth year. Do you think you could wait until then?"

"I can't believe I'm resorting to barter in order to lead my life." Chiara sat back in her chair, and sighed. "Besides, at this point I don't think Papà is ever going to like Adrian. It bothers me because I want him to."

"Believe me, *cara*, if Adrian relents a bit, I can't see how Papà wouldn't gain respect for him."

Chiara was full of doubt. "I'll talk to Adrian about it, Ma," she said. But she was sure Adrian wouldn't wait four years to get married. She knew Papà would never forgive her if she married sooner. A sinking feeling weighed her down in her chair, making her feel as if she were three hundred pounds. Mamma reached across the table and took her hand. "Everything is going to be fine, Chiara. You'll see."

Chiara squeezed Mamma's hand and nodded. But something told her things were *not* going to be fine.

She didn't want to think about her future with Adrian resting in Papà's hands right now, so she changed the subject. "How did your doctor's appointment go, Val?" Chiara asked.

"It went well. I start with the hormone patches next week. It's what happened later that ticked me off."

Chiara's interest peaked.

"What happened, *cara*?" Mamma said.

"I got a call at work from Sister Agnes. She fired me from teaching Sunday school at Saint Ursula's because she found out about my in vitro fertilization treatments from somebody I must have talked to about them in the parish. She said it wasn't "Christian–like" and I was setting a bad example for the kids."

Mamma slammed her hand on the table. "I have just about had it with that parish."

Chiara often questioned why they even bothered with church. Still, a part of her marveled at their strong faith. She thought of "the incident" never far from her mind and wondered how different her outlook on faith might have been if she had gone to a different school, if she had had a different science teacher.

Chapter 5

After Chiara left Gian Carlo's, she parked her silver Range Rover at the Three Rivers Stadium parking lot and dashed to the row of seats just behind the Pirates' dugout. Players and coaches were on the field, dressed in their black, white, and gold uniforms and baseball caps, playing catch like Little Leaguers. Chiara took in the smell of the freshly mowed grass cut in neat crisscrossing rows, and the sight of fans filling the seats. The smell of hotdogs permeated the evening air. Years ago, she and Valerie used to look down at the stadium from the Gian Carlo's floor-to-ceiling windows and make fun of it because it looked more like a flying saucer from an old sci-fi movie than a sports complex that was home to the world-champion Pittsburgh Steelers and Pirates.

Chiara had never thought that someday the love of her life would be a baseball player working there. Her heart fluttered like a hummingbird when she thought of the baseball season being over in a week. Adrian would then stay put in Pittsburgh until spring training. No more ten days home, ten days on the road. *Yippee!*

She thought she recognized him in the outfield—the players in their uniforms all looked alike from a distance—but then he stepped out of the dugout and looked into the stands.

"Hi, honey!" she called out to him.

"Hey, baby." He pulled off his cap, and his black hair caught streaks of light from the fading evening sun. He smiled and motioned her toward the rail down the first-base line, where they could be closer. "You're late. I kept coming out to look for you."

"I know. I got held up at the restaurant talking to Mamma and Valerie." She took in his gaze, his thick lips, his white teeth, and felt the urge to kiss him. Even after dating him for over a year, the sight of him still sent chills through her body, especially when he was standing this close and in uniform. *Wow.* His skin was such a rich shade of golden honey that it looked like the sun had plucked him up from earth with its rays and dipped him in a vat of sunshine.

"Gimme a kiss," he said.

She leaned over the rail and kissed him, tasting his sweat on her lips, wishing they were somewhere alone. "I'm sorry I didn't call you. I wanted to tell you in person about what happened with Papà last night."

"Ain't no problem, *amor*. But I was wondering all night if you told him."

"Hey, rookie!" the pitching coach yelled from home plate. He was a short, stout man with gray hair. "Why don't you get your head out of your ass? It's your turn to throw batting practice. Or would you rather go back down to AAA and be a hot shot down there for a few more years?"

There was laughter from Adrian's teammates.

Adrian squeezed Chiara's hand. "He knows it's my second year. Don't go. I'll be back in fifteen." He shot her a toothy smile and jogged toward the mound.

A few of the veterans laughed again as Adrian took the mound and picked up a baseball. He threw a pitch and the pitching coach slowly shook his head. Each pitch he threw made a loud *smack* as it hit the inside of the catcher's glove. Each time it did, the catcher gave Adrian an approving nod and tossed the ball back to him. Chiara marveled at the fluid motion of Adrian's body: muscles, bones, tendons, all working together to deliver a ball over a small plate at ninety miles per hour. She marveled at the rhythmical exchange between catcher and pitcher at such high speeds; it looked like a waltz between perfect dancing partners, like Fred Astaire and Ginger Rogers, or the intimate relationship between a fly fisherman and his rod as he casts and backcasts in a stream. She marveled at her feelings for him. Her eyes moved from his face to his thighs to his arms and back to his face again as if she were afraid he might disappear if she looked away once.

"Batter up!" the batting coach yelled.

Adrian made a sign of the cross on his chest, then wound up and threw a pitch to the batter. It was a fastball down the center of home plate and it connected to the bat with a *crack*. Chiara watched the ball take flight; it soared high and into the upper deck of center field and got lost in the glow of stanchion lights heating up for the game. Adrian looked over at Chiara and smiled. Chiara thought her heart might jump out of her blouse and join him on the field. It was fighting that hard to get close to him.

"Hey, Casanova!" the pitching coach yelled. "The batter's over here."

More laughs exploded from the coaches and players as they looked back and forth between Adrian and Chiara. Even a few fans chuckled, and Chiara found herself blushing.

Fifteen minutes later, the pitching coach called out another name and instructed Adrian to *go shag*, which was ballplayer talk for picking up hit balls.

Adrian handed the baseball over to the next pitcher and jogged back to Chiara.

"Your fastball looks great today," she said. "The speed gun clocked it at ninety-six and ninety-seven miles per hour."

Adrian took off his cap and wiped the sweat on his forehead with his shirt sleeve. "Yeah, I feel pretty good. What's going on with you and your dad? Did you tell him we wanna get married yet?"

"Last night."

"What did he say?"

Chiara looked off into centerfield. "He was pretty upset, stomped away. He walked right past me in the foyer this morning, ignored me at the restaurant tonight." She tugged at her pearl necklace Papà had given her for her eighteenth birthday. "We're supposed to have a *talk* tonight."

"Shit." He took her hand through the rail. "You want me to be there?"

"No, I can handle it."

"He just thinks he's losing his baby. If you were my daughter I'd have a hard time letting you go, too. It'll be okay, Chiara."

"I know," she said. But she was unsure. In the past, Papà's *talks* had managed to convince her that her boyfriends were wrong for her, or that it was the wrong time to get too serious with anyone. And in the past, he had been right. But this was different. Adrian was different.

"After I talk to him, I'm sure he's going to want to talk to you. You know how old-fashioned he is."

"I'm a big boy. I can handle your dad." He squeezed her hand again; the affectionate touch meant to tell her everything was going to be okay. "I told my mom that we've been talking about it too."

Chiara perked up a bit. "What did she say?"

"She said she knew we were in love, but that she didn't think we'd wanna get married so soon."

Chiara looked down at the rail. "Oh."

"Hey, look at me," he said. "Parents get weird when their kids get married. Don't worry. Everything's cool."

Chiara nodded, still unconvinced.

"I love you, okay?"

She leaned over the rail and stole a quick kiss on the lips. "I know you do. I love you more."

"I gotta get back to practice before I get fired."

They both smiled.

"You staying for the game?" he asked.

"Only for five innings or so. I have to study."

"But it's Friday night, *amor.*"

"I know, honey. But I have to. I was hoping you'd come to the house tomorrow morning, though. We could take the horses for a ride in the woods."

"I'd like that. It's been a long time since we did that. What time?"

"Around nine o'clock," Chiara said.

Just then Adrian looked up toward the stands and waved.

Chiara turned to see Adrian's mother descending the stadium steps toward them. She was a burly, bleached-blonde woman with massive breasts and thick legs.

"Hello," she cooed as she approached.

Her physique may have lacked femininity, but her voice, her voice was the definition of it. It was soft and seraphic, light, and pure. It could put a wailing baby to sleep in seconds. Aside from that beautiful voice, the only other feminine characteristics Cecilia possessed were her obscenely long French-manicured nails. But even they looked odd on her large hands.

Chiara took in the sight of them slicing the evening air as she waved to Adrian, wondering how she could do anything without their getting in the way. She imagined Freddy Krueger looking a them with envy.

Cecilia leaned over the rail and hugged Adrian as if it had been years since she'd seen him, not hours. "You look so handsome, son," she said, cupping his face in her hands.

"Where'd you go?" he asked.

"I was in the souvenir shop," she caroled. Then she produced a bobble head of Adrian from a plastic bag.

"There were a few other things I wanted but I didn't get them," she said, pretending to look sad.

"Why?" he asked

Cecilia gave a coy smile, pretended to pout like a child in a candy store without a penny. She held out her hands like she was asking for charity and her wrist full of gold bangle bracelets jingled. "No money," she said.

"I'll have one of the clubhouse boys bring some out to you in a little while," Adrian said.

Chiara looked over at the pitching coach. He was sarcastically tapping on his watch. Many of the players were making their way toward the dugout. "It's approaching game time. You better go."

"Okay, gimme one more kiss," he said.

Chiara leaned over the rail and gave him a quick peck on the lips. Cecilia looked away, but not before Chiara saw her face burn red.

"I'll see you in the morning," Adrian said. Then he disappeared into the dugout with the other players.

Chiara and Cecilia found their seats and sat down. Cecilia's arms were sunburned from sitting in the stands all day watching Adrian and the rest of the team practice. Chiara offered to go look for some aloe to soothe the burn.

"No, no," Cecilia said. "I'm fine. But I do want something to eat."

Chiara flagged down a vendor, and Cecilia ordered a hotdog and a box of Cracker Jacks. Chiara ordered a pack of M&Ms.

"I'm not supposed to eat ballpark food with my high cholesterol and blood pressure. But I can't help it, you know?" Cecilia said in her angelic voice. "I just love it. We never had money to go to major league baseball games and eat ballpark food when my boys was little."

"That'll be fifteen bucks," the man said.

Cecilia looked at Chiara, as if she wanted her to pay.

"Oh, of course," Chiara said. She reached into her purse and handed the man a twenty-dollar bill.

Cecilia took a substantial bite of the hotdog. "We was so poor," she said with her mouth full, "that I wouldn't even waste money to buy snacks at his Little League games." She swallowed, and then looked at Chiara. "But sacrifice is a good thing, you know? It makes you hungry. Look where my boy is now."

"Adrian told me about his childhood," Chiara said. "It must have been difficult raising two boys alone and working full time." She opened her pack of M&Ms. "My father's told me about his struggles growing up in Italy after World War Two."

"There's a big difference between hearing stories and living them," Cecilia said with a tone.

Chiara knew that. She was only trying to find some way to bond with Cecilia. She could almost see Cecilia constructing a brick wall between them by the second. Chiara didn't have to ask why; she knew. Chiara suspected that Cecilia would find the greatest satisfaction in drop-kicking her, like a football, right out of the stadium and out of Adrian's life.

Cecilia took another bite of her hotdog and a dollop of ketchup fell onto her Pirates jersey. Adrian's team number, thirty-six, was embroidered across her voluptuous chest. She *tsked*, scooped up the ketchup into her fingertip, and licked it off.

Chiara felt a wave of nausea rise and fall in her stomach, and she looked away.

"I made a lot of sacrifices for my boys. I don't make much money. I've been working like a dog in a grocery store in a fancy neighborhood for twenty years. You wouldn't want to know what that's like."

Chiara shifted in her chair. She believed Cecilia's life had been hard. Chiara knew what hard work was. She'd watched her parents toil in the restaurants, and when she and her sisters were old enough, they worked in the restaurants and went to school. There was no point in sharing this. Cecilia had already formed an opinion about Chiara and her family.

Chiara let go of Cecilia's prickly comment and changed the subject. "Adrian told me you were born in Mexico. When did you move to Florida?"

"My parents moved to Florida when I was five. When I turned eighteen, I moved to Orlando with my cousin. We got jobs at Disney World. That's where I met Adrian's father." Cecilia shook her head and *tsked* again. "That was a mistake. I moved to Tampa with my boys after I divorced him. They were only five and six."

"Oh," Chiara said. She was putting it all together. "I thought you lived in Mexico until you were much older. I've often wondered why your accent isn't stronger. My father left Italy when he was a teenager and never lost his."

Cecilia narrowed her eyes at Chiara. "You pick up on a lot of things when you wait on rich women coming into the grocery store dressed from head to toe in pearl necklaces and four-carat diamond rings that their husbands bought for them. My English is good, but not proper. Does our poor grammar bother you?"

This is going from bad to worse, Chiara thought. "No, oh God, no," Chiara said. *I was talking about accents, not grammar.* "I didn't mean it that way."

It was true Adrian's—and Cecilia's—grammar was less than perfect. But what did Chiara care? It was part of who he was.

"Adrian's grammar is how it is because I didn't have the money to send him and his brother to private schools like you went to. Didn't have the money to live in real nice neighborhoods like you do." Cecilia took her third and final bite of her hotdog. "Maybe you can help him with his English."

Chiara could barely stand her animosity one more second. She cleared her throat. "Cecilia," she said. "I know Adrian told you about our plans to eventually get married. I'd like to know how you feel about it."

The first batter in the lineup for the Houston Astros approached the plate. He swung at the first pitch. It was a fly ball to center field. The fans cheered, and Cecilia waited for the noise to die down before she answered. "Me and Adrian, we had a lot of plans when he finally got to the big leagues. Things are going to be different now."

The sadness in her voice disarmed Chiara, almost made her feel guilty for loving Adrian. She felt the urge to hug Cecilia and say, *Nothing has to change at all. All I want is to be part of your family, to be a daughter to you.* She took her hand. "Please don't feel that way, Cecilia. I'm sure—in fact, I'm positive—you and Adrian will still do all the things you planned to do together." She paused, looking for some sort of acceptance in Cecilia's eyes. "I'd like to be a part of them, too."

Cecilia winced at Chiara as if she were an annoying itch on her back. "He's happy now. That's all that matters. I just hope he doesn't forget about me."

She said nothing after that. It was as if she had suddenly contracted an acute case of laryngitis. Chiara sat rambling about nothing to fill the silent void between them for two more innings. At the bottom of the third, Cecilia was still mute. Feeling like a polar bear in a desert, Chiara excused herself to go home to study. Cecilia offered her a smile that wasn't exactly a smile and muttered goodnight.

Chapter 6

The alarm clock woke Chiara at six forty-five the next morning playing a jovial symphony. She loved Saturdays because there was no class and she could study at a slower pace. Within seconds she was wide awake, wondering why Papà hadn't called her down to the library for their talk. No matter. She was sure they would speak today. Looking forward to her ride and to seeing Adrian, she got out of bed, put on a pair of tan riding breeches and a cotton blouse, and washed the sleep out of her eyes. She checked her eyebrows, making sure stragglers hadn't sprouted overnight and thought about applying a little makeup so she could feel pretty when Adrian arrived. But there was no point; she would only sweat it off during her ride. Besides, Adrian liked her natural. She stopped in the kitchen to pour herself a coffee and then shot through the door, down the terrace steps, and toward the stable to exercise her horses before Adrian arrived.

After riding her four-year-old gelding for forty minutes, she tacked and walked Hemingway to the outdoor arena. By that time, it was eight o'clock. Already, signs of autumn were burgeoning all around her. Red sunset maple trees around the arena had caught fire overnight, their leaves boasting rich hues of burnt sienna, crimson, and orange-yellow.

They reminded Chiara of the crayons in the Crayola sixty-four pack. Patches of morning dew glistened in the grassy pastures, and the sun, rising slightly later every day, had just yawned its way up over a western Pennsylvania mountain in the distance.

I love cool autumn mornings. Chiara looked around the ring for a mounting block but didn't see one. She took the reins in one hand, grabbed hold of the pommel of her saddle, stepped into the left stirrup, and heaved herself up and over Hemingway's back. Before she could sit down, he trotted off in anticipation of their ride.

"Hemi," she scolded. "You know better than that." Sometimes she was intimidated by his hot temperament, but it felt great to be riding him again, like the first day of summer vacation.

After a few laps around the arena at a walk, Chiara squeezed Hemingway's sides and he transitioned into a trot. She posted along the track, listening to his hooves striking the sand with rhythmic regularity, compressing it with every stride.

Chiara relaxed, allowing her weight to drop into her heels to absorb the concussion of each stride as they trotted around the arena. Hemi let out a long, powerful snort, then another, as if he was clearing his throat, a sign that he was relaxed and ready to work.

In the breezy early morning, Chiara felt taken with a sense of calm and well-being. Even though Adrian would be arriving soon, she wasn't thinking about that now. She never thought of anything else when she rode. It was practically a spiritual experience for her, just as planting the sunflowers with her family once was. Sometimes she still thought of how similar the feelings were. But then she would recall Father Bob, how he'd shattered the association forever.

After some transitions between trotting, cantering, and walking, all useful for loosening Hemingway's back, Chiara took a strong half-halt in the walk—an aid used to redirect a horse's energy and center of balance. *Collect,* she thought. Hemingway lowered his croup, arched his muscular neck, and began to piaffe—a trot on the spot. They had both been training toward the execution of the difficult movement for years. He let out a loud, hard snort to alert Chiara that this was difficult work.

"Come on, we can do it, buddy," she told him. Hemi snorted once more, offering another four steps of piaffe before Chiara allowed him to relax and trot forward again.

"Good boy." She patted him on the neck, savoring the past few seconds. She wanted to ask him to do it again, but she didn't want to push him too hard so soon after his colic episode. So she gave him a loose rein instead, allowing him to stretch his neck long and toward the ground in the trot as a reward.

When she got back to the stable and saw Adrian's black BMW parked outside, she felt the familiar flutter around her heart. She looked at her watch, glad to see that he was on time.

In the stable, Julio was tacking Shadowfax and talking baseball with Adrian.

"Hey, guys," she said.

"Hemi looked good," Julio said. "I was watching from here."

Chiara patted Hemingway on the neck. "Thanks, Julio, I couldn't do it without you."

Adrian handed her a box of chocolates and kissed her on the lips.

Chiara held the box to her chest. "Chocolate...thank you."

Adrian smiled at her and looked around the stable. "I love the smell of horses."

Julio handed him Shadowfax's reins. "We do, too."

Adrian looked up at the huge gelding. "Hey, buddy, remember me? It's been a while since I rode you."

"Are you nervous?" Chiara asked.

"A little," he said.

"Don't be. You know he's a big puppy dog."

"I know, but he always looks like a really big horse before I get on," Adrian said.

They laughed.

"Are you ready?" Chiara said.

"Ready," Adrian said.

Taking in his rugged look, feeling her heart give her another reminder love thump, she wondered what he could possibly see in her. "Let's go, then."

When they got deep into the woods, Chiara looked him over once and giggled.

"What's so funny?" he said. He seemed to be admiring her legs in the breeches and tall black riding boots. It made her blush.

She giggled again. "Your western outfit."

He looked himself over once. He was wearing a Stetson cowboy hat and cowboy boots, a denim shirt and Wrangler jeans. "What's wrong with it?"

"Nothing's wrong with it. You look very sexy, it's just—"

"Just what?"

Chiara giggled again. "It's just weird seeing you dressed in western gear riding in English tack, that's all. It's like watching a hockey player skating around in figure skates."

She started giggling again, finding it hard to stop, partly because he did look a little funny and partly because she was so happy to have him there with her in the woods, alone and all to herself.

"Keep it up, hot shot, and you're gonna find yourself getting kicked in the rear end with this size thirteen boot," he said.

"Ouch," she said, still laughing.

Adrian fell silent. He seemed to be taking in her laughter, the quiet woods around them, enjoying every bit of it. As they rode, it grew warm and humid. The heat suspended a potent smell of sweet honeysuckle in the air along the coppice-lined path. It felt as if time had stopped just for them. Massive old pine and oak trees, wild blackberry bushes, and a variety of enormous weeds bordered the leaf-bedded path, offering Chiara a sense of respite from her daily obligations. She momentarily embraced the confused feelings she felt over Papà lately, then she let them go. Today she would be happy. She and Adrian were alone, no parents, no fans, and no guilt.

"I forgot how nice it is back here," Adrian said.

"It's definitely quiet compared to the ballpark and the restaurant and the hospital."

Adrian had a cool, unconcerned calmness about himself. His limbs moved, and he talked, unhurried, as if he was exactly where he was supposed to be at that moment in the universe. He was neither humbled nor made arrogant by this subtle knowledge. Chiara wished she could feel that way.

When they got deeper into the woods, an eight-point white buck shot out from behind a leafy brush several yards away and ran toward the hayfield ahead. Hemingway spooked and bolted in the opposite direction.

Chiara shrieked. "Whoa, Hemi!"

Hemingway galloped full force through the dense brush. Bent low over the saddle to dodge low-hanging branches, Chiara yanked hard on one rein trying to slow and turn him, to no avail. She pulled again and again, each time with more force. Tensing up, she lost one stirrup, then the other. She braced her thighs against the saddle and pulled again. Hemingway slowed and turned, transitioning into an animated trot on a small circle, stomping the ground beneath him, snorting. Chiara slid her feet back into the stirrups and stilled and relaxed her seat, willing herself to calm down, asking Hemingway to walk. Reluctantly he did, but his stride was quick and choppy. His back was as hard as a wooden plank underneath her.

Adrian was at her side in seconds. He looked petrified. "Are you okay?"

Chiara kept Hemingway on the circle. Her body was still tense, but she focused on relaxing. Hemingway would interpret any tension in her body as a sign of danger and bolt again. "I wish he would trot like that when I'm showing him."

"Chiara…"

"I'm fine, I'm fine," she said. But her insides were shaking. Hemingway had never bolted like that before. She had almost fallen off—something she hadn't done since she was a little girl.

"You sure?"

She gave him a reassuring smile. "I'm sure."

She rubbed Hemingway's neck and he slowed to a more natural walk. "You're okay, Hemi."

"Are you sure you're sure, *amor*?"

Amor. She took a deep breath and let it out quickly. Every time he called her that she felt a soft tickle in her heart and she had to smile. "Yes, I'm sure. Really, really sure." When Hemingway was calm, they walked on again.

"That buck came out of nowhere…He was white!" Adrian said. "I've never see a white deer. Have you?"

Chiara nodded. "We have a small herd of Seneca white deer that somehow made their way here from New York years ago."

"Was it an albino?"

"No, it's a recessive gene that makes them white. Did you learn about genes in biology?"

"Some," he said. "I never paid much attention in school. Are people allowed to hunt back here?"

"They're not supposed to, but they do anyway. We have 'no hunting' signs posted everywhere, but every year we always have a few overzealous hunters sneak onto the property to try and catch a poor buck."

"My dad would be one of those hunters if he lived around here."

"Have you talked to him?"

"No, not for months. He's a drunk."

"Sorry, I shouldn't have brought it up." She paused. "When I sat with your mom last night, she seemed as thrilled about our plans as Papà is."

"Forget it, Chiara. She'll be fine. It's about me and you."

She took a deep breath and let it out slowly. "You're right," she said trying to sound positive. She pointed toward another opening along the path. "Let's ride past the limestone temple. You know how much Papà loves Italian renaissance. He put a bust of Pan under it a few months ago. I think the path to it is the prettiest part of the ride. After that, we'll cross into the hayfield."

"Your dad sure likes limestone. Who's Pan?"

"He's the god of the woods."

"How much land do you guys have?"

"Around a hundred acres. We're on the edge of our property. We own the hayfield to the right and our neighbor, Chris Kaiser, whom we've known since we moved into Girasole, owns all the property to the left. But he lets us ride on his property, too. He plants thirty acres' worth of pumpkins every year for a Saint Jude's fund-raiser. He matches every dollar sold in pumpkins. They should be about the size of watermelons by now."

"That's pretty nice."

"It is. Valerie and I used to go over and help with the fund-raisers every year. The smile faded from her face. "He had a little sister who died of leukemia when he was a teenager." She wondered how anyone could believe in a god that allowed children to get sick and die before they could even learn to ride a bike.

Adrian stared at her, looking a little jealous, and Chiara found herself feeling a little more loved.

"Did you ever go out with him?" he asked.

"No, but friends tried to set me up with him for years. When I was a teenager I despised him because he rode his motocross bikes on Girasole pastures close to the stable when he had a hundred acres of his own to ride on. A few times his testosterone-motivated drive-bys spooked my horses while I was riding and caused me to fall."

"Why didn't you ever go out with him?"

"For one, he's almost ten years older than me. Two, he's so black and white about things, like Papà. And three, there was a time when I loved to do the opposite of what Papà wanted me to just for the heck of it. And Papà really likes him. It would've made him very happy if I eventually married Chris."

She raised her arm, punching the air with her index finger, mocking Papà's characteristic gesture when he wanted to pontificate. "*After* I finished *scuola di medicina.*"

They laughed and rode on side by side along an oak tree-lined path. Over forty feet tall, they formed a leafy canopy overhead, allowing the sun to peek through only in patches, as if they were telling it, "*You may be able to light the entire planet, but right here, in our little piece of the world, in these woods, we only want this much light.*" Chiara and Hemingway moved ahead of Shadowfax and Adrian. As she crossed one of the sun-drenched patches she glanced back at him, a mischievous grin spreading across her face.

"Last one to the hayfield buys dinner."

Adrian's eyes widened. "Are you serious?"

Chiara shouted, "Yaaaah!" Hemingway took off with a *boom, ba ba boom, ba ba boom* toward the field.

Shadowfax, close to twenty years old, apparently needed to be coaxed a bit but responded with a few *clopping* steps of his own before leading into a lazy, loping gallop. By then Chiara had already gained a considerable lead.

She glanced back under her arm like a thoroughbred jockey protecting her lead. It had rained the night before and Hemingway kicked up weighty mud balls with every stride. Some smacked Adrian in the face as they approached the clearing, reminding her of her mud ball fight with her sisters years ago.

"You're crazy, Chiara!" he called from behind. "Slow down!"

"Why?" she yelled back. "So you can pass me up? You can't win *everything*."

"I need to ask you something," he shouted back.

Adrian closed in on her lead. The horses now galloped side by side, their necks stretching forward with every stride, their tails flying like kites behind them.

"No time like the present!" she yelled.

"Okay!" he shouted looking between Shadowfax's ears at the path ahead and again at Chiara. "Will...you...marry...me?"

Chiara's mouth dropped. Her eyes filled with tears and she slowed Hemingway until they were walking. Until that day, she had lived her life like a math problem, relying on the predictable, finding faith in the concreteness of her studies. In an instant this had changed. She felt herself flying on wings of fate, surrendering to uncertainty and a longing for something she could never quite define.

Adrian hopped off Shadowfax and went to Chiara. He reached up and gently pulled her off Hemingway and set her down on the leaf-laden ground. They were breathing hard and Chiara was crying harder now, wiping tears and smearing dirt along her face.

He placed his hand under her chin and lifted her face to his. "I know we've been talking about it," he said. "But I didn't actually ask you." He took her hands in his. "Look Chiara, I know you want your dad's blessing, and I do too," he said with his deep velvety voice, "but I've wanted you for the rest of my life from the first time I saw you at the restaurant. I know we have something special. I love you, and I know you love me for me, not for my job or the money I might make someday. I want us to be official."

Chiara took in his expression, so strong and certain of them. Her heart was pounding so hard, she could barely breathe. *This is true love,* she thought. *When you feel as though all you will ever need to survive, to feel right in the world, is standing in front of you.* "Ask me again," she stammered. She needed to hear him ask her again.

"I'm taking off my hat, bending down on one knee, Chiara. Marry me."

Chiara stood motionless in the thicket, hoping to drag out the moment forever. She wanted to remember every minute detail for the rest of her life, the sound of the horses' muzzles sifting through fallen leaves for grass, sparrows chirping in the trees around them, the smell of the woods, the smell of his Carolina Herrera for Men, his hair, wet with sweat. But most of all, she wanted to remember his pleading eyes gazing at her as if to say, *This is our time.*

"Chiara?"

She kissed his full lips, so moist and soft against hers. "Yes. Yes, I will, Adrian."

"Yes!" he shouted. He picked her up and spun her around and around and around until they were both dizzy.

When he finally set her down, Chiara held him close, pressing her face against his chest. Hairs poked over the top of his shirt and tickled her cheek. It was as if they were inviting her to unfasten another button.

He cupped her face in his hand. "I love you."

"I love you too, Adrian. I don't ever want to be without you."

"We'll always be together, Chiara."

He ran his hands across her forehead. "Did I ever tell you I love everything about you?"

"Even my eyebrows?"

"Especially your eyebrows."

She smiled, kissed him, prayed he'd never see her teenage pictures.

He pressed the small of her back against him. Had he laid her down and wanted to make love to her right then and there in the thicket, she wouldn't have protested. But he didn't. Instead he growled and gently pushed her away. "You drive me crazy, Chiara."

She moaned, not letting go of him. "You drive me crazy too, Adrian."

He reached into his pocket and pulled out a purple velvet pouch trimmed in gold. Then he pulled a diamond ring out of it and slipped it on her finger.

"Oh, Adrian. It's beautiful," she said. It was a two-caret princess-cut stone set in a simple gold Tiffany setting.

"You really like it?" he said.

"Are you kidding? I love it. It's from you."

"I've been carrying it around for weeks trying to figure out the right time to give it to you. A couple of the ballplayers said I should propose at the ballpark, but I know you. You would've felt really shy."

She kissed him, her face lingering near his. "Today was perfect. Here was perfect."

"I think we should have a date in mind when we talk to your dad."

"Okay," Chiara said. Reality stung her like a swift smack with a wet towel.

"Well," he said. "When?"

When. What should she say? Papà had had control over that four-letter word for as long as she could remember. She had given it to him in the form of a promise when she was twelve. Papà was going to fight any sort of scheme that she and Adrian worked out. There was no doubt in her mind about that. It was as explicit as one plus one equals two.

A sense of malaise crept up from her feet and spread through her body, squelching the happiest moment in her life. How was she going to keep Adrian *and* Papà happy?

She lowered her gaze. "You know I want to become an obstetrician."

"I want you to, too," he said. "You can do both, don't you think? Be married and go to school? I'm not book smart or nothing, but I'll help you however I can."

She smiled at him, feeling full of hope. "I know you will, Adrian. I want to help you in any way I can with your profession too."

"But I don't want to wait until you graduate to get married, Chiara. Who knows how many times I'll get traded by then? I was thinking we should do it next year after the season ends, on your winter break."

She grew uneasy, and he stepped closer to her, as if to shield her from her father's impending reaction. "It's gonna be okay, Chiara. Your dad will get over it, believe me."

He wrapped his large hands around her slight arms and shook her gently left and right, coaxing her to smile.

She looked over at the horses that had strayed off looking for better grass. She gave a hesitant nod and smiled. "Okay."

"Awesome," he said hugging her again.

She took a deep breath, taking in his familiar smell. "I don't want this moment to end," she said. She meant it in more ways than one. As she stood wrapped in his arms, a scenario flashed through her mind. She imagined walking hand in hand with Adrian into Papà's library. *Papà, Adrian has proposed to me. We're getting married next winter.* Then a slew of Mafia hit men would appear out of nowhere and threaten to cut off Adrian's testicles. And that would be the end of the discussion until she was graduated from *scuola di medicina.*

"We'll have lots of times like this, Chiara, just you and me," Adrian said.

She pushed the ridiculous thought away. "I know we will."

"We better get back," he said. "My mom's at my apartment and she said she wasn't feeling good this morning. I should go spend some time with her."

Chiara clung to him for another moment like an insecure kitten. "Okay. If she needs anything, tell her to call me."

"I will. Can you go to a movie with us tonight?" he said.

Chiara managed a smile. "I can't, honey. I have to study a chapter for my medical interviewing class and one for my Intro to Physical Exam. Do you mind if we ride back through the hayfield? It's the long way home. I'm not ready to let you go yet."

"Whatever you want, Chiara, whatever you want," he said.

As she mounted Hemingway again, Chiara looked down at her finger. The ring's facets sparkled like the North Star on a clear night, radiating its symbolic promise. She hoped Papà would see it that way too.

Chapter 7

Isabella tamped coffee grounds into the portafilter of the copper espresso machine, placed a cup under the brew basket, and turned it on before sitting back down with Gian Carlo at the kitchen table. He was deep in thought. The train-track lines—as Chiara liked to call them—across his forehead had deepened over the years. Absently he stirred a cup of espresso; it was a daily morning ritual for as long as they could remember. There were times he would stir his coffee for so long that the *tink tink ta tink* sound of the spoon striking the sides of the cup could send anyone mad. Once, when Valerie was still in college, she flew into the kitchen and asked him for the spoon. When he handed it to her, she marched right over to the kitchen door, opened it, and threw the spoon as far into the garden as her strength allowed. Then she returned to her books in the family room.

Isabella placed her hand on his wrist, and he stopped stirring.

"Sorry," he said.

"What are you thinking about?"

"Chiara. We were busy at *il ristorante* last night. I got home too late to talk to her."

"She's home today," Isabella said.

"I know. I am waiting for Adrian to leave." He took a long, labored breath.

"You look pale, Carlo. Are you feeling all right?"

"I have heartburn."

Isabella went to a cabinet and returned with a pack of Tums and a cup of espresso for herself.

"I am so angry with her," he said. "This boy is not for her. I have a bad feeling."

Isabella set the pack on the table and placed her hand on Gian Carlo's arm. "Is it because you don't like him, or because you're afraid she won't finish medical school?"

"Both. I must protect her from him. I do not want to fail her again."

"You've never failed her, Carlo."

"I did not see through that *figlio di putana*. I was not there to protect her from that beast, and because of me, she was hurt. Because of me, she lost confidence in herself. Because of me, she lost faith in God."

"That is not true, Gian Carlo."

He paused for a long time. "It is the way I see it."

"Are you going to blame Valerie's infertility on yourself too?"

"No, that is different."

"Well, Chiara is happier now than she's ever been. Adrian makes her happy. He's a nice boy. Have faith in Chiara's decision."

"I have faith in her, but I know she does not have enough faith in herself. She puts everyone else before herself."

"That will make her a wonderful doctor someday."

"If it does not get in the way of her graduating first, eh." He leaned forward, placed his elbows on the table and rubbed his face with his hands. "This is her first year of medical school, Isabella. She needs to study, and he does not respect her time. He is always asking her to go here and there. He distracts her. Once they are married, he will want her to travel with him, to drink, to have children."

"She fits everything in she needs to do, Carlo."

"His lifestyle, the traveling, the drinking, the women chasing these sports figures, these things will all trouble her over the next few years, because she does love him."

Isabella rubbed the nape of her neck. "You can't babysit her anymore. She's a woman now."

Gian Carlo placed two tablets on his tongue and threw back the espresso like a shot of whiskey. "She must put herself first at this point in her life. She has no time to be married, *particolamente* to that *cafone*," he said pointing out the back window toward the stable.

Isabella gave him an all-knowing look. "She's going to marry him. There's no doubt in my mind."

"I know I cannot stop her. But I will not be involved in any way if she does so before she graduates. I will not attend the wedding, eh." He lit a cigarette and took a long drag, exhaling the smoke away from her.

Isabella crossed her hands on the table and gave him a long stare as if she had heard enough. Her cheeks were red, accentuating her cheekbones, and he was amazed how he could still be taken by her beauty after all these years.

"Carlo, you are going to put me in a very difficult situation if you refuse to be involved. I'm asking you to make some concessions. I've made many for you."

He looked at her as if she had a point. He opened his mouth to object anyway, but Isabella held up her hand.

He leaned back in his chair, muttering.

"I think Adrian is a nice young man with a fantastic career ahead of him in baseball. I think they could have a blessed life together."

Gian Carlo stood up and walked to the French doors. He took a long drag of his cigarette. Sections of the carved-stone balustrade on the terrace steps had darkened, and he made a mental note to have them sandblasted. He looked past the garden to his small patch of *girasoli* in the distance and listened to the landscapers trimming the bushes in the garden. For a second, he remembered the first time he saw Isabella, how he knew she was the *one*.

"Gian Carlo, all I am asking is for you to agree to a lengthy engagement." Her voice was calmer now, tender. "Perhaps they could get married in her third or fourth year. Would you consider that? During that time you might grow to like him."

He contemplated the idea. He thought about how he had not been particularly fond of Liam when he met him years ago. Liam was not *italiano* either. But now, Gian Carlo looked at him as a son. Gian Carlo looked forward to the day he would be a grandfather to his and Valerie's children, even if they were to be conceived in vitro. The science behind the process intrigued him.

"Maybe," she said, "if she has that commitment, she will feel less inclined to rush forward with wedding plans."

"We have worked so hard to give our girls opportunities, Isabella. I don't want hers to be taken away by a selfish boy who promises her the stars and the moon." He sat down at the table, took another long hit of the cigarette, and then put it out in the ashtray. He felt as if a five hundred-pound boulder had just been dropped on his chest from a three-story building.

"Please, *amore*, just think about it."

When he spoke, his voice was hoarse. "I will think about it."

"Thank you, Carlo. They should be back from their ride by now. Do you want to go down and see them for a few minutes? Then we can drive to the restaurant together. I have to pick up pasta for the spaghetti dinner at church tomorrow."

As they walked down to the stable, Isabella wrapped her arm around Gian Carlo's waist and kissed him on the lips.

Chapter 8

Papà and Mamma entered the stable arm in arm, and Chiara felt an agonizing ache growing in her chest. *It wasn't supposed to be like this.* Papà was old fashioned; he would have wanted Adrian to ask him for her hand in marriage. Chiara thought about inconspicuously taking off the ring until she could talk to Papà, but she knew that would hurt Adrian.

She purposefully un-tacked Hemingway, hoping Papà wouldn't take the news as hard as she thought he was going to, wishing there was something she could do to ease his hurt. Her face flushed and beads of sweat formed between her breasts and under her arms.

"Hi, Papà," she said, holding her saddle.

"Hi, Chiara," he said, extending his hand to Adrian. "Adrian, how are you? Did you and Chiara enjoy yourselves?"

"Yeah, Mr. Lazzaro. That statue of Pan you put in the temple is really nice."

"Thank you. I like to have whimsical things to see in the woods when I ride with my girls."

"How long did you ride?" Mamma asked, motioning for Chiara to wipe the dirt off her face.

"For a couple hours," Adrian said.

"Shadowfax can really jar your body. I hope you won't be sore for the game tomorrow night. Aren't you pitching?" Mamma asked.

Adrian offered her a smile. "Yeah, but I'll be okay."

"So," Papà said. "The baseball season is almost over; are you satisfied with your statistics?"

As Papà and Adrian made polite conversation, Chiara carried her saddle into the tack room, thankful to have something to cover the ring with. Papà's tone with Adrian was surprisingly cordial, perhaps—did she dare to say?—even *warm*. Chiara wondered what divine miracle Mamma had performed on him overnight. Adrian, on the other hand, sounded nervous. Chiara heard his deep voice quaver a few times. She couldn't leave him out there alone with Papà for long. She set the saddle on a rack, took a deep breath, and joined them in the aisle again.

"Adrian," Mamma said. "Chiara told me you have a day off today. We would love to have you and your mother over for dinner tonight, if you don't already have plans."

Mamma gave Papà a look like he should say something kind.

"Yes," Papà said, clearing his throat. "We could have a nice discussion about your future together. Chiara has informed me that you two have become very serious and would like to marry someday."

His eyes softened ever so slightly as he looked at Mamma. Chiara thought he was really trying.

"Perhaps we could sit down and come to a mutual agreement that would satisfy all of us." Papà's voice was calm, but when he looked back at Adrian, his expression demanded that Adrian agree.

Adrian tensed a little. "Mr. Lazzaro, I love your daughter, and I want to respect you, but I want to start my life with her as soon as possible. I'll help her get through med school in whatever way I can, but we don't want to wait until she graduates. I asked her to marry me today." He looked over at Chiara. "Show him the ring, *amor*."

Chiara reluctantly held out her hand. "It was a surprise, Papà," she said, her voice cracking, wishing she could soften the blow to his heart.

Mamma looked surprised, but Papà looked shocked. There was frantic look in his eyes. He stood motionless, staring at the ring. Absorbing the hurt on his face, Chiara regretted accepting the ring before Adrian had told Papà he was going to propose.

When he regained his composure, Papà's face grew ablaze with fury. "*A casa,*" he shouted at Chiara, pointing toward the house.

It was rumored in Italy that the Lazzaro family was distantly related to Mussolini; at that moment, looking at Papà, so erect and militant, it looked as if it might be true. If it wasn't, Papà had watched one too many war movies. He pointed at the stable doors and screamed at Adrian. "And you...go home!"

Chiara took a step toward him. "Please, Papà, don't be this way. We can work this all out."

"Mr. Lazzaro," Adrian said, "I'm sorry. I didn't mean for—"

Papà glared at Adrian. "Eh? Sorry? You are not sorry," he bellowed. "If you had *rispetto* for this *famiglia* you would never have permitted yourself such a selfish act."

"It's not how I wanted it to happen; it was just one of those things," he said looking offended.

"Just one of those things?" Papà roared. "Proposing to a man's daughter without his knowledge of it is not 'just one of those things.' You knew I would say no and you asked her anyway." He pointed toward the stable doors again. "Go home, and do not ever show your face on this property again."

Adrian handed the horse's reins to Julio and started down the stable aisle toward his car.

Chiara grasped his arm, trying to stop him from leaving, but he gently pushed past her. "Adrian, don't leave. How can you leave? Stay and talk to him about this."

Papà was still glaring at Adrian.

"Please," she pleaded. "Let's handle this like adults."

"Chiara, it's okay," Adrian said. "Talk to your family. I'll call you later."

Chiara followed Adrian to his car, begging him to stay. But he refused. Appalled, Chiara watched him drive away. When he was gone, she went back into the stable.

"Papà, why do you have to make marriage sound like a death sentence or something taboo that nobody in this family can talk about until you say it's all right?" Her vocal cords felt as tight as violin strings, as if they might break if she put any more effort into pleading with him to be reasonable. Her heart was pounding as though she were running a hundred-meter dash and she took a deep breath to steady her breathing. "Yours has been wonderful," she croaked, barely able to get the words out.

Papà glared at her through bloodshot eyes. If the wrath of God could be personified, it showed in Papà's face that very moment. "I married a wonderful woman," he said. "He is *un cafone*. What kind of man leaves the woman he loves to deal with her angry father over something like this? He is weak."

She drew her arms akimbo. "Why don't you like him? What do you think you know about him that I don't?"

"He drinks like a fish at *il ristorante*. Only problems can come of such overindulgence."

"He only drinks on the weekends when he doesn't have to pitch."

Papà took a deep breath. "Fine. Do you know he has a child he has nothing to do with?"

How did he find out? Adrian had told Chiara he had fathered a child when he was sixteen and although he wasn't a part of the child's life, he did pay child support.

"I knew. He made a mistake. He was young."

"He is irresponsible and selfish. These are character flaws," Papà retorted. He lit a cigarette and took a long drag.

She started to say, *everyone has character flaws,* but he held up his hand, motioning her to be quiet.

"He is not thinking of me, Mamma, or even you," he said.

"Maybe he didn't ask you for my hand because he was afraid you'd say no," Chiara snapped.

"Exactly."

The word punched the air, and Chiara had the feeling Papà had gained a slight advantage. She bit her lower lip.

"But he proposed to you anyway," he said, "creating problems for our *famiglia*. This is a sign of *un traditore*, Chiara—"

Chiara raised her voice. "Papà, he's not a traitor. He treats me like gold. If you give him a chance, you'll see that."

"I have seen everything I need to see." Papà squinted through the haze of his cigarette smoke.

"Do you see how happy he makes me? He empowers me…helps me feel confident."

Papà gave her a hard stare. "Chiara, your education, your accomplishments, and your self-esteem are what should empower you, not a man."

"I'm an adult, Papà. I'll choose who I want in my life."

He shook his head, looking disgusted. "You are an adult. A very naïve adult." He held up his index finger. "But I am your father. I will be respected."

"I do respect you. When don't I respect you? I go to class, I study, and up until this year, I've worked at the restaurant. What else do you want from me, blood?"

Papà's nose began to sweat. "No. Just a *degree.*"

Chiara tucked her hands in her pants pockets and stared down at the floor. "I can see we're not getting anywhere. You're resolved to hate him, to be cynical. Nothing I do or say will change your mind."

Papà shook his head. "Do you think I have always been this hard?" he said. "I have not. *La vita...*" he sighed. "*La vita* has shaped and molded me into what I am. *Sacrificio, povertà,* three daughters whom I love. I never thought I would have *i problemi* with you, Chiara. As a child you were always *calma,* reliable, obedient, and careful not to hurt anyone."

Chiara felt guilt rise in her throat. "I'm not trying to give you problems, Papà."

"I hope you never experience *i problemi* I have endured in my life. It has taken me thirty years of studying English to have this conversation with you, Chiara. Still, Italian words slip into almost every sentence I speak to remind me that *la America* will never be my motherland as you have come to see it."

Sweat seeped through the pores on Papà's face and for a moment his skin grew clammy and gray. "You are thinking about what he wants. I am thinking about what is best for you, your *futuro.* He is an asshole."

Her anger grew more intense. "He's not an asshole, Papà," she shouted. "I can see now, more than ever, all you care about is what *you* want me to accomplish. What about what I want for me? You're being so selfish."

"Chiara!" Papà shouted. "How dare you say that to me."

"Stop it, both of you," Mamma said.

"It's the truth," Chiara said, feeling a knot in her throat tighten.

Papà lunged toward her, his hands balled up in fists. "Everything I have done in this life, *con questi mani,* has been for Mamma, your sisters, and you! Not one penny have I earned without thinking about bettering the life of this *famiglia.*" His Roman nose dripped with sweat. He pulled a handkerchief from his pocket and pointed toward the driveway. "He is the selfish one," he said. "I have informed myself about him. I know what he and all the other baseball players do when they are traveling from *città a città.* They go from bar to bar and from woman to woman. You are not going to want that life ten years from now."

"I do know what I want ten years from now. I want to be an obstetrician married to Adrian. And he is not a womanizer!" Chiara yelled back.

"Stop, both of you!" Mamma shouted again. "We're not going to get anywhere now."

"Papà, I love you. But I love Adrian, too. I know it was wrong that he proposed without your blessing. And I'm sorry about that. But I am not sorry that I'm going to marry him. I will prove to you that I'll finish medical school."

"Men your age are not serious. He will use you and never look back," he shouted.

Chiara held up her left hand. "Does someone looking for a good time ask you to marry him?"

"You will never have my blessing to marry until you finish *scuola di medicina,* eh," he said, pointing in her face. "And you will never have my blessing to marry *him.* Never."

Chiara watched Papà march out of the stable as if he were heading into World War Three. When he left, she sank onto a bench in the aisle and let her tears gush like a geyser. "This is the best and worst day of my life," she cried.

Mamma lowered herself onto the bench and put her arms around her. "It's going to be all right, *cara,*" she said. "I'll talk to him."

"No, it's not. He'll never forgive Adrian for this." Tears poured down her face.

"He really should have talked to Papà first," Mamma said. "It is the way it's usually done in traditional families. Liam asked Papà before he proposed to Valerie. Do you think Adrian didn't know any better?"

"Yes, he knew better. I'd told him he would need to ask Papà's permission." Chiara sobbed.

"I'm disappointed that he left you alone to deal with Papà. He should have stood by you and tried to talk to him."

"I can't believe he didn't, Mamma." *How could Adrian have left me to deal with this mess all by myself?* "Why do men have such big egos?"

"Just tell me you didn't set a date."

"Next fall," she said, wiping her nose on her sleeve.

"*Aie*, Chiara, I'm not Moses. I can't part water."

"I know, I know." She took a deep breath, wiping her face, collecting herself. "I was just so shocked and thrilled that I agreed."

"What do you want to do?"

Chiara stood up and walked the length of the stable, stopping under the arched doorway to think. In the distance, Julio was schooling Amadeus, and Bibi sat under the gazebo watching him. Papà was so wrong about Adrian. Until she and Papà could come to an agreement about the marriage, she was going to have to find a way for him to tolerate Adrian.

She walked back to Mamma, watching her pet Papà's black gelding in his stall. "I'm going to make Papà an offer," she said. "I'll wait until my third year to marry Adrian. That's two more years."

Mamma stepped out of the stall. "Sounds fair."

"But—"

Mamma rolled her eyes. "There's always a but."

"Papà has to promise to be civil toward him."

"Who's telling him?"

Chiara looked down at the floor. "I will."

Chapter 9

Gian Carlo stomped into his library sweating as if he had just run a marathon. This was his favorite room in Girasole, where he loved spending time alone. Everything about the library was intimate and soothing: the subtle smell of cigarette smoke, the Persian Karistan rug that covered the walnut floor, the maroon walls and soft chandelier lighting. French doors opened to the terrace. In one corner stood a drink cart filled with liquors he never touched, and in the other a grandfather clock softly chimed every half hour.

A twenty-inch television in a floor-to-ceiling burl-wood bookshelf behind the desk was tuned to CNN. The station was airing a segment on major league baseball attendance, which was at an all-time low after the 1994 strike.

"Che sport stupido," he growled. He shot toward the television and smacked the power switch. He was livid, and he didn't notice Bibi, Julio's petite, dark-haired wife standing in the doorway with a steaming cup of espresso. She'd been working at Girasole since the Lazzaro family moved into the house, and she prepared a cup of espresso as well as any self-respecting *italiana.*

"May I come in, Signor Gian Carlo?"

He ran a hand through his thinning hair. It was still as black as ever. "*Sì*, Bibi, come in."

The expression on her face told him she was privy to what had transpired in the stable. She set the cup on his desk. He sensed she was attempting to placate him with the coffee. The caffeine would only fuel someone else's temper, but it worked like a calming agent on Gian Carlo. He sat down behind the desk and took a careful sip.

"Bibi, I do not understand Chiara. Sometimes I think it would have been less painful to never have had children at all."

Bibi's dark eyes fell to the intricate design of the rug.

Gian Carlo regretted his words as soon as they left his mouth. She and Julio had lost a child years ago.

"Pain, Signor, is a necessary evil in life," Bibi said. "It molds us and shapes us into who we are." She never looked up as she left the room, closing the doors behind her.

Gian Carlo chastised himself for not being more conscious of Bibi's feelings. He knew from experience that she was right, but he was so disappointed with Chiara. For the first time in his life, he realized, he was not thinking about the future or the past. He was just living, living in that very moment that defined who he was: a father who loved all three of his daughters; a father who had worked his way to wealth to provide them with a promising future; a father who wanted his daughters to have faith in themselves. Chiara placed too much faith in others.

He took a deep breath and let it out slowly, willing his anger away. He felt tightness in his chest, and his thoughts turned from Chiara to himself. *If I take away what I have accomplished, the goals I have for la mia famiglia, who am I?* That he might not know himself all that well was almost too vast a concept to comprehend.

He walked around the front of his desk to a wall of family diplomas and photos, taking a white handkerchief out of his dress pants pocket—he always wore a jacket and dress pants these days. As he wiped his face, a face still handsome but lined with many wrinkles, Gian Carlo's gaze fell upon a black-and-white photo of himself as a three-year-old boy in *Italia*. He was standing nude on a stone ledge in his mother's garden with his older brother Salvatore, then sixteen, sitting next to him. Salvatore's arms were wrapped around his younger self, one hand holding a large fig leaf to shield Gian Carlo's maleness.

Although their smiles revealed a comical family moment, Gian Carlo recalled that World War Two had begun two years before the picture was taken. The war had brought a famine so tremendous that it resembled a plague from the Old Testament sweeping through the village.

Gian Carlo shivered as he shifted his attention to another photo of himself and his seven siblings standing in the town piazza in front of the decrepit wooden church doors. Their clothes hung on them. There was a dusting of snow on the church steps, and uniformed German soldiers stood to one side, smoking cigarettes. *Natale, 1944.* There was nothing Christmasy about the photo. Gian Carlo chuckled at the thick cherrywood frame with gilded leaf corners. The frame cost more than his family had to spend that winter. *Italia mia, why do I love you when all I remember is pain when I lived in your arms?*

He sat back down in his leather desk chair and swiveled around to face the bookshelves. They extended along the entire back wall of the formidable library. He was proud that he had read every book on each shelf. Only those he had finished gained the right to join the others on the shelves, like an induction into an educational fraternity. Sometimes Gian Carlo wondered if he had learned enough through his own studies to merit a college degree. He reached for a paperback, contemplating the title: *Sprezzatura, 50 Ways Italian Genius Shaped the World.* It brought a smile to his face. *The authors of this book know why Italia is special*, he thought. Each chapter, an essay of its own, explored an Italian cultural achievement and how it influenced the modern world. Gian Carlo leafed through the pages, reading various chapter titles, basking in the pride he felt for his ancestors' accomplishments as if they were his own family members. He stopped at chapter ten, "Salerno and Bologna: The Earliest Medical School and University."

The title evoked a tender memory of his father, Patrizio. It had taken almost ten years for Gian Carlo's family to recover financially from World War II. Gian Carlo had worked for years in his father's vineyards. When Patrizio started turning a profit in 1954, he insisted Gian Carlo apply to the University of Bologna's college preparatory program for children and young adults who had fallen behind due to the war. Gian Carlo had planned to attend the university's medical school after he completed the program.

It was a warm late-September evening. Gian Carlo had ridden his bike as hard as he could to his father's vineyards, sure he would be there, overseeing the pickers. When Gian Carlo saw his father he dropped the bike and ran toward him, wildly waving the acceptance letter and his pageboy hat in the air. *"Papà, sono stato accettato."*

Patrizio Lazzaro, a thin, dark-haired man who always wore suspenders and a fedora, kept his eyes on the pickers, stroking his graying Hitler mustache. He kept Gian Carlo waiting a moment, then motioned for the letter. The experience of living through two world wars had hardened him, but the slight curl of his mouth as he read the letter was as much of a smile as Gian Carlo had seen in years, and it was enough for him. Days later, Patrizio had a heart attack. Gian Carlo was forced to take on more of the work. Two years later, shortly after Elena began university, Patrizio died. Parentless, Gian Carlo was sent to live with an older sister who had married and immigrated to Australia. His fleeting opportunity for a proper education was gone.

After all the stories he had shared with his daughters about his youth, could Chiara not see how fragile and fleeting her opportunity to become *una dottoressa* was, too? Being accepted to medical school did not assure her a medical degree. Did she think Adrian would not wait to get married until after she graduated? He believed this was so.

Adrian had no idea what sacrifices Chiara and he would have to make in order for her to reach her goals. Gian Carlo sensed Adrian would not want to make those sacrifices anyway. Adrian did not value education; he had once told Gian Carlo he never studied and had barely graduated from high school.

Gian Carlo's two Great Danes, Romulus and Remus, started barking in the foyer. He set the book down and looked up just as Chiara tapped on the library door, holding a cup of espresso as if it were a peace offering.

She smiled sheepishly. *"Permesso?"*

"Sì, come in," he said.

She looked at his coffee cup. "I see Bibi already brought you a cup."

He took off his reading glasses and set them down on the desk. "I will drink that one too."

Chiara set the coffee cup down carefully, as if it was a magical elixir concocted to make him concede to her wishes.

"Can we talk calmly, Papà?"

"*Si*," he said. But he was still angry. He felt a tightening in his chest, his temper rising. His face was sweating; he wiped it and placed his handkerchief back in his pocket.

"Are you okay, Papà? You look pale."

He emptied the overflowing ashtray into a trash bin next to his desk.

He took a long slow breath. "All this talk is giving me heartburn."

"Do you want me to get you an antacid?"

He nodded.

Chapter 10

Chiara hurried into the kitchen and grabbed a pack of Tums from the cabinet. The *tink tink ta tink* sound of Papà's spoon echoed into the foyer from his library. She remembered a quote by the great mathematician René Descartes: "*Each problem that I solved became a rule which served afterwards to solve other problems.*" *I'm going to solve this problem with Papà,* she thought

Bibi came in, pulled a horse show entry form out of her apron pocket, and handed it to her. "Julio needs to know by today if you want to go to the Virginia show."

"Tell him yes," Chiara said, "and that I'll be down in a bit. I just need to talk to Papà for a second."

A loud *crack* emanated from the foyer. Had Papà dropped his coffee cup? That was unlikely. She called out to him. No answer. She and Bibi walked back toward the library. When they turned the corner into the foyer they saw Papà sprawled on the marble floor, his arms splayed out to his sides as if he had been crucified.

"Papà!" Chiara screamed, lunging toward him, collapsing onto his chest, feeling for a heartbeat. He was breathing, but barely. She shook him, bellowing his name as if she could will him conscious.

"Papà!" she cried.

"Signor Gian Carlo!"

"Papà, can you hear me?" Her hands were shaking, her body convulsing. "Papà!"

Nothing.

Their cries summoned Mamma from upstairs.

"What is it? What's going on?" Mamma cried.

"Call 911!" Chiara shouted.

"Carlo!" Mamma screamed. She dropped to her knees at Papà's side, placing his head in her lap.

Bibi grabbed the phone.

"Papà!" Chiara shouted, smacking Papà's face, trying to gain eye contact. But his gaze was fixed on the ceiling, in his green eyes an expression of awe, as if he were admiring something spectacular, like a Michelangelo painting in the Sistine Chapel. Chiara put her ear to his chest. His heart fluttered like a million butterflies trying to escape a dark space. "Oh God…he's fibrillating!"

Then, just like that, Papà's heart stopped, and Chiara felt the complete nothingness of death. No text could have prepared her for that.

"Chiara, here!" Bibi shouted, handing Chiara the phone.

"What's the emergency?" the dispatcher said. It was a woman's calm voice.

Chiara's heart was racing. "My father!" she screamed into the receiver. "He's had a heart attack!"

"Is he breathing?"

"No!"

Mamma wailed and prayed, putting her hands on Papà's cheeks. Behind her Remus and Romulus paced and whined. Bibi cried too, as she dragged the dogs away.

"Can you perform CPR until the ambulance gets there, ma'am?" the dispatcher said.

Her hands were shaking violently and she gripped the phone, afraid to drop it. "Yes…but it's been so long. Oh God…what's the ratio?"

"Stay calm, ma'am," the dispatcher said.

"What's the goddamn ratio?" Chiara shouted.

"Thirty to two."

Chiara dropped the phone and ran her hand up to the triangular space directly under Papà's sternum. Tears flooded her eyes and fell on her father's chest. She started chest compressions, trying to concentrate on the task, trying to think of Papà not as her father, but as a patient, a person she needed to help, a life she needed to save. "One, two, three, four, five, six…"

"Gian Carlo…no!" Mamma cried.

"Ma, move!" Chiara shouted. Then she steadily blew air into Papà's chest. Once. Twice. *Breathe*, she thought as she started the chest compressions again.

Within minutes, Bibi ushered two paramedics through the front door, one carrying a black medic bag and defibrillator, the other pushing a gurney. Chiara moved over and held Papà's hand. "Right here, Papà," she said. "I'm right here."

After three attempts to start Papà's heart electrically, Chiara helped place him on the gurney, one paramedic still doing compressions as they wheeled him out of the house. The unhurried speed at which the ambulance pulled out of the driveway, its red siren lights flashing silently, told Chiara the paramedics' effort was more of a formality than an attempt to save his life.

Three days later, on the day of the funeral, Chiara sat on the back terrace, swinging back and forth on a gliding chair. Friends and family gathered in the kitchen behind the doors, but she barely noticed.

Papà was gone. *Gone.* She could barely believe it. She had been sure he would live to be a hundred. She had been sure there would be time to make up, to see eye to eye again. A sudden memory softened her heart and she was there, so present in the memory, a hormonal nineteen-year-old, standing outside the stable, freshly stung by a bee, quarreling with Papà.

"Are you okay, Chiara?"

"No, Papà, I'm not. Look at this." She held up her swelling arm. "I hate getting stung. Why can't you just plant a few sunflowers in the other garden?"

His eyes lit up emerald green and he blew a kiss toward the sunflower garden with both hands. "*É un giardino bellissimo.* I told Mamma I would plant it for her someday. *Io sono il—*"

Chiara raised her arms akimbo. "Papà..."

"Mamma loves *i girasoli*," he pleaded. "It is our tradition to plant the garden."

"No, you love the sunflowers and everything yellow."

"Chiara, people come from all over to pick them. They make people smile. If *Dio* has a favorite flower—"

Chiara rolled her eyes at him. "I know, I know, you tell us all the time. But they don't make me smile, and I'm sick of getting stung because you want a field full of them. What's wrong with a small patch?"

He winced at the sight of Chiara's swollen arm. "*Va bene*. This will be the last year."

Chiara had rarely won arguments with him. She wondered why he had given in so easily that time, especially when he loved the garden so much. Perhaps he was growing tired of planting such a big garden every year. Perhaps he loathed seeing her skin swell in the spots where she'd get stung. Perhaps he knew it was a constant reminder to her that God had failed her.

She closed her eyes, trying to find solace in the glider's simple rhythmic rocking and squeaking in the final days of the warm and sunny Indian summer air. The more she tried, though, the more she heard Papà's last fluttering heartbeats. Chills ran up and down her body, and she reached for the martini Bibi had set out for her earlier. She took a deliberate swig, embracing the vodka's sting. She hoped the alcohol would prove the analgesic it was reputed to be, blurring and numbing pain, befogging the memories she wanted to avoid.

Soft voices floated from the kitchen windows. "He was so young... early fifties. Heart attack...Isabella was after him for years to quit smoking...Chiara and Isabella saw it happen."

The intercom buzzed. More people had arrived to pay their respects. Chiara thought about getting up to let them in, but the vodka had already made her indifferent.

Valerie stepped out onto the terrace, wearing a black dress. "Hey," she said.

"Hey, how are you?"

Valerie offered Chiara a weary smile and leaned against the stone balustrade, her back to the garden. "I keep thinking this is a dream.

We're all going to wake up, and Papà will be sitting at the kitchen table, stirring his coffee."

If she could have, Chiara would have smiled back. That feeling inside her, the inescapable raw emptiness infecting and claiming her insides as its own, wouldn't allow her to. She took a deep breath, swallowed the nauseating taste of grief, and let the tears flow. "We'd just had an argument over Adrian," she said, her voice cracking. "This is my fault," she said, barely able to get the words out. "He was always stressed over work. I sent him over the edge."

Valerie went to her and embraced her. "Don't say that. You know it's not true."

"It is true."

"Chiara, listen to me," Valerie said, taking a firm hold of her arms. "This is hard for all of us, but I need you to help me with Mamma. She's a mess. We need to be strong for her. I need you to be strong for me, okay?" She loosened her hold. "We've got the restaurants to think about too."

Chiara nodded, trying to collect herself. "I'll do the paperwork, scheduling, whatever Mamma needs."

"Concentrate on your classes. Between Sylvia and me, we'll figure something out. "We're not selling, though. Papà wouldn't have wanted that."

They held each other for a long time in silence.

Finally Valerie said faintly, "It's time to go."

Chiara looked out toward the grassy field again, remembering Papà's expression before he died. There was a time Chiara would have been certain it was the expression of a man meeting his Maker. She wished for Papà's sake it was.

Chapter 11

October, 1996

C hiara tossed and turned in bed. It was two o'clock in the morning, and in less than twelve hours she would be a married woman. She would be a different person, living a very different life in a different home. Not bothering to turn on any lights, she rolled out of bed and hit the play button on the CD player. Her wedding song instantly began playing. It was the theme song from the movie *Titanic*.

She walked over to her silk wedding dress that Mamma had hung earlier so carefully from the top of her French armoire. Admiring it, she ran her fingers down its full length before she brought it down and laid it on the bed. It had been designed for her and she loved knowing it was a one of a kind, and it was hers. When she was a little girl, she wore homemade dresses all the time. Mamma would buy yards and yards of material and sew clothes fashioned from her imagination. Not a pattern. She did this to save money even after they could afford store-bought clothes. Back then, Chiara lacked an appreciation for Mamma's knack for making intricately embroidered cotton dresses and shirts, linen skirts with dainty pleats, and all the other pieces of clothing that came out of her creative mind. Instead, Chiara begged Mamma to buy her the popular designer jeans her friends were wearing: Jordache, Sasson, and Calvin Klein. The first time Chiara wore a pair of Gloria Vanderbilt jeans she must have looked down at the brand's signature gold dove on her hip pocket a hundred times. She was so proud to wear those jeans, not because she'd wanted them for so long, but because she felt like she finally fit in with her friends. She wore those jeans until she went through a growth spurt and the pant hem hovered around her willowy ankles.

Now, staring at the intricate details of her wedding gown, the fitted bodice, the full skirt, and the long train, hand-embroidered with a calla lily pattern and overlaid with Austrian crystals, she appreciated how many hours Mamma must have toiled to create those one-of-a-kind outfits. She slipped out of her nightdress and into the gown, listening to the zzzZZZZzzzz sound of the silk as it slid up and over her thighs. Then she walked to a large freestanding gilded mirror on the wall near the bedroom window. The full moon and stable lights on the far side of Girasole cast a slanting light through the window. It bounced off the gown's Austrian crystals like a thousand fireflies dancing around her on a hot summer night. Except for her candelabra-like image in the mirror, everything else in the room was a misty gray.

She marveled at her luminous reflection. A bride in her second year of medical school. *Is that me?* Her mind drifted to her childhood fantasy and suddenly she was there, wearing the gown, cantering Shadowfax through the plush green meadow, knowing her wooing prince was about to appear. But there was no need to fantasize anymore. Adrian was real. *Tomorrow my real happily-ever-after begins.*

She swayed back and forth to the melody of the music, the flowing gown undulating around her like rippling water in a stream headed for bigger things. She sensed a need to wave, to say goodbye, to the part of her that she would leave behind when she took her marital vows—in a church, for Mamma and Adrian—tomorrow.

Sylvia stepped into the bedroom room, rubbing her eyes. "What are you doing? You're going to have that thing on all day tomorrow as it is."

"What are you doing up?"

"I heard the music. If I have to hear Celine Dion sing that song one more time, I think I'll puke."

Chiara chuckled. "Only one more time. At the reception."

Sylvia pointed toward the hem of the gown. "It looks too long."

"I don't have my shoes on," Chiara said.

Sylvia yawned. "I'm surprised."

Chiara gave her a pretend snarl.

Sylvia hopped onto the bed. "The bridesmaids' shoes are uncomfortable."

"Valerie doesn't think so."

"Do you think anyone will notice if I wear a pair of Doc Martens instead?"

"Please tell me you're joking."

Sylvia smiled. "I am. It's going to be weird not having you in the next room after tomorrow. You've always been next door. I'll miss you."

Chiara felt a familiar sadness accumulate in the space between them. The same sadness she'd felt when Valerie got married and moved out of Girasole. She sat down beside Sylvia. For a while they sat shoulder to shoulder in the still darkness without saying a word.

"I know things will be different," Chiara finally said. "We were sad when Valerie moved out. But how silly was that? She's here all the time."

Sylvia studied the nap of the rug. "Yeah, but she and Liam live down the road. You're going to be living over a thousand miles away."

"Only during the baseball season. And that's after I'm done with med school."

"That's six months of the year, not including spring training," Sylvia said. "You'll probably end up living and working in the city he plays for all year round."

The yearlong rumor of his potential trade had become a reality when Adrian's agent called one afternoon in late August to tell him he had been traded, just minutes before, to the Texas Rangers. Up until that day Chiara had hoped—even though she knew deep down it was highly unlikely—that Adrian would play his entire career in Pittsburgh. Instead, she had spent the last two months planning the final details of their new life together around her classes with him a thousand miles away.

A sure smile spread over Chiara's face. "That's not going to happen."

"How do you know?" Sylvia said.

Chiara bumped her with her shoulder and smiled. "Because Adrian and I bought a three-acre lot down the road in June and we're going to start building a house right after the wedding." We'll still live in Pittsburgh during the off-season regardless of the team he plays for."

Sylvia's eyebrows shot up. "Where?" she breathed, full of relief.

Chiara dissolved into laughter at Sylvia's relief. Sylvia laughed too.

When Chiara finally stopped laughing she said, "The Rolling Meadows Estates," with a pompous English accent. For an instant, in her wedding dress, she felt like a character right out of a nineteenth-century Brontë novel.

"Why didn't you tell me?"

"Adrian told me not to tell *anybody* yet."

"Why wouldn't he want us to know? What's the big deal?"

She sensed Sylvia was hurt by her secrecy. "It had nothing to do with you guys. Adrian didn't want it to get back to his mother before the wedding, that's all."

"Why?"

Chiara stared at her, incredulous. "Why? You know Cecilia had been asking Adrian to buy *her* a house for years."

Sylvia shook her head. "Yeah, and he bought her one last month."

"Adrian said she'd be livid if she knew we bought property to build a home for ourselves before buying her house. He didn't want any problems before the wedding."

Sylvia cocked her head sideways at Chiara. "She bribed him into buying her that house."

"It wasn't exactly like that, Sylv. Adrian promised her a long time ago that he would buy her a place if he made it to the big leagues. Last month may not have been the best time for us to do it financially, but it's done."

Sylvia got up, switched on the lamp and turned off the CD player. "Telling your son that you won't attend his wedding in October if you don't own a house by September, Chiara? If that's not bribery, I don't know what is. She's a bitch. I don't like her. None of us do."

Chiara stepped out of the dress and hung it back up on the armoire. "Let's just forget it, okay? Cecilia is happy, we're happy, everybody's happy." *Except Papà*, she thought.

"Fine." Sylvia reached in her plaid flannel pajama pants for a pack of cigarettes. "Can I tell Mamma and Valerie tomorrow? They'll be so excited."

"Sure, if you promise me to quit smoking this instant."

"I'm trying." She quickly changed the subject. "How are your classes going?"

"Pretty well, I guess."

"Are you still in that Body Fluid Homeostasis class?"

"Sort of. Everything kind of intertwines in med school. We're now studying homeostasis within the pulmonary system. We'll learn a lot about organ systems this year." She watched Sylvia take another drag of the cigarette. "You promised me over a year ago you were going to quit. I'd do anything to help you kick the habit. Why don't you chew the nicotine gum I buy you?"

"I chew it till my jaw hurts, Chiara. It's helped me cut back to a pack a day," Sylvia said with an encouraging look.

"It's not enough, Sylvia," Chiara said.

"I'm glad you decided to wait to go on your honeymoon until winter break," she said, changing the subject again. "Not right after the wedding as Adrian wanted to."

Chiara slipped back into her white cotton nightdress. "There was no way I'd leave now. I'd never be able to keep up if I skipped ten days of class. Papà's worst fear would come true."

Sylvia put out the cigarette in a candle dish on Chiara's dainty writing desk and lit another. She rolled opened the window a little wider, took a long hit, and exhaled the smoke into the night. A brisk autumn breeze carried in the gentle hoots of a night owl from the garden, filling a long silence with its song.

"Something seemed really wrong with Adrian's mom tonight at rehearsal dinner," Sylvia finally said. "Did you notice?"

"I did. It looked like she was sucking on a lemon all night."

"I thought maybe she'd gotten into a fight with Adrian's dad or something for drinking himself into a stupor in front of everybody," Sylvia said.

"I'm sure that was part of it."

"You think she's still pissed off that you two are getting married tomorrow?"

"A little. When she was here last year, she told me she had *plans* for her life when Adrian finally made it to the big leagues." Chiara paused, remembering Cecilia's behavior at the ballpark last year. "I think she thinks I've encroached on her goals by falling in love with Adrian."

"What goals?"

"I know she asked Adrian if she could quit her job after he signed his last contract. He told her he wasn't going to make enough money to support her and prepare for the wedding. Adrian said she was pretty upset about that."

"She's such a selfish person."

"I just think she's had so little in her life that she thinks money is the answer to all of her problems in life. She's been waiting for Adrian to sign a big contract, and now that he has, I think she feels he's going to get married and leave her behind."

"That's ridiculous. He's not that kind of guy," Sylvia said.

"I know he's not. Regardless, she's been giving me the cold shoulder for months. When I call her to say hello, she gets off the phone as fast as she can, like she's afraid she's going to catch some deadly disease by talking to me."

Sylvia took another drag of the cigarette and exhaled the smoke out the window. "Unbelievable. It's crazy how all about money that woman is." She looked at Chiara. "Could you imagine what the rehearsal dinner would've been like if Papà was there too?"

"Yes, a disaster."

The phone rang and they looked at each other. It was close to three a.m. Caught off guard, Chiara hesitated for one more ring then rushed over to the nightstand and picked up the receiver.

"Hello?"

"Is Chiara there?" a woman said.

"This is Chiara. Who is this?"

"A friend," the woman said with a tone of sarcasm.

"Whose friend?"

"Adrian's."

Chiara's anger was instant. "Adrian's friends tell me their names, and they certainly don't call me in the middle of the night," Chiara said. "Who is this?"

Sylvia looked confused. "Who is it?"

Mamma wandered into the room looking as thin as a blade of grass. She still hadn't gained back all the weight she'd lost after Papà died. "Dear God, who is it?" she said.

Chiara tapped her index finger against her mouth, signaling them to be quiet.

"He's not the man he's promising you he'll be," the woman said. "He doesn't love you."

An uneasy feeling welled in Chiara's stomach. "What's that supposed to mean? Who the hell is this?" she said with her jaw set tight.

The woman laughed; she seemed to be basking in Chiara's distress.

Chiara clenched the receiver until her hand went numb. "If he doesn't love me," Chiara said, "he should be an actor instead of a baseball player, because he'd win an Academy Award for his performance as a loving fiancé."

"Hang up," Mamma said.

Chiara pressed her hand to her stomach, lingering on the phone while the woman spewed lewd remarks about a sexual relationship she claimed to have with Adrian. Finally Mamma grabbed the receiver from Chiara and slammed it on its base.

"Who the hell was that?" Sylvia said.

Chiara's legs grew weak and she sought support from the bed post. Who would call the night before someone's wedding and say such hurtful things?

She sank onto the bed and Mamma sat down beside her. Sylvia picked up the receiver and dialed star sixty-nine.

Chiara's tears poured like rain. "Who could do this?" She fell into Mamma's arms.

"I have no idea, *cara*," Mamma said.

"Things have been so tense between you and his mom," Sylvia said. "Do you think she'd put someone up to it as a last-ditch effort to cause problems, hoping you'll call off the wedding?"

"Adrian would never hurt you," Mamma said. "I'm sure of it. It has to be a fan."

"Did you recognize the voice?" Sylvia said, handing her a tissue.

Chiara wiped her tears, blew her nose hard. "No, but she had a Latin accent."

"The more I think about the way Cecilia carried on at dinner to-night, I wouldn't be surprised if she had something to do with it," Mamma said. "She looked like she was at a funeral instead of a wedding rehearsal. She cried on and off all evening."

Chiara nodded.

"Crocodile tears," Sylvia said.

"Tears of envy, *cara*. I swear to God, Chiara, if that woman lived in this city, and we'd gotten to know her, I would've had her straightened out by now, or there would be no wedding tomorrow."

Chiara rubbed her temples. Her head was throbbing. "Ma, there is no straightening out that woman. Adrian has tried. She's just plain dif-ficult. I'll talk to Adrian in the morning."

"The number's blocked," Sylvia said.

"I don't need to tell you how a jealous family can put unnecessary stress on a couple. You're experiencing it firsthand." Mamma squeezed Chiara's knee like she was kneading pizza dough. "I have a feeling this is just the beginning. You're going to go through a lot with Cecilia before she decides, if she ever does, to accept you. Are you sure you'll be able to deal with her on top of your studies?"

"I don't have a choice. Besides, she lives in Florida. I won't have to see her that often. I'm just shocked she can be so cruel."

Mamma tucked a strand of Chiara's hair behind her ear. "I know. You're going to have to be tough and win her over whether she she's behind this stunt or not."

Chiara nodded. "I can handle it."

They stayed up talking until close to five. When everyone finally went to sleep, Chiara turned off the lights and lay back in bed, think-ing about the woman who had called, about Cecilia and her meanness, about Papà and how disappointed he would've been with her at that very moment. Tomorrow she would marry a man he had loathed, and she didn't yet have her medical degree.

God, she thought, *if there is any chance You do exist, I'm sure Papà is pleading with you at this very moment to stop the wedding. Maybe he's asking you to send some sort of natural catastrophe to western Pennsylvania, an earthquake or a flood. Please tell him everything is go-ing to be okay.*

"Everything is going to be okay," she softly told herself over and over like she was counting sheep. Finally she drifted off into a restless slumber.

The next morning Chiara called Adrian as soon as she woke. His mother answered the phone on the first ring. She sounded less abrasive than usual. Chiara was glad about that.

"Good morning. Are you sure you want to talk to him? It's bad luck to talk to the groom before the wedding," she said.

Chiara could hear her insipid smile over the phone. She wanted to jump through the receiver and strangle her, but she remained as calm as she could, considering it was her wedding day and some unknown woman had called her in the middle of the night to tell her Adrian was cheating on her. "Thank you for your concern, Cecilia, but I think it's only bad luck if the bride allows the groom to see her in her wedding dress before the ceremony."

"Oh," Cecilia said, as if she didn't know that. "He's right here."

"Good morning, *amor*," he said, sounding as passionate as ever. He sounded so excited, as if he had just thrown a pitch to win the World Series. "You ready to spend the rest of your life with me?"

Chiara felt a calmness settle over her like a blanket left in the sun all day. "I'm more ready than I've been for anything in my life, Adrian. But I have to tell you something that happened last night that really upset me."

"What, baby?"

"Around three this morning, a woman called and told me not to marry you, that you're not the man you're promising me you are, that you were sleeping with her after you got traded to the Rangers in August."

"That's crazy," he sighed. "Shit."

"What?" Chiara said. "What is it? Do you know her?"

"No, *amor*."

"Well, it sounds like you know *something*." Her heart was pounding through her nightdress.

Adrian let out another sigh. "I was gonna wait to tell you after the wedding, but something weird happened to me yesterday, too."

"What?"

"Before we started rehearsal at the church, Father Vincent called me into the sacristy and told me someone called the rectory and told him not to marry us."

"What! Adrian, why didn't you tell me?"

"Calm down, *amor*. Father Vincent said it was a serious accusation and he was obligated to ask me about the things the girl said to him," he said. "I told them they weren't true and after we talked a while, he said he could tell how much I love you and that he believed me one hundred percent."

Chiara paused. "You should've told me."

"*Amor*, you looked so happy. I didn't want to upset you with that stupid crap."

"I still wish you would've told me."

"Well, I didn't want you to be upset like you are right now, right before our wedding."

"Adrian, for this woman to call the rectory and talk to Father Vincent, she has to either know you or else she knows someone who doesn't want us to get married." Chiara was about to ask if he thought Cecilia could have put someone up to calling her, but she bit her lip. Adrian loved his mother. She knew that. And to accuse her of something so malicious would definitely hurt him, anger him. It was his wedding day, too. Instead, she asked him again if he had any idea who might want to do something like this.

"No, nuh-uh."

The last thing she wanted to question Adrian about on their wedding day was his fidelity. She was sure of his loyalty. But there wasn't a bride alive who would not say something on the subject after what had happened. She had to. She wanted to. She took a deep breath and steadied herself. "Adrian, listen to me. I love you—"

"I love you too, Chiara."

"I know, but I have to say this." She paused. "I'm marrying you because I love you. You're everything I ever wanted in a husband. I would've run away and married you on a remote beach somewhere, or run down to the JP if you had wanted to, but I know you're a church-goer, and you love Father Vincent. I know there will be a lot of times when I'll have to give in on things in our life together. And I'm okay with that. But I could never accept or forgive a husband who cheats." Her voice cracked, oozing vulnerability. "Did you? Would you?"

"No, I did not. And no, I would not. *Amor*, I love you."

"Why?"

"Why what?" he asked

"Why do you love me?"

"I love you because you're beautiful, you're a good person, you make me laugh, and you love me for me, not for the cash I'm making, like a lot of women in the past did. I want to be with you for the rest of my life."

Chiara sank down cross-legged on the floor. "I want exactly the same thing, Adrian."

There was a knock on the bedroom door.

"Hold on," she said. "Come in…"

Bibi stepped into the room. She looked a little confused. "Father Vincent is here to see you."

Chiara felt panic rise into her throat, perspiration oozing instantly out of her armpits. She'd talked to Father Vincent at their marriage classes and at the wedding rehearsal last night, but she'd never talked to him one-on-one before. She hadn't talked to any priest one-on-one since she was twelve.

"Honey," she said to Adrian, "I have to go. Father Vincent is downstairs."

"He's probably gonna tell you what happened. Listen to me," he said. "I love you and we're gonna spend the rest of our lives together, okay?"

Chiara's shoulders eased a little. "Okay."

She leaned back against the bed, thinking. She refused to allow her mother-in-law or some crazy crank caller to ruin her marriage, her career, or her happiness with Adrian. She kissed him goodbye over the phone, put on a robe, and went downstairs.

Father Vincent was standing in the foyer. He had a kind face, with white hair he wore combed over. Still, seeing his black cassock, anxiety stabbed her in the stomach.

"Good morning, Chiara," he said, extending his hand.

Chiara shook it. "Good morning."

"I don't usually make house calls on a bride's wedding day," he said. "But I felt compelled to come and talk to you in person about something that transpired at the rectory yesterday."

"Oh, that. Yes, Adrian just told me about it."

"That makes me feel better."

He looked so relieved, Chiara couldn't help but smile. She actually felt sorry for *him*. He seemed as troubled as she was over the phone call.

"Dear, I believe that Adrian has no idea who called, but I felt uncomfortable that he wanted to keep it from you until after the wedding. Marriages should start with honesty."

Chiara relaxed a little. "Thank you for your concern."

He smiled wider. "Well, I guess I'd better go and let you prepare for this very special day."

As she closed the door, Chiara thought, *I'm actually getting married in a few hours.*

Chapter 12

May, 1997

Chiara lay in bed watching Adrian sleep in their new and unfurnished Texas apartment. It was past midnight, and after they made love he had fallen fast asleep. *There is no better feeling than lying in bed next to the man you love*, she thought as she studied his face in the hazy moonlit room. *It feels even better when he's your husband. And maybe just a little better when you're on recess from medical school until August.*

Her classes had ended yesterday. She'd worked since September like a busy squirrel gathering nuts for a long winter, memorizing the organ systems, taking exams every three weeks, learning clinical skills, trying to diagnose her pretend-sick patients' diseases in PBL, and preparing for the national boards. In spite of the excitement she felt over approaching her life goal of becoming a physician, she ached for Adrian. After he'd left Pittsburgh for spring training in February, they'd seen little of each other due to their schedules. She'd stolen a few weekend trips to be with him. It had been a mistake to take them; it had cost her a failing grade her Reproductive and Developmental Biology class. It was a huge blow considering it was her field of interest. She knew why she had failed; it was the least difficult of her classes, and she thought it required less of her attention than her other courses. It was that simple. When she should have been studying, she was spending time with Adrian.

She'd met with the dean of student affairs right before she left for Texas. He needed to gather information from her in order to aid the Committee on Student Promotions to decide her fate when it met again next month. It could dismiss her altogether for her poor judgment and bad academic performance. She had hoped her good academic standing up until February and her complete honesty with the dean might encourage him to persuade the committee to excuse her lovesick heart— once. She thought, *If Papà were alive, he'd be as livid as I am with myself.*

She sighed and caressed Adrian's lips with the pad of her index finger, thinking of the boards she'd have to take in June. She was going to continue studying for them regardless of whether she might be dismissed. If she didn't sit for them she would be denied promotion to her third year no matter what.

She pushed her academic troubles away and focused on the feeling of being in Adrian's arms for the first time in almost two months. She felt the breeze of his breath spilling over her face and loved the peace it gave her. Even though the air conditioning was on high, it was hot in the apartment and the paddle fan above the bed, spinning like a top, offered little relief from the heat. Chiara flipped onto her side, rested her head on her hand and placed the other on Adrian's hairy chest, feeling the rhythmic rise and fall of his ribcage as he breathed. He looked so content, like a hibernating bear. She contemplated each inhalation and exhalation he took, recalling from her body fluid homeostasis class the chemical reactions that take place during the process. She hoped the regular rhythm, the up-and-down movement below her hand, would relax her to sleep. But it didn't. Instead her mind wondered to Cecilia. She'd called earlier to talk to "her son" about visiting soon. Chiara wondered if it was purely coincidental that Cecilia had had a fainting spell just as Chiara started down the aisle on her wedding day. *Why didn't she visit him while I was away in Pittsburgh?* she thought. Chiara tossed between the sheets until Adrian turned over and spooned her into his arms. She took a deep breath and exhaled through her mouth, surprised at her own frustration.

Over the winter when Cecilia called, all Chiara had to do was listen to Adrian talking on the phone in his sexy Spanish, look at his lean muscular body, and her angst would get up and leave the room. Other times when Cecilia called, Chiara would shove her nose into one of her medical texts or start one of her new married chores, such as laundry or cooking, and that would help too. It was almost as if she could input *Adrian* as a function of x mathematical equation in her mind and happiness would automatically spew out of her heart as an output. It was that easy.

But lately that wasn't working, either. Over the last few weeks, an acidic taste rose up in Chiara's throat every time Adrian talked about his mother. She wasn't sure why, but Cecilia's dramatic fainting episode at the ceremony bothered her more now than when it happened. Perhaps because the initial shock of the event was over. Perhaps because Cecilia's daily calls to their apartment over the winter conjured up the memory. Perhaps because she never said a word about it afterwards.

Chiara pushed Cecilia back into a closet in her mind and slammed the door shut. Then she nestled in closer to Adrian, letting his chest hairs stroke her back like a thousand massaging fingers, determined to relax and enjoy every second of him and her summer break.

When that didn't work, she flipped onto her back again and stared up at the spinning paddle fan, hoping its predictable revolving motion might relax her. *I'm happily married and still in medical school,* she thought. *Forget Cecilia.* She rolled onto Adrian's naked body and kissed his cheeks, his mouth, and the dimple on his chin that was thinly veiled by a five o'clock shadow.

He stirred. "You okay, wifey?"

"I'm perfect when I'm with you, hubby."

"Then why aren't you sleeping?" he said in a low sultry tone.

Chiara ran her finger across the bridge of his long nose. It hooked slightly at the bottom. "I'd rather look at you," she whispered.

He pulled her closer and her heart played like a harp in her chest.

"I was watching *you* before and you know what ended up happening."

Chiara smiled, feeling his warm breath on her face. "And I loved it."

He stroked her bare shoulders and back. "Not as much as me. I love being married to you, Chiara. You make me so happy."

She bore her head into his chest, thinking she was the luckiest girl in the world.

He rolled her onto her back and kissed her breasts lightly. "Love being married to you."

She tensed.

"Are you feeling shy again?" he asked.

"No," she said. But she was lying. He was her first lover, and she still felt awkward when he complimented her, especially during intimate moments.

"Relax," he whispered.

She did, entwining her legs around his, marveling at how thick and muscular they were.

"What are you thinking about?"

"That I want you now, and that I hate that you're leaving in a few days," she said. "I should've booked the trips to San Diego, LA, and Arizona, too. I wasn't sure if I was going to have to take that elective class."

He gently ran his hands lightly over her breasts, her stomach, making tiny circles around her belly button and she moaned softly.

"I can still have the traveling secretary book the tickets for you in the morning."

Chiara kissed him. His coarse black hair tickled the side of her breasts, arousing her. "No," she said stroking his arm. "I checked on the prices. They're way too expensive now. Besides, I could use the time to study for the boards. I'll go on the next road trip." She kissed him again. "I can hardly wait to see New York. Do you know how long I've wanted to go there?" She sat up and straddled him, instantly bubbling with excitement and forgot she was naked. "Ever since I saw the movie *Splash* with Tom Hanks and Daryl Hannah. I think I was fourteen. The mermaid named herself Madison after a street in New York."

Adrian stroked the inside of her thighs. "I saw it," he said and laughed. "You'll like Chicago and Boston, too."

"When you're at practice at Yankee Stadium, I'm going to grab a cab and see everything there is to see in New York. I'm going to walk the same path as Jackie O did on her daily strolls in Central Park, shop in Soho like the Lennons did, drink wine in chic restaurants in Greenwich Village where all the actors hang out, and roam through the Guggenheim and the Museum of Modern Art because *I just want to*. Then I'll rent a pair of ice skates and skate in Rockefeller Center—"

"Chiara, it's spring—"

Chiara laughed. "I know, but I would if it were February."

He pulled her back onto him again. Her long brown hair fell into his face. "Come with me to LA, too. I can afford it."

She kissed his lips, his cheeks, and his strong jaw line. "No," she whispered, in his ear. "*Devo studiare.*"

Goosebumps erupted all over Adrian's body. "I love when you talk to me in Italian. It turns me on."

She laughed feeling the bumps on his legs. "Should I tell how we need to get some furniture for this place in Italian too? You've been here over a month and you still don't have a sofa or a fork to eat with." She looked around the bedroom and laughed. "All we have is this bed and the TV."

He moved his hands over her thighs and pressed her close to him. "It's all we need," he said. "Besides, I didn't wanna play house without you. I thought you'd like decorating our first real apartment together. The one in Pittsburgh was so stuffed with my things, you couldn't do that much with it. And I know you wanted to."

Chiara kissed him gently on the lips. "I'm glad you waited. By the time you get back, I'll have this place looking great. I'll have all of our suitcases unpacked, rental furniture delivered from the place the traveling secretary recommended, and food in the refrigerator so I can cook for my husband."

Adrian chuckled. "That sounds good, but I still hate leaving you alone. You've never been away from home."

"It'll be hell being away from you for another nine days. But studying for the boards and getting this place to look homey will keep me busy."

"Make sure you always lock the doors to the apartment, the car, everything."

"Don't worry, I'll be fine." She held him close and took in his scent. It was always a bit salty, reminding her of their Caribbean honeymoon during her winter break. Adrian rolled onto his side and perched his head in his hand, and Chiara fell into the crook of his arm.

A semi-trailer's horn blared as the truck passed along Highway 360 outside the apartment and light from a security light in the parking lot seeped through the white Venetian blinds in slanted rays. It made odd, angular shapes on the headboard and highlighted Adrian's face in the dark room. All of a sudden he looked concerned.

"Chiara, I mean it. I"ve been around. Some cities are crazy and this is one of them." He gently brushed a few strands of hair away from her face. "You can't just walk out the door and go for a jog like you do at home. Which reminds me, if you wanna join a gym, make sure you join the gym where all the team wives go. I'll find out the name of it tomorrow."

She ran her hand through his hair. "Okay."

"And I'll leave the team contact sheet that's in the team welcome packet on the kitchen counter. The traveling secretary's number, the clubhouse numbers, team players and their family numbers are all on that sheet. So if anything happens and you need to contact someone you can."

"Got it."

"I even had your mom's and sisters' numbers added to it as emergency contacts for you in case I'm flying and can't be reached."

"Thank you," she said. But she was only half-listening now. Her mind and body were concentrated on his plump lips, on making love to him again.

"And don't answer the apartment door if you don't know who it is, no matter who they say they are. Day or night."

"Adrian…enough, honey."

"I'm just saying lots of people know that the ballplayers rent apartments in this complex. Some fans get stupid. Like that crazy woman who was calling us back in Pittsburgh."

The caller, she thought. Her anonymous existence struck a nerve in Chiara.

"That's why I keep telling you how it is living away from home. You just see the good in people, Chiara, and I love that about you, but some people have another side to them."

She thought of Cecilia, wished she could see the good in her.

"You have to be careful," he said.

Chiara suspected that Adrian wasn't really doting on her as much as he was explaining the cold reality of life in a big city. It was true she had never lived away from home, never lived in an apartment—or even a college dormitory—before she married Adrian. She hated the part of herself that was, thanks to Papà's strictness, provincial. And although she loathed the idea of Adrian leaving for a road trip just as much, a part of her was secretly thrilled that she would be alone in a strange city for the first time in her life. No family, no husband, no friends, just her and the Lone Star State. It felt as if she was making an expedition to a foreign land, tantalizing her senses, waking the playful child in her, presenting a myriad of new things for her to experience.

Before she met Adrian, Chiara would read magazines like *Town and Country*, *Travel*, and *National Geographic*, and envy the people featured in them, people who packed a rucksack and ventured off to faraway places like India, Africa, or Bora Bora. Sometimes Chiara would imagine herself in those places: donning a robe and trying to pray in a Buddhist temple with His Holiness the Dalai Lama, or dressed in khakis traveling onTanzanian safari by Land Rover, or dancing on a Bora Bora beach all night to blazing tiki torches and Tahitian music with a handsome Polynesian.

Dallas wasn't as exotic or far away as any of those places, but it was a start. When she was in college, aside from family trips to *Italia*, her biggest getaway destination was at the University of Pittsburgh's Cathedral of Learning. Each of the second floor classrooms was donned to represent a different nationality. There she would study in a different room every day for a whole week, observe decorative tastes of other cultures and imagine what it would be like to be anything but Italian. Sometimes, after studying for hours after the cathedral had emptied, she would leave her science books on a century-old wooden desk desecrated by hundreds of ballpoint pens and mosey through one of the cathedral's archaic wooden revolving doors. She'd imagine the door as a rabbit hole opening into another world for her to explore. Sometimes she imagined she was Dorothy in *The Wizard of Oz*, stepping out of Aunt Em's house into the land of Oz. Except in Chiara's fantasy she was in no hurry to get back home. And the yellow brick road was another color. Maybe fuchsia or tangerine. Not yellow. She was sick of yellow. Anything but yellow.

"Look at me," Adrian said.

When she did, he kissed her long and tender on the lips, his tongue softly passing over hers. "I love you."

"I can feel that," Chiara said, smiling, feeling his maleness waking against her thigh.

"I'm not kidding, Chiara. You have to be careful."

He brushed her hair away from her face, and she focused on his gaze, so beautiful, so loving. "I know. I'll be careful...I promise." And she meant it. All she wanted to do was please him. Even if all it took to do so was something as simple as *being careful*.

He rolled onto her, wrapping his arms around her, entering her slowly. She wrapped her legs around his, feeling encompassed by his weight, his taste, his smell, and his body holding hers as he filled her. She had never felt so content.

Chapter 13

A few days later, Chiara dropped Adrian off at the ballpark's underground parking lot, kissed him goodbye, and watched him board the Rangers's chartered bus for the airport. He looked so handsome in a suit and tie; she wished she were going with him. After the bus pulled away, other players' girlfriends, wives, and their children lingered in the lot chatting. Seeing that she wasn't the only one who had stayed behind, Chiara felt a little better. As she took the stadium exit ramp behind the bus, she saw countless fans waving goodbye from behind an iron gate and noticed a Dallas news reporter interviewing a fan. She'd never seen this sort of bon voyage when Adrian was with Pirates. She thought even baseball was bigger in Texas

Driving home she was glad she hadn't gotten out of the car at the ballpark. She had thrown on an old pair of frayed denim shorts and a pink tank top for the brief ride, intending to go right back to their apartment for the season and start transforming the stark white space into a home.

She turned right onto Ballpark Way. Nervous about getting lost, she paid extra attention to the street signs. She had gotten lost more than she wanted to admit driving through the streets of Port Charlotte during her spring training visit. But she didn't blame herself for that. Florida roads were so flat and mundane; Dallas's were too. Nothing like the hilly streets of Pittsburgh that were connected by four hundred and forty-six bridges within the city limits. Each bridge was practically a city landmark. Perhaps that was why Pittsburgh was called the City of Bridges, even though there were other cities in the world that had many more than it did.

Dallas, on the other hand, was made up mostly of massive concrete under- and overpasses, fast expressways that never seemed to start or end anywhere, and brand-new construction booming at almost every exit along the freeway. Most of the new buildings were mini-malls with flagship stores like Home Depot, Linens and Things, and Barnes & Noble. It was easy to mistake an exit if your mind wandered for even a second. Life moved at a faster pace here than in Pittsburgh, too. She liked that. She knew that New York moved even faster; she could hardly wait to see it.

Suddenly a horn blared, and Chiara looked in the rearview mirror. A man driving a souped-up pickup truck was tailgating her, yelling things she couldn't hear and probably didn't want to. She looked down at the speedometer. She was driving under the speed limit. *Whoops.* She sped up, but he had already pulled up next to her. He gave her a nasty look, and then peeled off.

"Well, sorry," she said. *There are so many lanes in this city,* she thought. Approaching a red traffic signal, she cautiously maneuvered Adrian's BMW into the far left lane, flicked on her turn signal and waited for the light to turn green. It was a long light and the repeating soft *click* sound of the turn signal relaxed her. She looked in the rearview mirror again and took in the sight of the new ballpark where Adrian had been pitching since he was traded.

"The Ballpark at Arlington," she whispered in awe. The sight of it made up for the mundane roaring roadways. Many said it was one of the prettiest Major League baseball fields in the country. Chiara believed it, but she never expected this. Its massiveness and the salmon brick arcade that encircled the entire perimeter of the building made it look more like the Roman Coliseum than a ballpark. Chiara imagined Adrian and his teammates, muscular men dressed in red-and-white uniforms, taking the field like gladiators, carrying their gloves like shields, preparing for a momentous fight against a visiting team while adoring fans cheered wildly.

"Wow," Chiara marveled. She wondered how many bricks it had taken to build it and how many limestone archways encircled the perimeter of the building, making a mental note to count them on her first visit next week. She recalled the constantly cracking concrete ramps and rusted steel beams that held Pittsburgh's Three Rivers Stadium together. There had been talk in the past year by city planners of imploding Three Rivers and building a modern stadium. But change came slowly to Pittsburgh.

Papà would've loved this stadium, she thought, recalling his love of arches and how he had adorned the house and stable at Girasole with them.

Beep beep. A Volkswagen Beetle behind her politely signaled that the light had turned green. Chiara gazed in the rearview mirror at the arches of the stadium. They reminded her on a smaller scale of the arches at Girasole and of her father's love of them. When Chiara was a teenager he told her he'd built so many arches into Girasole's architecture because arches were invented by the ancient Romans. "They are strong, and preeminent, *cara*, just like Italians," he'd said. *Just like him*, Chiara thought. She smiled remembering his ways. Looking at the arches now, she felt that in a way they were an omnipresence in her life somehow acting as a reminder of who or what her father had wanted her to be. She made a left-hand turn and turned on the radio. Patsy Cline's intoxicating voice—the only *American* singer Papà loved—floated out of Y108, singing "Crazy." Chiara turned off the stereo again and drove back to the apartment in silence, wishing she had had a chance to make things right with him.

The apartment looked as if it had been ransacked. Opened suitcases stuffed with clothes, boxes full of baseballs, baseball bats, baseball cleats, baseball gloves, a computer, a dressage saddle from home in case she wanted to ride while she was in Texas, a new box of cookware Mamma had shipped to her, and what seemed like a thousand plastic hangers had been plopped in piles from the front door straight back to the master bedroom. *We really should've rented a house for the season.* Chiara rubbed the nape of her neck as she looked around the top-floor space. It had been her idea to stay in an apartment to save money for the new house that was going up that very moment back home. The apartment was a long and rectangular twelve hundred-square-foot space, and she liked it. She'd like it better after it was decorated. It had a small second bedroom to the left of a simple entry way and room for a dinette to the right. The front door opened to a view of the family room, which was separated from the kitchen by a long Formica counter. Directly across from the kitchen, in the family room, a sliding glass door opened to a small veranda that overlooked the complex's parking lot.

She took off her short strand of pearls and pulled her hair back into a ponytail. Even though she had no idea where to start, Chiara felt excited about organizing the apartment. It would keep her busy while Adrian was away and perhaps distract her from seething over Cecilia's upcoming visit, which was looming over her like a lead zeppelin.

She looked around at the white apartment as if it were a fresh canvas and thought about Girasole. In spite of its grandeur and perfectly placed Décor, Mamma always made it look so inviting. Chiara was sure she could create the same peaceful atmosphere here.

Outside, beyond the sliding glass doors, the wind picked up and it began to rain, slowly at first, the drops making uneven *tink tink* sounds as they hit the aluminum gutters. She slid the glass doors open and stepped barefooted onto the patio to let in some fresh air; she hated air conditioning but it was as necessary as toilet paper in Texas. She made a mental note to buy some pretty potted topiary plants for the outdoor space tomorrow.

The cherry trees that had been planted as a privacy fence, separating the parking lot from Highway 360 in the distance, began to blow violently, though it had been calm a minute before. Within seconds the humidity dissipated and it was pouring, masking the discharge of dark pollution from trailer rigs as they passed on the highway.

Chiara felt an overwhelming relief whenever it rained, as if life somehow slowed down allowing her to live and breathe in the moment. She crossed her arms and leaned over the railing, watching a middle-aged, red-headed woman in the parking lot below lock her car door and struggle to open a flapping umbrella, then scurry toward the apartment stairs. It felt strange to know that there were at least thirty other people living under the same roof whom she knew nothing about.

She was looking forward to making new friends. So far she had only met a couple of Rangers's wives in passing during her short spring training visits to Port Charlotte. Alicia Patterson seemed very pleasant. Surprisingly, she was also a dressage rider.

Over the sound of the rain she heard the faint ringing of the phone. Chiara went back inside to answer it. "Hello...? Hello...?" She heard someone snicker.

Click.

Chiara thought of the woman who had called the night before her wedding. *No,* she told herself. *This is not happening again. It was just a silly hang-up. A wrong number.* She grabbed the handle of a heavy black suitcase, dragging it into the master bedroom closet, and began the slow process of turning the apartment into a home.

Late Sunday night Adrian called from the airport to tell her he had just landed in Dallas. Chiara waited for him on the couch in a long black sheer negligee, thumbing through characteristics and pathophysiology of common diseases of the skin and musculoskeletal systems in her USMLE prep guide. She placed the take-out Chinese she'd bought earlier, a bottle of uncorked cabernet, and two wine glasses on the cocktail table in front of the TV. There was only one lamp on in the family room and when Adrian walked through the door thirty minutes later, he looked extra tan in the dim lighting.

He loosened the knot in his tie, looking impressed. "Damn, girl, you been busy," he said.

And she had been. She'd bought furniture instead of renting it, and within a week she had managed to have everything delivered and put in place. A brown walnut-and-leather sofa was placed against the long wall in the family room. She'd dressed it up with three green, gold, and crimson pillows she found on sale. Above the sofa she'd hung a large wooden-framed acrylic of horses grazing in a pasture. She'd placed a high-backed walnut-and-leather chair in front of the sliding glass door and draped a hunter green throw over it. On the walnut cocktail table in front of the sofa she placed their wedding picture, a set of pillar candle-holders, and a set of horse-head bookends Sylvia had given them as a wedding gift. Sandwiched between the bookends were leather-bound copies of her favorite classics: Jane Austin's *Sense and Sensibility*, Charlotte Bronte's

Jane Eyre, and Maya Angelou's *I Know Why the Caged Bird Sings.* She planned on rereading all of them over summer break, a welcome respite from the medical texts she'd been poring over for the past year.

On the end tables on either side of the sofa she placed smaller framed pictures of Adrian and Cecilia, Chiara's family, and her horses. Adrian's only request was that she buy another TV for the family room. He loved watching movies until dawn. She loved sleeping in his arms while he watched them. She had bought the largest one that would fit into the matching neoclassic armoire.

"You like it?" she said, feeling proud. "We can use all of this stuff in the new house. All I have to buy now are some plants, and I think we're set."

"I like you," he said, taking off his suit jacket and strolling over to her with his head cocked. He picked her up and buried his head into her neck, growling. Her hair was still damp from the shower and smelled faintly of lilac. "I used to have to do this stuff by myself and it never looked this good."

Chiara wrapped her legs around him and kissed him. "I'm glad you like it."

He set her down. "What else did you do while I was gone? Did you study?"

"Put in seven hours every night. I got through almost a quarter of the USMLE manual."

He smiled, impressed. "Good job."

"I also had time to drive through downtown Fort Worth, downtown Dallas, and meet Alicia Patterson at her stable to watch her ride."

"I saw your Rover in the parking lot," he said. "When did it get here?"

"Yesterday."

"I know you didn't want to take Hemi away from Julio, but I wish you would've shipped one of your horses from home too."

"He loves training him. He's so excited with his progress. But the more I think about it, I'd like to ship Amadeus here. I already miss riding."

"Go for it, baby, bring him down."

"Julio would love for me to get in a few shows this summer on Hemi so I can try to qualify for the regional finals in November. I only need one more score."

"What do you want to do?"

"I want to be with you, study the class I failed in case I'm given the chance to repeat it, and show Hemingway, too."

"It's your sport, baby. You shouldn't give it up. We'll figure out how to make sure we're not apart too much. One or two weekends over the next three months are okay. You can use that time to check on the house since the team won't give me no extra days off for something like that."

"I thought of that, too."

Adrian pulled her onto the couch next to him. "Did you ask the builder how far he's got?"

"I left him a message on Thursday, but he hasn't gotten back to me yet. Mamma called me yesterday, though, and said she drove by it on her way back from the restaurant."

"How's she doin'?"

"Okay, I guess." Chiara rolled her eyes. "She goes to church twice a week praying for strength. She's constantly worrying if she and my sisters are running the restaurants as Papà would've wanted them to. She misses him so much." She paused. "So do I."

She noticed Adrian's eyes and mouth soften, as if they were taking in her hurt.

"Tell your mom if she needs anything, all she has to do is ask." He took her in his arms and held her close. "You okay?"

She took a deep breath, swallowing the sadness. "I'm okay," she said. "Mamma said they started on the blue boards."

When Adrian released her, his eyes were wide and full of encouraging excitement. "Damn, they're moving fast. I think we'll be in by October."

"I think so, too. Did you tell your mom we're building it yet?"

Adrian looked away. "Nuh-uh, not yet. I'll tell her when she gets here."

Chiara was disappointed but didn't say so. Instead she leaned over and emptied a container of chicken with garlic sauce into a dish and handed it to him. "Did she tell you when she's coming? How long she'll be staying?"

"She called me this morning," he said.

I'm sure she did, she thought, feeding him a bite of chicken with her chopsticks. He placed the dish on the table and poured himself a glass of wine. It was dark and opaque and smelled spicy. "She said that she wants to come and stay for a few weeks, maybe a month."

"A month?" she croaked.

"I know it's a long time, Chiara, but she's depressed. She got fired from her job and just needs to get away."

Depressed, my rear…she's wanted to quit since you signed your contract. Chiara poured herself a glass of wine and took a long swig. She wanted to tell him that she only had three months to be with him without having her head buried in books. *And your mother wants to come and stay for one of them? Your mother can't stand me.* She'd been nothing but kind to Cecilia, even after she pulled that stunt at the wedding—*which, by the way, everyone who saw it said was an act*—yet Cecilia said something offensive every time they spoke on the phone. *And now she wants to stay with us, in this small apartment, for a whole month? A whole fricking month?*

"You okay with that, wifey?"

She took a deep breath before she answered. "Honestly, honey, I'm not sure."

His eyes lost their sparkle for a moment, and it almost made her want to cry.

"I mean, I'm fine with her visiting, really I am," she said trying to sound reassuring, as if everything was fine between her and Cecilia.

But he wasn't buying it. "You don't want her to come," he said, then took a long, deliberate swallow of wine.

Chiara sighed. "Adrian, that's not true. I'm fine with her visiting. It's just that I only have three carefree months with you before I start classes again. Next year I'll be spending more time on wards in clinics and I won't have as much time off in the summer. I know it sounds selfish, but my first reaction is that it's a long visit, considering you and I have seen so little of each other since you left for spring training." She looked away. "I just wanted more time alone with you, that's all."

Adrian's expression softened. "*Amor*, we have the rest of our lives together. Besides, she's really down."

"Uh-huh."

"Come on, baby," he said. "You guys got to get to know each other."

Does it have to be a mother-in-law 101 crash course? "I know," she said.

He squeezed her chin softly. "How about I make it up to you by taking you to Cancun over winter break?"

Chiara looked down at the carpet. "You don't have to do that," she said, but she'd already given in. "She can come and stay."

"I'm taking you to Cancun."

Chiara smiled. "Okay. When does she want to come?"

"After we come home from the next road trip."

"All right. I'll prepare the spare bedroom for her."

He kissed her on the lips then took another sip of wine. "*Amor*, I really appreciate it. You guys are really gonna get along great after she gets used to us being married."

She wanted to believe him, but she knew as well as she knew her own name that Cecilia would never, ever want to be close to her.

Chapter 14

"Here you go, miss," the cab driver said in a thick Indian accent. "Grand Hyatt Regency on Forty-Second Street. Enjoy your stay in New York."

"Thank you, Mr. Gupta," Chiara said.

"Don't forget that you are right next to Grand Central Station. You should stop in and see it. Many, many movies have been filmed there."

Mr. Gupta drove like the stereotypical New York cab driver. Reckless and dangerous. Chiara felt sick from the hasty accelerations and abrupt stops. He wove through traffic like he was a race-car driver vying for first place in the Indianapolis 500. But she never said a thing about it. He was a jovial and genteel man who had wholeheartedly recommended so many sights and restaurants for Chiara to visit, that after the first twenty places she felt obliged to pull out a pen and paper and start jotting them down. But with one eye on the road the whole time, she doubted anything she'd written was legible.

"Take my card," he said. "Next time you need a cab, call and request me. I will drive you."

"Thanks again, Mr. Gupta, I will," Chiara said, sparing his feelings. But this would be their first and last trek through New York City together. If she had to choose between a ten-mile hike through the city in her stilettos or a ten-minute drive with Mr. Gupta, she would happily grab a box of Band-Aids and head out on foot.

She paid the fare and included a generous tip. Seeing that the doorman was busy helping another guest, she rolled her over packed suitcase into the hotel lobby, and made a mental note to ask Adrian if her bags could be shipped on the Rangers's chartered plane to Boston. She had expected to get to the hotel by three o'clock at the latest, but New York City traffic *was* insane. It was almost five. Adrian had been waiting for her in the hotel room for well over an hour.

As she walked toward the elevators, Chiara looked around the congested lobby. It was pretty and adorned with cream marble. At the center, an enormous fountain emptied into a basin the size of a Grecian bath. A set of preschool twins dressed in pink were tossing pennies into the water and she smiled, looking forward to the day when she'd have her own children.

"Chiara!" a woman called out.

Chiara turned. Alicia Patterson was walking towards her wearing a Ramones tribute t-shirt and jeans. Alicia was Chiara's age but much shorter, with black spiked hair and fair skin. There was a hard edge to her and Chiara wondered if she'd once been a rebellious teenaged rocker who dressed in black and colored her hair pink.

"How was your flight?" Alicia said in a husky voice that contradicted her petite frame.

Chiara gave her a hug. "The flight was fine. It was the cab ride that almost killed me."

Alicia laughed. "Let's plan the next road trip together."

Chiara smiled. "I'd like that."

"No game tonight. What do you guys have planned?"

"I don't know. Adrian said it's a surprise."

"That's cute. It's so obvious you guys are newlyweds." Alicia looked at her watch. "Judd and I are going to a new restaurant he heard about called Havana. He said the food's authentic. Do you guys want to meet us there later? We're not heading out until about nine o'clock."

"I'd like to, but I'll have to see what Adrian has planned first."

"Okay. I'll leave the name and address on your cell phone later."

"Great."

When Chiara reached the hotel room, she set her bags down and ran her fingers quickly through her disheveled hair before knocking.

Adrian opened the door with a cocky grin. He was dressed in a cream cotton dress shirt and a pair of dark dress pants. Chiara caught a wisp of his cologne. *Yummy.*

He smiled. "What took you so long? I was on time."

She knew he was teasing her; Major League Baseball teams flew in chartered planes and rode on chartered buses to keep them on schedule.

"Very funny," she said. "Next time, I'm booking direct flights. Connecting flights are killers, especially when they're on the opposite sides of the airport. The cab ride here is another story."

Adrian laughed as he wheeled in her suitcase. "When I played in the minor leagues, we had to bus it everywhere. Now *that* sucked." He kissed her on the lips. "You hungry? I made dinner reservations for six and bought tickets for *Cats*. It starts at eight o'clock. You think we can make it?"

"*Cats*!" She leapt into his arms and kissed his face until she was sure she hadn't missed a spot.

"Okay, okay," he said, as if he'd had enough. But she could tell he was enjoying the attention.

"Can we make it? We're in New York! You bet your cute ass we can make it," Chiara said. "Give me fifteen minutes." She tore off her jeans and a white silk blouse she had bought just for the trip, unzipped her suitcase, and pulled out a simple black dress and a pair of strappy black sandals.

Adrian seemed amused. "You're silly."

"I can't believe it. We're going to a *Broadway* show. Do you know how long I've wanted to do that? How much this means to me?"

Chiara had seen *Cats* in Pittsburgh once, but the prospect of seeing it—or any show for that matter—on Broadway was blood-tingling. There was an expectant excitement about it. Chiara pictured herself calling out the address to a cabby like a starlet from a 1930's blockbuster black-and-white film. "The Majestic Theatre, please," or "the Gershwin Theatre on West Fifty-First Street between Broadway and Eighth." It sounded so chic, so sophisticated.

Adrian laughed. "That's nothing. We have a day game tomorrow so I bought tickets to tomorrow night's Nets vs. Knicks game at Madison Square Garden. Fourth-row seats."

Chiara's mouth dropped. "You're kidding. How did you finagle that?"

"I know one of the player's agents. He hooked us up." He looked at her heels. "We're gonna be out late. Those shoes comfortable?"

"Yep." She was feeling around the suitcase for a black evening clutch. She sensed him eyeing her lacy panties and bra.

He sighed. "I better go downstairs like now and call for a driver or we won't be going anywhere tonight."

"No cab?"

"The hotel's got cars lined up in front that you can rent for the night. It'll be easier than catching cabs."

Chiara slipped on her dress and motioned for Adrian to zip up the back. He finished with a soft kiss on the nape of her neck. She turned around and faced him, pecked him on the lips. "You're so good to me."

He kissed her again. "I'm gonna go grab a drink. I'll meet you at the bar."

Chiara washed her face at record speed and reapplied her makeup—making sure her eyebrows hadn't sprouted any stragglers during her stressful ride with Mr. Gupta—before dusting on a shimmery eye shadow for a smoky evening look. When the curling iron was hot enough, she rolled a few large romantic locks into place. Wearing her hair curled always made her feel sexy. When the phone rang she realized almost half an hour had passed. *Shit.* She unplugged the curling iron, screwed in her pearl studs, and hopped to the phone, slipping into her sandals along the way.

"I'm walking out the door right now, sweetie," she said, sure it was Adrian telling her to hurry.

The woman on the phone asked if she was speaking with Chiara Peruviso.

"Oh…I'm sorry," Chiara said. "Yes, yes it is."

"Well, hello, bitch," the woman snapped, emphasizing the B. "Remember me?"

Chiara felt an uneasy feeling well in her chest. Her voice cracked slightly. "Who is this? Why are you doing this?"

The woman laughed. "Why are you doing this?" she mocked in a high-pitched tone. Then her voice deepened again. "I'll tell you who this is. This is your worst fucking nightmare, bitch. That's who."

She was engulfed in anger again. "How did you know I was here?"

"How did you know I was here?" the woman parroted back.

Chiara felt her confidence unravel a notch. "What do you want from me? Why don't you leave us alone?"

"Aw...are you crying, bitch?" the woman said.

"Over someone like you? No."

"Why don't you just go home to your rich mommy and daddy? Oh I forgot, your daddy's dead, isn't he? Found him lying on the floor like a dead dog, didn't you?"

"You little tramp," she shot back. Her hands trembled around the phone. "I'm with my husband and I'm not going anywhere. You can tell that to whoever put you up to harassing me."

"I'm with my *husband*," the woman mocked again. "You think you're so *perfect*, don't you? *Perfect* animal-loving Chiara, with her *perfect* high cheekbones, and her *perfect* life, and her *perfect* baseball-player husband."

Chiara's hand choked the receiver; she tried to remember if she had ever heard the woman's voice in person.

"You don't fit in, *Snow White*," the woman said. "You or your stupid horses. Go home."

"You're nothing but a little trouble maker!" Chiara said.

The woman laughed. "Oh, you're real tough, princess—"

"I will find out who this is," Chiara said.

The woman snickered. "Oh, yes you will," she said. Then she hung up the phone.

Chiara was left seething, holding the phone.

When she met Adrian downstairs, the bartender saw the look on her face and gave her a sympathetic smile.

Adrian got up from his bar stool. "What's wrong?"

"The woman who was harassing us on our wedding day...She called again."

Adrian seemed caught off guard and flinched. "What? Where? At your mom's house?"

"No, just now. In our hotel room."

"What?"

"I'm worried, Adrian. She sounds wicked. How could she know we're staying here?"

"I don't know."

Chiara grabbed a bar napkin and dabbed at the tears that were glid-ing down her face. "Do you remember telling anybody we'd be staying here?" she asked.

"No…I don't think so. I mean my family, but that's it."

Bingo, Chiara thought.

"What did she say to you?" Adrian demanded.

"She called me a bitch and told me to go home because I don't fit in."

"What the hell is that supposed to mean?"

"I don't know." Chiara was about to ask Adrian if Cecilia could have put someone up to the crank calls, but she stopped herself.

Adrian wrapped his arms around her. "You okay?"

"I think so. Let's just forget it and go have some fun. I want to see New York."

Adrian paid his bar tab and led Chiara to a black Lincoln Town Car. A few minutes later, driving down Forty-Second Street, he took her hand and pointed toward a street sign. "Look, wifey, there's Madison Avenue."

Chiara slid in closer to him and he wrapped his arm around her as if he were securing her under his wing. She looked up at the street sign, then at the busy streets of New York City. Her expression softened, but her mind was still on the voice of a woman whose words cut like a knife, bleeding droplets of doubt on her marriage.

Even though Chiara was feeling anything but social after the show, she and Adrian met Alicia and Judd at the restaurant. It was a busy candlelit Cuban restaurant with wooden tables, cognac-painted walls, and parquet floors. Habanera music played loud and the heavenly aroma of garlic, cumin, and sweet plantains hung like heavy clouds over the tables. Handsome waiters dressed in black-and-white uniforms floated from table to table serving patrons. Every one of them looked exotic, like Greek gods. *Being good-looking must be a prerequisite to work here*, she thought. She presumed many of them were aspiring actors and models trying to make a little extra cash. A waiter in his thirties carrying a tray of tropical drinks breezed by and winked at her. Chiara smiled back. *Wow. He's Cary Grant reincarnated.*

"Hey, you made it," Alicia said when they reached the bar. She was standing next to Judd nursing a drink.

Mike Hogan, the team catcher, got up from his bar stool so Chiara could sit down. He was a broad-bodied blond Texan in his forties with twenty years of baseball experience. He had a friendly demeanor and everybody in the Rangers organization respected him.

"Hey, rookie, what's up?" he said to Adrian.

"What's up, Hogan?" Adrian replied.

Mike took a puff of his cigar. He motioned toward Judd who was tall, lanky, and eating something with lots of beans in it. "You hungry?" Mike asked. "The food's great here."

"Naw, we already ate," Adrian said.

Mike then turned to Chiara. "Have you met my beautiful wife, Lindsay?"

Chiara smiled at Lindsay. "Hi, it's nice to meet you."

Mike flagged down the bartender. "Good. Gentlemen, who's pitching tomorrow?"

Judd gave Hogan a look like he was crazy. "You think I'd be drinking if I were pitching tomorrow?"

"You, rookie?" Hogan said to Adrian.

"No, day after. And I ain't no rookie. This is my fourth year in the big leagues."

"Good man," Hogan said. "Then what are you drinking? I'm buying."

"Jack and Coke," Adrian said.

"And you, young lady?" Hogan asked Chiara.

"Thank you, I'll have a Coke."

When the drinks came, Hogan held up his glass. "To the World Series…"

Judd and Adrian held up theirs. "To the World Series," they said.

"Keep this guy out of trouble, Chiara," Hogan said. "We need his arm to go all the way this year."

Chiara smiled and wrapped her arm around Adrian. "I'm trying."

"If I can give you two newlyweds some good advice after twenty years married and in the big leagues, be good to each other and put each other first."

Adrian smiled at Chiara. "We will."

Hogan took another puff of his cigar and exhaled the excess smoke toward the ceiling. Then he glanced around the restaurant. "It's easy to get caught up in all the partying and fancy restaurants when you first get started in the majors. Every city has something crazy to offer; it's hard to stay grounded."

"Don't you know it," his wife chimed in.

Hogan nodded. "I was nuts when I first started in the majors," he said. "I was twenty-two and fresh off my daddy's cattle ranch. Lindsay put me back on track again. Got me walking a straight line. I don't know what I'd do without her."

Lindsay gave him a wry smile. She was a tall, attractive blonde around Hogan's age with a warm Texas drawl. There was something nurturing about her. Chiara liked that.

"You sly thing, it had nothing to do with me," she told Mike. "Your daddy fixed your ass when he finally got sick of hearing about your shenanigans in the papers back home."

Everybody laughed.

Lindsay turned to Chiara. "Now tell me, Chiara, how are you getting along in Texas? Do you like it so far?"

"The roads are a little confusing, but I really like it. The ballpark is beautiful."

"You'll get used to them," Alicia said.

"I'm so glad I finally got to meet you," Lindsay said. "I didn't go to spring training because we have two small boys in school. They're six and eight. I hate pulling them out for camp or the start of the season." She took a sip of her martini and winced. "But I've heard so much about you from Alicia. I feel like I know you."

"I've heard a lot of nice things about you, too," Chiara said.

"You're in medical school, right?"

"I am," Chiara said. "I'll be starting my third year in August." *I hope.*

"What field?"

"I'm interested in obstetrics and pediatrics. I love kids. I can hardly wait for Adrian and I to start our own family."

"I'll drop off my boys with you for an afternoon. You might want to change specialties after that."

Chiara laughed.

Lindsay shook her head. "They're so bad." She adjusted her green strappy dress and Chiara noticed a diamond ring the size of a bottle cap on her finger. Even in the dim bar lighting it shone like a torch.

"Your ring is beautiful, Lindsay."

Lindsay fluffed off the compliment with the wave of her hand. "Thank you, darlin'. I earned every carat of it."

Alicia laughed at Lindsay's remark. "Tell me, is it true you're a dressage rider, too? Did you bring your horses down from Pittsburgh?"

"I'm shipping my five-year-old, Amadeus, next week. He'll arrive in Texas the day we get back from the trip."

"Well, that's real nice, but what I'd really like to know is if you like to shop?" Lindsay cocked her head toward Alicia. "All this one ever wants to do is ride that damn horse of hers. I'm lucky if can get her to go shopping with me twice all summer."

"I shop," Alicia said. "I just don't make it the meaning of my whole existence like you do, Lindsay."

"And it shows," Lindsay said with a wry smile..

Chiara laughed. "I take it you two have known each other for a while."

"Our husbands have been with the Rangers for three seasons," Alicia said.

"Lindsay, I love to shop *and* I love to ride," Chiara said. "Unfortunately my wardrobe shows little proof of it. We're pretty limited in Pittsburgh."

"You hang out with me and I'll show you some great places. When you go back to Pittsburgh, you'll be dressing for your classes looking New York chic."

"I can't wait," Chiara said. "I love clothes, even though I spend most of my time in sweats, studying."

As the men talked Chiara's mind wandered back to the caller, and for a second a part of her looked forward to getting back to Pittsburgh and immersing herself in her studies. That would at least give her a small respite from the gnawing suspicions devouring her from the inside out. She had spent the entire length of the play contemplating if it was possible that Cecilia really had nothing to do with the calls, if it was possible that Adrian was lying and he knew this woman, if it was possible that the woman calling was nothing more than a fanatic, an inconvenience a major league baseball player's wife has to put up with from time to time, like the common cold. She had decided one thing for certain, though: she was going to find out who this woman was.

Chapter 15

On their first morning back in Texas, Adrian woke Chiara with a kiss on the lips. "Good morning, sleepyhead."

"Good morning, hubby," she mumbled.

"I have to be at the ballpark by eleven for a team autograph-signing session," he said. He got up and pulled a pair of white Calvin Klein briefs out of the nightstand drawer. "It's fan appreciation day. You wanna get up and have a cup of coffee with me before I gotta go?"

Chiara had been awake until almost four a.m., reading through her reproductive and developmental biology material, knowing she'd have to retake the course if she wasn't dismissed. Mastering the material would be helpful for the USMLE too. She was still in bed when the coffee had finished brewing. In the kitchen, Adrian started banging pots and pans, telling her to get out of bed.

"Okay, I'm up," she said and wandered into the kitchen. She was wearing one of the negligees she had received as a bridal shower gift. This one was ivory silk and lace and fell to her ankles.

Adrian lifted her off her feet and sat her on the kitchen counter. "I'm up, too," he said, with a devilish grin.

Chiara shook her head, rubbed her eyes. "You're silly." She pulled her hair back in a ponytail, and then took a sip of coffee. He had made it just the way she liked, with cream and sugar. She watched him toss ham, onions, and tomatoes into a frying pan sizzling with olive oil.

"You want an omelet?"

"All right. You need help?"

"Naw, I got it."

"It's going to be a long day for you at the ballpark. Are you coming home before practice?"

"Naw, I'll just stay and get a rub from one of the trainers."

Chiara turned and looked out the sliding glass doors. Even though it was only the beginning of June, temperatures all over the South were tipping one hundred degrees. It was overcast outside. "I heard we're supposed to get a bad storm later."

Adrian seemed unfazed, cracking eggs over the frying pan.

"It's just rain, baby."

"The news said to expect high winds and hail, too. Maybe they'll cancel the game and we can go to a movie."

"That almost never happens. You know that. They'll probably just pull the tarp over the field and wait it out. I hate rain delays. We just sit around the clubhouse doing nothing until the coaches tell us to go out again." He tossed the eggshells into the trash can. "But if it does get bad, don't you go driving to the stable. Wait it out."

"I will."

"I talked to my mom last night. She said her flight lands at eleven a.m. the day after tomorrow. Said you two talked yesterday. How did that go?"

Chiara sighed. "A bit better. She seemed excited to visit. She asked me to pick up a few things at the grocery store so she can cook for you while she's here. She loves cooking for you."

"She does. What did she ask you to pick up?"

"Limes, lemons, shrimp, cilantro, tomatoes, onions, lard, cornmeal, green peppers, eggs, sausage, sirloin strips, potatoes—"

"I hope she makes seviche and tortillas."

"What's seviche?"

"Didn't Bibi teach you anything about Latin cooking? It's like Latin sushi."

"Papà was always such a picky eater. Bibi learned to cook Italian to help Mamma once she and Julio moved in. Besides, they're from Argentina."

He flipped the omelet, then went over to the CD player and popped in a Juan Gabriel CD. Adrian loved Latin crooners, especially Juan Gabriel and Luis Miguel. Most of his favorite music was in Spanish, which had always struck Chiara as strange since he was only half Mexican and was born and raised in Florida. Chiara preferred American top forty and classical.

He strolled back into the kitchen, humming along with the song, and pulled out a bottle of vodka from the pantry to make a stiff Bloody Mary. Chiara wondered if she should say something. Lately he'd been starting every day with one.

"By the time she goes back home," he said, "you guys will love each other, believe me."

And Moses parted the Red Sea. "I hope so."

The phone rang. Chiara hoped it was Mamma calling to read the letter from the dean of student affairs. Chiara had been waiting for it to arrive at Girasole for almost a week. Her future lay in the lines of that letter. *Here we go.*

Adrian reached for the phone while pouring the Bloody Mary mix into the glass of vodka. "Hello...? Hello...?"

Click.

"They hung up," he said.

"God, this is driving me crazy," Chiara said.

"Baby, it was just a hang-up."

Chiara was sure it was more than coincidence. She gave him a look. "That's easy for you to say. Nobody is calling you to say I'm sleeping around."

Adrian raised his eyebrows at her tone, but she couldn't have cared less. She hopped off the counter and took her coffee with her to the couch in the family room. She turned on the TV and flipped to the Weather Channel. She'd practically become obsessed with it since hearing stories from Alicia and Lindsay about the violence of Texas storms.

Adrian turned off the stove and followed her into the family room, kneeling on the floor in front of her. As tall as he was, he was still looking down at her. "Hey, I'm sorry. I know it sucks."

"I need to find out who she is, Adrian. I want to hire a private investigator."

Adrian rubbed his forehead and moved to sit down next to her on the couch. "Baby, I know you want to find out who she is. I do, too. You think I'm not worried for us? I am. But don't you think hiring a PI over some crank calls is a little drastic? Why don't we wait a while? If she doesn't stop by the end of the season, then we'll hire one. I promise."

Pensive, Chiara sought relief in the warmth of her coffee.

"You need to concentrate on studying for the boards and I need to concentrate on my game so I can get more wins. I'll be a free agent after this season and if I get a lot of wins, I can sign with a team that's closer to Pittsburgh."

Chiara blew air from her lips, thinking about the added distractions hiring a PI would cause so close to her board exam at the end of month. "Okay. But can we at least change the phone numbers?"

"No problem." He paused. "I love you, Chiara."

"I love you too." She leaned her body into his. She thought of Cecilia, how stressful things were going to become when she arrived on Monday. "What do you think your mom would like to do while she's here?"

"Don't plan anything. All she's gonna want to do is go to the games, believe me."

Good. "Okay." Chiara looked at the kitchen clock. "You have to leave soon."

He pulled her negligee straps down over her shoulders and kissed her breasts lightly, one by one. "We still have time for a quickie," he said.

"Chiara wrapped her arms around him and gave in to laughter. "You're so silly. I love you."

"Hey, guess what?" he said.

"What?"

"The Rangers manager told me that I'm gonna make bank next year if I keep up this winning streak. If I do, we'll be able to pay off the new house with one fat check."

"That's awesome, hubby."

She tousled his hair. His hairline was starting to recede a bit near his temples, and she wondered what he would look like fifty years from now, when he was old, when they were old together.

"After the house is paid, we'll have everything I ever wanted, except—"

Chiara looked at him. "What?"

"Nothing."

She drew her knees up and wrapped her arms around them, intrigued by his hesitation. "Tell me, except what?"

"Well I know it's a touchy subject with, well, you know, Valerie's troubles having a baby and everything like that, but—"

"But what?"

"Well, we always said when we were engaged that we were gonna start trying to have a kid after we got married. And we've been married eight months."

Chiara's eyes widened. "I want them too, honey. But I didn't think you meant it literally. I only have two more years of med school. We'll have plenty of time after that to start a family."

"Do we?" Adrian challenged. "Look at what happened to your sister. She waited, thinking she wasn't gonna have no trouble and now they've been trying for what, five years?"

"Almost. It isn't fair. People who have no right having children have them without any trouble. My sister, who would be the best mother in the whole world, can't hold a pregnancy."

"Life ain't fair, Chiara."

"I know. You don't know how much time I've spent wondering why it's not."

"Me too."

"I mean, if there is a God, why couldn't he have made life fair? If He created everything on this planet and us in his likeness, what would've been so wrong with going a step further and making life fair? Good people would get what they deserve and bad people, well, they would, too."

"Sounds nice."

"Better yet, why couldn't he have made life on earth a utopia?"

"Back up," he said. "What's Utopia?"

"It just means an imagined perfect place."

Adrian looked perplexed. "Wasn't the Garden of Eden supposed to be that?"

Chiara said, "Are you kidding? You believe the Creation story?"

"I do. Did you ever?"

Her voice softened and she looked down at the carpet. "I used to, a long time ago, but not anymore."

He seemed to be contemplating something. "If life was a utopia, then there'd be no hell."

Chiara hesitated a moment. "I don't believe in hell, or heaven anymore. When we die, we die. Thomas More had it right, I think—"

"Who's Thomas More?" Adrian asked.

"He wrote a book called *Utopia* during the Renaissance about an imagined perfect place. It was an island named Amaurote."

Adrian took a long swig of his drink. "My Chiara, always reading."

"Well, you have to admit, it would be nice if the world was a perfect place, wouldn't it?"

"It would."

"Anyway, Valerie told me this last in vitro treatment didn't take and that's it, they're done. They're not going through any more procedures. That ought to make their church happy."

"Why?"

"The Catholic Church is against alternative ways of bringing children into the world. It has to be natural or nothing. Personally, I think it's as ridiculous as the Creation story. Do you know there are actually two different creation stories in the Bible? In the same book of Genesis?"

Adrian seemed to be weighing this. "Really?"

"Really. I mean, why didn't they just give one? It would give it more weight, you know?"

Adrian gently pushed her back against the couch and kissed her. "I don't wanna talk Bibles, I wanna talk babies. Let's start trying." He fluttered his eyebrows up and down as if he were Charlie Chaplin. "I want my own baseball team."

Chiara gave him a look like he was crazy and laughed. "You're nuts."

Adrian grabbed her and playfully wrestled her to the carpet, tickling her everywhere: under her arms, up and down her waist, between her thighs, all the way down to her toes.

"If you want to throw in a couple of cheerleaders," he said, ducking her flailing hands, "that'd be cool, too."

Chiara was in tears, she was laughing so hard, trying to push him off of her, but he was too strong. "STOP! STOP!" she screeched. "I'm ticklish…I'm going to pee my pants."

Adrian whooped and howled and tickled her even harder around her tummy and her ribs. "I wouldn't be tickling you if you weren't silly, girl. Besides, you ain't wearing underwear."

Still fighting him off, she said, "The most you're getting out of this belly, *hee hee*, is three...four tops!" Then she gasped for air. "There's... *haaa!*...no...way in hell I'm going to be pregnant...*Aghh!*...*Stop!*...for the next twelve years of my...life!"

He stopped tickling her and wrestled her hands above her head. They were eye-to-eye panting, trying to catch their breath. "Well?" he asked. "When? When are we gonna start a family, *amor?*" His voice was now as delectable and sweet as maple syrup and made her fall even more in love with him.

"Wait." She paused to catch her breath. "The second I complete my residency. I promise."

Adrian's eyes lost their sparkle, making her want to say, *Okay, okay, let's start now.*

"I was hoping for sooner, but I understand. It would be a lot to handle now." He kissed her again. "You swear you want to wait because of school and not beause you feel bad for your sister?"

"I swear. My sister and Liam would be happy for us if we got pregnant," she said.

"I say, screw it, then, let's start practicing now." Adrian yodeled like Tarzan, tossed her over his shoulder and carried her into the bedroom.

After Adrian left for the ballpark, Chiara called Mamma at Girasole. When nobody answered, she tried Gian Carlo's. Enzo answered on the second ring and handed the phone to Mamma.

"Hi, *cara,*" Mamma said. "I was just about to call you. I had to leave early for the restaurant, but I brought the letter with me." Mamma sounded down.

"Are you all right, Mamma?"

Mamma's voice cracked and slowed. "It's been a tough morning, Chiara. Today, two people came into Gian Carlo's asking for Papà, wanting to say hello. I relive the day he died every time people ask what happened. I got mail for him at Girasole and at two of the restaurants this week." She cleared her throat like she was holding back a storm of tears. "I see his name on an envelope and I burst into tears."

Chiara bit her lip hard to hold back the urge to cry, but it didn't stop it from happening. She sat on the couch, staring at a picture of her parents on the cocktail table. "I think about him constantly too, Ma."

"The only thing that keeps me going is my faith that I will see him again someday in heaven."

Chiara wished she could have that comfort. "I keep studying knowing it would've made him proud."

Mamma sniffled. "It would've, *cara*. He always taught you to never give up. Even if this letter brings bad news, you have to keep trying. God always shows us a way. I remind myself of that every time I look at my yellow sunflower border in the kitchen."

Chiara heard pots and pans clanging and someone call Mamma's name. It was almost lunchtime in Pittsburgh.

"Listen to us crying like it just happened yesterday. We have to be tough, *cara*. I have over a hundred people I have to feed in the next hour."

Chiara was so thankful Sylvia and Valerie were there to help. "I know, Mamma," Chiara said, wiping her tears.

Chiara held her breath as she listened to Mamma tear open the envelope. She heard Mamma sigh, long and slow like a deflating balloon.

"What? What's it say? Was I dismissed?"

Mamma read the letter.

Dear Miss Lazzaro:

After careful consideration, due to your unsatisfactory performance on the reproductive and developmental biology curriculum section of your course work, the Committee on Student Promotions has voted to place you on academic probation for the entirety of the next academic year. During this time you will be required to repeat the deficient course work. You will be informed by letter prior to the committee's meeting again to review your academic performance and discuss your promotion.

The faculty here at the University of Pittsburgh School of Medicine is dedicated to assisting you to graduate in any way it can. Please take the rest of the summer recess to reflect on what steps you can take to better perform during the upcoming academic year. I strongly encourage you to meet and work closely with your advisory dean, as she will know firsthand of many helpful resources for you to take advantage of at the university to ensure your success.

Sincerely,

Joshua Stremple MD, PhD
Associate Dean for Student Affairs

Chiara breathed a sigh of relief. *They didn't kick me out. I still have a chance.*

"Chiara," Mamma said with a critical tone in her voice, "this is not good news."

"Mamma, believe me, I know. But the faculty could've dismissed me altogether if they wanted to."

Mamma paused at her admission. "You never told me that."

"I'm sorry, I didn't want you to worry. I know it's still serious, but I won't make the same mistake again."

"*Cara,* listen to me," Mamma said, as if she were squeezing Chiara's hand through the phone. "I've never wanted to preach like Papà did, but I must tell you, you cannot be traveling like a vagabond on weekends to be with Adrian and think you're going to breeze through medical school."

"I know, Mamma. It was stupid. I was stupid."

"Aie… this is exactly why Papà wanted you to wait until you graduated to get married. "If he were alive, he'd be saying—"

"Ma, stop. Please." She knew exactly what Mamma was going to say. And Chiara thoroughly hated hearing "I told you so."

Chapter 16

Late that afternoon, Chiara waved good-bye to one of the trainers at the Argyle Equestrian Center. She was glad she had shipped Amadeus to Texas. All day she had been stressing over the added pressure of being placed on academic probation. Riding was a great stress reliever for her, and now, after a long training session, she felt tired and as relaxed as she could feel under the circumstances.

Alicia was waiting for her by the car, smoking a cigarette. They had carpooled over together. As usual it was hot and unbearably humid. Drizzle began to sprinkle a stardust mist into the Saturday evening air. It landed softly on Chiara's face as she looked up at the high wispy cirrus clouds in the sky. Chiara recalled a walk with Papà past the sunflower garden at Girasole when she was fifteen. He'd been talking about cirrus clouds. *Did you know they are also called mare's tail clouds? I read about cloud types in your sixth-grade science book.*

She tossed her riding boots and a backpack into the backseat of the car and shut the door.

"I'm starving," Alicia said as they got into the car. "You want to grab something to eat?"

Chiara started the engine and turned the air conditioning on high. Air blasted from every vent in the SUV. "Are you kidding? Look at me. I'm a sweaty mess. It must've been a hundred and ten degrees in that indoor arena. And like an idiot, I forgot to bring a change of clothes."

Alicia had already changed into a pair of faded jeans and a Nirvana T-shirt. "Oh come on, you don't look that bad."

Chiara smelled her armpit and wrinkled her nose. "Yeah, right. I stink." She looked in the rearview mirror. "And look at my hair. It's drenched. I'm sweating so bad I turned my tan breeches brown." She put the car in reverse. "After I drop you off, I'm going to stop at the grocery store to pick up a few things I forgot to buy yesterday for my mother-in-law. Then I'm heading straight home and hopping in the shower so I can get ready for the game."

"I heard we're supposed to get a bad storm tonight," Alicia said.

Chiara's eyes widened. "So did I. You and Lindsay have made me paranoid about the storms here. I'm becoming obsessed with the Weather Channel."

Alicia chuckled like she understood. "Don't. Sometimes they skip right over us. What do you have to pick up at the store?"

"Limes, a bundle of cilantro, and a container of animal lard."

"You eat pig fat?" Alicia looked mildly repulsed.

"Never have," Chiara replied, "but I guess I'm going to."

"You better open all the doors and windows before she starts frying with it because, let's just say, it has a *very distinct* odor."

Chiara laughed. "Is it that bad? How do you know?" None of the oils Mamma and Enzo used at the restaurants or at Girasole ever smelled bad. Girasole always smelled of extra virgin olive oil, garlic, fresh basil, and red, ripe tomatoes by early evening, often mixed with the aroma of percolating espresso, and it never smelled anything less than divine.

"My sister-in-law's from Mexico and she uses it to cook everything. I'm surprised my brother hasn't keeled over from a heart attack. He gained forty pounds the first three years they were married."

"Maybe your brother just really likes to eat," Chiara teased.

Alicia pulled down the visor mirror. Her normally short, spiky hair had been flattened by the heat and her riding helmet. "I'm convinced it's the lard." She ran her hands through her hair a few times, trying to get it to stand up again. When it wouldn't, she flipped the visor shut.

Obviously it was no use. "Aside from her cooking practices, how do you like your mother-in-law?"

Chiara turned onto Highway 114. The rain was falling harder now. It thumped against the car with heavy drops and she increased the speed of the windshield wipers, trying to think positive thoughts about Cecilia before she answered.

"Honestly, I barely know her," she finally said. "We talked over the phone pretty often the first year Adrian and I dated. But when Adrian and I started talking about getting married, our relationship sort of fell apart all of a sudden. I guess our engagement changed some plans she had for Adrian and herself."

"I'm not surprised," Alicia said.

Chiara gave her a quizzical look. "What do you mean?"

"She probably wasn't ready to let her son go, that's all. A lot of women are like that. She'll get over it."

"I don't know about that. I feel like ever since we got married, she pretty much hates me. I can't seem to do or say anything right around her."

"I don't know you all that well yet, Chiara, but it's pretty obvious you're an open book. I don't think you'd intentionally hurt anyone. I don't think you could kill a roach."

Chiara laughed. "Oh, I could definitely kill a roach. Especially the ones I've seen here in Texas. They're humongous." They both laughed. Chiara turned down the air conditioning. The temperature outside had dropped rapidly—it was down to eighty. "Besides, there's a lot more to it than that."

Alicia gave her a knowing glance. "Like what? Money?"

Chiara's mouth dropped. "You, too?"

"Oh, yeah. We barely speak to Judd's brothers. When Judd broke into the big leagues, they started asking for money constantly."

"That's how Adrian's mother is. It's incessant." She began mocking Cecilia's high-pitched voice. "*Son, I can't make my cell phone payment, can you help me out? Son, I need this, son, I need that.*" Chiara squeezed the steering wheel. "We sent her three thousand dollars this month alone, for God only knows what. I don't mind helping, but it makes it hard to budget. I'm not working right now."

"I've heard it all before. It's pretty common in the baseball scene."

Alicia reached for her cell phone to check her messages, and Chiara realized that she had left hers back at the apartment.

"I'm so glad to have someone to talk to about this," Chiara said. She brought one hand to her chest. "I mean, I always get a little upset with myself for getting angry when Adrian sends her large sums of money because I do want to help her out. Really, I do. He bought her a house last September right before we got married and I was really happy for her."

"Wow—"

"It's her frivolous spending that drives me crazy." Chiara was now on a rant. "And then Adrian has to bail her out of debt. Last month she told him she *accidentally* ran her cell phone bill up to a thousand dollars again. How do you repeatedly accidentally run your cell phone bill up to a thousand bucks?"

"It won't end unless you put a stop to it, Chiara."

"I don't feel it's my place, Alicia; she's Adrian's mother. I think he should do it, but he doesn't. Every time she tells him she needs money, he just sends it. No questions asked. It's like he's pacifying her for getting married or apologizing for finally earning a decent living." She shook her head. "He's so good-hearted. But I'm always nervous to buy anything for the house we're building in Pittsburgh because I don't know what she's going to throw at us next. Do you know she actually had the nerve to ask Adrian to send her three thousand dollars last week because a cousin of hers—a cousin Adrian said she's not even close to—needed money to repair his truck? I mean, how is that our responsibility?"

Alicia laughed. "Now, that's funny. Did he send it?"

"No." She took a deep breath to thwart her temper from rising. "I got involved for that one and I think she hates me even more for it."

"I don't have any trouble saying no, or being hated for it." Alicia cocked an eyebrow at Chiara. "I've been with Judd a long time—since high school. And no one cared when we could barely make our rent." She pointed to a road on the right. "I know a short cut, turn at this light."

Chiara was glad she did. The raindrops were pelting the car as if they were rocks.

"When Judd was in AA ball, he stocked grocery shelves at night after the games, dreaming of a shot at the big leagues. I gave music lessons."

Chiara was impressed. "What do you play?"

"Violin. It didn't come easy for us."

"I didn't know Adrian when he was in the minor leagues," Chiara said.

"It's hard. The competition's tough and the pay sucks. When Judd signed his first major league contract, it was major league minimum, one hundred and twenty grand. We thought we hit the lottery, though, and so did some of our *friends*."

Chiara hoped Alicia would share her stories. Lately, so many people wanted a piece of Adrian—he was leading the American League in wins at six and one, and it was only June. Alicia's experiences might help her navigate through some of the problems she was bound to encounter being married to a sports figure.

"Don't get me wrong, we've met some really cool people over the years, but that first year—" Alicia shook her head "—we met some very shady people. Some asked for money. Some asked for free tickets to the games. Some just tagged along, wanting to be friends with a big leaguer." She rooted through her bag and pulled out her cigarettes. She smoked Marlboro Ultra Lights, just like Sylvia. But she never took one out of the pack, just twirled it between her fingers. "I won't even go into the women I've had to deal with." Alicia winced.

The women, Chiara thought. *Should I tell her about the crank calls?* Cecilia was probably behind them; Chiara believed that. She just had to figure out a way to win Cecilia over so she would call off her attack dog.

But what if it is someone else? Technically, I have no proof it's Cecilia. Had Alicia ever experienced anything like this? She had to ask.

"You're just getting your feet wet, honey," Alicia said. "You wait. A couple more years and you'll be spewing out the word *no* in your sleep."

Chiara kneaded the steering wheel in her hands, cleared her throat. "Alicia, you mentioned women. What kind of problems did you have?"

Alicia creased her forehead, frowning at Chiara like she was an idiot. "There's only one kind of problem with women, Chiara. Why? Something happen to you, too?"

Chiara realized her question sounded ridiculous. "Well, sort of." She glanced at Alicia then fixed her eyes on the road again. She could barely see anything out the window with the rain coming down so hard. "I've been getting crank calls from a woman since the night before I got married. She even called the church the day before my wedding to tell the priest to stop the wedding. That Adrian was sleeping with her."

Alicia raised her eyebrows, looking apologetic. "Wow. That's pretty bad. What did Adrian say?"

Chiara cleared her throat again. It felt like she had a hundred cotton balls stuck in it. "He said it wasn't true. And I believe him. They stopped after the wedding, but since I moved here, they've started again. The more she calls, the more doubt starts creeping into my head. I even got a call from her in our room in New York."

"Phhh. Someone's got to be pretty ticked off to call the priest. Do you know if Adrian has an old flame that never got over him?"

"I asked. He said he doesn't." Chiara wanted to tell her there were only two people she knew of that hadn't wanted them to get married: one was Papà and the other was Cecilia. Chiara wanted to tell her she thought Cecilia was behind the calls. She refrained. *No proof.*

"You guys should change your phone numbers."

"We're going to."

"And Adrian should put his name under an alias at the front desk in the hotels. Judd does. It keeps pesky fans and loose women from calling the rooms."

"I mentioned hiring a private investigator, but he asked me to hold off until after the season ends."

"He must not be too worried about it. The guys are used to being badgered."

"He's not. Besides, he wants me to concentrate on my boards coming up at the end of the month, and he wants to work on getting as many wins as he can this season. He'll be a free agent again at the end of this year."

"If it gets to the point where you need a PI, you won't have to hire one. The Major League Baseball Players Association provides that kind of help to its players. I guess enough of the star players have been stalked over the years to warrant it. The money to pay for it comes out of the players' dues. Just have Adrian call his agents. They'll get you in touch with the firms the association uses for stuff like that."

"I didn't know." Chiara was relieved. "Thanks. Alicia?"

"Yeah?"

"How did you get through those tough times?"

Alicia opened the pack of cigarettes and pulled one out. "Cigarettes and the man upstairs," she said. "I started going to church and Bible study classes at the ballpark. You should come."

Chiara's throat tightened. "No thanks, I'm not a Bible study kind of person."

They merged onto Highway 360 and headed south toward Arlington. The wind picked up, and ominous pitch-dark clouds rolled and churned toward them like a filthy avalanche.

Alicia fixed her eyes on the clouds. "Ho-ly shit. They're rockin' and rollin'."

Leaves, branches, and debris swirled in every direction along the highway.

"Is this a bad storm for Texas?" Chiara was starting to feel uneasy. She had never seen a sky stir like this before. She drove the car steadily through the rain, but she could hardly wait to get back to the apartment.

Alicia shrugged, turned on the radio, scrolled through the stations. "I've seen worse. What do you feel like listening to?"

Chiara doubted her, but she acted just as stoic. "Anything but jazz. What's your favorite?"

"Alternative."

"Should've guessed," Chiara said.

"Why?" Alicia asked.

"The T-shirt. My sister Sylvia has the same one."

"That was a great concert. Did she go?"

"She did." Chiara pointed at the sky. "Does that look like a funnel cloud to you?"

Alicia laughed at her naiveté. "You've obviously never seen one. That's not even close."

"I have on *Storm Chasers*." She double-checked to make sure her headlights were on—with the rain falling so hard it was hard to tell— and then clutched the steering wheel again with both hands. She was trying so hard to maintain a carefree attitude that she started sweating again. "The clouds—" She paused. "—they look spiteful."

In an instant the rain turned to golf-ball-sized hail, pelting the SUV. Chiara wondered how two little hydrogen atoms bonded to an oxygen atom could cause so much havoc. Without warning a car in the left lane hydroplaned and Chiara swerved her SUV toward the shoulder of the highway to avoid getting hit.

"Watch out!" Alicia screamed.

Chiara screamed and turned the wheel again just inches before hitting the guard rail. She stopped the car. "You okay?"

Alicia was still gripping the car handle, but her shoulders eased back a little. "God…that was close."

Chiara stared into the rearview mirror and waited for a few cars to pass before she eased back into the right lane.

"I can't see a thing out the window. Still going to the grocery store?" Alicia asked, obviously attempting to lighten the mood.

"She'll have to wait for the lard." Chiara's clothes were still wet from her ride and she felt a chill shoot down her back.

"Just keep breathing. We're almost home."

A roar of thunder reverberated through the car with such a force it shook Chiara's insides. She felt the urge to go to the bathroom. "Find a station reporting the weather."

Alicia tuned into Fort Worth's Y108 and turned up the volume just as a bolt of lightning creased the sky in half. "You're more than welcome to stay at my place till it lets up," she said.

"I'll be okay." Chiara sat up straighter, acting like she was fine. "I'm only another five minutes from your place."

As they pulled up to Alicia's building, the storm abated.

"Call me when you get home," Alicia said. She grabbed her riding boots, heaved her hobo bag above her head, and dashed toward her apartment.

By the time Chiara got home the rain stopped all of a sudden; the wind, too. *Odd*, she thought. She opened the car door, taking in the eerie quiet in the air. She looked around, feeling as if she were alone in an old haunted house or stranded in a black hole somewhere. Cherry trees, usually alive with chirping sparrows at this time of day, stood quiet. Cicadas, normally welcoming in the evening, were silent.

She stepped onto the steaming asphalt, shaking her head at the dents the hail had made on the hood of her car. Early evening streaks of fuchsia, tangerine and cobalt blue streaked the western sky behind clusters of blue-black clouds. She grabbed her backpack and riding boots and hurried up the apartment steps two at a time. At the third-floor landing, she took off her leather clogs, leaving them on the straw mat outside the door to keep the smell of horse hair and manure from permeating the apartment. As she dug for her keys in her purse, she noticed a sunflower wreath on the apartment door next to hers. It didn't look new. She wondered *Why didn't I notice it before?* She stood there a moment, staring at the wreath, remembering how Papà used to go on and on about sunflowers, how he believed that God uses the Golden Ratio present in the flower and so many other things in life, as a guide for his flock. She felt her stomach grow heavy inside her. She'd do anything to see Papà again, to say she was sorry for arguing with him, to tell him one last time she loved him and she wasn't going to let him down. But it was too late for that.

The wind picked up again and Chiara unlocked the door, stepped inside and latched both the lower and upper locks. Then she hurried to the phone in the kitchen. The answering machine was blinking off the phone cradle; maybe Mamma or her sisters had called to ask about the weather. Maybe it was Cecilia, asking her to pick up something else at the grocery store. She'd check the messages after she called Adrian at the ballpark. She just wanted to hear his voice. No answer. He was probably working out. She turned on the TV which was still tuned to the Weather Channel and dialed Alicia's number.

"You have reached eight one seven…" It was the answering machine.

Chiara left a message and hung up thinking Alicia must have hopped into the shower. She glowered at the television. It was showing a map of the United States with parts of Texas, Kansas, and Oklahoma lit up like a Christmas tree in shades of red, yellow, green and orange. A meteorologist pointed to the red sections explaining the phenomenon of tornadoes. Within seconds a ticker flashed across the bottom of the screen: a tornado warning for Denton County, not so far away. She was about to check the messages when the phone rang.

"Hello?"

"Hello, pretty girl." It was Lindsay. "I was calling to check in on you. You northerners aren't used to this kind of weather."

Her southern drawl was so American; it made Chiara think of rural summer barbecues and homemade apple pie. She was relieved to hear Lindsay's voice. "Hi, Lindsay. I'd feel a lot better if I wasn't looking at the entire northeast part of Texas on the Weather Channel covered in red and orange."

"I know. I've got it on too, darlin'. Me and the kids were just watching the terrific-size hail balls crashing into the swimming pool. They look like meteors."

"I just dropped Alicia off. We were at the stable and got some of the hail on our way home. My car has some pretty big dents."

"Don't worry about the car, it can be fixed."

Chiara took in Lindsay's casual voice. "I know, I'm just a little frazzled from the ride home."

"Oh, bless your soul, you poor thing. It was pouring out there. I couldn't see a thing out the window. You all right?"

"I'm fine. It seems to be moving out of here. How are you and the kids?"

"We're fine, and oh no, it isn't movin' out of here. Texas skies don't let you off *that* easy, sugar. The rain stopped here, too, for a bit, but we just started getting hit again about five minutes ago."

Chiara walked over to the sliding glass door and pushed back the vertical blinds. A dark funnel cloud was forming to the west of the building, about a mile away. Around it the sky was glowing in violent hues like a Van Gogh painting, complete with sinister swirls. In spite of her terror, the scientist in Chiara thought it was the most awesome skyline she had ever seen. It was real and surreal at the same time.

Chiara's voice rattled in her throat. "Oh my God, Lindsay. I'm looking at the craziest-looking cloud I've ever seen. The Weather Channel is talking about a tornado that just touched down in Denton County."

"That's not far from here." Lindsay sounded grave. "I can see the counties in trouble blinking across the screen." She paused. "Okay, stay calm. The Metroplex area of Tarrant County hasn't had a tornado in over fifty years, so what you're seeing probably isn't going to turn into a tornado. I guess all the big buildings break up the wind or something."

"That sounds promising, but I'm still pretty nervous."

"Don't be. I talked to Mike a few minutes ago. He said they're probably going to cancel the game tonight. He said Adrian was trying to call you on your cell phone to tell you, but you didn't answer."

"I forgot it here at the apartment earlier." She let out a heavy sigh. "I feel like I'm forgetting to do a lot of things the past few days." *Things like studying*, she thought.

"Stop being so hard on yourself, Chiara. I've been in your shoes. It's hard getting used to new places and people. I can't wait for Mike to retire this year. I never thought he'd still be playing in his forties. I swear, at the end of the season I'm going to throw out every suitcase we own, even if some of them are Louis Vuitton."

Chiara laughed, but her eyes were still focused on the cloud. She forced herself to change the subject. "Hey I stopped by the little boutique at the Galleria that you told me about the other day. They do have great stuff."

Lindsay's voice brightened. "I told you so! Did you see that shimmery silver dress in the window?"

"Oh, yeah, very sexy, and very out of my price range." Chiara embraced the sound of Lindsay's warm voice through the receiver as if she were hugging her favorite childhood teddy bear.

"Good, 'cause I'm buying it tomorrow."

Chiara smiled, fell silent. She could hear Lindsay's sons calling for her in the background. "Lindsay?"

"Yeah?"

"Thank you."

"You are welcome, darling. Hey, isn't your mother-in-law coming in soon?"

"The day after tomorrow."

"Okay, we'll get together this week and take her shopping with us. And don't you be shy to call me if you need anything, ya hear?"

Chiara hung up and stood staring out the sliding glass door at the strangely lit sky. It swallowed up the funnel cloud as quickly as it formed. Chiara felt little relief. It was raining hard again, the wind blowing harder, stripping the trees in the parking lot of their leaves. Hail knocked on the door like a persistent salesman. On the TV, a tornado warning flashed in red for Denton County, Tarrant County, and the entire Dallas–Fort Worth Metroplex area. She thought *Unbelievable.* She moved away from the door and dialed Adrian's cell phone number again, her fingers trembling.

Calm, stay calm, she told herself.

A tornado siren sounded somewhere in the distance. The phone rang and a roar like a thousand stampeding horses boomed somewhere outside.

"Oh my God!" Chiara shrieked. She dropped to her knees and crawled frantically toward the bathroom. Something hit the glass door, shattering it into a million pieces and shooting glass shards everywhere. She felt a quick sting as her hand passed over one. Wind sprayed the apartment like a fire hose, hurling pictures, books, plants, and anything else in its way like a merciless betrayed lover. In the tub, Chiara ripped the plastic shower curtain from its rings and covered herself with it, praying the Lord's Prayer over and over again as she waited for the storm to pass.

Later, waiting to be seen by a physician in Arlington Hospital's packed emergency waiting room, Chiara first wrapped her sliced hand with some gauze she'd requested from the triage nurse, and then helped make other patients comfortable until they could be seen by a doctor. A little girl, her face framed with ringlets of hair, badly cut by something from knee to ankle, sat on her mother's lap, still bleeding, still shaken. Chiara wrapped the little girl's leg. While she soothed the child's fears, sounds of the tornado echoed in Chiara's ears like whispers from a seashell reminding her of her own terror and of how she'd found comfort in prayer.

Chapter 17

On Tuesday, the storm was still the highlight of the local news stations. Waiting for Cecilia to freshen up so they could go to lunch, Chiara and Adrian sat on the couch, their eyes glued to the TV, watching the news.

"It's hard to believe," said a blonde reporter in an editorial voice, "that I am here in downtown Fort Worth, standing amid an incredible amount of debris, covering clean-up efforts caused by an F5 tornado that touched down right smack in the middle of the city on Saturday, ravaging everything in its path."

"That's some crazy shit," Adrian said, shaking his head at the destruction on the screen.

"Three days have passed since the horrific night," the reporter continued, "and clean-up crews have barely made headway. President Clinton declared a state of emergency and ordered the city shut down until further notice."

As she spoke, the camera zoomed in on tall office buildings with blown-out windows. Computer monitors, office furniture, and other debris could be seen strewn across streets. Car roofs were smashed. The violent winds had uprooted trees and smashed them into buildings, and thousands of pounds of glass mixed with tree branches, trash, books, and a plethora of other debris flowed toward clogged gutters in a steady stream of flood water.

"Our Channel 7 meteorologists confirmed that the tornado that touched down only one hundred yards from an apartment complex in Tarrant County the same evening was a F3 and caused considerably less damage—"

"Please turn it off, honey," Chiara said.

Adrian clicked it off with the remote and wrapped his arms around her. "The apartment manager told me this building was hit the hardest with debris. You sure you don't want to move into a first-floor unit?"

"I'm sure. What are the chances we'd get hit again?"

"True."

She hugged him tight. "Just promise me no more third-floor apartments after this year."

"I promise." He kissed her forehead. "I wish I'd been here when it happened."

"I'm glad you weren't. What if you had gotten hurt? You might have been out for the rest of the season." She looked down at her bandaged hand. Her right palm had received double-digit stitches and reminded her of Papà's lined forehead. She missed him so much and knew if he were alive, he would've told her she would never have gone through this ordeal if she'd listened to him. She looked at all the scratched furniture and the open space that used to house the sliding glass door. She had taped it up with black garbage bags until the maintenance crew could replace it.

Adrian kissed her hand. "What are you thinking?"

She didn't want to hurt his feelings, so she said, "I wanted everything to look perfect when your mother got here, and instead it looks like a tornado hit." They looked at each other and burst into laughter.

"We'll get new furniture," Adrian said, laughing. He stroked her cheek and gave her an amatory gaze. "I called the apartment manager while you were getting dressed. The door came in. The new carpet, too. The carpenters are gonna come by around two to put them in. Then you can toss the broken stuff and put everything that ain't broke back exactly like it was."

"I'm ready," Cecilia sang as she emerged from the guestroom. She was wearing an oversized red-and-white Texas Rangers jersey with Adrian's new number, thirty-eight, sewn across her gargantuan bosom—the same type of outfit that she'd worn in Pittsburgh—and a pair of obscenely tight-in-the-crotch blue jeans. Her claws were painted Texas Rangers red.

Chiara wanted to smack herself in the head. *Stop being so critical of her. Try harder to love her.*

"Where do you wanna eat, Ma?" Adrian said.

Cecilia wrapped her arms around Adrian's neck and kissed him on the cheek. "I wanted to cook for you here, but this place is a mess, you know?" She observed Chiara's reaction out of the corner of her eye.

Chiara avoided her glance. She felt as if she was intruding on a personal mother-son moment, even though it looked farcical. Really, did Cecilia think she needed to dramatize her love for her son? Chiara made herself smile. *Nice*, she reiterated to herself. *Be nice.*

"The carpenters are coming later to put new carpet in and fix the windows and door so we can get this place cleaned up right," Adrian told her. "Then you can cook all you want."

Cecilia released Adrian from her grip and looked down at the carpet. "I stepped on glass three times already, you know?"

"I am so sorry, Cecilia," Chiara said. "I've vacuumed over and over. It just keeps surfacing."

Cecilia gave her a tight smile. "Maybe one more time would've done the trick," she said, turning to Adrian. "Where do you want to have lunch, son?"

Chiara smiled politely as Cecilia wrapped her arms around Adrian again. He had definitely gotten his height from Cecilia. But his face, so kind and benevolent, was doubtless a paternal genetic contribution.

He looked at Chiara. "Where do you wanna go, baby?"

"You guys go ahead. You haven't seen each other since spring training. I think I'll wait here and make sure the carpenters don't break anything else when they move the furniture around."

"They'll handle it," Adrian said.

"If I stay I might be able to get everything back in order before the game and Cecilia—" Chiara gave her a glance, "—can have a nice, neat kitchen to cook in tonight when we get back from the game. It's tiny but we got tons of pots and pans as wedding gifts. Adrian says you're a great cook, so you'll have everything you need to make dinner."

Cecilia seemed mildly content that Chiara was going to stay behind. "Actually, your kitchen is very modern and high class compared to the kitchen in my old apartment. I cooked in it for twenty years for my boys before Adrian bought the house for me and my son Mario. You should appreciate it, you know?"

"Oh, I do, Cecilia. I just meant—"

"Ma, stop," Adrian interrupted. "Let's go eat. You come too, Chiara."

"No, really," Chiara said. "You guys go ahead. I'll get some studying in while I wait for the carpenters and you two can catch up on some quality time together."

Cecilia smiled at Adrian.

"You sure?" he said.

"I'm positive." *One hundred percent positive.*

Adrian strode over to Chiara, picked her up as though she weighed nothing, and kissed her on the lips before setting her down again. Cecilia looked away, but not before Chiara saw a rush of blood rise to her face.

"I have to be at the ballpark for the three-fifteen stretch, so I'll drop my mom back off by three."

Cecilia pouted like a child. "I want to watch batting practice, like I always do."

"Ma, it's hot here, worse than Florida," Adrian said. "You can't be sitting in the stands all day, especially since you've been feeling sick with your high blood pressure and everything."

"But I feel good today," she cooed. "I want to watch you practice. I can always go into one of the restaurants if I want a break from the heat. Besides, I can't wait to see the stadium."

Adrian rolled his eyes. "Okay, okay, but you better call Chiara if the heat starts getting to you."

He took Chiara's hand in his and kissed it, looking as sexy as ever.

"I guess I'll see you after the game," he said, looking reluctant to leave.

"Good luck, honey. Get another win."

"I don't know about tonight. It's the Yankees again."

He kissed Chiara on the lips once more, and then he and Cecilia were gone. Chiara rubbed her cheeks. Her face ached from pasting on a smile since Cecilia had arrived. In fact, the only time Chiara had given Cecilia a sincere smile in the past twelve hours was on the ride home after picking her up at the airport. Cecilia had told them her best friend's daughter was having her confirmation next Sunday back in Tampa and would be livid if Cecilia missed it. Cecilia would have to leave next Thursday. *Smile.* Chiara was instantly thankful for that sacrament and every other pious occasion she could think of. Now she would only have to deal with Cecilia for nine more days. She could have more time to study and be alone with Adrian before she headed back to Pittsburgh to take her exam, check on the house, and show Hemingway. *Smile.*

She walked around the family room, rummaging through piles of scratched and cracked picture frames, damp books and magazines, and other knick-knacks spoiled by the rain and wind. When she picked up her wedding-cake-top figurine of a bride and groom, she felt her stomach churn. It was a wedding gift from Valerie and Liam. Part of the bride's train was cracked and the left side of the groom's face was missing. She placed it on the dinette table, hoping to find a place that could repair it, and then began placing the rest of what she could salvage on the kitchen counter. She reluctantly tossed into a trash bag the things that were ruined. When she picked up a Bible given to Adrian, wet and swollen, pages ink smeared, she stopped and stared at it, unable to throw it away. She remembered her invocation. Was there still a little faith left in her after all? *Papà,* she thought, *if there is an afterlife, and you are alive in spirit, pray for me. Pray that I can ignore the crank caller tormenting me so that I can concentrate on my studies. Pray that I can ignore Cecilia's insolence. But most important, pray that I get myself off academic probation, because I feel like I'm starting to lose my way.*

The carpenters arrived at two o'clock sharp.

"Wow," one of them said, looking at the blown-out door. He was a tall, rugged Texan with a Fu Manchu mustache. He asked if she'd been home when it happened.

Chiara held up her bandaged hand. "Unfortunately, yes."

"Ouch," he said.

"It's not so bad. I just can't ride my horse until it heals."

"I can see why." He scratched his head, looking around the apartment. "We'll get this place cleaned up real fast for you." He winked.

"Apartment manager says you've got an important ballgame to go to tonight."

Chiara looked down at the carpet and smiled, proud of Adrian. "I do."

"He's good. Real good. Leading the American League pitchers for most wins for the season."

She beamed with pride. "So far, so good."

"Well, good luck to ya both. He seems like a real good guy—and a lucky one, too."

Chiara felt her cheeks grow warm. "Thank you."

The man's eyes rested on her, and an awkward moment lingered between them.

"It's so hot in here," she said. "Can I get you guys something to drink?" She pointed toward the plastic bag covering the doorway. "As you can see, there's been no point in turning on the air conditioning."

"Maybe some water," he said.

"Make that two," the other carpenter added. He pulled a hammer out of a red toolbox and walked over to the screen door, arms akimbo, as if wondering where to start.

Chiara brought them two large glasses of ice-cold water and then excused herself when the phone rang.

"Hello?"

"Hello, Chiara," the woman hissed.

Her voice shot down Chiara's spine like a winter chill, a voice that miraculously appeared and disappeared of its own will, intruding on her conscious and subconscious existence, sprinkling doubt on her happy marriage.

"I see you're still alive, bitch. I was hoping the tornado killed you," she said.

"Unfortunately for you, it didn't," Chiara retorted and hung up.

The phone rang again, and Chiara couldn't resist answering it. She stormed into the bedroom and closed the door so the carpenters would not hear what she was about to say. "Leave me alone," she demanded *sotto voce.*

"Not until you and Adrian break up," she snapped. Then she cackled, long and hard. "You stupid cunt, you white bitch. Nobody likes you in his family, not his mother, not his brother."

So you know Adrian's family.

"I'd watch my ass if I were you. There's no telling what might happen to your skinny little white ass when your pretty-boy husband is on the road and you're in that apartment late at night all by yourself."

"I'm not afraid of you," Chiara said. Her blood was boiling. "If you were a real woman having an affair with my husband, you wouldn't be hiding behind a phone."

"He's stopping by to see me before practice starts."

"Oh yeah? Well, tell him to pick up a gallon of milk on his way home tonight," Chiara said with a clenched jaw and hung up.

Chiara sat on her bed, seething, long after the carpenters left. The USMLE guide lay open in front of her. She hadn't read a word all day. *What would Papà's advice to me be right now?* she thought. *Could it be possible he was right about Adrian all along?*

By the time Chiara arrived at the ballpark, it was game time and still a hundred degrees. The early summer sun was steadily sinking into a cradling cerulean sky just behind the Jumbotron, and the stadium lights were heating up in anticipation of another sold-out game. The smell of freshly mowed grass and hotdogs permeated the air. Her stomach growled and she thought about buying one, but she'd lost her desire to eat after her conversation with "Miss Latin America." Besides, she wanted to be in her seat when Adrian threw his first pitch.

She squeezed by strolling fans toward section 202—the designated Rangers's family seating area. Just as she reached the landing, Arlington High's 1997 valedictorian was introduced to sing the national anthem. Chiara stopped at the landing and waited respectfully. As the young woman began to sing, Chiara felt the boulder-like tension she'd been carrying on her shoulders ease. The young girl had the voice of a harp; it was the loveliest rendition of the anthem Chiara had ever heard. And she heard the anthem a lot. Every night, before every game. After the song, the crowd cheered wildly. *Another sold-out night. Texas fans are amazing,* Chiara thought as she started down the steps again towards her seat. When she saw Cecilia, she painted on a smile even though she felt deflated and confused. Cecilia was fanning herself with a scorecard with one hand and nursing a beer in the other. Was there a chance Cecilia was innocent in the matter? If she was, Miss Home Wrecker could be lurking nearby, watching her, watching Adrian, watching them.

Chiara stepped into her row and a few Rangers wives stood up so she could get to her seat.

"Good luck, Chiara." The second baseman's wife patted her on the back.

"Thanks, Shelly."

The left fielder's girlfriend crossed her fingers. "We're rooting for him, Chiara. Lucky seven."

Chiara squeezed her arm. "Thanks, Beth."

Alicia and Lindsay both hugged her.

"How's your hand?" Alicia asked.

"Better, thanks."

"Good luck," Alicia said.

Cecilia watched her approach, smiling like she had just bitten into a lemon, droplets of sweat running down the side of her face. "I was wondering when you were going to get here," she said, moving a bag full of souvenirs from Chiara's seat so she could sit down. "Did you study? Adrian told me you're gonna get kicked out if you don't do really good next year. He said you have to put in extra time now studying."

"Hi, Cecilia. I'll have to retake the class I failed last semester so I'm trying to study that material and prepare for the board examination at the same time. But that's not why I got here a little late. It took me a little longer than I expected to clean up after the carpenters left."

"Call me Cici. Everyone in the family calls me Cici." Cecilia said this as if she had been tortured into saying it. Still, she said it.

Chiara looked at her, surprised. *Could this be an effort on your part...Cici?* "Okay, thank you...Cici." *Are you responsible for the crank calls? Could you be innocent? Could Adrian be having an affair? If he is, it would've started before we even got married. And that makes no sense. Why would he go ahead with the wedding? No one was holding a gun to his head. Why would he want to buy the property and build the house? Why would he allow this woman to call me?*

A Pittsburgh Pirate's wife had once told Chiara about a groupie who made crank calls and stalked her husband for three years before the police identified and arrested her. Her husband had never even met the woman. The Texas Rangers were all over ESPN and FOX Sports News every day. Of course Adrian was going to get a lot of attention as one of the newer players on the team. *I should expect things like this.*

Cecilia's stared down at Chiara's white linen sundress and orange patent-leather sandals, pursing her lips so tight they disappeared into her pudgy face. Her disdain for Chiara was palpable. She was still wearing the Rangers jersey and jeans she'd had on in the morning.

"It must be extra hard for you to get through your classes with that problem Adrian said you have," Cecilia said.

Chiara blushed and sat on her hands to avoid chomping on her nails. "It's not too bad, Cici. I have little tricks I was taught in school as a little girl that help me with that."

It has to be her. Nobody else dislikes me this much. If she could win Cecilia over, perhaps their relationship would improve and Cecilia would call off her attack dog. Chiara resigned herself to trying to be kinder to Cecilia. She tucked away her doubts about her mother-in-law, the caller, and Adrian. It was his night.

The Rangers trotted onto the field and took their positions. The crowd cheered. Fans chanted Adrian's name. Cecilia shot out of her seat, whooping and hollering at the top of her voice. "Go, *hijo!* Go, *hijo!*" She sounded like a man. Chiara had no idea her voice could drop so low, almost to male bass range. *This woman missed her calling; she should've been a singer.*

When Adrian started throwing his warm-up pitches, Cecilia sat down and took a swig of her beer. "So the apartment is back to normal?" she said. Her voice was back to its sweet soprano range.

"Yes," Chiara said. "The kitchen is ready for your culinary expertise. How was your day? Where did you and Adrian have lunch?"

Cecilia fanned herself with the score card again. "Macaroni House." She paused. "You know, Adrian's right. It is hotter here than in Florida." She stared off at him adoringly. "Oh, look how good he looks."

Hey, something we agree on. Adrian was in his white-and-red uniform, the letter T embroidered on his red baseball cap, his wedding band hanging from a thin gold chain around his neck. *That's my husband.*

The umpire motioned for the first batter. Adrian made the sign of the cross over his heart, then threw his first pitch. It was a ninety-five-mile-per-hour fast pitch down the middle of the plate to Yankee Derek Jeter. The ball hit Mike Hogan's glove with a *smack*...and the sound reverberated through the stadium. The fans roared.

Cecilia jumped out of her seat, caterwauling, *"Woo-hoo! Way to go, son!"* She buzzed her lips into her closed fist with the expert embouchure of a military bugler. The earsplitting shrill erupted through the stands and caught the attention of everyone in the section. Chiara was shocked by how loud and piercing the sound was, like a real bugle. She looked around to see who was watching them. Three Rangers wives a few seats over were huddled together, laughing. Despite her mortification, Chiara wanted to say, *Hey, back off, this is my mother-in-law.* But then she thought how ridiculous Cecilia's reaction was. It was only the first pitch of the game. Of course they were going to laugh. Was Cecilia going to carry on like this for the whole game?

The next pitch was another fast ball on the outside corner of the plate. It also went in for a strike.

Still standing, Cecilia bellowed, "Yeah! Way to pitch, son!"

Chiara looked up at Cecilia and back down at her bandaged hand, tapping her foot on the concrete, wandering how long her mother-in-law was going to go on like this. The next pitch, a slider, hit Hogan's glove even harder and the scoreboard lighted up with a pitch speed at ninety-seven miles per hour. The umpire threw up a leg, punched the air, and called, "Strike three!"

Phil Collins's hit song "Home by the Sea" blared, "Sit down, sit down, sit d-o-w-n" from the stadium speakers, and Derek Jeter walked back to the visitor dugout twirling his bat, his head slung low like a defeated lion. Chiara clapped along with Cecilia and the fans. Cecilia finally sat down and Chiara was thankful that she had taken Phil's cue.

"I could cheer like that for him every pitch, but Adrian told me to behave myself while I'm here." Cecilia laughed as if she knew she was embarrassing but couldn't care less, and her watermelon breasts jiggled under her jersey.

Chiara let out a sigh of relief. *Thank God.*

Cecilia pulled a box of Cracker Jacks out of a bag and offered her some. "So we can use the kitchen now?"

"Yes, Cici. *Mi casa, su casa.* The kitchen is officially open."

"Good, 'cause I invited a few of the Latin boys over to eat after the game. I hope that's okay. Sanchez and Lopez said they don't get to eat authentic Latin food much."

Chiara bit her tongue, thinking it would've been nice for Cecilia to run it by her first, considering the earlier condition of the apartment. "No problem." But what if the carpenters had canceled? The place would've been a mess. *Calm, stay calm*, she told herself. The apartment was clean and neat and in order. Everything was fine.

"I'm going to make fish tacos," Cecilia said. "I sent one of the clubhouse boys to the store to pick up some cod."

"Then I guess we're set."

By the top of the seventh inning, the Rangers had a five-nothing lead over the Yankees and Adrian had only given up two hits. When Chiara's cell phone rang with a restricted number, Chiara thought it must be Mamma. Chiara answered it. "Hi, Ma."

"Hi, *cara*," Mamma said.

"You don't usually call me during the games. Everything okay?"

"Everything is fine, Chiara. I'm actually having a good day for once. How are you?"

"I'm fine. I'm sitting here with Cecilia…I mean, Cici." She looked at Cecilia for some sign of approval but her mother-in-law's eyes were glued to the field, watching the game.

"Tell her I said hello," Mamma said. "I wanted to call and tell you Liam, your sisters, Bibi and Julio, Enzo and some of the waiters and waitresses from Gian Carlo's are all here at Girasole watching the game. I guess everybody wanted to keep me company tonight," she said sounding grateful. "We just saw you and Cecilia on the TV, *cara*!"

"Really?" Chiara laughed. "That's funny."

"We're all praying Adrian gets the win. He's doing great. Can we call after the game to congratulate him?"

"Of course you can, Ma. Hold on…Cici, my mother says hello. She said she just saw us on TV." Cecilia nodded while marking a strike on her scorecard. Chiara turned away when Cecilia didn't respond. "We're up so late anymore, Mamma. You can call anytime. Besides, Cici invited some players over after the game. I have a feeling it's going to be a very late night."

When the crowd started singing "Take Me Out to the Ball Game," Chiara couldn't hear. She told Mamma she'd call back and hung up the phone.

Chiara smiled as she thought of everyone sitting around the family room at Girasole keeping Mamma company, rooting for Adrian. It made her tingle inside.

"How is your mother?" Cecilia said.

"Oh, she's hanging in there, Cici. It's been hard for her since my father died. They were very close. Together since she was twenty. She just loves watching baseball now."

Cecilia raised an eyebrow at her as if to say how Mamma *dare* impose on her sport.

"It keeps her mind occupied at night when she comes home from one of the restaurants to an empty house. She says watching the game gives her three solid hours of distraction. By the time the games are over, it's usually close to eleven. She watches the news and then heads up to her room to get ready for another day at work." She smiled, thinking of Mamma watching the games at night.

"What's so funny?" Cecilia asked.

"Nothing, really. It's just that nobody in my family ever followed baseball before I met Adrian. We were a soccer family," she said. "Now my mother has the special MLB sports package through our cable network so she gets all the games."

"That's nice," Cecilia said with a tone, fixing her eyes on the field. "You can only imagine how proud me and Mario are of him. We waited so long for him to get to where he is now and…Well, it doesn't matter, does it?"

Chiara pretended that she had missed the intentional low blow, but her anger was sudden. She fought the urge to grab Cecilia's hands and rip off her synthetic red fingertips one by one. *Why do you have to act like this? He's taking care of you. Why don't you want me to be part of your family?*

"My heart bursts with pride every time he takes the mound," Chiara said. "I can only imagine what you must feel like being his mother." And she meant it, too. All parents beam with pride when their children achieve the pinnacle of success in their endeavors. As the thought crossed her mind, Chiara's anger shifted to guilt. She had not reached the pinnacle of anything. In fact, she felt she was beginning to dive toward rock bottom. She'd failed her faith in God, let Papà down by breaking her promise, and could fail medical school and end up feeling like a useless mote in the capacious world if she wasn't super careful next year. And now, she was losing faith in her husband.

Her cell phone rang again, but she didn't answer. Forty-five thousand fans were all standing and chanting, "For it's one, two, three strikes you're out at the old…" Chiara peered into the bullpen and saw a relief pitcher warming up. It was number eighty-six, Miguel Lopez, a stocky player with thick bowed legs.

"I don't think they're going to let Adrian pitch the eighth," Chiara said.

"I know. That makes me mad, you know? He's only thrown a hundred pitches; he's not tired."

When the eighth inning started, Adrian walked the lead-off batter and then gave up a single. The bases suddenly had two runners on them for the first time all night, but Adrian remained cool, as if his seventh win was a sure thing. Once he told Chiara that he learned to be a master of his feelings in Little League by acting as if things were always going his way, and ever since it helped him keep his mind clear, on and off the field. Chiara admired that about him, how he stayed cool under pressure. She wished she could be more like that. Right now, it was taking the energy of every cell in her body to keep trying to befriend Cecilia.

When the Rangers's manager, Mike Hogan, and the first baseman jogged over to the mound, Adrian handed the manager the ball. The manager gave him a congratulatory pat on the back, and Adrian walked toward the dugout. The crowd was on its feet, giving him a standing ovation. Just before he entered the dugout, Adrian turned toward the crowd and tipped his hat. The crowd roared again as he disappeared into the clubhouse.

Chiara and Cecilia were on their feet applauding, too, Cecilia bugling again.

"Way to go, son!" she screamed. Then she made the god-awful sound again. And again. "Let's just hope Lopez can get him out of this little jam!"

The crowd settled back into their seats as Lopez warmed up on the mound. Chiara's cell phone rang again. Restricted. Mamma again. *Shit.* "Hey, Ma…"

"Hi, whore, you still at the game with Cecilia? Adrian told me today he's gonna leave you—"

The batter hit a line drive down the right field line, allowing two runs to score easily, and the woman's voice drowned in the groans and boos of the crowd. Chiara flipped the phone shut. *Unbelievable…She has my cell phone number.* She felt nausea grip and churn her stomach, and her mouth dropped into her lap. Cecilia noticed.

"You okay?" Cecilia asked, a fleeting look of pleasure falling over her face like a veil.

"Fine, Cici. Everything's fine. I'll be back." Chiara stood up and rushed up the stadium steps, holding her stomach, afraid if she slowed down she'd vomit all over the fans. Alicia and Lindsay saw her and followed. They caught up to Chiara in the ladies' room.

"Hey, what's wrong? What happened?" Alicia asked. "You looked like you were about toss your cookies down there. You okay?"

"Hey, guys. I'm fine," Chiara said, placing a wad of wet paper towels to the back of her neck. The room felt like it was two hundred degrees. "I got really queasy. I had to get up and walk."

"Are you pregnant?" Lindsay asked.

Chiara shook her head.

"Did you have a misunderstanding with your mother-in-law?" Alicia asked.

"No, that's going all right," Chiara said. She looked at Lindsay. "I've been getting crank calls from a woman for almost a year. Alicia knows all about it. Whoever it is was able to get a hold of my cell phone number, too. She just called me on it."

"Oh, you're kidding," Lindsay said. "That's terrible."

"It caught me off guard. I wasn't expecting her to call my cell."

Lindsay looked at them as if she was afraid to ask the question but was going to ask it anyway. "Do you think Adrian's doing something wrong?"

"I never thought so. But this girl is so persistent. It's starting to make me wonder."

"Now you listen to me, Chiara," Lindsay said. "I'm not in the habit of airing anybody's dirty laundry, but I can tell you story after story of players' wives who have had problems with women chasing their husbands." She grasped Chiara by the shoulders. "And believe you me, after twenty years in baseball, I've got a few of my own. So don't you go letting some good-for-nothing tramp affect your marriage and your studies, until you know something's going on for sure. You hear me?"

Chiara nodded, gave her a pitiful smile.

"I told Chiara about the MLB Players Association, how they'll provide a PI at no charge if she wants one," Alicia said.

The game was over and a mass of women flooded the bathroom. Chiara tossed the wet napkins she'd been clutching in the trash.

"I think you should give them a call, Chiara," Alicia said.

Chiara rubbed her temples. "I'll do it first thing in the morning."

They walked through the crowd down to the Rangers's daycare room to pick up Lindsay's boys. The stadium monitors along the way had a picture of Adrian on them, his seven-one record posted under his name.

"He did it, Chiara," Alicia said, opening the daycare door. "He's seven and one and it's only June. Judd would kill to be in his shoes."

Chiara nodded. Her face softened and her mood lifted when she saw the children playing. It looked like *Romper Room*. It seemed every couple on the team had children except Chiara and Adrian. Lindsay's boys were wearing army pants, shooting at each other with pretend machine guns that sounded like the real thing. Chiara grabbed the younger one and gave him a bear hug, reluctant to let him go.

"You are too cute for your own good, do you know that?" she said, tousling his bowl-cut hair.

Garret looked at her, so blond, so jovial, and so six years old. He threw up his hands. "Why does everybody say that to me?"

Chiara stole another hug before letting him go. Something told her he was going to break a lot of hearts when he got older.

"Let's go, boys." Lindsay said, clapping her hands and sounding like a drill sergeant.

"I can hardly wait to start a family," Chiara said.

"Not me," Alicia said. "My horse is my baby. I don't want any kids."

Lindsay laughed. "I think it's 'cause you've been around my boys too long."

On the other side of the room, one of the team's babysitters was rocking her own newborn in a bassinet while keeping an eye on two little girls playing a board game.

Chiara leaned over to get a better look at the baby. "Look how beautiful she is. How can you not want one?"

The girl saw them looking over at her and avoided their eyes.

"I don't want the responsibility of kids the way we move around. And I'm thirty," Alicia said. She motioned to the babysitter. "I don't know how anyone her age can take on that responsibility. What is she, eighteen?"

"Just turned," Lindsay said and picked up a GI Joe action figure. "The baby's barely a month old."

The babysitter looked over at them again and Chiara smiled at her. "She's beautiful," she mouthed, avoiding yelling over the children.

The girl gave her an insipid smile, mouthed a thank you, and looked away.

Okay, Chiara turned her attention back to Alicia and Lindsay. "Adrian's mom invited Sanchez, Lopez, and their girlfriends over for fish tacos. Do you guys want to come over, too?"

Lindsay stroked one of her boys' blond heads. "Thanks, Chiara, but I have to put these monsters to bed." She stepped away to talk to another player's wife.

"I'm going home, too," Alicia said. "Those guys will keep you up drinking till the crack of dawn. Besides, I'm riding early tomorrow."

"That reminds me. I have to ask you a favor," Chiara said. "Will you ride Amadeus for me until I get back from Pittsburgh? I'll have my stitches out by then."

"Of course I will. Are you still going to be able to show your other horse back home after you take the boards?"

"Yeah, I think so. I get my stitches out next Wednesday. Honestly, though, I've barely thought about the show. All I can seem to think about is whoever's calling and the boards. Starting tomorrow I'm going to buckle down and study longer hours."

"You're on break," Alicia said. "Why do you have to study so much?"

Chiara was embarrassed to tell her, but she couldn't be dishonest. "I failed a class last semester, Alicia. I'll have to retake it, so I'm studying for the boards *and* that class. It also takes me longer than my classmates, I think, to grasp the material. I have dyslexia."

Alicia rested her hand on Chiara's shoulder. "You do what you need to do and don't worry about Amadeus. I'll ride him and take care of him until you get back. Concentrate on passing those boards."

"I'm leaving, horsey girls," Lindsay said as she made her way to the door with her sons. "See ya tomorrow."

Chiara stole a kiss from Garrison, Lindsay's eight-year-old son. Then she walked with Alicia to the players' underground parking lot to meet Adrian and Judd. Judd and a few other players were already showered, changed, and waiting for their wives to come down from the stands. Cecilia was already there, too, standing with Lopez's girlfriend, Alita, looking enthralled by their conversation. She never looked that interested in anything Chiara had to say.

When she saw Chiara, Cecilia went over and handed off her purse. "Why'd you leave so fast?" she said, her eyes narrowing to slits. "I was waiting for you in the stands."

"Sorry about that, Cici. I needed some fresh air. This is Alicia, Judd Peterson's wife."

"Hello," Alicia said. Her tone was matter-of-fact.

"Hello," Cecilia said.

Judd walked over and took Alicia's hand. "Hey, Chiara...Adrian did great! Congratulations."

Cecilia's face turned purple as Chiara humbly accepted the compliment. "Thanks, Judd."

"You ready, sweets?" he asked.

Alicia nodded. "Yeah, babe. I'll see you tomorrow, Chiara." Then they were gone.

It was after five a.m. when Lopez, Sanchez, and their girlfriends went home, and Adrian and Chiara went to bed. All night she had wanted to pull Adrian aside and tell him about the woman calling on her cell phone, but they were never alone and he was drinking. A lot. At two o'clock she had excused herself to study. As she read, the letters in her texts flipped and somersaulted practically out of the books and onto her bed like Olympic gymnasts. Chiara concentrated, trying to ignore the loud music playing in the next room. By three o'clock, she knew there was no use and she gave up. Now, as Adrian slept, she held him close for what was left of the night. His heavy snoring left his throat and fell over her face in loud and long bursts. Chiara could barely tolerate the potent smell of Buchanan's scotch coming off his breath and stinging her nostrils. She stared up at the monotonous revolving motion of the white paddle fan, feeling a soft breeze caressing her face with its every revolution, fighting off the depression knocking at her mind's front door.

Chapter 18

When morning came, Chiara woke to Cecilia tapping on the bedroom door and the smell of fried fish lingering in the air.

"Wake up," she sang. "I'm making breakfast."

Chiara kissed Adrian on the cheek and nudged him.

"Hmm," he groaned.

"Wake up, honey. Your mom just knocked on the door. She's making breakfast."

Adrian's eyes flickered open. "Didn't we just eat?"

Chiara rolled onto his chest. "Well, no. But that's probably what you remember. How do you feel?"

"Terrible…that scotch is brutal."

"I'm sure it is when you drink a bottle of it," Chiara observed. "Do you want an aspirin?"

"Naw, I'm okay."

"Adrian, I'm worried about how much you've been drinking lately. Do you think you're developing a problem? If you do, let me help you."

Adrian cupped Chiara's buttocks in his hands and pressed her against him, instantly excited. "I do not have a drinking problem. I just like to drink. There's a difference." He flipped her onto her back and pulled down her panties. "Are you mad at me, baby? Let me make it up to you."

She pulled away from him. "Honey, not now—"

"Yeah, now." He rolled on top of her, kissing her lips, her neck, her ear.

She pushed him away. "No, Adrian, I mean it. Stop. I need to talk to you."

He pulled her close again. "And I need to make love to you."

Chiara rolled away and sat up. "Stop it. I'm serious," she whispered, afraid Cecilia might hear. "I really need to talk to you."

Adrian sighed and flipped onto his back and stared up at the ceiling. "Okay, what?"

"That girl called again yesterday. Three times, Adrian. She called here at the apartment, then on my cell phone while we were at the game. When my mom called back last night after the game she told me she was getting crank calls at Girasole, too." She shook her head. "I'd been trying to keep this from her so she wouldn't worry. She has enough to deal with at home."

Adrian ran his hand through his bedraggled hair. "How could she get your cell phone number?"

"I don't know. Have you given my cell phone number or the apartment number out to anybody new?"

"Nuh-uh...no."

"Then how could she know how to get a hold of me so easily?"

He sat up. "Fuck—"

"What?"

"The player contact sheet in the Rangers's welcome packet. All our numbers are on it. Our cell phones, the apartment, your mom's number, my mom's—"

Chiara exhaled heavily. "I can't believe I didn't think of that. Do you think it's someone in the organization?"

"Maybe, maybe not. Whoever it is definitely got a hold of that sheet, though," he said.

"How many copies did you give out?"

"Just a couple. I gave one to my brother. He wanted some of the players' numbers after meeting them that first road trip to Tampa. And one to my mom. Everybody on the team gets a copy before the season starts, though."

"I'm fed up, Adrian. We have to do something. I want to call the police and contact the Major League Baseball Players Association. Alicia said the association has its own investigators for things like this, since players and their families have been stalked in the past. You pay into it through your dues. It won't cost us anything."

"Okay, I'll call my agent later. He'll get us hooked up. I know the police won't do nothing over some crank calls, though."

Chiara's shoulders relaxed a little.

"What did she say to you?" Adrian said.

"Same things…that I'm a whore, that you're sleeping with her."

Anger formed around his mouth, tightening his lips. "Let's just change the phone numbers."

"Okay. Has she called your cell?"

"I got some hang-ups yesterday, but that's it."

"Why didn't you tell me, Adrian?"

"'Cause I didn't think anything of it at the time. I'm just now thinking it could be her calling my phone, too."

He motioned for her to lie back and she did, laying her head on his chest. "I couldn't stop thinking about her last night," she said. "Who she is, what she looks like, why she's doing this, and—"

Adrian stroked her hair. "And what?"

"If it could be true."

He closed his arms around her. "Chiara, how could you think that?"

"How could it not cross my mind? You're on this great team now, on TV all the time, girls asking for your autograph everywhere we go."

"Chiara, I love you. I wanted you from the day we met. We're always gonna be together."

"I know. I love you too."

She wanted to say, *Ever since I met you, you've made me feel so secure and proud to be your girl, but ever since she started calling she makes me doubt you, doubt us, and doubt me.*

"Can we change the numbers today?"

"We'll do it after breakfast."

"Speaking of phones, we have to call my mom back. Do you remember she said last night the powder room at our house looks like it's going to be too small? She wanted to know if she can go ahead and put in a change order for us so they can move the partition over a bit."

"I can't remember. I was ripped. But yeah, tell her to go ahead."

"The builder's going to charge us seven hundred dollars to do it."

"No problem."

She tucked herself under his arm, caressed his hairy chest. "When do you think we should tell your mom about the house?"

Adrian pulled her onto him and kissed her. "How about now?"

At the dinette, Cecilia shoveled scrambled eggs onto the dishes with a vengeance, steam practically shooting out of her ears. "Why in Pittsburgh? What was wrong with Florida?"

"Ma, Chiara's really close with her family—"

Cecilia's eyes were hard and narrow. "And you're not?"

"Ma…Chiara still has a few more years of school left in Pittsburgh."

I hope, Chiara thought.

"The new house is just down the road from the house where she grew up," he said. "She'll be close to Pitt and to her horses at Girasole so she can keep training with her coach. It would cost a ton of money to board all of them in Florida—"

Cecilia muttered, "Um-hmm."

"And I'll still be able to work out with my old Pirates trainers during the off season."

Cecilia grabbed a frying pan full of sausage patties and emptied them onto Adrian's dish with quick deliberate strokes. At five, Adrian asked her to stop.

"How big is it?" she asked, fighting back tears.

"A nice size, but it's not done. It's still being built, won't be done till October."

"Bigger than the one you bought for me?"

"Yeah."

Chiara sat twirling the tie of her robe under the table. She felt guilt standing behind her like an evil dementor from a Harry Potter novel, waiting to swallow her up alive. Mamma would have felt the same way if they had decided to live in Florida. But Adrian hadn't just left home. He'd been living on the road, traveling in the minor leagues, the major leagues, since he was eighteen. He'd once told Chiara he barely knew where home was anymore.

"How many bedrooms?" Cecilia asked.

"Four," Adrian said.

"Cecilia, you're welcome to come and stay with us during the off season whenever you like," Chiara blurted out, hoping to keep the growing tension in the room at bay.

Cecilia straightened her robe, red as her face, smoothed back her hair, which was still in a piglet tail, and sat down. "I have to find a new job, Chiara," she said with an irritated tone. "Whoever hires me isn't gonna give me time off any time I want to go traveling."

The room turned silent and Chiara stared down at her eggs, wishing Cecilia would just go home if she was going to continue like this.

"Come on, Ma, don't be like that. If you think about it, it makes the most sense."

"I lived my life, son. Do what makes you happy."

They ate without saying a word, the sound of their forks scratching against the plates like fingers running down a chalkboard. Chiara could barely wait to excuse herself so she could get in a few hours of study. She'd gotten nothing accomplished last night. The boards were only three weeks away.

Adrian finally spoke up. "You wanna check out some malls, Ma? Do some shopping?"

Cecilia perked up instantly. "Okay. I need a new purse."

"Great," Chiara said, feeling relieved that Cecilia seemed to like to shop as much as Adrian did. She looked at Adrian. "Why don't you take her to the Galleria, honey, while I study?"

Adrian smiled at her. "Okay, but I want you to come with us for a little while. We'll go in two cars. Me and my mom can go to the ballpark from there and you can come back and study."

"I should really stay home—"

"I want you to come with us," Adrian insisted.

Chiara conceded to keep him happy.

"Isn't the jeweler going to show the players gold chains at three o'clock?" Cecilia asked. "I want to get back to the ballpark in time for that."

There was a jeweler who rented space at the ballpark and sold jewelry to the players in the clubhouse. A few of the players on the team had purchased gold chains so thick they could restrain King Kong. Chiara hoped Adrian would avoid following the trend; he had already surprised her a few days earlier by coming home with blond highlights in his beautiful dark hair. She thoroughly loathed them.

Cecilia plopped a few flour tortillas onto their plates. "Hurry up then, eat, *hijo,* so we can go."

Adrian picked up the pace, recapping the parts of last night's game where he threw some bad pitches. He told Cecilia that he had shaken off a few pitches that Hogan wanted him to throw, and it had led to the lead-off walk at the top of the eighth.

After pushing her eggs around on the plate, Chiara got up, placed her breakfast in a Tupperware container, and put it in the refrigerator. The white linoleum floor felt sticky under her bare feet from last night's spilled scotch. She made a mental note to clean it up when she got home from the mall. She poured a half-empty glass of wine down the sink and placed the glass and her dirty dish in the dishwasher. Then she rinsed out the sink and went to take a shower. Adrian joined her a few minutes later.

"That didn't go too bad," he said and pulled the curtain back, stepping into the shower.

Chiara moved under the shower head so he could get wet. Between his size and the modest dimensions of the shower unit, the two of them barely fit.

"No, but I still feel bad about it," she said, lathering his back with some soap.

"She always acts like that when she doesn't get her way. We'll buy her some nice stuff at the mall, and she'll forget all about it. You'll see."

"I hope so," Chiara said.

Adrian was right. Cecilia wove in and out of the mall stores with the dexterity of an earthworm in mud after a summer storm. She found something she absolutely had to have in almost every one, too. Chiara was taken aback by Cecilia's avarice but followed along anyway on Adrian's account, helping to carry their growing collection of shopping bags as they went from store to store. She felt like a golf caddy.

It was almost two o'clock when Chiara remembered that they still had to stop at an AT&T store to change their cell phone numbers. She reminded Adrian under her breath.

"I'll take your phone with me and stop on the way to the ballpark," he said. "Ma, you ready to go, or do you want to keep shopping with Chiara?"

Cecilia gave Adrian a theatrical disappointed look. *This woman could win an Oscar if she acted.*

"I didn't buy my purse yet," she trilled in her songbird voice.

"Just stay and shop with Chiara then, and I'll see you at the game tonight."

Cecilia held her hand to her chest and furrowed her eyebrows at Adrian as if she were about to take her last breath. "I wanted to see the jewelry and watch batting practice, *son.*"

"Aren't you gonna want to go back to the apartment and change before the game?" he asked.

Cecilia looked down at her jeans and running shoes and then at Chiara's flowery sundress and wedge sandals. "I don't need to impress anybody."

Chiara looked away, wishing she'd stayed home.

"Okay, but you're gonna be hot in those jeans," he said.

"I'll be fine. Real quick, where can I find a purse like Chiara's?"

"Her backpack? That's Gucci," Adrian said.

Chiara looked at Adrian, hoping he would tell his mother she had spent enough money for one day. Instead, he winced at Chiara as if to say he was sorry and pointed toward the Gucci boutique. *Unbelievable.* When they reached the store, Chiara opted to wait outside. She absolutely loved Gucci's handbags and clothing and wanted to avoid the temptation of buying something. Adrian had developed a particular penchant for shopping since he signed his new contract, and Chiara found herself saving for both of them so they could furnish the new house. They were going to need furniture for every room, as well as curtains and other home accessories.

Chiara sank onto a bench, planning to wait, but the smell of fresh ground coffee cajoled her into following the scent. She thought she'd have a quick espresso for Papà. She grabbed Cecilia's bags and headed toward a coffee shop a few doors down. A red-headed woman took her order.

"Are you sure you don't want a flavored coffee?" she said. "They're on special and they're *so* good."

Chiara read the menu board. "Mocha Madness Mondays and Wednesdays: Take one dollar off any regular mocha, vanilla mocha, raspberry mocha, peppermint mocha or caramel mocha, all day." She thought of how Papà used to scoff at all the flavored coffees that were so quickly becoming trendy. In his mind there were only three ways to serve it: espresso, cappuccino, or latte.

"No thanks, just a plain espresso, please."

"All right then, that'll be three dollars and fifty cents," the woman said.

Chiara reached into her purse and pulled out her wallet. When she opened it, she felt a small wave of panic swell in her chest. Last night she had two hundred dollars in her wallet. It was gone. Could Adrian have taken it this morning and forgotten to tell her? That was unlikely; he never went in Chiara's purse.

The barista gave her an all-knowing look. "Goes quick in this mall, doesn't it?"

Chiara was only half-listening. How could she have lost two hundred dollars since last night? The only thing she remembered buying was a beer for Cecilia. She rooted around in her backpack. Maybe it had fallen out of her wallet and floating around in bottom-of-the-purse limbo. She checked. Not there. Then it hit her. *Cecilia.* Chiara had left her backpack with her when she rushed to the ladies room last night. She stood there frozen faced, like a person found dead somewhere in the arctic. *My mother-in-law, a thief?*

Chiara dropped her wallet back into her purse. "Could you please direct me towards an ATM machine?"

The woman pointed down the hall. "It's right next to the escalator near the food court."

"Thanks, I'll be right back."

"Take the coffee with you, sweetie. Looks like you're having a day."

Chiara gave her an appreciative look. "Thank you."

Chiara grabbed Cecilia's bags and marched toward the ATM machine. Her hands were balled in fists. Sweat formed between her breasts and dotted her dress in spite of the cool temperature in the mall. Chiara had only stolen one thing in her life: a ten-cent pack of chocolate-flavored gum in a grocery store after her family moved to Pittsburgh. She was only six, but she remembered the incident as if it were yesterday.

When Mamma saw her unraveling the pack in the passenger seat of their old yellow station wagon, she had marched Chiara right back into the A&P. "Stealing is wrong, Chiara, a sin," she had told her. "It is so important not to steal that God put it on his top ten list of rules to live by: the Ten Commandments."

"The Ten Commandments?" Chiara repeated.

"Yes, the Ten Commandments. And now, what you've done is out of my hands, *cara*. I can't help you. It's up to the check-out girl to decide if she is going to call the police. You might go to jail and never see me, Papà, and your sisters ever again." Chiara still remembered that walk into the grocery store as one of the scariest moments of her life. She cried for days after the incident anytime Mamma so much as left the room. But she never stole a thing again.

After Chiara paid for the coffee, she went and sat on the bench outside the boutique again. She told herself to stay calm, to be the better person in all of this. But what she really wanted to do was charge into the Gucci store and yell at Cecilia, regardless of how many people were in there. *Listen here, you overbearing, controlling, materialistic, jealous, wedding-crashing sorry excuse for a mother! Why are you doing these things? Why can't you just be nice? Then I'd go out of my way for you.*

But she didn't; she sat there fuming, biting the skin around her nails, wondering if Adrian would believe his mother was capable of stealing. She wondered if she should even tell him.

When they came out of the store, Cecilia was carrying another bag. "I love that store," she cackled like a hyena.

The high-pitched shrills sent shivers down Chiara's spine. "I've never been able to buy anything like that, you know? Everything in there is, like…beautiful."

Chiara looked at her watch, stood up, and started walking with her eyes on the floor. "That's why I waited outside."

Wrapping his arms around her, Adrian gave Chiara a quizzical look. "You okay?"

"I have to go home and study."

"I know. I gotta leave for the ballpark now or I'm gonna be late for batting practice."

They left the mall and were hit with the blinding heat. June in Dallas felt like a Saudi Arabian desert at high noon. It was at least a hundred degrees. Chiara put on her sunglasses as they walked toward the cars in the parking lot.

"Why don't you ever go to the ballpark early, Chiara?" Cecilia said.

Ah, because I'm not obsessed with baseball, Cecilia. "I usually study or go to the stable and ride while Adrian practices. I'm always there by game time, though, whether Adrian pitches or not."

Cecilia stroked Adrian's back as they walked along. "I've always watched your practices, son, haven't I?"

"Uh-huh," Adrian said.

Cecilia gave Chiara a tight smile and a sideways look. "Ever since he was in Little League."

Chiara's eyes started to water. Her heart felt tender and swollen in its space. She wanted Cecilia to stop it already, but she knew it would take a stun gun for it to happen. *Are you trying to tell me I'm not a supportive wife too?* "You've been very supportive of Adrian, Cici. I wish I could join you today, but I have to go home and study. I have to take the boards at the end of the month. Anyway, none of the wives go to the ballpark four hours before game time," she snapped. "Neither do the players' mothers. In fact—"

"Baby, you got the phone?" Adrian asked, looking as if he was about to play referee.

Chiara reached in her backpack and handed him her cell phone. *Should I?* she thought. *Oh, what the hell.* "Hon, I'm missing some money from my wallet…" Chiara started. Cecilia's face caught fire and she planted her eyes on the cement walkway as if she was studying every crack.

I knew it.

"Did you by chance take it and forget to tell me?"

He looked at his mother and back at Chiara. "No. I got my debit card. You sure it's not in one of your other wallets?"

"I'm sure. I haven't changed wallets since I came to Texas."

"Why are you taking her phone, *hijo*? Is it broken?" Cecilia said, fanning herself with her Congo red claws. "What if I start feeling sick in the stands? How will I get in touch with her?"

Adrian unlocked his car door. "We're changing our cell phone numbers," he said.

Cecilia cocked her head at him as if she didn't understand. "Why are you doing that? All your friends and cousins will be calling me for months to get the new ones."

"It's nothing," Chiara said.

"Well, if it's nothing, then why do you want to change them?" Cecilia insisted.

"Ma, Chiara's been getting some nasty crank calls from some woman on her cell phone and at the apartment. We're just gonna change them so whoever's calling stops bothering her."

Cecilia chuckled like it was the funniest thing she'd heard all week, her breasts bobbing up and down under her jersey like buoys in white water. "So that's why you left the stands so fast last night. I can't believe you'd let something silly like that get to you—" She made a disapproving tsk-tsk-tsk sound. "Do you know how many women would love to be in your shoes? Married to a Major League baseball player?"

At least one—you.

"Do you know how many times you're going to have this kind of silliness come up in Adrian's career?"

Chiara grit her teeth. Who was she to tell her it was a silly matter?

"Are you going to go changing your numbers every time a girl gets infatuated with my *hijo* and tries to mess with you?"

Chiara felt like a reprimanded child. She wanted to lash out at Cecilia, tell her mother-in-law that she knew she'd taken the money, tell her that she was behind the calls, tell her to call off her female thug. But she held her tongue. The pragmatic side of Chiara wanted to be sure before she made any accusations—for Adrian's sake. But as for the missing money, Chiara felt she did have proof: Cecilia was the only person who'd had access to her purse in the past twelve hours.

"Ma, please," Adrian said in his deep drum-like voice. "We wanna change 'em."

"Fine," Cecilia said, looking offended. "I know it's none of my business. I just think it's silly."

"I don't think it is," Chiara rebutted. "Whoever is calling is trying to tear Adrian and me apart."

"Ma, it was my idea," Adrian said. "She doesn't need to be putting up with that shit."

"Okay, okay, I was just saying…"

Adrian looked antsy, annoyed. "Look, I gotta go, you coming?"

Cecilia smiled. "Just let me get my new purse out of the bag," she caroled. "I want to wear it to the ballpark." She pulled out a medium-sized black cloth pouch with an upper case G pattern on it. When she pulled the draw-strings apart and pulled out the purse, Chiara gasped.

*You have got to be kidding…*It was the exact same purse Adrian had bought for her. The very one she was wearing that very moment.

"I hope you don't mind," Cecilia said with a coy smile. "I just love yours."

Chiara looked on in disbelief as Cecilia emptied the contents of her purse and stuffed them into the backpack. *Of all the beautiful bags in that boutique*, Chiara thought, *Why? Why the very same bag Adrian bought for me?*

Cecilia seemed to be basking in Chiara's disappointment like a robin in a birdbath. Adrian felt bad. Chiara could see that. "She really wanted it, baby," he said. "I said no, but—"

"But I always get what I want, right, *hijo?*"

Adrian ignored her, kept his eyes on Chiara.

Chiara looked at Adrian, disappointment all over her face. "It's okay, Cici. How could you not love it? It's a beautiful bag. The horse-bit closure is my favorite part of it."

She smiled, but something coiled around her windpipe, squeezing tighter and tighter until she surrendered to the anger and only felt hurt.

Adrian smiled. "There's something in the bag for you too, baby."

Chiara regained a little composure, even though she felt like giving in to tears, pushing against the back of her eyeballs like a ready-to-overflow dam. "You didn't have to get me anything, honey."

"I know. I wanted to," he said.

Chiara feigned a smile. "Thank you, I'll open it when I get home."

Adrian looked at his mother and then at his watch. "You ready, Ma?"

"Ready," she said.

Chiara handed Cecilia her bags and she placed them in the back seat of Adrian's car.

"Baby, I'm thinking I'll be late if I stop at the store to change the numbers now. Can you do it?"

"There's no way. I have to get back to the apartment to study," Chiara said.

"Is it okay if we do it in the morning then?"

Chiara nodded. "Okay."

He handed the phone back to her and kissed her good-bye. "I'll see you at the game."

Watching them drive away, a wave of nausea rose and fell inside her, and her heart was flooded with a tender sadness. She'd never realized how hard Papà had worked to make her life uncomplicated. Now it was anything but uncomplicated. She'd misunderstood his firm guidance, balked at his fatherly love.

When she got home, she made a pot of coffee, threw on a pair of sweat pants, grabbed her study guide, and started with her easiest subject, gross anatomy. Sitting on her bed cross-legged, medical texts splayed all around her, page by page she scanned and processed the information like a computer. While she read she kept reminding herself that the boards were a summary of everything she had already learned. A review, so to speak.

At seven o'clock, still on a roll, she wondered if she should blow off the game and keep studying. When the phone on the nightstand rang, she stared at it for a moment, reluctant to answer. *It could be Mamma or Valerie or Sylvia. It could be Cecilia or Miss Hoochie Coochie.* She gave in to her curiosity.

"Hello?"

"Hi, whore—"

Chiara hung up.

It rang again. This time Chiara let it ring until it stopped—on at least at the tenth ring. A few minutes later it rang again. Chiara counted the rings: five. Then it stopped. Then it rang again. This time it rang until she got up, yanked the phone cord out of the wall and did the same with the phone in the kitchen. *You are not ruining my marriage or my career, you tramp.*

She went back into her bedroom and sank down on the edge of the bed near the window. Her legs and arms felt heavy, as if she had been swimming for months in a sea of confusion. She sat in the stillness thinking, *Should I just go home? Who is she? How would you handle this, Papà?* She pressed her hands to her forehead. Looking down at the carpet, she noticed a shape made by the evening sunlight slipping through slats in the venetian blinds. It looked like a parallelogram and it puckered in the middle of one side, folded in like an envelope. It reminded her of a cyclopentane ring, one of thousands of hydrocarbon compounds she'd studied in chemistry classes over the years.

She leaned over and picked up her study manual again, recalling the last arguments she'd had with Papà. "You will never finish *scuola di medicina* if you marry him," he'd said. "You will have too many distractions with him."

Sure, I knew there'd be distractions, but who could've imagined this? Especially as a newlywed.

Her cell phone rang in the kitchen. She opened her manual and read, ignoring the rings until they faded into the walls of the apartment like the chimes of the grandfather clock in Papà's library. For a moment she wished she were back at Girasole, in her old bedroom studying, Hemingway's neighs floating through the windows, her only care in the world the desire to deliver babies.

At midnight Chiara heard the front door open. Adrian bolted into the bedroom looking frantic. "Chiara, where were you? I've been calling you between innings for hours! Why didn't you come to the game?"

Her eyes were puffed out like a moor fish from crying over her books all night, and when she saw him, the tears gushed over her face like Niagara Falls all over again.

He rushed to the side of the bed, shoved her books aside and sat down beside her. "Shit, Chiara, what's wrong? What happened?"

"I can't take it anymore," she said and sobbed into her hands. "Your *girlfriend's* been calling all night."

He seemed moved by her distress. "Chiara, I don't have a girlfriend."

He was freshly showered and smelled like the fabric softener she used in his clothes. She wanted to kiss him and smack him at the same time, the dichotomy of true love. "Don't you? Then why does she know so much about you? Why is she being so persistent?"

"I don't know, *am*—"

"She left ten messages on my cell phone. Go ahead, listen to them!" She went to the dresser, picked up her cell phone, and threw it at him. He caught it without looking.

Adrian listened to one of the messages and hung up. "I have no idea who that is, Chiara."

"I don't believe you. She has to know you, and you have to know her. She knows too many things about you not to."

He motioned for her to sit down, but she just stood there wiping her wet face, glaring at him with suspicion.

"Look, Chiara, I'm telling you I don't know—"

"I don't believe you anymore," she said and headed for the bathroom.

Adrian shot towards the door to keep her from locking it behind her. "Chiara, please—"

"She knows about the beauty mark on your ass, Adrian."

He avoided her glare, an odd expression in his eyes that Chiara had never seen before. Was it guilt? A distant memory recalled? Anger suppressed? She was unsure.

"So what, Chiara? All of the ballplayers walk around naked in the clubhouse. Someone could've told her…"

"That's ridiculous!" she shouted.

She moved toward the bedroom door. Cecilia was in the kitchen clanking pots and pans, but her eyes were on Chiara. They looked at each other for a moment, and when a look of satisfaction blossomed across Cecilia's face, Chiara slammed the door shut.

Adrian peered down at her with arms akimbo, an angry frown joining his eyebrows. "So you're gonna believe that shit over me?"

Chiara lowered her voice. "Unless she's psychic or someone in your family told her about the birthmark on your ass, yes." She hissed like a wet cat and pointed toward the kitchen. "I'd be an idiot not to. It started before the wedding, didn't it?"

She searched for the slightest hint of guilt in his eyes, but she could only see anger and disappointment, uncertain if it was with her or himself.

"Chiara, you're not thinking straight. Relax." His face softened. "We're gonna figure out who this is. Let's relax, go into the kitchen, eat something, then we'll come back in here and talk."

"I'm not hungry," she said. She held her hand to her heart. "How can I have an appetite, how can I study when there's a girl torturing me by telling me she's sleeping with my husband, that you two are in love, and that you don't love me…that you're not the man you're promising me you are?"

He reached for her and placed her face in his hands. A pleading look filled his eyes, and it made her want to throw herself into his arms. He was so good-looking, rugged.

"You know me, Chiara. I didn't have to get married. I got married 'cause I love you, 'cause I wanna spend the rest of my life with you."

"I don't know anything anymore, except that she's calling every day: here, on my cell phone, at Girasole—"

"I called my agent today. He said he's gonna get on it right away. I don't know what else you want me to do."

"You could start by being a little more selective about who you give our phone numbers to."

"Look, tomorrow we'll change the cell phone numbers and the apartment number and everything will be fine after that."

"It won't make a difference."

Adrian looked caught off guard. "What? Why?"

"Because if there is the slightest chance you haven't been cheating then your mother is behind all of this. She'll have the new numbers as soon as we get them." *There, I said it. Proof or no proof.*

"Whoa, wait a minute. Don't go bringing my mom into this. She wouldn't do that—"

"Oh no?" Chiara shot back. "In case you haven't noticed, she can't stand me. The way I see it, if you're innocent, then she's guilty. No fan would know about your beauty mark. It's either you or her."

"My mom is a pain, Chiara, I know that, but she wouldn't try and fuck up my marriage. And she doesn't hate you."

"I guess you haven't noticed how she talks to me. She would love for you to be single again, so she could have you and your money all to herself. She 'had plans,'" Chiara said, making imaginary quotation marks in the air, "for when you finally made it to the big leagues. I seemed to have screwed them up for her."

Chiara heard the front door slam. Cecilia had apparently heard enough and left the apartment.

"Adrian, she hates me," Chiara said. "If she had to pick between saving me from a fall off the balcony and burning your breakfast, she'd make a mad dash for the frittata!"

"Not true."

"Yes, true. I might as well tell you, while we're on the subject, that she's a thief. She took the money from my wallet."

His face turned bright red. "What did you call her?"

"I left my bag with her when I rushed out of the stands last night. She's the only one who could've taken the money. Who else could've taken the cash and replaced the wallet, too?"

"That's messed up." He ran his hands through his hair and sat down on the edge of the bed.

"Messed up? Messed up? It's the truth—"

"Relax, Chiara, or I'm not gonna talk about this anymore."

Chiara took a breath, but she couldn't stop the flow of tears. "All I've done is fall in love with you. All she's done since we got engaged is punish me for it by causing tension between us."

"I don't need this shit, Chiara. I got married 'cause I love you, 'cause I want to be with you. I can't have you questioning me like this. I got a career to concentrate on."

"And I don't? What about the *shit* I'm being dragged through? She started counting on her fingers. "I'm taking my board in three weeks. I'm dealing with crank calls, my father's death, being on academic probation, and *your* mother."

He looked her up one side and down the other, got up, and stomped into the kitchen.

Chiara followed. "If you're telling the truth, your mother is the only other person who could provide this girl with the information she has about us. It's the only thing that makes sense."

He opened the refrigerator and took out a beer. "I'm not talking about this no more."

She knew he'd heard enough, but she couldn't stop her rant. She needed to get every last thought off her chest. "Whoever is calling knew I wasn't at the game tonight, Adrian. She knows that my father is dead, that I have horses, that I have two sisters, their names, and things about them. How could she know all that unless you or your mother told her?"

"I have no idea."

"She has a Latin accent, did you hear it?"

"Yeah."

"Did you recognize her voice?"

Adrian never looked at her as he took a swig of his beer. "Naw… not at all." Anger crossed his face again in shades of red, but his tone remained even. "Look, Chiara, drop this for now. I've been at the ballpark all day and I'm tired."

"And I've been studying all day, and I'm tired *and* upset, Adrian. I'm tired of her calling to tell me to watch my ass when you're not around. I've been trying to fluff it off for almost a year, and I can't anymore. I don't want to."

Adrian slammed the beer on the kitchen counter. "What the fuck do you want me to do, Chiara?" he shouted in her face. He looked like he wanted to grab her and toss her into a closet so he wouldn't have to listen to her anymore. "We're changing the phone numbers. I called my agent today about the PI. You wanna call the police? Call the police! I don't know what the fuck else you want me to do!"

Chiara stepped back, shocked at how mean he could look. For a moment everything was quiet, and she could hear her heart beating out of her chest.

She swallowed hard. "Would you talk to your mother?" she said, her voice shaky.

"And say what? 'Ma, Chiara thinks you're a home-wrecker and a thief, but you two should try and get along?'"

He grabbed his beer and stormed toward the front door.

"Where are you going?"

"For a drive."

"So that's it?" she said. She was still crying, and she wiped her cheeks with the back of her bandaged hand. "You're just going to leave every time we have a fight?"

Halfway down the apartment stairs he yelled back at her. "No! Just when you're acting stupid. I'm somebody now; I can't help it if people wanna know me. It's part of being famous."

Part of being famous? You asshole! Speechless, she ran out to the landing overlooking the parking lot. His back to her, he unlocked his car door. She felt like plucking every last blond highlight out of his head one by one. When she found her voice, she yelled down at him. "Hey, Mr. Famous! I'm not stupid; I'm in medical school, you jerk!" She turned to go back into the apartment. Under her breath, she added, "And you were always somebody to me."

Chapter 19

On Friday, Adrian and Chiara drove to meet with the private investigator assigned to their case by the MLB Players Association. They said nothing to each other the entire way there. Adrian looked pale from another late-night drinking binge with a few teammates. When they walked into the coffee shop, the smell of fresh percolating coffee made Chiara's stomach rumble. She'd eaten little the past few days. A man sitting at a corner table jotted something down on a legal pad and waved them over. *He must have recognized Mr. Famous*, Chiara thought.

He introduced himself as Conner O'Grady. He was a tall, thin man with freckled skin and strawberry hair, and he spoke with a dry authority. He asked them a slew of questions: When did the crank calls begin? How often does she call? Does she call at certain times of the day? What does she say? Has any of your property been vandalized? The last question made Chiara feel idiotic because nothing of theirs had been damaged—except her confidence and pride.

"We're gonna change the phone numbers, Mr. O'Grady," Adrian said. He didn't look at Chiara. "We just haven't gotten around to it yet."

"Call me Conner. And don't, not yet. I'm going to put a tap on them. "

Chiara's spirits lifted. *There might actually be an end to this year-long drama.*

When the meeting was over, Conner said he'd contact them as soon as he had any information. Chiara thanked him, feeling content for the first time in days.

On Sunday morning, she woke in bed to Adrian's hands massaging her back. It felt divine. She rolled over and looked at him, her eyes full of remorse. "I'm sorry," she said softly.

"It's okay. I'm sorry too. I shouldn't have walked out on you."

She rolled over and wrapped herself around him, holding him tight as if he might disappear into thin air if she let go. She never wanted to fight with him like that, ever again.

"All the things that have happened in the past year or so," she said, feeling that familiar sadness rise in her throat. "Papà dying, the crank calls to Girasole and the church before the wedding, your mom fainting at the most important moment of my life, failing the class...It all just got to me the other night when the calls started again. I think I've made too many assumptions." She kissed his cheeks, his lips, and lay back on his chest, her body shedding the anger and disappointment like an old coat. "There are some pretty evil people out there. I see that now. A savvy thief could easily have pick-pocketed your mom. Someone none of us even know could be calling."

"Chiara, my mom probably took the money."

Chiara blinked, sat up, shocked. "What?"

He wiped a tear welling on her bottom lid. "I was too embarrassed to tell you, but she's taken money from my wallet before, too. She's stolen stuff from the grocery store where she worked too. She'd been working there so long the owners just ignored it, but they couldn't anymore; it was happening more often." He rubbed his forehead with his hand. "When they first found out though, they called and told me about it. I asked her if it was true, and she didn't lie. She said it was, and that she thought she was a klepto."

"So, she was fired," Chiara said.

Chiara lay back on his chest, stunned by his admission, by Cecilia's disease.

"I got her therapy for it, and she'd been really good for awhile. But sometimes she has setbacks. I think it's why I do too much for her sometimes. I don't want her to feel like she ever needs anything, or can't have anything, or whatever she's feeling when she steals."

Chiara sat up and shook her head. She felt terrible. "Adrian, that's a sickness. She can't help herself."

"I know. That's what the psychologist I sent her to said."

"If you had told me, I would've understood why you spoil her. I wouldn't have felt violated by her taking the money."

"Baby, it's embarrassing." He opened his arms and she lay down beside him. "She may be a klepto, but I can tell you she'd never put someone up to calling you. She'd never do that to me."

Chiara took in his maple-syrup skin, his blue eyes, and felt an amorous chill run through her. "What do you mean, to you?"

"I got talking to her about the crank calls once after the wedding. I told her if you ever left me over it, over anything, I'd never be the same." He kissed the top of her head, held her a little closer. "She wants me to have a great career in baseball. She wants me to be happy. And she knows you make me happy."

Chiara reached up and kissed full bottom lip. "You make me happy too," she said and smiled. "Let the PI take care of it. You're pitching today."

"Going for eight and one, baby," he said. "For you." He rolled on top of her and pulled up her negligee, spread her thighs apart with his. He pressed his lips against hers, kissing her deeply, rhythmically.

"Ummm…Adrian." Everything about him was so sultry. The way he kissed her, the way he danced with her, the way he made love to her.

"Talk to me in Italian," he whispered in her ear. "It drives me *crazy*."

She giggled softly. "I think you're the horniest man alive."

"Because I love you, and you're sexy, and I want to be the father of your babies," he said in his milk-chocolate voice.

"Hmm, babies," she whispered in his ear. "Let's practice making babies."

Later, Chiara lay in bed quizzing herself with a six-inch stack of note cards while Cecilia fed Adrian a breakfast fit for a Viking going to war. Today was renal study day. She read the questions on the front of the cards aloud and answered them before flipping the card over to check the answers. "What section of the renal tubule reabsorbs sixty-seven percent of the fluids and electrolytes filtered by the glomerulus?" *That's an easy one,* she thought. *PCT.* She flipped the card over. *And I am correct.* "What segment of the renal tubule is responsible for concentrating urine?" *No brainer: collecting duct.* "What segment of the renal tubule is always impermeable to water?" *Thick ascending limb.*

When Adrian called from the kitchen to say he was leaving, she got up and went to say good bye and wish him good luck. Chiara ignored the Bloody Mary he had in a to-go cup. "Go get 'em, honey," she said and kissed him.

"Gonna get number eight today," he said.

"Good luck, *hijo,*" Cecilia said.

"Thanks, Ma. See you guys there."

When he left, Chiara, still in her robe, reached for the empty coffee pot and filled it with water. She thought of Bibi and how she always had coffee brewed by the crack of dawn. She missed her as much as she missed Julio. "Has he always drunk this early?" she asked Cecilia.

Cecilia was washing dishes at the sink. It was almost a week since Chiara had surrendered the kitchen to her. "Off and on, when he's under too much pressure. He controls it, unlike his father."

Cecilia's coldness told Chiara she was still angry with her for upsetting Adrian Wednesday night.

"Why didn't you leave with Adrian? The game starts at 1:35. He's pitching today."

"It's Sunday."

Chiara gave her a quizzical look. *Why doesn't she go to the ballpark on Sundays?* Only the apocalypse could keep Cecilia from baseball. Especially on a day Adrian was scheduled to pitch.

"I always go to church on Sunday, like your mother and sisters. No matter what." Cecilia gave Chiara a scornful look, reminding her she was a heathen. "I see you like to sleep in on Sunday."

Chiara walked to the sliding glass door and placed her hand on the glass. It was only a little after ten, and the Texas sun was already baking the pane. Her voice came out sounding small and vulnerable to her ears. "I...I'm sorry I said those things you overheard the other night, Cecilia. I've been under a lot of pressure, but...well, it's no excuse. I'm very sorry for hurting you."

"Will you drive me to mass?" Cecilia asked. Her voice had softened a little and Chiara took this as a good sign.

Chiara stared out to the highway. *Mass? Do I have a choice?* "Yes, but we'll be late for the game if you go to mass."

"Not if we go to an eleven o'clock service," Cecilia said.

Chiara looked at the kitchen clock. "I'll never be ready for the eleven o'clock mass."

"Then we'll have to go to a later service and be a few minutes late for the game."

"Cecilia, I don't even know where there's a Catholic church. Did you ask anyone at the ballpark if there's a Catholic church in Arlington?"

"No, but we'll find one."

Chiara was less sure. Texas was full of Baptist and Methodist churches. But Catholic churches? Not so easy.

"Why don't you know of any?" Cecilia asked. "Don't you go?"

Here we go again. Cecilia knew Chiara's history with the Catholic Church perfectly well. Adrian had told her what had happened.

"I used to, but I don't anymore."

Cecilia put her hands on her hips. "Well, you should—"

"I have an idea." Chiara strode across the room, gritting her teeth. She had a feeling today would be no different from any other day with Cecilia. Even after an apology.

"What are you doing?"

Chiara picked up the welcome packet on the kitchen counter and waved it. "I'm going to see if churches are listed in here. It lists just about anything anyone new to Arlington might need: nail and hair salons, restaurants, physicians, babysitters, malls, all the team player and family *contact* information. Yep, you name it, there's a phone number for it."

Cecilia looked at her as if she were not right in the head and said, "Good. Then you won't have any trouble finding a Catholic church."

An uncomfortable silence suffused the room as Chiara flipped through the pages of the packet. She tried to think of something positive about having to take Cecilia to church. She could think of only one: it would be a full hour of silence. *A sacrifice, but definitely worth it.*

Chiara pulled out a sheet of paper from the packet. "Ah. Here we are: churches." She ran her finger down the page. "Baptist, Episcopalian,

Lutheran, Methodist, and last but not least, Roman Catholic." Chiara picked the first church under the heading and jotted down the address and phone number on a separate sheet of paper.

"Do you know how to get there?" Cecilia asked.

"I'll call the parish for directions."

At noon they pulled into the Saint Maria Goretti parish parking lot. *Why does that name sound familiar?* Chiara thought. The eleven o'clock mass had just let out and parishioners were moseying to their cars. People moved so slowly in Texas. It had to be the searing temperatures and over-consumption of red meat. A few teenagers lingered outside the vestibule, chatting with the priest. He was wearing a white cassock and a broad green cope. Ordinary Time. Chiara remembered it from her years at Saint Ursula's.

Chiara looked at Cecilia out of the corner of her eye, this hardened woman who wasn't exactly hard. She was wearing a red floral-patterned sundress and a few extra gold bangle bracelets she'd bought at the mall and added to the collection on her wrist. Aside from her wedding day, Chiara had never seen Cecilia in anything but jeans. She looked nice.

"You look pretty, Cecilia."

Cecilia rooted through her stuffed backpack and pulled a rosary out of it as if she were yanking a rabbit out of a magic hat. It was baby blue and silver and Chiara recalled having one just like it when she was in junior high.

"Thank you. You can still call me Cici."

Chiara looked down at the steering wheel, feeling terrible for the way she felt about Cecilia. *Try, Chiara. Try to tolerate this woman, your husband's mother, no matter what Conner O'Grady finds out.*

"We're a little early…Cici. But the sun is blinding. Would you rather wait here or go ahead inside?"

"Let's go inside," Cici said in her soft soprano voice.

They walked toward the gothic entrance of the small stone church. In the bell tower a copper bell, green with age, tolled the final seconds of noon. Chiara felt her feet grow heavy with reservation, as if she were dragging cement blocks chained to her ankles.

"Maybe we can leave mass a few minutes early to make it in time for the first pitch?" Chiara said.

"No, no," Cecilia said. "God comes before baseball, even if my son is pitching."

Next to the entrance of the church, on a grassy knoll, there was a life-size statue of a young girl, perhaps twelve or thirteen, holding a bouquet of lilies. Someone brought up outside the Catholic faith might easily have mistaken her for a statue of the Virgin Mary. But Chiara knew better. Her name sounded so familiar. Perhaps because it was Italian.

Chiara motioned toward the statue, trying to make polite conversation. "It seems she was canonized pretty young. Do you know who Saint Maria Goretti was?"

"No," Cecilia said with a flat tone, heaving her overstuffed backpack over her shoulder.

Well, that takes care of that. Chiara wiped her hands on her pale-blue cotton sundress as they entered the vestibule. She wished she had left her bandage on. She could've used it wipe away the sweat that was pouring out of her skin. She was relieved that the priest was gone. She took a step into the church aisle, peeked in, really, to get a feel for things. It was in dire need of refurbishing and smelled of musk and incense. The dark wood-paneled altar and faded wooden pews, all worn by Texas sun and heat and parishioners, made it look somber in spite of the sun streaming in slanting rays through stained-glass windows. On either side of the altar, potted sunflowers flexed and bent their heads toward the high-noon sun. Chiara took another step and stopped. She couldn't explain why, but lately, she was seeing those yellow buggers everywhere. She thought about Papà's God and wondered why her scientific mind could never quite dismiss Him entirely.

Cecilia was a few feet in front of her and turned around. "What?" she said.

"You go ahead, I'll wait here."

"Come on, Chiara—"

"No really, it's my stomach," she lied. *Lied in church. Oh well…God probably gave up on me a long time ago.* "I have to use the restroom."

"Fine," Cecilia said.

Then Cecilia did the oddest thing. She dropped to her knees, made the sign of the cross, her gold bracelets jingling and echoing through the empty church, and shuffled, still on her knees, toward the altar. *What are you doing, Cici? People don't even do that at the Vatican.* Backing into the vestibule, Chiara looked on in disbelief as Cecilia continued all the way down to the altar and bowed her head to the cool marble floor. The only time Chiara had ever seen anyone crawl in a place of worship was in a picture taken at the Temple of Guadalupe in Mexico. Chiara remembered Father Bob telling her seventh-grade religion class that the temple had been constructed after a poor Indian named Julio Diego claimed to have been visited by the Virgin Mary in the hills of Tepeyac, Mexico. The Virgin instructed him to tell the Spanish bishop to build a temple on the very spot where she had appeared. Mary had supposedly left an image of herself on Diego's poncho as proof of her visitation.

Chiara had been intrigued by the cloth. It had remained intact for over four hundred and fifty years and the image and hues on it were said to be as vibrant today as they were four centuries ago. In junior high, before the Father Bob incident, Chiara was convinced it was proof of the grace of God in action, proof of science and God in action together, proof that the soul lives on after the body dies. Back then, in spite of her growing love of the scientific world, Chiara's regard for great thinkers like Aristotle and Saint Thomas Aquinas had strengthened her belief that she could love and believe in both science and God. But why was she even thinking about that now? And why couldn't she stop thinking of those sunflowers as more than just flowers when she saw them lately? *So there are some sunflowers on the altar. Who cares?*

"Excuse me," Chiara heard a small voice say. She turned and saw an elderly nun wheeling another even older nun in a wheelchair. They were waiting to get by. Aside from Cecilia in the front row, they were the only other people who had come to attend the service.

For no logical reason, Chiara grabbed some pamphlets on an old wooden table against the wall and walked out into the hot sun as the opening hymn began. She had an hour to waste. She wished she'd brought her note cards for more than one reason. She sat on a bench near the statue and fanned herself with one of the pamphlets. When she noticed a stained-glass figure of Saint Maria Goretti pictured on the front leaf of one of the pamphlets, she took a closer look. *The window must be somewhere in the church,* she thought.

Seconds after she sat down, searing UV rays attacked her skin like a swarm of bees, stinging every inch of her body. She fanned herself with the pamphlets for another minute, but when the sun began burning her skin, she got up and forced herself to go back into the vestibule.

She sat down on a folding wooden chair next to the table where she had picked up the pamphlets, placing them back on the table. Looking into the church again, high up and to the left of the altar, she saw the stained-glass image of Saint Maria Goretti shining rays of red, blue, yellow, and green into the church. The saint looked younger than she did in the pamphlet. She was dressed in a white peasant dress and wore a yellow sash around her waist. In one had she held a bouquet of lilies and in the other she clutched a knife. *Italians*, Chiara thought. *They always mean business. Even the pious ones.*

That's when it hit her. *That's the saint—the very same saint—Papà told me about when I was a little girl! Unbelievable.*

Stunned, a certain nervousness rose in her throat and escaped as a loud chuckle. She instantly clamped her hand over her mouth, but not before the nuns in the last row of pews turned and shot her a disapproving glance. She was too intrigued by the depiction to care. As she took in the saint's visage, her eyes, her cheekbones, her long brown hair, an eerie feeling overcame her. *She looks like I did when I was a little girl.* For a fleeting moment she wondered if it was a sign. Believers or not, Italians always believed in signs. *But of what?* Suddenly, she felt her intestines grumble, and she bolted for a bathroom.

Chapter 20

On Wednesday morning, after dropping Cecilia off at the airport and stopping at the doctor's office to have her stitches removed, Chiara drove back to the apartment thrilled that she was going to have it and her husband all to herself again. She felt a rush of shame for being dizzy with happiness that Cecilia was on a plane back to Florida. But it passed. Driving along sweltering Interstate 30 with her sunroof open and the windows down, a song she liked came on the radio. She turned up the volume until the music was blaring from the speakers. "Just one look at you," she sang, "and I know life is good, life is good, life is good …Cecilia's gone, Cecilia's gone…"

Lately, Chiara felt as if the blissful marital momentum she and Adrian had set in motion almost the day they met was stalling. Chiara worried it was her fault for not being able to ignore the calls and Cecilia's insults. But it was more than that. Adrian had lost Sunday's game, allowing six runs to score in the first two innings. He'd been in a bad mood ever since. Still, she was determined to do everything she could to nurture their relationship back to normal again. If she had caused their happy momentum to shift backwards, then she was going to shift it into fast-forward again.

On Friday night, after Adrian's second poor performance in a row, Coach Williams pulled him out of the game in the second inning for giving up seven runs to the subpar Kansas City Royals. In the dugout, Adrian and Mike Hogan exchanged heated words, Hogan pointing in his face. They looked like they wanted to tear into each other. Chiara watched from the stands shocked, wondering what they could be fighting about. The fans caught on and booed them both for unsportsmanlike behavior. Adrian threw a water cooler clear across the dugout, barely missing the batboy, and hit the showers. Chiara graciously accepted condolences from two Ranger wives, and then she went home.

Change the momentum, she repeated over and over to herself as she rushed around the apartment dimming lights, lighting candles and incense, and dabbing his favorite perfume on her neck and wrists, trying to feel sexy and happy in spite of what had just happened. It was going to be a struggle to get him in a romantic mood after his terrible performance. But she had to try. He was leaving for Baltimore tomorrow.

Change the momentum, change the momentum. She was practically chanting now. And just like that, while searching through her pajama drawer for the raunchy negligee one of her med school friends had given her as a bridal shower gift, a momentum theorem from her college physics class popped into her head, word for word. *The linear momentum of an object is the product of the object's mass and velocity. Linear momentum is a vector quantitiy that points in the same direction as the velocity.* She slipped into the negligee, surprised at the easy recall. *God, I can't believe I still remember that stuff.*

When Adrian opened the apartment door, his mouth dropped open.

"Wow," he said, stepping into the apartment. He slowly closed the door behind him, taking in the dim candlelit room. "What's all this?"

Chiara had bought a fifty pack of votive candles at the pharmacy on the way home and lit every one of them. She'd bought dozens of roses, too, plucked the petals and spread them over the carpet like fallen autumn leaves.

She stepped out from behind the kitchen counter with a bottle of cabernet and two wineglasses.

"You like what I've done with the place?"

"I do." He sauntered over to her and kissed her on the lips.

Even with nothing but the soft hazy light of the candles, Chiara could see Adrian looked stressed. She hoped what she was wearing would get his mind off the game. Her negligee was red, fitted, and it barely reached her thighs. It was also very sheer.

Adrian looked her over and Chiara dropped her gaze to the carpet. "You look great," he said.

She looked up at him again. "So do you."

"What made you decide to do this tonight? I got my ass kicked out there."

"I just wanted to do something nice for you. Want a back rub?"

He leaned over, picked up a rose petal, and smelled it purposefully, giving her a devilish smile. Chiara knew what was on his mind now.

"I love you," he said.

Chiara knew that. But something told her she loved him more. Everything about him sent her spinning into romantic nirvana when he looked at her that way.

He picked her up with a quick swoop and set her on the couch, sitting down next to her.

Chiara placed the wine bottle on the cocktail table and helped him take off his shirt. She pressed her hands into the nape of his neck and massaged outward, toward his shoulders, in even, circular strokes. They felt taut from his outing and he looked more muscular than usual in the sepia light. She admired every inch of him, every muscle, every tendon, every ligament, as he uncorked the bottle and poured the wine, the oaky aroma rising from the bottle like a genie. She glanced around the apartment. Everything looked perfect, felt perfect.

"You feel tight," she said.

"I am." He leaned back against her. "I'm so fuckin' pissed I lost again."

"I saw you and Hogie yelling at each other. Want to talk about it?" she said softly.

"Naw. He's an ass."

Chiara tried to sound encouraging. "So you've had two bad outings. You're seven and three, your record's awesome."

"It ain't that easy, Chiara. My arm's been bothering me. It feels tired. It's taking me a lot more pitches to get the batters out because my velocity's down."

"I know." Chiara moved her hands down to his pitching arm. "Where exactly is it bothering you? Does it hurt when I rub it?"

"No."

"Did you tell your coaches?"

"I told them. They just said if it keeps bothering me, I should go get an MRI."

"Should I be rubbing it?"

Adrian smiled. "It's fine, baby." He seemed to be enjoying the attention. "It just feels...I don't know how else to explain it...tired."

"Adrian?" she paused. "Maybe you should start taking vitamins and eat better. Maybe drinking less would help too."

"Maybe..."

"Do you want me to schedule an MRI for you?"

"Not yet. I'm gonna give it a little more time." He pressed his face into his hands. "I'll be so fuckin' glad when the season's over. I'm not gonna do nothing all winter except relax and be with you."

Chiara turned on the CD player with the remote control and Vivaldi's "The Four Seasons" pranced into the apartment like a jester.

"Sorry, I know you hate classical." She hit the *next* button on the remote. The CD player made a *ca click ca click* sound and Luis Miguel's smooth Spanish-crooning voice poured through the speakers singing *adagio* a melody of lost love. It was beautiful. His voice coated Chiara like warm honey pouring onto her skin, slow and sweet. She thought, *This is happily ever after.*

"Turn it up," Adrian said.

She raised the volume and went back to rubbing his back. "Honey, you've had two bad outings. I know it's hard, but you have to try to shake them off. Besides," she paused, "it's not entirely your fault you've been struggling."

"Then whose?"

"Mine," she said full of regret. "I was hard on you."

Adrian *tsked*. "Chiara, you haven't done anything wrong."

"Yes, I have. I've badgered you about the crank calls for months, bugged you almost daily about calling the investigator to find out if he has any leads, and bickered with and about your mom when I should've been letting things go. None of that helped you concentrate on your game."

"That don't have nothing to do with it. It's my velocity, my mechanics."

"Well, I think it has a lot to do with it," she said barely above a whisper, the sound of regret lingering. "I know you're disappointed I didn't get along with her like you thought I would. We barely spoke from Sunday on. I've been putting a lot of pressure on you and...I'm sorry."

He took a long drink of wine. "Chiara, I know my mother. She's moody, she wants things to go her way all the time, and if they don't, she acts like a kid. Me and my brother have been dealing with her attitude ever since we were little."

Chiara moved her hands over his shoulders and he moaned. "Sorry, too hard?"

"No, it feels good. When I was a kid, I used to have to go out and pitch while my mom and dad fought in the stands, him drunk and her pissed off. I got pretty good at ignoring things. Hiding things. I was glad when he moved back to Ireland for a few years."

"Hiding your feelings?"

"Yeah."

Chiara sighed. "That's terrible."

"Well, sometimes that's the way things go. I wish you could ignore the crank calls for a while so I don't have to see you so upset, because that does bother me."

She leaned over and kissed the nape of his neck. "I love you, Adrian. I'll try. I'll really try."

"I promise if we don't find out who's calling before the end of the season we can go at it harder over the winter."

"Will you promise me something else," she asked.

"What?"

"After tonight, will you promise to cut back on your drinking?"

"Yeah, I promise."

She ran her fingertips through his dark hair, kissed the nape of his neck. "Deal."

"It would help me out if you could handle the investigator stuff. You can call him and tell him what's going on when that bitch calls."

"I can do that," she said and wrapped her arms around him. "I want us to be happy."

He sighed. "I know. I do, too." He lay back on the couch and pulled her on top of him, kissing her. "Just let me concentrate on my game. And you concentrate on school. We've got three months to go. Then we'll go back to Pittsburgh, move into our new house, and put all of this shit behind us."

Chiara kissed him again, taking in the taste of wine on his tongue, thinking how lucky she was to have him in her life, feeling like she was finally finding her tiny place in the world.

They made love to candlelight and by the time they fell asleep dawn was streaking heavenly shades of citron, fuchsia, peach, and aqua blue across the wide Texas sky. In the afternoon, Adrian left for Baltimore.

On Monday morning, after studying a stack of flashcards two feet tall all night, Chiara awoke to the sounds of garbage trucks in the apartment complex parking lot and morning traffic whizzing by on Highway 360. It made her wish for double-paned windows. She heard an adjacent apartment door slam and the sound of a pair of pumps rushing by her front door. Waking up in an apartment was different from waking up at Girasole. Very different. All she ever heard at home in the morning was the sound of horse whinnies floating through her bedroom windows. Often, a family of doves woke her. They had a certain predilection for perching on Chiara's bedroom window sill at the crack of dawn. They would land there and coo until their songs cajoled her out of bed to greet them. She always kept sunflower seeds on her writing desk for their morning visits. She got out of bed, pushing away her study material, feeling a sense of total contentment. Her studies had been going well—she'd scored over ninety percent on every practice test so far, including the developmental bio material. Aside from attending the games and checking in on Amadeus, she'd barely left the apartment since Cecilia left, studying, studying, studying for the boards.

She hurried to the small walk-in closet to pack for her flight. The plan was to meet Adrian in Baltimore later that day and then fly home for a week to take the boards, show Hemingway, and see how the new house was coming along. Mamma and Valerie said the builders were moving fast, and it looked great. Chiara could hardly wait to see it. *Let's see…what do I need?* She opened a suitcase and tossed in three blouses, a dress, a pair of strappy sandals, a sexy negligee, shorts, a skirt, matching panties and bras, toiletries. Her competition boots and show clothes were at Girasole, so that was taken care of. *What else?*

"Ah, my study material. That, I'll carry on."

It was after seven o'clock when she arrived at the Baltimore Marriott, late because of a flight delay. Lindsay had left a message on her cell phone asking if she'd read the Arlington newspaper. Chiara pushed herself through the hotel revolving door with bags and books in tow to the registration desk. The woman working behind the counter was stubby and stout, around fifty with short black hair. She wore a royal blue suit and matching heavy eye shadow.

"The person registered to that room has already checked in with his keys," she said. She looked at Chiara with a raised eyebrow.

"I know. I'm his wife. There should be a notation in your computer that I'd be arriving later."

The woman tapped on her screen with stubby bitten-down fingernails and then asked, "Are you Mrs. Chiara Peruviso?"

Mrs. Peruviso. She loved hearing her new name.

"Yes."

"I'll just need to see some identification," the woman said.

Chiara handed her a driver's license.

The woman looked back and forth between Chiara and the photo and her expression softened.

"Thank you for your patience, Mrs. Peruviso."

"No problem," Chiara said, offering a smile.

"We sometimes get groupies in here pretending to be players' girlfriends and spouses, trying to get access to the young men's room numbers and keys. It's ridiculous really," she said. "You're in room 1121. Enjoy your stay."

The hotel lobby was adorned with Asian art and bonsai trees. Chiara walked through the lobby and down a long hall toward the elevators. On a long table between two sets of elevators, arranged in a colossal oriental vase, was a bountiful sunflower arrangement. *Not you guys again,* she thought. *Helianthus annus,* she could almost hear Papà whisper over her shoulder. "If God had a favorite flower, Chiara, it would be *il girasole.* It is a symbol of *il Signore,* God, at work among us, guiding his flock."

As she waited for the elevator, Chiara thought of the oral biology report she had presented in high school, how Papà had insisted she do it on the sunflower, on how its seed pattern followed the Fibonacci sequence, and the golden ratio. Even after all these years she could remember the report like it was yesterday because Papà had made her research and include so much more material than her teacher had required. The night before she presented the report to her class, she had recited it to him.

"Chiara, make sure you explain in the *presentazione* that the sequence was introduced to Western Europe in the 1200s by *un italiano,* a mathematician named Leonardo of Pisa, known as Fibonacci," he'd said. "Explain how the sequence is defined mathematically by $F_n = F_n - 1 + F_n - 2$ and show this on the diagram of the sunflower head."

"But Papà, I read that Indians have been using the golden ratio since before Christ. Shouldn't I mention that?"

"No. Mention *le architetti, musicisti,* and *artisti italiani* that used the golden ratio in their work during the great Renaissance period: Leonardo Da Vinci used it to paint the beautiful Mona Lisa, to draw the Vitruvius Man sketch; Pacioi, the Franciscan friar who was also a mathematician, wrote *De Divina Proportione* in the 1500s. Did you know he was convinced there was a Catholic religious significance in the ratio?"

"Well, how about Vincent Van Gogh? While I'm at it, shouldn't I mention him, Papà? He was famous for painting sunflowers."

Papà gave her a mischievous grin. "No, Chiara. Of course not, he was Dutch."

At the time, Chiara was furious at Papà for practically writing the presentation for her, making her talk about how this Italian did this and that Italian did that. But now, looking at the arrangement, cradling the memory of him pontificating and punching the air with his pointing finger, rubbing his graying five o'clock shadow while she recited the presentation, she found the memory, all of a sudden, amusing. A smile blossomed over her face, thinking of him, thinking she was less than twelve weeks away from entering her third year of medical school, and how proud he would have been. She was proud, too. She was married *and* in medical school.

She took a flower from the arrangement. A woman waiting for the elevator poked her husband and gave Chiara a disapproving look. Chiara started counting what seemed like an infinite number of florets.

Fibonacci series, she thought. *Probably the Lemon Queen variety, not as large as the Gargantuan types Papà had us plant at Girasole.*

When Chiara got to the room, she swiped the card and let herself in. She liked the neutral shades of white and caramel on the walls and bedspread. Two pictures of geishas hung on either side of a centered window. On a corner desk adjacent to the window, were magazines, a phone, and a large nearly-empty bottle of Jack Daniels. A tall open armoire with a TV and minibar was situated in the middle of the wall across from the king-size bed. Adrian had already raided the minibar. *I'm not letting this go,* she thought. *He just promised. How's he trying?*

Chiara calmed her nerves and made a mental note to look through the room-service menu later and order a bagel for the morning. She had started her own mini-contest to see which of the hotels she had visited served the best bagels and cream cheese. At the end of the season she'd rate them. It gave her something small to look forward to when she was alone in the room, as she frequently was after Adrian left for promotions or practice at the ballpark. So far the Ritz Carlton in Chicago was winning hands down. *Yum.*

She changed into a cotton miniskirt and sleeveless lavender blouse and freshened up at record speed. As she opened the door to leave for Camden Yards, she saw a note on a Marriott hotel napkin on the carpet. She must have rolled right over it with her suitcase. She picked it up and read:

Call me if you want to have some fun again, Jen.

Chiara placed the note in her pocket and took her time walking to the ballpark. Thoughts of Adrian with another woman rammed against each other in her mind like a swarm of bees trapped in a mason jar. She'd felt the same emotional blow every time Miss Hoochie Coochie called, like a boxer knocked down from a sucker punch to the gut. Usually she could get up, shake off the anger, jealousy, and suspicion, and steady herself for the next round of life. But lately it was getting harder. She felt like staying down.

At Camden Yards, she stopped to look at the statue of Babe Ruth. Sad or not, she wanted to take it in; he was a legend. Then she went to the section where Lindsay was saving her seat. When she finally caught sight of her bright blonde hair, she feigned a smile and made her way over.

"What took you so long, darlin'?" Lindsay said, getting up to hug her. She was dressed from head to toe in Pinky Tuscadero pink—blouse, jeans, and pink patent-leather sandals. She looked ready to head straight to a *Grease* tribute after the game.

"The plane was late," Chiara said, taking her seat between them.

"Girl, we've already downed two beers apiece."

Alicia held up a fifteen-ounce cup. She was wearing a pair of Gap jeans and a Moody Blues T-shirt. "Want one?" she asked.

"No, thanks."

Lindsay looked uneasy. "Well?" she said. "Did you read the paper this morning?"

Chiara gave them both a quizzical look. "No, what happened?"

Lindsay sighed hard. "Last night Adrian had the bases loaded, Mike and Coach Williams went up to talk to him on the mound, and Mike smelled alcohol on Adrian."

Chiara shook her head, not surprised. *Unbelievable. On his day to pitch.* "I asked him after the game why Mike was yelling at him in the dugout and he said he didn't want to talk about it."

"Well, now he won't have to, 'cause a reporter near the dugout heard the whole thing and printed everything except the swear words."

Chiara looked at both of them "I'm so sorry, guys." *Why was he doing this to himself? To his team?* "What did the paper say?"

"Mike said somethin' about the rest of the team still loving the game and wanting to win. Then somethin' about Adrian reserving his drinking for days he doesn't have to pitch."

Chiara felt her face flush and her muscles in her neck clamp tight. She gave them an apologetic look. "He's been drinking a lot lately. I've asked him if he needs help and he keeps telling me that he doesn't have a problem."

Lindsay patted her on the lap and sighed. "It's alright, darlin'. Lord knows Mike was no saint years ago. I think it's the pressure to win that gets to some of them. Just talk to Adrian, get him some help so it doesn't get out of hand."

"Hey, you got your stitches out," Alicia said.

Chiara was glad she had changed the subject.

"Let me see," Lindsay said.

Chiara held out her hand.

"You can barely tell," Lindsay said.

"It's healing great. The doctor took them out on Wednesday."

"When are you going to start riding Amadeus again?" Alicia asked.

Lindsay rolled her eyes. "Oh, for the love of God, Alicia! Do we have to talk about horses tonight?"

"When I get back from Pittsburgh," Chiara said. "Is that still okay?"

"Yeah, I'm having fun riding him. He's really talented."

"Thanks, Alicia…I owe you."

Alicia smiled at her. "No you don't."

"Now, you two listen to me," Lindsay said in her adorable southern drawl. "I am not gonna spend one more minute—not one more second—of this trip with either one of you if that's all you're gonna talk about tonight." She threw up her hands in frustration and her diamond ring twinkled as brightly as the field lights. "I have been trying to work my way off a farm since I was fifteen, and all I've heard since I've been hanging out with you two is horses, horses, horses. I mean, they're cute and all, but it's annoying as all get-out."

"Oh, relax, Lindsay, don't go losing a fingertip over it," Alicia said.

Lindsay blinked, surprised by her smart remark. She changed the subject. "Now, Chiara, Alicia and I were just talkin' about how we should plan for the next road trip a little better. We should book our flights together. What do you think?"

"I'd like that," Chiara said. "I'll be able to go on more trips after the boards."

She sat back and stared into a cheerful crowd dressed in black and orange, wondering if Adrian was hiding something, feeling confused, angry, jealous. She fought off a sudden urge to burst into tears. At the top of the third inning Mike Hogan went up to bat. He swung hard at the first pitch and the ball soared into the upper deck of right field. Lindsay and Alicia shot out of their seats, cheering.

"Way to go, Mike!" Lindsay shouted.

The Oriole fans booed and groaned around them. Chiara barely noticed. Her eyes were glazed over, envisioning Adrian in someone else's arms.

"Number twelve for the year," Lindsay said, sitting down. "Not bad for an old geezer."

Alicia gave Lindsay a high five, and they sat down.

"Are you two jockeys going to Seattle from here?" Lindsay asked.

"I am," Alicia said. She held out her hands as if she were holding a set of reins. "Chiara is going home to take the boards and show her *blank* in a competition."

"Very funny," Lindsay said.

Lindsay leaned over to Chiara.

"You all right, honey?" she asked.

"I'm fine," Chiara said. She avoided their stares by adjusting her blouse, telling herself that in the grand scheme of life, with all the injustices in the world, her problem was small. But her heart, as usual, was stronger than her mind.

Lindsay squeezed Chiara's hand and gave her an encouraging smile. "Don't worry. If he keeps pitching well, the team, the papers, and the fans will forget all about it."

Chiara nodded, even though she knew no coach on earth was going to let such an offense to his team go unpunished. She felt like going back to the room and pouring every ounce of alcohol from the minibar down the sink. But what was the point? There was a full bar in the lobby.

Alicia leaned in close to her. "Everything is going to be okay, Chiara, you'll see. Have you gotten any more crank calls?"

"Yes, last night. And I just found a note slipped under our room door from a girl named Jen. It said, 'Call me if you want to have fun again.' I'm wondering if it's her." As she told them, she felt her heart grow heavy.

"Chiara, I think all the crank calls are starting to get to you," Lindsay said. "Just because you found a note under the door doesn't mean Adrian's having an affair or that it was written by whoever's calling you. Besides, that note could have been left by someone Adrian met years ago. I told you how persistent some women are."

"I know," Chiara said. She grabbed a tissue out of her purse and dabbed at her watering mascaraed eyes. "I think the 'again' part set me off."

"Chiara," Lindsay said, "I've picked up close to a hundred notes under hotel doors in twenty years of baseball. Why the hell do you think I go on all these road trips? You think I like leaving my boys at home or that the shopping is better in Maryland than in Dallas? *Please.* After twenty years of marriage to Mike, I could definitely go without seeing him for a week or two here and there when he goes on the road." She looked at her diamond ring. "But…when you say 'I do' to a professional athlete, you get women chasing them as part of the package. So I protect what's mine. I travel with him all the time."

"How would she know the room number?" Chiara asked. I know it's possible she slipped it under the wrong door and it wasn't meant for him at all."

"Oh, God, stop being so naïve, Chiara," Alicia said. "If it was meant for him, all she had to do was offer someone at the front desk fifty bucks to cough up the info."

Chiara remembered what the woman at the front desk had said. She sat up straighter, took a long deep breath. "You guys are right, I'm sorry. I'm going nuts wondering who's calling me, wondering if it could be true. Don't you guys ever wonder if your husbands have cheated?" Chiara asked.

Alicia cringed like she'd bitten into a lemon. "Judd did once—that I know of—but we got through it."

Chiara stared at her wide-eyed. "How? I could never get over it."

"Chiara, he said it was a one-night stand. I've been with Judd since I was sixteen and I wasn't willing to let go of him over it." She took a sip of her beer. "Besides, he didn't have to tell me. I would never have known." She gave Lindsay a quizzical look. "Has Mike?"

Lindsay shifted in her seat. "He was a nut before we got engaged, so I'll never know for sure. But I think he's been true to me since we got married. He knows I'd wrap his penis around his baseball bat if I thought he ever cheated." She made a wringing motion with her perfectly manicured hands.

Chiara didn't doubt it; she feigned a smile.

Alicia cringed again and looked up at the scoreboard. "Tell us how you really feel."

"Look," Lindsay said. "It's not that I don't trust my husband, because I do. But I travel with him whenever I can to keep an eye on the women. I know it'll be hard the next few years with your schooling, but you should too, Chiara."

"The temptation's always there, Chiara," Alicia said. "You're new to the baseball scene. You don't know yet how far some women will go to get their hands on these guys. That babysitter in the family center with the newborn? She's only eighteen and rumor has it she'd been trying to get pregnant by a baseball player since she started working for the Rangers last year. For financial gain." She shook her head, disgusted. "I mean, who thinks like that as a kid?"

"I was still jumping rope and playing hopscotch," Lindsay said. "I guess she has a boyfriend now, but my point is, you have to be careful, gold diggers come in every shape, size, and age. And they're everywhere."

After the game, which the Rangers won 10–2, Chiara waited a while after Adrian got into bed to mention the note, and the whiskey.

She cleared her throat. "Honey, you promised you were going to cut back on your drinking. That bottle is almost empty."

"Sanchez stopped by last night. He drank most of it."

Chiara didn't believe him. "Lindsay told me your fight with Mike was in the paper this morning. You've got to cut back, or it's going to cost you your career."

He took a deep breath. "Sanchez brought the bottle over. It wasn't full when he got here. Can we relax now?"

She gave him a suspicious look. "Not yet. When I got to the hotel today there was a note under the door from a girl named Jen. Who is she?"

He had been stroking her hair while they watched the game's highlights on ESPN news and he barely flinched.

"Jen…" He shook his head. "That girl is crazy. What did it say?"

Chiara felt the familiar stab of jealousy in her stomach. "Call me if you want to have some fun *again*. It's on the desk, next to the phone. Do you know her?"

"Yeah, I know her. I hooked up with her once when I played in Baltimore, when I was in the minor leagues. I guess she thought I might want to again. She probably doesn't know I got married."

Whew, she thought, feeling the jealousy subside. She turned off the lights and snuggled in close to him. "Is she pretty?"

"Not really, and stop it. She was just somebody to have a good time with under the sheets a few years ago. I love you."

"Love you, too."

Around ten the next morning, after they made love, Adrian went into the bathroom to shower. They planned on having breakfast in the hotel restaurant and then walking to the Babe Ruth Museum.

"Take a shower with me," he said.

"I'll be right in. I have to cancel the bagel I ordered last night."

Adrian smiled and shook his head as he headed for the bathroom. "Chicago Ritz still winning?"

Chiara nodded. "Hands down."

Chiara heard a gush of water shoot out of the showerhead as she picked up the hotel phone. Just then her cell phone rang, too. Julio had been calling all week with last-minute tips to help her prepare for the competition. This was the time when he was done riding Hemingway and full of ideas.

"Hello?"

"Hi, whore. Did you fuck my boyfriend last night?"

Chiara's anger was instant and her hand trembled around the phone. Within seconds it felt like a hundred degrees in the room.

Think quickly. "Actually, I fucked my *husband* last night *and* this morning. If you're fucking him too, that makes *you* the whore."

"Well, ain't you getting witty," she said. "I'm impressed."

"Listen here, you little tramp. You might as well stop calling, because I'm not playing this game with you anymore. I'll hang up every time you call. You're not going to ruin my marriage."

"Marriage? You don't have a marriage. Husbands in a *real* marriage don't fuck around on their wives. Yours does."

"Adrian would never do that to me."

"You don't know how to make him happy under the sheets; I keep him coming back for more."

"Oh yeah? Well if he can't get enough of you, why can't he wait for the season to end so we can go home to Pittsburgh? He's counting down the days."

For a moment there was silence.

"Oh, poor girl, you don't like hearing that?" Chiara said, full of satisfaction.

"You're a whore," the woman said.

"I'm in a monogamous relationship with my husband."

"What's mononomagamos?"

"That's what I thought," Chiara said, more to herself than to the woman.

"You may be book smart, bitch, but you're stupid when it comes to the real world," she said. "Adrian ain't going nowhere, and he knows it. He's mine."

"He's mine," Chiara shot back. "I'm married to him, you pig." Her hands were clamped and numb around the phone. She was surprised at the anger she was capable of. Not even in her angriest moments with Papà, Father Bob, and the Catholic Church had she ever felt such rage.

Sounds of women laughing in the background on the other end of the receiver trickled through the phone line. They seemed to be basking in her distress.

"Well I'm fucking him," the woman said and laughed.

Chiara could almost see the wry smile in her voice. It nauseated her, and she felt an urge to vomit.

"If you are sleeping with Adrian, why don't you come right out and tell me who you are so I can get this out in the open with him? Then you could have him all to yourself because *I*, unlike *you*, will not share my lover." Chiara knew the exchange was getting ridiculous and immature. But she couldn't help herself. She wanted to find out something, anything, about this woman who was chiseling away at her happiness, at the person she was, making an insecure monster out of her.

Adrian came out of the bathroom wearing a towel around his waist. Droplets of water were still dangling from his chest hairs. "Who you talking to?"

Chiara handed him the phone. "It's your girlfriend."

"Hello…hello?" he said into the receiver.

No response.

Adrian held the receiver between Chiara's ear and his own. "Hello," he demanded again.

Again, no response.

Adrian handed the phone back to Chiara.

"You still there?" Chiara said.

"I'm here, stupid—"

"This is your chance. Adrian and I are both standing here. What's your name?"

"*Adrian and I are both standing here*," she mocked. She was purposely trying to sound sophisticated. "I was in Baltimore with him Saturday night while you were reading your books. He had on a black Armani shirt and jeans."

"Are you Jen?"

"No. I'm Nonya," she said.

Chiara looked at Adrian. "Do you know a Nonya?"

He shook his head.

"*Nonya* business," the girl said. Laughter exploded through the receiver again.

Chiara stood there, feeling stupid. "I will find out who you are, you tramp." She hit the END button on her cell phone.

She looked at Adrian. "I've given you the benefit of the doubt, but I will find out who she is. And, if she is telling the truth, you can pack your bags and go straight to her, because I will not tolerate an unfaithful husband."

Adrian gave her a long steady stare and walked away.

Chiara threw the cell phone on the bed.

"Why do you keep falling for that shit, Chiara?" he said. "You're just making it more fun for her to call and mess with you."

"Adrian, she said she was with you Saturday night. I packed your suitcase for the road trip. I packed what she said you wore Saturday."

"Here we go again." He reached into his suitcase for a pair of khaki shorts. "Didn't we just talk about this in Texas?"

"How could she know I wasn't with you this weekend?"

"I don't know, Chiara. I'm just ignoring it. I don't know why you can't."

"I can't because I'm in love with you. If a man was calling to tell you he's sleeping with me, could you ignore it? Are you having an affair?"

"How many times do I have to fucking tell you no?" He held up his hand to show her his wedding band. "This means something to me. I got married to be with you and start a family."

He put on a black shirt and a thick gold necklace he'd bought from the jeweler at the ballpark. It had a gold-and-diamond number thirty-eight charm hanging from it and it seemed by wearing it, he had branded himself, identifying himself by what he did for a living instead of who he was as a person. Chiara looked at it sparkling against his chest, at Adrian's blond highlights, wondering who he was becoming.

"Did you call the investigator?" he said.

"Yesterday. He said he tapped the apartment phone but she's using a calling card. I don't think you understand how much this is affecting me, Adrian. I can't seem to think straight, study, or even smile lately."

He grabbed a tiny whiskey bottle from the minibar and poured it into a plastic cup. "I don't think you know how much this is affecting me either. I'm trying to deal with it too, but you're making it tough." He opened the door.

"There *you* go again, drinking and walking out every time we fight."

"I also understand something you don't," he said. "It's about until death do us part. And that's why I don't need this shit right now."

"This isn't shit, Adrian."

"I need to concentrate on my game, win some games so I can pay for the house I'm building for us. I can't help it if people want to know me now that I'm somebody," he said. The cocky expression he'd worn the week before spread over his face.

"You're starting to change, Adrian. You're letting your popularity go to your head."

"No, I'm not. I'm pissed because you keep fighting with me. You're getting jealous of me."

"Jealous! Are you kidding me?" She wanted to charge him like a bull. He was the matador in total control standing in the doorway, waving a red flag in her face—she, the taunted and doomed beast, nostrils flaring, enraged. "How could you say that, Adrian? I could never be anything but proud of you and your success."

He stepped into the hallway.

"Adrian, don't leave. We're supposed to be a team." She pointed to Camden Yards outside the window. "You understand the rules of baseball. What about the unspoken ones in our marriage? You wouldn't walk out on your team."

"My team's always got my back."

"I have your back. Do you have mine?" She questioned that more and more lately.

She waited for him to say something like, "I do have your back, and I'm sorry we're going through this" or "You're right. I shouldn't leave." But he didn't.

"I want you to go home," he said. "I'm pitching on Wednesday and I need to be relaxed and concentrated."

She took a step toward him, feeling like she had just stepped into an empty elevator shaft. "What? Why?" Her voice was shaky.

"You heard me. I can't lose again. I don't want to be sent to the bull-pen to be a reliever. I'm a starter, and I can't concentrate on my game if you're gonna keep riding me every day, every time the phone rings."

She folded her arms across her chest, feeling lost for words. "Fine," she said. "I'll change my flight. I'll leave today."

"Fine." he said, slamming the door behind him.

Chiara sank onto the edge of the bed, sniffing back tears, feeling as if he had just trampled over her heart. After a moment there was a knock on the door. She looked at the door, thinking Adrian had had a change of heart and come back, but instead she heard, "Room service." She had forgotten all about the bagel.

Later, with her suitcase in tow and a backpack full of study material slung over her shoulders, Chiara got on the elevator and hit the lobby button. Within seconds the elevator doors opened to the lobby and she found herself in an eye-to-eye stare-down with the sunflower arrangement. She thought, *don't you dare say a word*. If there really was such a thing as signs, Papà was preaching to her loud and clear through those flowers. And she knew exactly what he was saying.

Chapter 21

"You weren't supposed to come home until Thursday," Mamma said, paying the airport parking attendant. "Why am I picking you up three days early?"

It was pointless to lie. Nobody got anything past Mamma. She could read people, especially Chiara and her sisters, faster than she could chop an onion, which she did at lightning speed.

"I got into a fight with Adrian...about the calls."

"No news from that private investigator?"

"Not really. He said he tapped our apartment phone, but she's using a calling card to call and he can't trace the number back to anyone."

Mamma hit the accelerator hard, merging onto the highway. If feet could talk, hers were saying, "We're taking matters into our own hands." Minutes later they emerged from the Fort Pitt tunnel onto the Fort Pitt Bridge and a postcard view of downtown Pittsburgh exploded into sight. Chiara looked over at Three Rivers Stadium. Above it, Gian Carlo's stood like a sprite on the woodsy hillside of Mount Washington, overlooking Point Park. She thought about how before she got married, she would look down from the restaurant windows at the stadium, counting down the seconds until her shift ended so she could dash to the ballpark to be with Adrian. He would always be waiting anxiously. Now, he didn't seem to care where she was.

Mamma looked annoyed. "You should've stayed and worked things out with him, *cara*. You don't just pack up and leave when you argue with your husband."

"He does it all the time." She reclined her seat, taking in the late afternoon sun coming through the sunroof of Mamma's Mercedes sedan, listening to the sounds of Pittsburgh's familiar congested five o'clock traffic.

Mamma shook her head. "The ticket must've cost a fortune."

"It did, but he told me to leave. So I left."

"Chiara, that's not how you work at a marriage…*Aie*."

Chiara closed her eyes tight, took a deep breath. "Ma, please. I know that. I didn't want to leave. I just thought he could concentrate on his next outing a little easier if I came home."

She looked out the window at the Point Park fountain bubbling into the sky like a freshly uncorked bottle of champagne, marking the spot where the Allegheny, Monongahela, and Ohio rivers converged. Three boats raced by; she imagined the people on board laughing and carrying on, enjoying the summer. It felt like ages since she had enjoyed anything. Lately, loneliness and suspicion hung over her shoulders like a heavy black cloak.

She looked down at her hand and fiddled with her wedding ring. "I didn't really have a choice."

Mamma shook her head. "You had a choice." She looked away, beyond the traffic, and Chiara could tell she was somewhere else.

"You remind me so much of myself when I was your age." She patted Chiara on the knee. "You should've stood up to him and told him you weren't going anywhere. But instead, you did exactly what he wanted you to do." For a moment her voice sounded distant and dreamy. "You're a hopeless pleaser when it comes to your husband. Like I was. "

"You and Papà had a great marriage, Mamma."

"We did. But I sacrificed a lot for him, *cara*. I've had a lot of time to think about things since he passed." She focused her stare on the road and Chiara noticed fine lines on Mamma's face that had surfaced since she last saw her.

"Like what, Ma?"

"I wish I'd have had some of my own goals in life." She gave Chiara a reassuring look. "Don't get me wrong, I don't regret one thing, because Papà's intentions were always so good. But I always allowed his goals to become my goals. My only goals. I never took the time to think what I would've liked to do for my own personal satisfaction." She tucked a few straying strands of hair into her chignon. "When you're like you and me, Chiara, it's easy to put everyone else first. If you're not careful, you end up losing yourself. Here I am, almost fifty, and I don't know anything else but cooking in restaurants."

It was true. Mamma had always worked side by side with Papà, never really took time to pursue any interests of her own. Chiara thought how lost and misplaced in the world she must feel now without Papà.

"Ma, it's not too late. If you want to take up a class, or try something new, I'll help you in whatever way I can."

Mamma smiled at her appreciating the offer. "Don't worry about me, *cara*," she said. "I'm telling you this because I want you to stick to your guns when you want something. Whether it's medicine, or staying in Baltimore with your husband. Don't let anyone push you around. Not Adrian, not his mother, and not that crank caller."

Chiara nodded at her mother, taking in her wise words.

"Papà looks after us from a different place now. We may not be able to hear him or see him, but we can still think of his *girasoli*, remember what they meant to him, and remind ourselves to be tough. God has a master plan for all of us. No matter how trying life is sometimes."

Chiara looked out the window at the city buildings and bit her lip, fighting back an urge to cry. She was doing that a lot lately and uncertain why she was struggling not to, now. Perhaps it was because she couldn't find comfort in those helianthuses, as Mamma did. Their yellowness just didn't enlighten her about anything in her life. Perhaps it was because she was feeling sad that she missed her father and mentor. Perhaps it was because Mamma's voice resounded with longing for Papà, and it echoed her own sentiment for Adrian.

Mamma tapped the turn signal and merged into the left lane, waving through the rearview mirror at a car behind hers. "God sent me another cross to bear lately."

"What?"

"Sylvia just told me she's gay, but you already knew that."

Chiara sat up in her seat, gazed at Mamma openmouthed. "Who told you?"

Mamma scratched her sky-high cheekbone mindlessly. "She did, last week. I've been at church every night since then praying for guidance on how to handle this. Papà would've been livid."

Chiara cleared her throat. "He wasn't."

Mamma turned her eyes from the road and glared at Chiara for almost a bit too long.

"He knew, Mamma. Didn't Sylvia tell you?"

"No, she didn't, Chiara. Why didn't he tell me?"

"He knew you'd take it badly. He wanted Sylvia to tell you when she was ready."

Mamma's eyes were darting back and forth between Chiara and the road. "Well how did he take it when she first told him?"

"He seemed okay with it after he read up on it and realized there's a genetic predisposition for it. He said he'd always had a feeling anyway." Chiara shook her head. "I'm surprised Sylvia didn't call me to talk to me about this. I know she's upset."

Mamma furrowed her brow at Chiara, gave her a sideways look. "That takes a lot of nerve, Chiara, considering it took her ten years to tell *me*." She evened her tone. "I'm sure she felt like I do, that you've had your hands full studying for the boards and dealing with Cecilia and that *putana* harassing you."

Chiara felt a familiar tightness in her chest rise to her throat, knowing how difficult this must be for Mamma and Sylvia. "Ma, it wasn't my place to tell you about Sylvia. She kept saying she was going to. Did you lose your temper?"

"I did." Mamma's hands clenched the steering wheel. She looked so disappointed.

Chiara looked away; she was thinking about the hell Mamma must've put Sylvia through the past week, telling her it was wrong in the eyes of God. "I knew you would."

Mamma took a deep breath and let it out slowly, unclenching her hands from the steering wheel. "I think I always suspected, but the finality of *knowing* is what set me off."

"What did you say to her?"

Mamma focused her eyes on the road. "I was hard on her. We're barely speaking."

"Ma. What did you say?" Chiara insisted.

"I told her from what I've seen in the restaurants, the gay lifestyle seems very unstable. I told her that it's not a Catholic way of living, that it's a sin."

"A sin—"

"Yes, a sin, Chiara."

Chiara gave her an all-knowing look. "Ah, the truth comes out. It's the Catholic part that's *really* bothering you."

"Everything about it bothers me, Chiara."

"Child molestation is a sin, but Catholic priests engage in it all the time. Nearly fourteen thousand molestation claims have been filed against Catholic clergy since the early fifties and the Catholic Church has paid out over two billion dollars in legal expenses for abuse-related cases instead of using the funds to help the poor, sick, and needy. That's a much worse sin, if you ask me."

"The money goes to fund a lot of good things too, Chiara. Therapy programs for victims, support and rehabilitation for the offenders. Priests are human too, Chiara."

"True, and when they molest kids they're criminals."

Mamma's brow furrowed as if she was contemplating something larger than herself. "I know. I was blinded by his cassock too."

Chiara's voice softened. "Ma, don't. It's okay. Nobody suspected he was capable of something like that. Let's worry about you and Sylvia. How is she holding up?"

"Aside from being uncomfortable around me, she seems fine."

Chiara felt a small sense of relief. "Okay, good. I'll talk to her tonight. And Valerie? How's she?"

"Disappointed because she's on a three-year adoption waiting list." She shook her head, incredulous. "I don't understand why there's so much infertility in your generation; it's like an epidemic." She kneaded the gold cross around her neck with her free hand, as she often did when she was pensive. "You rarely heard women were infertile when I was a little girl. When couples decided to get married and have babies, they got married and had babies. Today, everybody's infertile."

Chiara rubbed the nape of her neck. It was sore from leaning over her books all night. "It's always existed, Ma. Back then there were few treatments for the known causes of infertility. People were more private about it." She recalled some causes of infertility that she'd read about in her developmental and reproductive biology texts over the past week. "Lots of things can cause it: salpingitis, which is fallopian tube damage or blockage; thyroid disorders; sexual diseases like chlamydia; ovulation disorders caused by tumors. Also polycystic ovary syndrome, early menopause, fibroids, hyperprolactinemia, pelvic adhesions..."

Mamma gave her a wide smile, revealing almost every tooth in her mouth. "Okay, okay, doctor. Nothing will keep me from believing that all the preservatives in the food have something to do with it, too."

"Articles are constantly coming out about that. "How's my house coming along?"

"It's looks nice, but I don't think it'll be ready by the end of September. You and Adrian will have to live at Girasole for a month or so, but I'm sure you'll be in by Christmas."

If we're still together.

"I have to admit, it'll be nice to have the company. It's so lonely at Girasole now that Papà's gone. Sylvia's always out with her friends, and I'm home alone at night. I thank God every night for baseball and cable."

A soft sadness fell over Mamma's face and for a fleeting moment she looked older than she was, her high cheekbones sallow. Chiara felt guilty. Lately, she had given so little thought to anyone's suffering but her own.

"I'll be home soon, Mamma. Classes start first week in September. We're only about eight weeks away."

"I'm fine, *cara*. You concentrate on those boards."

"They're Friday morning. I've been studying for them like crazy."

"I don't know how you absorb all that material day after day, *cara*."

"If I want to become a physician, I have to, Ma." She took her cell phone out of her purse and phoned Adrian to let him know she had landed in Pittsburgh.

No answer. She hung up.

"Are you prepared?"

"I think I am, but you never know exactly what's going to be on an exam."

"Good. Don't let Julio distract you. He's so excited for the show. He's kept Hemingway in tip-top shape for you. I think he and Bibi are more excited to see you than Liam and your sisters. They're all at Girasole waiting for us."

Chiara smiled at the thought. "I can hardly wait to see everybody, including Shadowfax and Hemingway. Maybe I'll hop on Hemi for a few minutes after dinner."

They merged onto Route 28, heading north. The smell of ketchup from the Heinz 57 plant suffused the car and Chiara felt a pang of hunger. "What's for dinner anyway?"

"Spaghetti bolognese."

Yum.

After dinner everybody sat around the walnut-paneled family room watching the Rangers-Orioles game on ESPN. Chiara sandwiched herself between her sisters on the sofa, and her brother-in-law, Liam, sat cross-legged on the floor near Valerie. Julio and Bibi sat arm in arm on the love seat. Once the camera zoomed into the Rangers' dugout, and Bibi call out "There's Adrian!" She must've remembered that Chiara told her about the argument because she instantly fell silent.

Chiara noted how relaxed Adrian looked, how unfazed by their argument he seemed. She clenched her fists to avoid throwing something at the TV. How could he argue with her, send her away like an unwanted pet, and then just continue as if nothing had happened? Was he giving a stellar performance of hiding his feelings again? No, he was relieved she was home. She could see that.

Mamma was on the leather button chair near the fireplace, a *Bon Appetit* magazine open on her lap, rambling from subject to subject as if it had been two years since she saw Chiara, not two months. She talked about Enzo and Gian Carlo's. She talked about the construction of Chiara's new house, how she and Valerie were going over there almost every day to make sure it was being built exactly as Chiara and Adrian had planned. But mostly she talked about Papà, how nothing was the same without him.

Chiara felt his absence more, now that she was home. She looked at her sisters, at Bibi and Julio, at Liam in his predictable, after-lawyering clothes—a polo shirt and jeans—and felt a sense of complete belonging. Outside, the cicadas were calling in the night and it had begun to drizzle. The soft pitter-patter of raindrops tapping on the windows made Chiara feel more relaxed than she had been in months. She looked up at an oil painting of Shadowfax above the dark walnut mantel. Papà had it commissioned the year he bought the horse for her. The bookshelves on either side of the mantel were lined with leather-bound encyclopedias, knick-knacks, and family pictures. On one shelf was a picture of her and Adrian on their wedding day. She wondered whether it would be there if Papà were still alive.

"Earth calling Chiara," Valerie said. "You okay?"

She leaned into her older sister. "I'm great." She got up, dimmed the lights, and sat back down. Chiara caught a whiff of cigarette smoke from Sylvia's clothes; she loved its familiarity.

Just then Mac Shooster, the Rangers's shortstop, hit a home run, bringing in a batter ahead of him.

"All right!" Liam shouted. "We're up seven five."

Sylvia took Chiara's hand, studied the scar. "I thought it would look worse," she said. "How many stitches?"

"Fifteen," Chiara said.

"You must've been so scared. Did you think it was going to hit the building? That you were going to, you know, die?"

Mamma eyes narrowed and she smacked the magazine on her lap. "Now what kind of question is that?" she said, glaring at Sylvia.

The tension between them was palpable.

Sylvia gave Mamma a long flat stare. Her raven eyes were lethal when she was angry. "A legitimate one."

"Come on, guys," Chiara said, trying to soften the tension. "I must've, Sylv, because I found myself praying. I feel like such a hypocrite…"

Mamma went back to leafing through the magazine. "There's nothing wrong with that. Sometimes it takes a catastrophe to help you find your way to God. Have you learned anything from it?"

Chiara gave Mamma a modest smile. "I did: no more third-floor apartments."

Everybody chuckled.

"That was pretty good," Valerie said.

Bibi pointed at the TV. "There he is again," sounding almost disapproving this time.

"I've been praying more than usual myself," Mamma said, not looking up from the magazine. "I've been praying Sylvia realizes what a mistake—"

Sylvia got up and strode out of the room. Chiara got up to follow, but Valerie pulled her back down.

"She'll be okay, just give her a minute," Valerie said.

"She needs more than a minute. She needs her head examined," Mamma said.

"Okay, Ma, that's enough," Valerie said. "You might not be okay with it, but we are. If you keep this up, you're going to alienate her from all of us."

Mamma smacked her lap with the magazine again. "I can't help it." She was acting hard, but Chiara thought she looked more confused than angry.

Valerie peered at Mamma. "Yes, you can."

"Relax, hon," Liam said.

Bibi focused her attention on the Persian rug, and Julio scratched his head.

Mamma glared at them. "Did you two know?"

Julio frowned, looking apologetic. "We never saw her with a boyfriend, so we had our suspicions. We thought you did, too."

Mamma sighed. "Of course I *knew,* but I didn't *know.*"

Liam laughed. "Sounds like something an attorney would say."

Mamma rolled her eyes at him. "You would know," she snapped.

"Oh, come on, Ma," Valerie said. "It would be one thing if you never had an inkling, but you did. What are you going to do? Shun your daughter for the rest of your life because she's attracted to women?"

"No...but—"

"But what?" Chiara said.

"*Aie...*" Mamma slapped the magazine on her lap a third time, crossed her arms, and looked into the fireplace. "If I accept it, I have to question my faith."

Valerie blew air out of her lips. "You're acting like a fanatical Christian fundamentalist. You can't take every doctrine of the Catholic

Church literally." Valerie leaned forward on the sofa. "Saint John said, 'The seed that bareth not fruit the Lord taketh away.' Does that mean I should be waiting to be struck by a lightning bolt—or that I should throw myself in front of a bus—because I'm infertile?"

Mamma tilted her head and nodded as if she recognized that Valerie had a point.

"Times have changed, Ma, and the Catholic Church should too, if it wants to thrive," Valerie said.

Sylvia walked back into the room and sat on the floor between Bibi and Julio. She planted her dark eyes on the TV.

"God existed before the Roman Catholic Church," Valerie insisted. "He didn't create Catholicism, and neither did Jesus. The Roman emperor Constantine did. He used the impact Jesus made on humanity for his own political gain."

Mamma rubbed her forehead with both hands. "I don't know what to believe anymore, where to compromise."

"God isn't religion, Ma," Valerie said. "He couldn't care less if we eat meat on Good Friday, miss church on Sunday, choose to share our lives with someone of the same sex, or try to bring a baby into this world to love via a Petri dish. Love is love. Faith is faith. I go to church to share that love and faith."

Liam reached back and patted Valerie on the knee. "Relax...let's watch the game."

Valerie made a growling sound. "Sorry. I'm just disgusted with St. Ursula's right now."

Love is love...faith is faith...God isn't religion. Chiara let Valerie's words settle on her tongue as if she were tasting wine. It had never even occurred to her, an educated person, that she could've believed in God and Jesus without being part of any religion at all. *Imagine that.* The idea that God and Jesus went hand in hand with Catholicism had been drummed into her as a fact of life during her years at Saint Ursula's.

Sylvia's eyes were fixed on the carpet, her long ebony hair draped over her wide, angular face, her fingers kneading a silver-and-leather bracelet.

"How long have you known?" Mamma said.

Sylvia looked up, stoic. Sure. "Since I was fifteen."

Mamma held her gaze, closed the magazine and folded her hands thoughtfully on her lap. Her face softened and when she spoke, her voice was softer, kind. "I'll try, *cara*, okay? I'll try."

Sylvia nodded, and Julio tousled her head as he used to when she was a little girl.

When Chiara's cell phone rang, she grabbed it from the cocktail table. "Hello?"

"Hi Chiara, ready for the boards?"

It was Li from Chiara's PBL team. Oh, hi Li." Chiara had hoped it was Adrian, sneaking a call from the clubhouse. When she realized it wasn't him, the disappointment showed in her voice.

"Nice to hear from you, too," Li snipped. "I was just calling to make sure you knew we moved the exam group-study session to Josh's place."

"I'm sorry Li. I was waiting for a call from Adrian. I'll be there. What time?"

"Nine o'clock," she said.

"Perfect."

"I'll see you there," Li said and hung up.

When the phone rang again, Chiara picked it up, assuming it was Li again. "Hi, Li," she said with more enthusiasm.

"Hi, Snow White. I just wanted to let you know that I'm gonna be fucking your husband tonight while you're at home playing with your stupid, smelly horses," the woman said.

Chiara's lips tightened as thin as a paper cut, and her mouth suddenly felt as if she had a mouthful of glue. "You sure get around, tramp."

Everybody stopped watching the game and stared at Chiara.

"Hang up," Valerie told her.

The woman heard Valerie through the receiver. "Who's that? One of your sisters? Why don't you tell them to mind their own business?"

"I am their business," Chiara said. "Just like they are my business."

"What's that *putana* saying?" Mamma said.

"Tell them it's me, bitch," the woman said. "Tell them I hope you die."

"Give me the phone," Sylvia said.

Valerie grabbed the phone out of Chiara's hand and shot off the couch. "Listen here, you little whore. You've been calling this house, our restaurants, and Chiara's phones for almost a year. When we find out who you are, and believe me, we will, I am personally going to take the greatest satisfaction in beating the living shit out of you," she said, pacing the family room. "Until then, keep calling, keep digging your grave!" She hung up. "That's it. We're getting this whore. We're hiring our own investigator because the one you have, Chiara, frankly sucks."

For a moment nobody said a word. They just sat there stunned, staring at Valerie.

Sylvia finally spoke up, looking impressed. "Nice."

Liam gave Valerie an approving nod. "I know just the guy," he said. "Our firm's used him in the past for some criminal cases."

"Is he good?" Chiara asked.

"The best. He's a retired FBI agent."

"Let's do it," Chiara said. "I think the PI in Texas must have too many cases and ours is at the bottom of his list."

"I think it's a good idea to get an independent guy who will work for us exclusively," Liam said. "You've got some sort of stalker on your hands."

Sylvia looked relieved. "None of us feels comfortable that you're alone in Texas dealing with this."

Julio gave Liam a heavy stare and nodded. "Make sure the investigator will work fast. If she is a stalker, there is no telling what she will do next."

Chiara looked at them, so worried over her. She felt embarrassed by the drama she had inadvertently caused her family.

"I'll get his number for you tomorrow," Liam said. "Call him and tell him you're my sister-in-law and that I referred you. Then tell him what's going on."

"Okay," Chiara said. "I'll do it tomorrow."

Valerie sat down on the floor next to Liam and he wrapped his arms around her. "It's either that," he said, "or Commando here will take matters into her own hands, and I'll be bailing her out of jail."

Sylvia laughed as she pulled her hair back into a ponytail.

Mamma said, "Do you think Adrian will be all right with us getting involved?" Chiara knew she was only asking for propriety's sake. Her family was Italian through and through and was getting involved regardless of what Adrian thought.

"I don't know, but I need answers, and I can't wait to get them anymore. I've exhausted enough energy worrying." She started picking at what was left of her nail polish. "Classes start again soon and I want this behind me before then. How often is she calling here anyway?"

"Often this past week," Bibi admitted. "She hears my accent and tries to talk to me in Spanish. I just hang up."

Chiara shook her head, confused. "Let's say that he's been having an affair since before we got married. Why would he have gone through with the wedding? And why wouldn't she give her name? She'd have nothing to lose and everything to gain. On the other hand, if she is a crazy stalker, of course she wouldn't give her name. She'd be charged with harassment."

"Exactly," Mamma said.

"I'm playing the devil's advocate here, Chiara, but it could be true," Liam said. "I've seen some crazy things in the years I've been practicing law. You never know what makes people tick. I always say hope for the best, but prepare for the worst."

Chiara forced a smile and nodded.

Sylvia looked at Liam and pulled a pack of cigarettes out of her jean pocket. "Don't you think if it was true she'd have no trouble telling Chiara who she is?"

"Not necessarily," Liam said. "He may have promised her something. He may be paying her to keep quiet. Maybe when it looks like their deal is getting shaky, she decides to cause problems, put the pressure on him by crank-calling you."

Julio and Liam exchanged glances that ensured Chiara that, as always, they would do whatever it took to protect the family.

Chiara made a mental note to check the bank accounts for any suspicious transactions. "She knows some pretty personal things about him."

Valerie eyes stood at attention. "Like what?"

"She mentioned a birthmark he has on his rear end," Chiara admitted.

Mamma looked away.

"Sorry, Ma," Chiara said.

Valerie dismissed it as trivial. "Cecilia could easily have told her something like that."

"I know. I'm just so tired of coming home to her squeaky little voice on my answering machine. I'm tired of wondering if it could be true.

Tired of worrying if he could really do that to me and have no trouble lying in bed with me at night."

"That must be difficult," Bibi said.

"Adrian loves you, Chiara," Mamma said. "I'm sure of it. He wouldn't have gone to an investigator if he was guilty. I still think Cecilia has something to do with it."

Chiara stared at the television screen, saw Adrian chewing and spitting out sunflower seeds in the dugout. "Lately he looks at me like I'm a thorn in his side."

"He's probably under a lot of pressure to win, *cara*," Mamma said. "When your father and I were newlyweds, we were constantly fighting and making up. Things will get better when the season ends, you'll see." She nodded at Chiara like it was a sure thing. "I thought for sure the investigator would've had some news by now, though."

"I did too, Ma," Chiara said. "I did, too."

She flipped open her cell phone and called Adrian again, leaving him a message to call her after the game. He never did.

On Friday morning Chiara took the boards. As soon as she left the testing room, hopeful she had passed, she called Adrian—even though he'd been ignoring her calls since Monday. She had never met anyone who could hold a grudge, let alone this long.

He picked up on the second ring. "Hello?"

Hearing his voice after days, she grew nervous, her knees weakened, and she sat down on the center's front steps. "Hi, how are you?"

"I'm good, you?" He sounded indifferent.

"I...I just took the boards. I think I passed," she said trying to sound optimistic.

"That's good," he said, sounding uninterested.

That's good? I follow you and your career all over the United States to show my support, and when I pass my boards, that's all you have to say? That's good?

She swallowed hard, trying to understand what he was going through. "How's everything going with you?"

"Not too good. If I don't win on Monday, they're putting me in the bullpen."

"I've been wondering for days how your arm is. Is it still sore?"

His voice softened a little. "Yeah."

"You sound tired. Was it a long night?" She could hear the hangover in his voice but was not about to mention it.

"No. What are you, my mom?" His voice sounded like venom.

Chiara ignored his tone. "I didn't mean it that way. I worry about you, that's all." She cleared her throat. "Look, I'll let you go so you can rest."

He made a *tsk* sound. "I'm not tired. I'm still pissed off at you."

"Well, I guess I'll just see you back in Texas on Thursday," she said.

Chiara looked up at the sky. A soft steady drizzle began to fall, and a breeze picked up and swirled dirt across the street.

"That's fine. I'll see you at home."

Chiara got up and walked to Mamma's car, refusing to shed a tear.

That evening she and Julio loaded Hemingway and the rest of her gear into the horse trailer and left for the show grounds in Cleveland. She was glad Mamma had decided to drive out the following morning with Valerie and Sylvia to watch her show. She had been lecturing Chiara, telling her to postpone showing and join Adrian on the road, regardless of what he said.

Chiara had refused.

At eight thirty the next morning, dressed for the competition, Chiara led Hemingway out of one of five temporary showground stables past the concession stand and vendor tents to the white-fenced warm-up arena. It was hot and muggy and oddly windy. Occasionally the sun peeped out from behind enormous banks of swiftly moving puffy clouds. Seven other riders were already in the arena warming up for their classes.

Chiara hopped on Hemi and went to the inside of the track, watching one of the riders practicing an extended canter down the long side of the arena, leaving a small dust storm in her wake. Like Chiara, they were all dressed in traditional dressage attire: black shadbelly, top hat, tall freshly shined boots, white breeches, blouse, stock tie, and gloves. They looked so pretty, proper.

After a few laps around the arena at a walk Chiara transitioned to a trot, keeping in mind the part of the German dressage training scale that gave Hemingway trouble, relaxation. As she did, her top hat slid over her eyes, and everything went black. *I hope this isn't how the rest of my ride goes*, she thought. She pushed it back up a few times, finally stopping Hemingway to readjust. Then she went back to work.

Julio approached the ring with a cup of coffee in his hand. He always dressed nicely for shows. He looked handsome in his khakis and a royal blue Ralph Lauren oxford.

"Ride him deeper," he said softly as she passed him on the track. "Ask him to relax through half -halts."

She kept a steady rhythm at the trot, flexing Hemingway's head and neck subtly with her reins, encouraging him to relax his head. A *little left, a little right, a little right, a little left* she thought, ignoring her sore hand.

When the wind picked up, Hemingway tensed in his back and resisted her aids. A king-size drop of rain thumped her top hat. She wondered if there was such thing as God, was He shedding a tear of disappointment in people like her? If it was going to rain, she hoped it would hold off until after her ride. But then again, perhaps it was her fate for the heavens to unleash every water molecule in existence on her special day. Now was not the time to dwell on her issues with God. There were seven other twelve hundred-pound horses warming up in the arena with her. A moment of lax concentration on her part could cause a catastrophe.

Without warning a plastic bag skipped across the arena in Hemingway's path. Hemingway took a few sideways steps, glaring at as if it was a semi-trailer barreling towards him. Just then the show secretary made an announcement over the intercom. The speakers squealed and crackled and Hemingway spooked again, rearing onto his hind legs. "Easy boy," Chiara said, pushing him forward with her legs, getting him back on his four legs and insisting he trot forward.

When he did, she patted him on the withers. "Good boy."

She performed a half-halt to get Hemingway's attention, and he relaxed again in his trot. His eyes grew soft. His gaits grew more expressive and buoyant like a ballet dancer's, his ears flicking back and forth with attentiveness to Chiara. When he was relaxed enough she asked him to canter.

"Good, Chiara," Julio praised as she trotted by him on the rail again. "Ride each stride, each half-halt. A true dressage rider rides from half-halt to half-halt, not from letter to letter."

When her competition number was called, she entered the show ring. She looked into the stands, saw Mamma and her sisters, Liam, and Bibi. They looked so proud of her. She was almost embarrassed. She was glad they were there. They always were. Chiara saluted the judge and began the test. Hemingway felt divine under her, his articulating joints bending and flexing as he held a collected trot around the arena. When she wanted to piaffe, she gave Hemi the aid and he lowered his croup, arched his neck, proud like a swan, and performed beautifully. When she wanted to go forward into passage, she gave the aid with her whole body, collecting his energy underneath her. Hemingway responded with an elevated forward trot down the long side of the ring.

The sense of control as she rode Hemingway, this bouncing red-blooded beast willingly surrendering his vigorous will to hers, filled Chiara, if only for a few moments, with inner strength and confidence. She had lost so much control of her life over the past year that it felt wonderful to be able to control something in a positive way.

Chiara gave it her best in the competition ring. Hemi was a star, and he responded with enthusiasm and superb agility to each of the compulsory movements she asked him to execute with her aids. When the test was over she praised Hemi, patting his neck over and over and stroking his black mane. She felt it was the best test they'd ever ridden and her smile revealed how proud of him she was. She saluted an approving judge and as she and Hemi left the ring, Chiara looked over at her cheering family and blew Julio a kiss, knowing she had him to thank for all the work he did with Hemi. Later, when the show secretary announced the scores over the intercom, she learned they'd won the class with an impressive 73 percent.

On Monday morning, the new PI Liam had recommended knocked on the door at Girasole. He introduced himself as Mack Crosby and he looked like Santa Claus in disguise. There was something about his earnest brown eyes that inspired trust, and Chiara liked him instantly. At the kitchen table she told him about the crank calls and how Conner O'Grady seemed to be missing in action—she'd left three messages for him, all unreturned.

"The good news, young lady," he said with a grandfatherly smile, "is that I'll be happy to look into your crank caller. The bad news is, I'm already working on a case that's consuming a lot of my time." He placed the notes he had taken into his briefcase. "If you're willing to wait a few weeks so I can finish it up, I *guarantee*"—he laid particular stress on the word—"I'll find out who this woman is."

Sold! Chiara thought.

After he left, Chiara drove down the road to her new house to see how the construction was coming along. Sounds of carpenters pounding nails into blue boards and baseboards echoed through the empty rooms. It was going to be pretty when it was done, but right now it was just an empty salmon-brick house, not a home. She breezed from room to room, smelling plaster and construction dust, thinking that she should be the happiest person in the world. But she wasn't. Not even close. How could she be happy with the crank calls tormenting her, with a mother-in-law looking for a reason to criticize her every chance she got, with Adrian livid with her, with *academic probation* stamped in red on her medical school file?

She spent the rest of the day riding and helping Julio around the stable, hoping Adrian would call so they could talk. By late afternoon she had ridden five horses, cleaned the tack room, and washed and re-filled all the horses' water buckets. Minutes started to feel like hours. When she couldn't think of anything else to do to distract her from call-ing Adrian, except for going inside and tweezing her eyebrows, she sat down in the tack room and called Conner O'Grady's number instead. He didn't answer, and she hung up without leaving a message. She was thankful when Julio came in and hung two fistfuls of bridles on a bridle hook near the sink.

"Wipe down and condition these," he said. "And don't even think about picking up that phone. He should have called you to see how you did at the show."

He called Adrian a bad name in Spanish and walked out.

Chiara grabbed a bucket and filled it with water. She could hear Julio in the feed room scooping grain into feed buckets for each of the fifteen horses with a vengeance—some of which belonged to boarders who took lessons from Julio. Shadowfax let out a deafening whinny for his dinner, as if he hadn't been fed in days, not hours. Julio always fed on time. It was six o'clock. *Still no phone call from Adrian.*

She wiped sweat from her forehead onto her breeches and then ran her fingers down one of the black leather bridles. It was sticky with horse sweat. She placed the water bucket in the sink, grabbed a sponge and some saddle soap from a cabinet above it, and applied the sudsy soap to a set of reins with long sweeping strokes. Every few strokes she rinsed the dirt from the sponge, lathered it in the saddle-soap container again and started a new section of the bridle. Before long she was engulfed in the process, and after about the fourth bridle, she felt an almost therapeutic effect in cleaning them. She wished she could wash away all her doubts in life if she kept on scrubbing. Doubts about Adrian. Doubts that she would be strong enough to give her marriage and her career what they needed to survive. Doubts that Papà was wrong about Adrian, and that she was right about God.

She thought of her marriage; it was anything but the happily-ever-after she had naively thought it would be. She wondered what the woman calling looked like and what her name was. She thought of how she and Papà had parted on such bad terms, all because of her romantic notions about love and marriage.

"Hey, Chiara," a voice said.

Chiara looked up and saw Chris Kaiser, her long-time neighbor, standing in the tack-room doorway. He'd let his hair grow since she last saw him, and it gave him sort of a surfer look. It really suited him, and she liked it. His eyes hadn't changed a bit though; they were sapphire blue as ever and looked extra bright against his untucked white button-down dress shirt.

"Hey, Chris," she said, looking surprised to see him. She took in his clean, freshly showered scent and grew self- conscious about the way she looked. Her polo shirt was sporting armpit stains from working in the heat all day and her hair looked like a bristle broom that had seen better days. "I haven't seen you since my wedding. How are you?"

Chris smiled and a hint of nostalgia crossed his face. "Hard to believe it's been almost a year, huh?"

She grabbed a towel from the counter and wiped her hands before she reluctantly gave him a hug. "I'm sorry I'm such a mess. "It's really good to see you." She meant it and she could tell in his expression that he was happy to see her too.

"You look great."

Chiara shook her head and smiled, knowing he was being polite. "Well you look great *and* smell great."

Just then a noxious smell suffused the stable. Chiara wrinkled her nose. "Do you smell skunk?"

"Yeah, that's why I stopped by."

She was relieved that there was a reason for his visit. He had never married, and taking in the look in his eyes she wondered if even after all these years, he still wanted more than friendship from her.

"I was riding the quad through my fields, trying to figure out how many pumpkins to plant for the kids this year and I came across two Danes. They jogged right up to me. They didn't look like Remus and Romulus, but I read their tags and knew they were yours. I think they had a pretty good altercation with a skunk."

Chiara blinked hard and smiled. "I can smell that."

They both laughed.

Chris pointed outside. "I tied them to the lamppost with a couple of horse leads that were out there. I guess it wasn't far enough."

"No, it's fine. Thank you for bringing them back. Those two are always getting into stuff. I couldn't get Remus and Romulus to leave my side if there was a fifty-pound dog bone sitting twenty feet away." She smoothed her hair, trying to look more presentable, taken with his new look. For a second she wished she had plucked her eyebrows, and she felt guilty for even thinking it. "But Sasha and Jadey are a different story. It doesn't help that Sylvia isn't exactly the best disciplinarian when it comes to dog training."

He looked around. "Where are Remus and Romulus?"

Chiara looked away, felt the familiar pang of loss in her belly. "Remus died last year. Romulus died just days after Papà passed."

"I'm sorry, Chiara," he said.

"It's okay. They were really old. They both lived to be ten, which is a long time for Danes."

"About your father, too. I really liked him. He always did a lot for my charity. And he never gave me a hard time when I rode my bike through your fields when I was a kid."

Chiara smiled at him. He sounded so sincere. Maybe it was just his voice. It was warm and sweet, like a puppy. "He liked you a lot too, Chris."

At that moment she felt an urge to summon every memory of Papà she could conjure up in her mind. Perhaps it was because Chris had known him. Perhaps it was because of the guilt she felt for arguing with him right before he died. Perhaps it was because in recent months the people in her new life, her married life, had never known Papà. Except, that is, for Adrian. And naturally, he never wanted to talk about Papà after what had happened between them.

"It's nice to talk to someone who knew him," she said.

Chris had loved his sister with a passion and he wasn't able to save her either. They had that feeling in common, the helplessness of watching someone you love die. When he looked at Chiara, she felt that mutual understanding in his eyes.

"Anytime," he said. He started toward the stable doors, moving slowly like there was glue stuck to his feet. "Are you still competing?"

"I just won my first Grand Prix competition, on Saturday."

"I knew you'd get there…Well, I better go. Don't be a stranger, okay?"

Chiara thanked him for bringing the dogs back. As she watched him cross through the arched stable doorway, she wondered what direction her life would've taken if she hadn't been so fixed on irritating Papà and gone out with Chris, just once.

Chapter 22

On Thursday morning, exam taken, show won, nails done, and eyebrows tweezed, Chiara flew back to Texas. After Adrian's loss on Monday night, ESPN announced on Tuesday that he had been relegated to the bullpen. He was now a relief pitcher and Chiara was sure he was incensed about it. Almost an hour into the flight a sense of angst ignited in her and spread through her like a forest fire. She fought the urge to pick at her nail polish by sitting on her hands. She took a few deep breaths, thinking it might be time to start taking yoga classes or maybe kick-boxing to relieve her ever-increasing bouts of anxiety. She closed her eyes and leaned her head against the window, trying to get some sleep, but the two women next to her were going on and on about the President Clinton and Monica Lewinsky scandal.

She looked out the window at a cluster of billowy clouds in the distance. How would she feel when she saw Adrian? A part of her wanted to run into his arms shouting, *I believe you, I believe you, and I'm never going to let anyone come between us again.* But another part of her was growing more suspicious and wanted to hijack the plane, turn it around, and go straight back to Pittsburgh. She started retracing Adrian's daily

Arlington schedule in her mind like the jealous wife she was forced to become.

If she lives in Arlington, when would he even have the time to see her? He leaves for the ballpark at the same time that Hogie and Peterson do. And we leave the ballpark together at night. Maybe...

NO. STOP IT, CHIARA. He is not doing this. She is either a friend of Cecilia's or some weird fanatic. You're not going to let her get to you.

When Chiara arrived at the apartment, she found Adrian lying on the couch in a pair of jeans and a T-shirt, watching ESPN. Looking at him, she swallowed an urge to burst into tears, again. *Don't you dare*, she told herself. *Don't even think about crying.*

Adrian sat up when he saw her. He looked sad, apologetic. It surprised her.

"Hi," he said.

Chiara rolled her suitcase over the threshold and set her backpack down. "Hi," she said, barely hearing herself say it.

"I was gonna pick you up at the airport, but I had a promotion at the Ford dealership from nine to eleven."

"It's all right. I caught a cab."

"I only have like about five minutes, but I wanted to see you before I left for the ballpark." He motioned to a check on the cocktail table. "I made four thousand bucks signing autographs for about two hours. I thought you could go buy some things you want for the new house with it."

He got up, walked tentatively over to her, and took her in his arms. "I'm sorry."

She held him close, wondered if he could feel her heart pounding in her chest.

"I'm sorry, too. I missed you."

He sighed and kissed her, gently. "I missed you too, but I have to go. I've got a meeting with Coach Williams. I'm gonna talk to him about putting me back in the rotation. Can we talk after the game tonight?"

She wanted him to stay. She wanted to talk about their marriage, not his position on the team, but she knew how important it was to him. She could wait a few more hours to talk.

"Okay," she said softly into his chest. "Do you think he will?"

"I don't know, but I have to try. I'm a starter. I hate relieving."

"Will you call me after you talk to him and tell me what he said?"

"Okay," he said. He loosened his hold and looked down at her. "It's fireworks night. You coming to the game?"

She smiled, hesitant to let him go. "I'll be there."

"Sounds good. Peterson's wife asked when you were coming back."

"What did you tell her?"

"That you got held up with all the stuff going on at the new house."

She smiled, nodded. "Thanks."

Adrian leaned over and kissed her again. "I'm glad you're back. We'll talk after the game, okay?"

He never called after his meeting with Coach Williams, and Chiara thought it must've gone badly. When she got to the ballpark around seven, the stadium was packed. She rushed down to the first row of seats along the third-base line, finagling her way through a crowd waiting for autographs. She saw Adrian in center field catching with Sanchez and flagged him down. He jogged over to her, looking irresistible as usual in his red-and-white uniform, and Chiara couldn't help but lean over the fence and peck him on the lips. A group of fans looked at them and smiled, and Chiara felt a little bashful about the attention she had attracted.

"What's up?" Adrian asked.

"Hi, I just wanted to know how your meeting went."

"Sorry I didn't call you, I was just so fuckin' pissed. He said he needs some time to think about it. How much time does he need? I need some wins."

She was hurt that he didn't call her, but she didn't let it show. "It's better than a no," she said trying to sound optimistic. "I bet he'll put you back in before the month is over."

Adrian rolled his eyes. "He doesn't want to give me a chance. He wants the call-up from AAA in my spot."

She wanted to tell him she didn't think this was true. She wanted to say that the newspaper article had gotten a lot of media attention. She wandered if Coach Williams had demoted him for the rumors of his drinking binges and not for a few subpar performances. Perhaps he wanted to prove a point: if Adrian was abusing alcohol, great pitcher or not, he was out of a job.

Adrian shook his head. "Thanks, baby. I got to go shag balls. I'll see you after the game. I heard the wives are allowed to sit on the field for the fireworks, so come down."

Chiara brightened up. "That's pretty neat. Will you be able to come out and sit with me?"

"If I don't relieve too late in the game. If I do pitch late, I'll wanna get some treatment on my arm before we go home."

"How does it feel?"

"It feels better."

"Good. I'll sit near home plate in case you can make it out."

There is nothing more American, Chiara thought, nothing that better expresses summer, than a fireworks show at the ballpark at Arlington amidst forty-nine thousand wound-up Texas Rangers fans. Seconds after the Rangers won the game, the stadium lights shutdown like a blackout, blanketing the sold-out ballpark in darkness. When the first *boom* sounded, fans hooted and whistled and sent crazy stray catcalls into the night.

Chiara made her way down to the field and found a spot behind home plate. She sat down on the grass cross-legged just as an explosion of red, white, and blue hearts lit up the ebony sky and free fell toward the field to George Strait's new country hit song "Carrying Your Love With Me" blasting out of the stadium speakers. Rangers players and their families slowly poured onto the field while Chiara waited for Adrian. Lindsay's sons were running the bases, Hogie and Lindsay chasing after them in the dark, herding them in as if they were untamed mustangs. Alicia and Judd sat snuggling a few yards away.

Chiara looked toward the dugout for Adrian. He hadn't pitched, so she was sure he'd surface any second. She pulled a few sprigs of grass from the field and kneaded them in her fingers, taking in the different shapes and sounds of fireworks exploding and expanding against the night sky, of smoke spreading across the wide Texas sky. After about twenty minutes, Chiara realized Adrian wasn't coming out. She felt her stomach knot, her mood dip. It amazed her how alone she felt with thousands of people around her, how the only thing she had to keep her company was the potent smell of freshly mowed grass beneath her, and a wish for things to be as they used to be between her and Adrian.

When the fireworks were over, she negotiated her way through the crowd toward the clubhouse family waiting room. Her ears were ringing from the noise of fireworks and cheering fans. She told herself Adrian must have decided to have the treatment for his arm after all. But when she got there, Lindsay told her Adrian had just left. *Why did he leave without me? What is wrong with him?* she thought. Chiara thanked her, went to her car, and called him. He picked up on the first ring.

"Hey, we're on our way to get something to eat," he said.

Her body grew hot from the anger rising in her chest. "Who?"

"Me and Sanchez. Meet us at The Grill."

I'm not following you around like a puppy dog for one more second of my life, she thought. "No thanks. I think I'll just head home."

"Come on, baby."

"I said no. You're leaving for the road again tomorrow. I thought we were going home to talk tonight. I made lasagna for you this afternoon."

He sounded surprised at her tone. "Oh, okay. I'm just gonna have one beer and vent about Williams. Then I'll come home."

Chiara fell silent.

"Okay, Chiara?"

She steadied her voice, hiding the desperate neediness and suspicion in it.

"Fine." *I can see where your priorities lie.* She started her car, weaving through the bumper-to-bumper traffic that was leaving the ballpark and did what any suspicious wife would do. She drove past The Grill. When she saw Adrian's car there, parked next to Sanchez's, Chiara breathed a sigh of relief. She drove the rest of the way home yelling at herself for distrusting him.

Around two o'clock in the morning, she blew out the candles on the cocktail table, went into the kitchen, and stripped the aluminum foil off the pan of lasagna. Without bothering to slice it, she stabbed at it with a fork and forced herself to take a bite. It was good. Mamma would be proud. Then she went back to the couch, rolled herself in the green chenille throw and stared at their wedding picture on the table until she dozed off. Hours later, the sound of Adrian's jingling keys in the breezeway woke her. She walked to the front door in her nightgown. *Stay calm,* she told herself. Outside, morning was gently lifting the sun to the sky, casting creamy tones of crimson, tangerine, and gold on the apartment walls. When the door opened, Adrian sauntered in like nothing was wrong. He was inebriated.

"Hey, what's up, baby?" he said. He went to the couch and sat down, patting the cushion and inviting her to sit next to him.

She stood stock-still at the front door. Her heart banged against her rib cage like a furious jailed convict, screaming things at him she was glad he couldn't hear. It wasn't so much from anger as it was from hurt and sorrow. Sorrow for what he was doing to himself. Sorrow for what he was doing to them.

"What?" he said.

"You'll never get back into the rotation if you don't stop drinking. And, not that you care, but you're going to lose me, too, if you keep it up. I've had it, Adrian. I know I put pressure on you with—"

Adrian belched. "Here we go again—"

She narrowed her eyes at him and dug her nails deep into her palms until she felt a stab of pain in the one that was still tender. "Here we go again? Here we go again? You know what? That's it. I'm going home."

Chiara stomped toward the bedroom. "I'm going to have some peace with what's left of my summer break."

He got up and blocked her path. "Chiara, you're not going anywhere. I'm sorry; I've got a lot on my mind. A lot of stuff I'm going through. I'm constantly thinking about my position on this team."

"Well, now you can add thinking about how to resurrect our marriage to your list because I'm done trying."

"I don't have to. You're my wife and I love you. Till death do us part, you understand, *amor*?"

"I understand I'm your wife," she shot back. "I was trying my best to be a good wife. But I'm not a doormat. You can't just come and go whenever you feel like it without any consideration for me. Maybe you need to call Father Vincent and get some Cliffs Notes from the Catholic marriage class you made me take on what it means to be a good husband." He stood there staring her, shocked at her tone. "And don't you dare call me '*amor*,'" she yelled, glaring up at him, "until you're ready to be the man I married. You might want to think about that long and hard when you go on the road tomorrow."

"I got married for a reason."

"Really?" she shot back, proud of how strong her voice was. "And what reason might that be? To come and go as you please? To have a warm body to come home to when you decide to roll in, smashed? To disregard me and do whatever else you may be doing when I'm not around? Which one is it? Or is it all of the above?"

"I am not doing anything wrong, Chiara," he said.

"So, I guess you must consider not returning your wife's phone calls and coming home late and drunk acceptable behavior for a husband."

He stepped away from her and scratched his head, wobbling. "Well, not really."

"Ever since we moved here you look at me like I'm a thorn in your side."

He collapsed onto the couch. "No, *amor*," he said. "That's not true."

She looked him up one side and down the other. "You've become so full of yourself, acting like you're God's gift to Earth."

Adrian snickered and belched again. "Like you know anything about God."

She stabbed at her lower lip, shook her head at him. *You ass.* "Maybe I don't," Chiara retorted. "But you think *you* do and look at how you're behaving. You make the sign of the cross over your heart before every outing, and then you act like an egocentric monster the minute you leave the ballpark."

"Well, I'm somebody now."

"And you think that gives you the right?" She blew air from her lips, disgusted. "Just forget it. I'm done talking, done sounding like a broken record."

"Good," he said.

She charged into the bedroom and slammed the door shut behind her. Adrian jiggled the doorknob, but his reactions were slow. She'd already locked it.

"Open up!" he shouted and punched the door.

Chiara got into bed. She took his pillow in her arms and held it close, sincerely hoping he used his left hand, not his pitching hand, to punch the door.

At eight o'clock, while he snored away on the couch, she packed an especially light suitcase for his ten-day road trip, and set it in the family room before locking herself in the bedroom again. *He likes to shop,* she thought as she climbed back into bed. *Now he can shop for a week's worth of clothes.* Later, on his way out, he tapped on the bedroom door and said goodbye. She ignored him. For the first time since they'd met, she was glad he had left.

After a few days, he called. Chiara refused to answer the phone. By the fifth day, he called incessantly, leaving messages, apologizing. Chiara listened to the messages and deleted them. *There's no way he had a marital epiphany this soon.*

During that time Conner O'Grady called, too. He told her he was swamped with two other very serious cases and had to drop hers. Chiara was hardly upset. She felt more comfortable with Mr. Crosby, anyway. She thanked O'Grady for his effort and before he hung up, he recommended she change the phone numbers. From what little he had done with the case, he was sure the woman was still using a calling card when she called.

On Tuesday afternoon Chiara disconnected the apartment phone all together. Feeling hungry for the first time in weeks, and oddly in better spirits too, she got dressed in a pretty pink cotton mini dress and matching wedge sandals Lindsay had picked out for her in a shop in New York and drove to Dallas's posh Highland Park Village to have a nice Italian dinner. It was August third, Papà's birthday. She thought she'd have an espresso in his memory too. Maybe she'd top off the day by buying herself something really expensive in one of the boutiques to boot. Not that it would take much effort. Highland Park Village was a shopper's paradise with couture boutiques like Chanel, Hermès, and Ralph Lauren and could turn even a heartbroken person into a jolly shopaholic for a day.

When she got there, she parked the car and walked a short distance in the scorching heat to La Trattoria, a simple, Tuscan-style restaurant nestled behind a wrought-iron gate covered in wisteria and grapevines. It had peach-colored walls embellished with picturesque photos of Tuscany's countryside. French doors near the entrance were wide open to a cozy terrace with umbrella-covered tables and a European three-tiered fountain splashing water into its basin. As hot as it was outside, the indoor dining area was still cool. Chiara was certain the electric bill must be exorbitant.

The waitress seated Chiara. As she was about to open the menu, she noticed a dwarf-sunflower arrangement on the table. It seemed to be

staring at her, smiling as if it was happy to see her, as if it had been waiting for her all day to get there. She made a tsk sound and thought about
moving, but the other tables were set with the same type of arrangement.
She gave the flower a sidelong look and turned it to face the back of the
restaurant, telling herself this was not a sign from anybody. Telling herself that Papà had just made up the story of sunflowers being a symbol
of God guiding his flock. Telling herself that there was no way God
was working through that irritating golden ratio and persistent Fibonacci
pattern that made the sunflower turn its face towards the heavens every
day. August was simply the time of year when sunflowers were in season.
Plain and simple. Still, she couldn't explain their convenient presence
away. For a moment she allowed herself to wonder. *If there is the slightest chance He's out there somewhere in the universe, what was He telling her?
Was everyone's personal path in life supposed to be lined with suffering?*

She ordered fettuccine Alfredo. She knew it was a mistake the second she did. It came out looking and tasting like glorified macaroni and
cheese. It was terrible. After a few bites of the gooey concoction, she set
it aside. Texans prepared the best steaks in the world, but they didn't
know a thing about pasta.

By the time she got home it was dark. Adrian was calling on her cell
phone again. She hated to admit it, but she was actually getting a little
satisfaction from his distress. She smiled to herself. *He must be going to
the locker room and sneaking calls between innings.*

She set the phone down on the cocktail table next to their wedding
picture and flipped it the finger. After changing into a long sheer nightgown, she went into the family room and popped one of Beethoven's
symphonies into the CD player before going onto the veranda with a
bottle of cabernet and a wineglass.

In the dark, pouring the wine, the warm Texas night felt like the
arm of a friend over her bare shoulders. She took a sip of wine. It tasted
strong and oaky and gave her the chills in spite of the heat. She chugged
it anyway, as if it were an analgesic that could cure the suffering in her
heart. She filled the glass again and leaned over the railing, gazing up
at the moon. It was a clear night for the Metroplex area. Stars sparkled
white against the midnight blue sky. She knew little about astronomy
aside from the Big and Little Dippers. One brilliant star caught her
attention.

"Are you the pretty Lone Star of Texas?" she said, lifting her glass to the star, feeling the effects of the wine. "I know you see what's going on down here, but you're not saying a thing, are you?"

She sat down on a chair and rocked it back onto its hind legs against the outside wall of the apartment, looking out onto Highway 360. The trailer rigs passing in the distance sounded louder at this time of night. She thought of all the nights she had spent as a teenager pent up in her bedroom at Girasole studying words and phrases that teased her with their orientation on the page, looking out the window on her breaks, beseeching the heavens to bring her someone to love and find strength and faith in, because she lacked it in herself. In some skewed form, for better or for worse, her dream had come true.

When she looked up at the star again, she made another wish: *Let me find out who she is, why she wants to strip away my happiness.* Then she chastised herself for allowing Adrian's existence to have become the reason for her breathing over the past couple of years.

She thought about the tale of the water nymph, Clytie, and the god Apollo, whom Papà had told her about at one of the sunflower planting parties years ago. He had read about it in Ovid's *Metamorphoses.* She knew better than to love anyone more than herself. But it was so much easier.

When she grew tired of watching the trailer rigs pass, she went inside, fighting the urge to feel sorry for herself. The second movement of Beethoven's seventh symphony was playing. She raised the volume. *Thanks for the piano lessons that I quit, Papà.* She emptied the rest of the bottle into her glass and sank to the floor, leaning against the couch, taking in the complementary sound of brass, winds, and strings. Her cell phone rang and rang, and in her tipsy state it seemed to be an additional wind instrument in the symphony. *Sounds nice,* she thought as she drifted off into a dreamless sleep.

On Monday night, Cecilia called Chiara and told her she was upsetting Adrian by not taking his calls.

Oh well.

On Tuesday, Mamma, the marital peacemaker, left a message threatening to fly to Texas if Chiara didn't take Adrian's next call. Mamma never made empty threats, so Chiara gave up and answered her phone.

"Hey," Adrian said warmly.

"Hey."

"Boy, you sure let me know how it feels," he said. He was trying to sound funny.

Chiara didn't laugh. "I wasn't trying to make you feel anything," she said. She kept her voice even, as if she were talking to one of her professors.

"Chiara, things are gonna be different when I come home. Better, I promise."

"Uh-huh." She wanted to stay angry but knew she couldn't. His sweet and pleading voice made her believe him, and her heart ached again like the first moment she knew she love him. She wanted to say that all she wanted was a peaceful life with him, but the words were tangled in her emotions.

"I'm good now, Chiara. I haven't had a drink since I left Texas, I promise. Did your mom tell you I'm back in the starting rotation?"

"Yes," she said, barely above a whisper. "I'm happy for you."

"Be happy for us." He paused. "I'm sorry, Chiara. For everything. When I get back, everything's gonna be different. You'll see...I'm gonna make everything up to you."

Chapter 23

I t was after ten on Thursday night when Mamma called again to see how things were going between her and Adrian. Chiara was in the kitchen scrubbing a baking pan. She could tell something was bothering Mamma the second she answered the phone.

"Is he home yet?" Mamma said.

"Not yet. He called earlier and said his plane would be landing around midnight. He'll be home between one and two o'clock. I just pulled some pork chops out of the oven in case he wants to eat something when he gets home."

"How has he been, *cara?*"

"On the phone, he's been great. We'll see who comes home, though, Dr. Jekyll or Mr. Hyde."

"Give him a chance, Chiara. He's been under a lot of pressure, too."

Chiara rolled her eyes. "I know, Ma. I just hope he's not drunk. He always drinks on the plane."

"Well, if he is, don't say anything."

"Ma, please."

"I'm sorry, I'm just trying to—"

"I know, it's okay."

"Have you talked to his mother?"

"I called her today. She'd left me a message when I wasn't returning Adrian's calls."

Mamma sounded protective. "How did it go?"

"A little better. She asked me how I did on the boards and wanted to know when my classes start. I asked her if she'd like to come to Pittsburgh for Christmas, and she said yes."

"Well that's good news, *cara*."

"I think so," Chiara said. "She's thrilled Adrian is back on the starting rotation. What about you, Mamma? You sound stressed."

Mamma breathed deeply. "Sylvia and her new friend went to mass at Saint Ursula's on Sunday, and I got a call from Sister Agnes that night. She said she'd heard from a parishioner about Sylvia's romantic predilections and her new 'lady friend'. She told me it was inappropriate for them to attend mass together and that perhaps they should come separately. That was it for me. I lost my temper, Chiara."

Chiara's jaw dropped imagining what Mamma might have said to her. "You didn't—"

"Oh yes, I did. And you know what? It felt wonderful."

Chiara stopped scrubbing the pan; she was grinning from ear to ear. "What did you say to that old witch?"

"What didn't I say is more like it. I told her off for what she'd said about Sylvia. I told her how despicable it was for the parish to fire Valerie from teaching Sunday school because she was going through in vitro fertilizations, and how I feel it's never wrong to bring a child into this world, no matter how they get here. And I told her if the Church can't keep up with the times, I'll find another church."

"Way to go, Mamma!" Chiara cheered into the phone.

There was a pause on the other end of the line, then Mamma said, "I also told her how Papà and I forgave the parish after Father Bob did what he did, even though his transgression clearly violated one of the Ten Commandments. I told her how we struggled to help you work through your emotional scars while remaining good Catholics, and that after all that, the parish was turning its back on my family by the way it was treating Valerie and Sylvia. The way it treated you. I told her I would never step foot in that parish again. Then I hung up."

"Wow. It must've been hard for you, Ma."

"Surprisingly, it wasn't. The Catholic Church doesn't have the final say in my family's happiness."

"So, now what?"

"I'm going to find another church, one that's more accepting."

"Good for you."

Mamma sighed. "I feel good about what I did, Chiara. I think Papà would've been proud of me. I miss him so much, you have no idea."

"I know he would've been proud, Mamma."

Later, after she'd finished reading her old developmental class notes for the night, Chiara lay in bed staring out the window, waiting for Adrian to come home. It was cloudless and windy outside. The moonlight entered the bedroom unabashed, casting its glow on the walls. The dark shadow of a maple tree swayed back and forth on the wall transforming the flat surface into a three-dimensional passage to another world. As Chiara stared at the gray blowing tree on the wall she thought that it looked like an attainable place, that if she cared to, she could step inside, into another world. Maybe that place was different, maybe suffering, regret, and guilt didn't exist there, only joy. She thought how lonely Mamma must be at this very moment after having shared her bed with Papà for thirty years. She thought of the challenges Valerie faced with her infertility, the challenges Sylvia faced with her sexuality. Princess Diana had just died in a car accident, and Chiara thought of the two young sons she had suddenly left behind. She wondered if there was an afterlife. Was it a happy place where troubles were nonexistent? Then, gradually, she nodded off to sleep.

She woke to Adrian sliding naked into the sheets behind her. It was two o'clock in the morning. He was sober.

"Hey, baby," he whispered as he scooped her into his arms.

"Hi," Chiara said softly, only half awake.

"I missed you."

He turned her to him, entwined himself around her, kissing her lips, her shoulders, her neck, her cheeks. Chiara felt the armor around her heart melting.

"I got you something," he whispered in her ear. There was a tender excitement in his voice.

She opened her eyes. His face was close to hers and his teeth glistened white in the amber light. She smiled. "What is it?" she whispered

He sat up and wrapped a bracelet around her wrist.

"It's a diamond tennis bracelet, six carats."

She held her hand toward the window to admire it and get a better look. "Oh, Adrian, it's beautiful. It must've cost a fortune. What's the occasion?"

"It's because I love you," he whispered and kissed her lips.

Tears welled in her eyes. She kissed his lips tenderly, stroked his five o'clock shadow with her face. "Thank you, but you didn't have to buy me anything." She was quiet for a moment.

"What Chiara? What is it?"

She stared at the bracelet for a minute before she answered. "All I want is for things to be like they were before we moved here."

Adrian secured the clasp. The diamonds reflected the moonlight and danced on the walls around the bedroom.

"Me too, Chiara," he said softly. "And they're gonna be. We're always gonna be together."

He cupped her chin in his large hand. "Look at me, *amor*."

She couldn't. She felt too vulnerable.

"I said look at me," he told her.

Reluctantly, she met his gaze and noticed that his hair was solid brown again.

"Chiara, I know I've been an asshole," he said. He wiped away the tears that were streaming out of her eyes. "And I'm sorry, for everything. I'm gonna be better to you because you deserve the best. You've been good to me. We're gonna find out who this bitch is who's been trying to break us up, okay?"

Chiara nodded and drew herself closer to him, feeling as if her heart might explode from wanting him. "Adrian, I—"

"Shhh..." He kissed her forehead. "It's okay. I can't believe I acted the way I did. You not talking to me made me realize how much you mean to me." He lifted her face to his. "Look at me," he said again.

Chiara raised her head and looked at him.

He kissed her lips, and she savored their fullness. "Before then, you were always there, and all I could think about was my career, my popularity, about how you're my wife and you're always gonna be there for me, about how this was my time to shine with my boys, and about finally being somebody."

"I've told you so many times how important you are to me, Adrian—"

"I know that, Chiara, but for a while there, for some reason, it wasn't enough. When you come from nothing, struggling for years in the minor leagues, making a couple of hundred bucks every couple of weeks and sending most of it home to your family, you get bitter. Then you finally start making some cash and you feel like you got your head above water. Next thing you know, *bang!*" He punched the air. "You get a big contract and you're making bank and you feel like you're on top of the world. Everybody all of a sudden knows you, and the people who don't, want to. Everybody wants to be your friend and you got the money to do anything and go anywhere you want." He was starting to get excited, but he caught himself. "Well, it's no excuse, but I let it get to me."

"My parents used to tell me stories about how they struggled—"

Adrian shook his head. "Chiara, they were just stories to you. You never lived it. You were too little to know what was going on. You never had to feed anyone."

Chiara lowered her head. "I know, you're right."

"Your dad busted his ass so his kids didn't have to, so you could concentrate on school. I could never concentrate on school." He sounded frustrated. "I had to think about helping my mom pay the rent starting when I was, like, thirteen." He ran his hands through his hair. For a moment he seemed to be recalling something from his childhood. Then his voice softened again. "Look, all I'm trying to say is that I fucked up and—"

"Oh, Adrian," she said. She clutched his face with her hands, kissed his mouth, his eyes, chin, like he was water quenching her ravenous thirst. "I love you for who you are, where you've been, and where we're going, together."

"I love you too, Chiara, and I'm never going to hurt you again, okay? We're gonna go home next month, and hopefully over the off-season I'll get traded to a National League team so we never have to come back to this city again. I hate it here."

She hardly believed she was looking at the man she'd married last year. Everything about him was as it had been before the start of the season, the way he was looking at her, talking to her, holding her. It was almost as if some evil spell had been lifted from her handsome prince and he finally recognized himself and her again. His expression was so soft and warm—so Adrian. *Valerie was right. If I hung in there, things would work themselves out.*

The next few weeks were a blur. When Adrian wasn't on the field, they were together, on the road, in Texas, having fun. They shopped for furniture for the new house, made love, ate out, ate in, made love, went to dance clubs, made love, and watched movies. Mamma was still receiving crank calls at Girasole, but Chiara never said a word about it to Adrian. She wanted him to concentrate on getting as many wins as he could before the end of the season and she wanted to squeeze in as much time as she could have with Adrian before her classes resumed.

On the last, and hottest, day of August, Chiara and Adrian got up early, threw on shorts and T-shirts, and started packing the belongings that Adrian could do without for the next month. The plan was for movers to ship the contents of the apartment to Pittsburgh the day before he left for his last road trip two weeks from now. Adrian could then go straight home to Pittsburgh after the final game of the season without having to go back to Texas to pack up the apartment alone.

"I can't believe all the stuff we've collected over the past few months," Chiara said, taping a box shut. She pointed at a large one he was about to close. "What's in there?"

Adrian had been dropping things into it all summer when he got home from the ballpark. He looked inside. "Baseballs, baseball cards, a baseball bat, baseball gloves, baseball cleats, and a promotional bobble head of me." He picked up the bobble head and shook it. Its head bobbed up and down and all around. He laughed. "It looks just like me."

Chiara walked into his arms and held him tight. "You're better looking."

He kissed her and dropped the bobble head into the box. "Did you schedule for the cars and Amadeus to get shipped back yet?"

"It's all done," she said.

He looked around. "What's next?"

Chiara frowned, reluctant to remind him. "Me. Classes start the day after tomorrow."

"*Amor*, it's only for a few weeks. Then I'll be home until spring training.

Chiara forced a smiled. "I know. I think I'm just a little nervous about the start of classes."

"Don't be. It's your chance to prove to them you deserve to be there."
She hoped with all her heart she would be able to.

Chiara had heard from students ahead of her that the third year of
medical school was a pivotal point in training. After only four weeks
in, she could see why. It was in the third year that students develop the
professional skills and attitudes toward patients. Chiara already had a
stack of index cards, one for each patient she had been assigned in the
last week. Li was referring to her patients by their diseases. It troubled
Chiara. She thought it was dehumanizing, demeaning to the patients.
Even though she would be flying through seven clerkships in under
a year, she vowed to make time for each patient and never allow her
empathy or bedside manner to deteriorate. So on Sunday, even though
she had seen all of her patients at the hospital and was done for the day,
even though Adrian was scheduled to pitch his last game of the year in
an hour in Cleveland, Chiara dropped her car keys into the pocket of
her white coat and went back to Mr. Matthews's room. He was usually
grumpy and loud, and when she'd checked in on him earlier, he was
quiet. It didn't sit well with her.

She knocked on his door and walked in, "Hello, Mr. Matthews."

"You again. Now what do you want?"

He seems to be feeling more like himself again, she thought. "I just
thought I'd drop in and say hi before I go home for the day."

He gave her a surprised look, as if he didn't know what to say.

"May I sit down?"

He nodded, crossed his arms over his round belly to show he didn't
care one way or the other.

Chiara looked up at the TV. "What are you watching?"

"Judge Judy. Damn kids have no respect for their elders. Glad I
never had any."

"Any pets?" Chiara could tell she hit a soft spot.

His expression softened. "My old dog died last night, while I was
stuck in this joint."

Chiara leaned forward in her chair. "Oh Mr. Matthews, I'm so sorry. Losing your pet is one of the worst feelings. I lost two of my dogs
within a year. It makes you never want to own another one so you don't
have to go through the pain of losing it. What breed was he?"

Mr. Matthews looked down at his nightgown, white as his hair. "He was a shepherd mix, hips as bad as mine."

"They're one of the smartest breeds out there. I have a friend who has one. Poodles are supposed to be super-smart too, but I've never been around one."

He shook his head. "He used to get the paper for me on the curb every morning. Even when it hurt to get up."

"It's because he loved you."

He looked out the window, and Chiara could tell he was fighting the urge to cry. She quickly changed the subject. "Hey, do you like baseball?"

"You're not a good American if you don't."

"My husband is pitching for the Rangers against the Indians in about an hour on channel twenty-two. I'll miss a few innings driving home." She grabbed a piece of paper and pen from his food tray and jotted down her cell phone number. "Will you call me and tell me how he's doing after the third inning?"

Mr. Matthews seemed to like being given a task, because he perked up instantly. "Sure, I'll do that for you."

"Thank you. I appreciate it so much." Chiara got up and adjusted his pillow. "Now, no sneaking any candy tonight. Your sugar levels were great today. I'll see you tomorrow."

When she left his room, Dr. Roland, a tall, lanky, senior professor with keen blue eyes was waiting outside in the hall.

"Hi, Dr. Roland," she said, standing a little taller, trying to look professional.

"Hello, Chiara. I see you stayed behind again today."

They started toward the elevators. "Mr. Matthews didn't seem himself this morning. I thought I'd check in on him and sit with him for a few minutes."

"I've noticed you've done this often with your patients."

Chiara's eyes widened. "I didn't think to ask, sir. I hope that it's all right."

He held up his hand as if to say don't worry. "No, it's fine, Chiara." He smiled. "A few patients in your clinical rotation have commented how personable you are and what a fine doctor you'll make some day. I've been watching you since you came back. Keep up the good work."

Chiara looked down at the floor. "Thank you, Dr. Roland."

Chiara got back to Girasole at the bottom of the fourth inning. Mamma and Valerie were on the sofa, their eyes taped to the TV. Liam and a few of his friends had driven to Cleveland to watch the game and drive Adrian back to Pittsburgh. Chiara didn't even consider going. The weight of being on academic probation hung over her like a winter coat in August. She sat down between Mamma and Valerie and when Chiara's cell phone rang, the three of them looked at each other as she pulled it out of her backpack and answered it.

"Hello?"

"Hi, *amor*," Adrian said.

Chiara smiled at Mamma and Valerie. "What are you doing, honey? You're about to pitch the fifth inning."

"I ran to the clubhouse for a minute," he said. "I wanted to hear your voice."

Chiara smiled. "I'm glad you called. Guess which one of your favorite Italian dishes Mamma's making for you tonight."

Adrian paused. "Gnocchi?"

"Yep. You think you guys will be back by eight?"

"If the game lets out at, like, four thirty, and Liam helps me with my stuff, I think it won't be no problem."

Chiara sensed a certain something in his voice. Was it nerves?

"Are you all right, hubby?"

"I'm cool," he said.

Chiara was skeptical. "Don't be nervous, okay? You said you wanted to finish the season with eleven wins. You did that."

Adrian sighed. "I know."

"Good. So go out there and kick some ass."

Adrian laughed. "Okay."

"Did you see Liam yet?"

"Yeah, I had breakfast with him and his buddy, Aidan, before I came to the ballpark. I gave him a suitcase to put in the car." He cleared his throat. "Strike three. I gotta go, baby."

"Okay, I'll see you around eight," she said, feeling her heart flutter and remind her she hadn't seen him in weeks.

"Chiara," he said.

"Yeah?"

There was a long pause. "I love you more than anything in the world."

Chiara felt her heart swell. She could almost smell Adrian's sweet cologne. "I love you too, Adrian, and I can hardly wait to see you."

The Rangers lost the game, three to two.

"He got a no decision," Valerie said. "Do you think he'll be disappointed?"

Chiara followed her and Mamma into the kitchen. "I don't think so. He gave up two runs in seven innings. That's a good outing." She reached into the refrigerator for a Coke. "Besides, he got his eleventh win in Toronto. He told me as long as he finished the season with eleven wins he'd be satisfied. Not thrilled, but satisfied."

Mamma wrapped an apron around her khaki cotton dress and grabbed a bag of flour and a large mixing bowl from the pantry. "Well, *figlie*, I guess we can start the gnocchi," she said.

"You guys have no idea how relieved I am the season's over," Chiara said as she cracked the tab open.

"Oh, yes we do," Mamma said.

Chiara and Valerie gathered around the kitchen island and watched Mamma add the ingredients for the gnocchi to a large bowl and mix the concoction by hand, not bothering to take off the wedding band she still wore. Chiara and Valerie instinctively pulled their hair back—Chiara into a ponytail, Valerie into a chignon like Mamma—and waited for their cue to help.

Valerie peered at the growing ball of dough in the bowl. "It looks like a lot. There are only ten of us tonight, not the US Army."

"I'll freeze the rest," Mamma said. "Adrian and Liam love gnocchi."

Mamma mixed the ingredients until the dough was firm and soft, but not sticky. Then she sprinkled the counter with flour and plopped the dough onto it. She sliced it into smaller sections which she rolled into thin baguettes and cut into one inch cubes. When she was far enough ahead, she nodded to Valerie and Chiara. They began rolling the cubes one by one between their thumb and forefingers until each resembled the fat dimple on a cherub's chin.

When Sylvia walked in, Mamma smiled and motioned for her to roll, too. Now they were all rolling. They placed each dumpling, one by one, on a white cotton tablecloth on the far side of the island. When

Liam and Adrian arrived, Mamma would cook them in boiling water and then mix them in a basil-infused marinara sauce, topping them off with a few handfuls of Pecorino Romano cheese. *Yum.*

Every so often Sylvia stopped rolling. "They're always mushy, even when they're cooked," she said. "How do you guys know when you're supposed to take them out of the water?"

Valerie shook her head, looked up at Mamma's sunflower-bordered wall. "This must be the thousandth time we've made gnocchi, at home, at the restaurants. Pray tell, how can you not know the answer to that question?"

Things had been going well between Sylvia and Mamma, and Chiara frowned at Valerie inconspicuously—the last thing they needed was for anyone to cause any sort of tension between Mamma and Sylvia. "They float to the top, Sylvia," she said with a cool, casual tone.

Sylvia tore a piece of bread from a homemade loaf and dipped it into a pot of tomato sauce that had been simmering on the stove since morning. She blew on the bread to cool it off and took a bite. "Wow, that's good."

It was after eleven o'clock when Chiara saw headlights brush across the foyer walls and ceiling from the family room. Liam's car pulled up to the porte cochere at Girasole. He was alone. Nobody had touched the gnocchi. Sitting on the couch, she felt numb with confusion and didn't get up; she just sat there in her jeans and T-shirt, petting Jadey and Sasha lying at her feet.

When Liam walked into the room he looked half frightened, half livid. "Did he call?"

Mamma paced the family room. "No. Something must've happened to him. He wouldn't just disappear."

Chiara doubted that. Adrian was as unpredictable as a hurricane and back to the way he was before. She fixed her eyes on the Karistan rug, studying the design as if it were a textbook that could explain the intricacies of male psychology. "I don't understand," she said. "Everything was fine."

"Chiara," Liam said gently. "We waited for hours, called security, the police. Nobody saw him after he left the clubhouse. The ballpark was deserted by the time we left. There wasn't a soul around."

"What the hell's wrong with him?" Valerie hissed. "Does he have schizophrenia or something?"

"Did you call his mother again?" Liam asked.

"I'll do it," Sylvia said. "Bottom line is, she's not going to answer. Hasn't all night."

"Don't bother," Valerie said. "After all, even if she answers, do you really think she'll tell us anything?"

Chiara went into the kitchen and came back with her wallet. She pulled her credit card from it and motioned for the phone.

"What are you doing?" Sylvia said, handing her the phone.

Everyone was looking at Chiara. She didn't look at them, afraid she'd break down. "Calling our credit card company to see if there are any recent transactions on it."

She listened as the account representative told her that two had just been posted to the account. One was a cash withdrawal of three hundred dollars at six o'clock at the Cleveland International Airport. The other was a charge at a local restaurant in Dallas, around nine.

Chiara slowly sat down with the help of the sofa arm, feeling as if she had been eviscerated; her heart gnawed by scavengers.

Mamma rushed to her side. "*Cara*, what's wrong?"

"What is it, Chiara?" Sylvia said.

Chiara looked at her wedding picture on the mantel, blurry through watering eyes. "He left me."

Chapter 24

When life went awry, Chiara and her family found comfort in different things. Mamma immersed herself in work at Gian Carlo's and prayed. Valerie read mystery novels. Sylvia ran. For Chiara, it was always the horses.

When she wasn't at Presbyterian Hospital on her geriatric clerkship, she spent the days following Adrian's unexplained disappearance at the stable, working and riding.

On Saturday, Mr. Crosby came to Girasole to give her news about the investigation. He found her in the outdoor arena schooling Amadeus.

"That looks like a lot of fun," he called out. "Is it?"

Chiara trotted over to him. "Hi, Mr. Crosby, you're early."

He looked at his watch. "No, no, I'm right on time."

She looked at her watch and winced. "I'm sorry, I lost track of time." She hopped off Amadeus, took off her riding gloves, and shook his hand. "Did you find out who she is?"

He nodded, looking disappointed to be the bearer of bad news. "I did."

They started toward the stable, avoiding puddles in the gravel from an autumn rainstorm that had swept through the area earlier in the day.

Mr. Crosby stroked Amadeus. "They're such beautiful creatures. Sometimes I think I like animals better than people."

"I know what you mean. You're about to give me pretty bad news, aren't you?" Chiara asked.

He nodded.

"It's okay, Mr. Crosby, I can handle it. I need to know the truth."

He patted Amadeus again, took a deep breath and let it out. "Her name is Nina Encarnación."

Chiara repeated the name under her breath. "Why does that name sound so familiar?"

"She is—well, was—, one of five babysitters who watched the ballplayers' children in the ballpark's family center. She has an infant daughter." He paused, giving her a look of regret. "Adrian's child."

Chiara stopped dead in her tracks. She stared at him blankly, recalling the girl in the clubhouse who had been rocking her child in the bassinet. Her mouth grew dry and sticky and her stomach sank into her riding boots. *Her? A teenager has been tormenting me all this time?* Chiara's lips trembled a little. "I saw them once," she croaked. "That baby girl is his?"

He nodded. "I tracked Adrian down in Florida." There was a tone of sympathy in his voice. "He's living with his mother. I had a talk with him."

She swallowed hard, holding back tears. Waiting.

Mr. Crosby looked bashful for a moment. "I asked him how the relationship began and he told me he first slept with her when he was traded to the Rangers. He said he met her one night when he was out having drinks with his new teammates. He said it was a mistake, that he had had too much to drink, that it was supposed to end that night. But it didn't and soon she got pregnant."

Chiara looked at him incredulously, pressed her free hand against her stomach. "Why did he let her call me and torment me for so long? Why did he go along with it when I decided to go to the MLB for an investigator?"

Mr. Crosby rubbed his forehead and sighed. "I asked him that, too, dear. He said he couldn't stop her from calling. He said she fell for him and she wanted him to leave you. When he said he wasn't leaving you, that he loved you, she told him she would call until she drove you mad, if that's what it took to break you two apart."

"Why didn't she just tell me who she was?"

"Because he threatened never to see her again if she did. He said he went along with hiring an investigator because he didn't want you to get suspicious. He knew you'd leave him if you found out the truth."

"I hadn't found out anything, so why did he leave me?"

"He had every intention of coming home on the last day of the season until she showed up at the ballpark."

"In Cleveland?"

He nodded. "Adrian said she threatened to tell your brother-in-law who she was if he went back to Pittsburgh. Adrian flew back to Texas, knowing his number was up, finally convinced that you were going to find out the truth."

Chiara shook her head, shocked. "That girl is street-savvy beyond her years."

"She definitely knew what she wanted," he agreed.

"Did his mother have anything to say?"

"Just that you thought she was behind it all."

"I did. Did she know what was going on?"

"Adrian told her toward the end of August, but made her swear to secrecy." She said she didn't return your family's phone calls because she didn't know what to say."

At the stable's entrance, Chiara called for one of the boarders and asked her to take Amadeus.

"I can't believe he kept the lie going for a whole year." There was a tone of regret in her voice. "Why did he marry me? There was no need."

Mr. Crosby crossed his hands behind his back and looked down at the ground. "That, my dear, I do not know. He did say he filed for divorce as a resident of Florida, so you might have to travel for the proceedings."

Chiara shook her head. *How on earth am I going to be able to do that?*

That night, after she'd studied until her head felt like it couldn't possibly absorb one more piece of information and her fingers stung from paper cuts she'd acquired flipping through note cards all evening, Chiara went and sat in the family room with Mamma and her sisters.

Sylvia got up to light a fire reluctant to disturb Sasha and Jadey laying like bear rugs at Valerie's feet.

"Did you get much done?" Valerie asked Chiara.

"Very little," Chiara admitted.

Sylvia poked at the logs and blew into the fire. "I can't believe Cecilia didn't have anything to do with it."

Mamma looked up from her cooking magazine and took off the reading glasses she was wearing lately. "No, but she certainly didn't help things between the two of you, either."

Chiara got up from the couch and went to the heavy mantel, taking in the smell of burning embers. She looked at the photograph of her and Adrian dancing at their wedding, so happy. *He had already slept with her.* She took off her wedding ring and placed it on the mantel, too. When she reached for the photo, her hand shook as if it was saying, *Don't you dare make me touch that picture.* When she grasped it, she wanted to hurl it across the room as hard as she could, to shatter it and every memory she had of Adrian into a million pieces. But she didn't; instead, she slowly placed it face down and leaned her head against the mantel.

"I am such an idiot," she said.

Valerie gave her a quizzical stare. "Chiara, why would you say that?"

"Because Papà was right. He wasn't for me. If I had waited to get married until I graduated, like you did—" She turned and looked at Valerie. "—I would probably have figured that out along the way and I wouldn't be going through this crap right now."

Valerie gave her a sympathetic smile.

"During that time I would've learned Adrian's weaknesses."

Valerie got up and gave her a long hug. "Oh Chiara, Papà wasn't right about everything. If you remember, he said you'd never finish medical school if you married Adrian. In spite of everything, you're in your third year, trooper. He'd be so proud of you."

"Damn right he would be," Sylvia said.

"Mamma," Chiara said, "I know how you feel about divorce, but I'm getting one. And I'm selling the house. I'll live here until I'm done with med school."

Mamma gave her an approving nod. "That's the best news I've heard all day, *cara.* If Adrian doesn't know what gems I raised you and your sisters to be, then that *figlio di putana* doesn't deserve you. He can go on sleeping with *that* kind of girl for the rest of his life for all I care."

Sylvia smiled. "Thanks, Ma."

Chiara sat back down on the couch with her sisters. "I am going to need to get rid of anything that reminds me of him."

Mamma shot out of her seat and started scanning the bookshelves to the left of the fireplace, searching for pictures of Adrian or trinkets that he had bought for Chiara. Sylvia took her cue and hastened to the shelves to the right.

Chiara followed them with her eyes, amused at their look of urgency to help her with the matter. She laughed in spite of feeling miserable. "Guys, I didn't mean right this second, just at some point."

The next evening, after an exhausting sixteen-hour day at the hospital, Chiara walked into the foyer at Girasole to find a gigantic mound of Adrian's things at the foot of the staircase. She dropped her backpack and stared at the pile, feeling the agonizing heartache of lost love. *My family,* she thought. *Always trying to help.* Mamma and Sylvia must have spent the entire day scouring the house, looking for things that might tug at Chiara's heart. Her family's thoughtfulness never ceased to amaze her, and she appreciated it now.

Determined to facilitate the transition to a life as a soon-to-be-divorcée, she took off her white coat and hung it on the newel post, marched to the stable, grabbed a wheelbarrow and some lighter fluid, and rolled it back into the foyer, creating thick mud tracks along the marble floor. She began loading it with the pile, tossing the suitcase Adrian had given Liam into the barrow first.

Bibi must've heard the commotion because she came walking into the foyer. Her eyes widened when she saw the fat mud tracks on the polished marble floor. "What are you doing, Chiara?"

"Cleaning up."

Bibi gave her a crazed look. "It does not look like you are cleaning up."

"I'll be back."

Chiara rolled the wheelbarrow to a shallow fire pit on the west side of the property. She and Sylvia had made it years ago with some Belgium block left over from the construction of Girasole. She tipped the wheelbarrow forward, spilling everything into the pit. She stared at the contents of the pile for a long time: posters of Adrian when he was a Pittsburgh Pirate, baseballs he'd signed for her family, pictures of their engagement party, his bobble head, stuffed animals he'd won for her at Kennywood Park, and a plethora of other things. There was a part of her that wanted to go and pull everything out of the pit, place everything one by one carefully back in the house, as if each object were a wounded bird that needed a safe place of refuge. Then, maybe someday when her grandchildren came to her suffering from a terrible break-up, she could ease their pain by showing them her mementos. "You see, sweetie," she'd say showing them a picture, "I was once young and loved somebody with all my heart, too. But sometimes things just aren't meant to be, and we have to move on or be sad forever."

And *moving on* was exactly why she had to burn everything.

But first she grabbed one of Adrian's favorite Louisville Slugger bats from the pile and used it to smash and beat every single thing she'd unloaded into the pit until she was out of breath. Then, panting, she poured the lighter fluid over the pile and lit a match to it. The fire ignited with a *pouf.* Chiara watched the flames rise and the pictures melt and become part of the blaze. When the fire was high, she tossed the bat into the inferno. *You don't really need it, AMOR,* she thought. *You're a terrible batter no matter what bat you use.*

When the fire was raging, scorching her face, she took her wedding band out of her pocket, looked at it one last time, and tossed it into the fire too. She understood why pyromaniacs couldn't stop setting things on fire.

It felt so good.

Over the next few days, Mamma and Sylvia kept watch over her like protective mother bears. Valerie stopped by every day, too. Chiara was sure they were expecting her rage to erupt again with the strength of Mount Vesuvius, blasting her red-hot fury into the atmosphere, or waiting for her to fall from the sky like Icarus in her suffering. But there was something settling and oddly calming in knowing the truth—even if her calmness was tinged with heartache. She would never have to wonder where Adrian was again, never have to be nervous about answering the phone, and never have to feel that gnawing suspicion churning in her stomach as she lay in bed next to her husband.

The truth will set you free. Whoever it was in the Bible who had coined the phrase, she thought, had probably been lied to a lot, too.

On Halloween morning, excited to have a day off from the hospital, Chiara got up early. She planned to study for a while, because it was taking her twice as long to retain anything since Adrian had left. But when she cracked open her bedroom window, a warm Indian-summer breeze drifted into the room. It tugged at the scrubs she had fallen asleep in, wooing her like a childhood friend to go outside and play. She looked out toward the gazebo and riding arena. The leaves on the red sunset maple trees surrounding the arena were so vivid they looked as if they were on fire, and the crape myrtle, cherry, and pink dogwood trees in the garden below were exploding with shades of scarlet, sienna, and gold among the Roman concrete statues. It looked like the perfect place a fairy might want to frolic. Chiara gave in to her temptation, deciding to take Hemingway for a hack in the woods before beginning her studies for the day.

These are the days I live for, she thought. She pulled on a black rugby shirt with *ITALIA* embroidered on the back in alternating colors of green, white, and red and a pair of black riding breeches. Taking two steps at a time, she jogged down the staircase.

"Good morning," she said as she passed Mamma and Sylvia arguing about something in the foyer. Even though Sylvia towered over Mamma, her expression told Chiara she was losing the battle. They seemed to be at a loss for words when they saw her looking so cheerful.

Chiara swiped a banana from the fruit bowl on the kitchen table and skipped down the terrace steps toward the stable, cutting through the garden, slowing for a moment to say good morning to a bust of Julius Caesar Papà had tucked behind a bed of azaleas long ago.

When she got to the stable, Julio was grooming Amadeus. "Morning, Julio," she said.

"Good morning," he said.

"Is Hemi in or out?"

"Out. Pasture two."

"I was going to take him for a hack if we're not going to work him today."

"Take him. He worked all week."

Chiara walked to the pasture gate and whistled. Hemi came galloping toward her at full speed as if she were an enormous carrot. "Whoa!" she yelled as he got closer, afraid he might jump over the gate to get to her. He'd done it before.

She opened the gate and led him to the stable, talking to him and patting him the whole way. "How are you, buddy? You want to go on a hack, huh? Would you like that?"

Hemingway trotted full of exuberance at her side. Chiara had to walk extra fast to keep him there. He snorted, spraying her with a mixture of dirt, grass, and warm mucus.

"Yuck! Thanks a lot, big guy." She wiped her face with her shirt and led him into the stable. The clomping sound of Hemingway's steel shoes hitting the brick floors as she led him to his stall felt comforting to Chiara and she laughed at him, feeling better than she had in months. Julio must've noticed because he laughed too.

Chiara collected her grooming box and Hemingway's tack from the tack room and placed them near his stall. She stepped into his stall and began brushing him while he drank out of his water bucket. On the radio, two morning DJs were discussing last night's World Series game, a win by the Florida Marlins over the Cleveland Indians. "Good thing the Rangers didn't make it to the series," one of them said, "Peruviso might've decided to just take off without telling anybody when it was his turn to pitch." They both laughed.

The story of how Adrian had left her was all over the papers in Texas, according to Lindsay and Alicia. Apparently the news had spread east, too.

Chiara and Julio exchanged glances as she brushed Hemingway's forelock and mane. She shrugged like she didn't care. But it would be a long time before she could watch baseball again. She was humiliated.

"Lesson with Amadeus when you get back?" he asked.

She tightened Hemingway's girth and he pinned his ears in disapproval.

"Yes, and be very tough on me. I want to go the regional finals with him next year."

Outside the stable doors, she mounted Hemingway and rode into the woods. The thicket had grown dense over the summer. Hemingway carved a new path with every stride he took, trampling branches like a bulldozer, crushing everything that got in his way.

They went deeper into what seemed untrodden territory, and Chiara made a mental note to come out over the weekend with the tractor to clear the path. Alone in the quiet woods, the sounds of swooshing leaves and dead branches cracking under Hemingway's feet sounded like burning kindling. She breathed in the smells of autumn, stroking Hemingway's neck from poll to wither. It felt good to know there was nobody there to analyze her every action, to look for signs that she might retreat into her own deep dark place.

When they reached her favorite part of the woods, she looked up into a canopy of trees that were playing hide and seek with the sun. "I love it out here!" she called out.

Hemingway spooked at her sudden outburst and trotted off a few steps, letting out a powerful snort.

She smiled and patted him on the neck. "I'm sorry, Hemi."

She turned onto a path she had taken after a bad fight with Papà over Adrian shortly before he died.

It had been a day much like this, calm and sluggish, with a warm breeze whipping up every now and then, swirling fallen leaves up into funnel shapes, sweeping them across the ground and settling them in a different spot on the forest bed. She could hardly wait to get out of the house and away from Papà that day.

He is not for you, she heard Papà's words echo through the trees.

At the memory, all Chiara's newfound serenity drained away like oil through a funnel. Disappointment and regret opened their greedy mouths and swallowed her whole again.

The reservoir of tears she had been holding back spilled from her eyes and flowed over her face like a broken dam. She halted Hemingway and dropped the reins, surrendering to her broken heart, her broken pride.

"I can't," she cried, leaning over and burying her face in Hemi's mane. "I can't do this. I can't handle medical school *and* travel back and forth from Florida for divorce proceedings. I can't be away that long. I'm on fricking academic probation. I'll never make it through. Never."

She cried there for a long time, acknowledging that her life pursuit to become a doctor was up, her dream gone. She'd call the office of the dean of student affairs when she returned from her ride. When she finally stopped crying, her head felt waterlogged, and she promised herself that was the last time. No more tears over Adrian. She picked up the reins and trotted off, wishing she could bury her sadness in the very spot where she had just unleashed it minutes ago. Then she could avoid ever riding past it again. *Maybe I could post a sign: "No riding beyond this point, misery spot ahead."*

Hemingway moved off fast and sure through the woods, his hooves covering the ground with strong elevated steps, crunching dry leaves beneath him, one diagonal pair of legs hitting the ground, then yielding to the other pair through a moment of suspension. His eyes and ears flicked back and forth, focusing attentively on Chiara and the woods. Chiara loved feeling his power beneath her.

She directed him toward the part of the property where the whimsical bust of Pan reposed beneath a domed temple. She liked passing it when she rode in the woods. There was a pond nearby where she always let the horses drink. As they approached, Hemingway's ears pricked forward toward something in the distance. In an instant his body grew tense and she sensed his reservation.

"Relax, Hemi," she said. "It's only Pan. We've been through here a thousand times."

She squeezed her legs against his sides, urging him forward, but he tossed his head in objection, refusing to go any farther.

She gave him a quick kick. "Trot on, Hemi…"

He softened to the reins and trotted a few feet before slowing until he was trotting in place, snorting guttural warning signs to something in the distance.

Chiara looked around but only saw Pan. She squeezed his sides. "Come on, Hemi, it's all right, trot on."

His nostrils flared, and he snorted again like a boar, a warning once again for whatever he saw in the distance to stay back. Chiara knew then something was truly scaring him.

Chiara patted him on the neck, trying to comfort him. She looked around, balancing herself in the saddle as Hemingway pranced in place underneath her. *What does he see?* She was about to urge him forward again when a man appeared like a ghost from behind a coppice of trees sixty yards away. He was pointing a rifle at a deer in their direction, but didn't see them.

"Don't shoot!" Chiara screamed, just as he pulled the trigger.

The bullet left the rifle with a thunderous *crack*. Hemingway turned and bolted in the opposite direction.

"Whoa boy! Whoa!" Chiara yelled.

Hemingway galloped, terrified, at full speed, dodging trees, fleeing from the danger. Chiara ducked to avoid low-hanging branches and pulled hard on the reins, trying to slow him down. Finally, he broke into a trot. But just as the woods gave way to the hay field there was another shot.

Hemingway bolted again and tripped. Chiara flew from the saddle, landing in the field on her back, striking her head hard against the ground. For a moment, her head throbbed and the base of her back felt as if it had been struck with a sledgehammer. Steadily though, everything around her grew blurry and shadowy, and the pain, bit by bit, subsided. The better she felt, the more the field around her came back into focus. When the pain was totally gone, she felt relieved. But something told her this wasn't normal. She could be paralyzed. She told herself to remain calm and still so she could assess her situation. But the colors in the field had all of a sudden grown more vibrant than she could've ever imagined, even for autumn. She was overwhelmed with the brilliant shade of golden yellow the hayfield had suddenly turned and she sat up and ran her hands over what was left of Julio's final cut. It felt like velvet. She got up, carefully, and looked wide-eyed toward the woods. Every part of each tree that lined its entrance was sprinkled with tiny specks of light sparkling with life and joy, tickled to see her, as if they'd been waiting centuries for her to arrive. They made her feel loved just the way she was. That she was a perfect being, just the way she was. It warmed her heart, made her feel special. She thought, *This is unbelievable.* She gave into her intrigue and smiled at them.

She looked down at her feet again to get a better look at the golden hay and noticed, just to the left of her, her body lying supine and still. Her riding helmet was cracked in half. She realized what had happened, but why didn't she feel...dead? Hemingway was a few feet away. He had stepped on his reins and broken them, and he had a

small cut on his front leg, but otherwise he seemed fine. She heard him
tearing hay out of the ground and chewing it. She heard the sounds of
motor vehicles approaching too. Chris was driving at full speed ahead
on his ATV from one direction, Julio in a jeep from another, panic in
their eyes. She saw, felt, heard, and understood everything happening around her. It defied every intellectual aspect she'd studied and
believed to be true about the human body and death. It was humbling
and thrilling at the same time. Oddly, she felt no desire to go back to
her body.

What a year I'm having, she thought.

She heard someone call her name. She turned toward the sound of
the voice, squinting at the brightness of the sun. She was surprised to
see a large, dark-haired man dressed in a toga—and with muscles as
chiseled as the statue of David—standing in front of her, smiling. He
was beautiful.

"Hi," she said when she could manage to speak.

"Hello," he said.

His voice was strong and sure, his face exquisite and stoic, like a
work of art. Chiara didn't know whether to walk toward him or run in
the opposite direction. Truly there was no point; his calves were the size
of a tree trunk. All she could do was stand there and stare at him.

"My name is Andrew," he said.

"Andrew," she repeated, bewildered.

He nodded.

For a moment she wondered if there was the slightest chance her
sisters were playing a joke on her since it was Halloween, but her body
on the ground next to her assured her this was no joke.

"I…I'm Chiara," she said.

"I know," he said.

He took her hand and she gazed into his copper colored eyes, feeling stupefied. She could think of nothing but how magnificent he was.
Nothing. Zero, zip, *niente.*

"Come," he said.

He led her down a wooded winding path lined with stone paves that
she had never seen before. Confused, Chiara walked with him, looking
him up and down, taking in his Roman garb.

I have to be dreaming, she told herself. *I have to be.*

At the end of the path, the woods gave way to a view of a sunflower field that went on for as far as she could see, for infinity. Chiara gasped. She'd never seen a sunflower field so immense, not even in calendars. Every single head, each more yellow than the next, reached for the cobalt blue sky with a certain conviction, a certain regard.

She turned to Andrew, still taken with his beauty. "Andrew, what's happening? Who are you?"

He looked down at her and smiled again. "I'm your guardian angel, Chiara. I'm always with you. You just can't normally see me."

Chiara smiled. "My guardian angel? Does everybody have one?" she said, hoping the answer was yes.

Andrew smiled reassuringly, his square jaw softening.

When they got closer to the field, Chiara saw a group of people standing in a grassy area around a picnic bench near the front row of the sunflower field. They were talking and laughing and seemed to be having a great time. She squinted, trying to get a better look at the man smoking a cigarette. He looked familiar.

"Oh my God! It's Papà! Papà, Papà!" She started toward him like a racehorse out of the starting gate.

Andrew gently grasped her arm. "Later, Chiara," he said. "There is someone waiting to see you."

"I'll talk to whoever you want me to talk to, but please, please, just give me one minute with Papà. One minute. Please…"

Andrew shook his head and nudged her. "This way," he said.

She had no desire to fight with him, so she reluctantly followed him. She stopped once to touch the velvety grass beneath her, but when she saw Papà again, in the space framed between Andrew's legs, her excitement got the best of her. She ducked past Andrew and made a mad dash toward Papà and the sunflower field, screaming his name, arms flailing, hoping to get his attention before Andrew swooped down on her and carried her away.

It worked! She could hardly believe it. Papà saw her and started walking toward her.

"Chiara!" he called. He was smiling like she had just graduated from *scuola di medicina*.

"Papà! Papà!" Chiara cried, running into his arms. She was so happy to see him, she was shaking with exhilaration. She saw Andrew approaching from the corner of her eye and felt an urgency to say everything that she was thinking as fast as she could. "I miss you so much. Mamma misses you, Valerie and Sylvia miss you. Everybody misses you. She took in his green eyes, his cigarette smell. "And I'm sorry, sorry for everything, Papà. I'm sorry I broke my promise. I'm sorry I let you down."

Papà wiped tears rolling down her face. "Eh?" he said, looking confused. "You did not let me down, *cara*," he said.

"I did, Papà. I didn't keep my promise."

"Everything will be fine and you will graduate, *cara*."

"No...I'm here now, Papà. Here with you, and I don't want to go back."

His eyes looked greener than she'd ever seen them, his train-track grooves along his forehead, gone. "I did not raise you to break, *cara*," he said. I did not raise you to fail. *Forza, tesoro*. Be tough. Go back. Finish what you started."

"It's too late. I can't. It'll be too hard now."

Papà tapped his hand over his heart. "You can. Papà will always be here for you. Every time you see *girasoli*. Every time you see yellow. You must go Chiara. Now."

Andrew was now standing next to them. He stepped toward her. When he took her hand, a shot of pain gripped her body so violently it sent her reeling toward the ground. In an instant she was freefalling though a dark empty space with no ground in sight, reaching for something to slow her fall, afraid of where she was going next, of what it was going to feel like when she hit the ground this time. She heard someone scream in the darkness, "We got her!" She blinked her eyes open. A team of doctors stood over her, looking relieved, one holding EKG paddles. She breathed in the medicinal smells of the ER, heard the beeps of the monitor measuring her pulse and heartbeats.

"Come on, Chiara! Stay with us." Was that her classmate Josh?

She moaned in pain. Blinding ER lights burned her eyes, making her pray for darkness. Throbbing pain in her body made her wish for drugs.

Over the next few days she lay conscious and restless in Presby's intensive care unit going through a battery of tests on her brain. Her ER doctor told her she'd flatlined twice the day of the accident. Once in the field. Once in the hospital. He said that miraculously, the trauma to her head was minor. He explained she had a concussion and a broken tailbone, but no permanent injuries. Had he asked, she wouldn't have been able to explain what happened during those humbling moments while she was dead.

Three days later, she was moved to a regular room for observation. She felt dizzy with restlessness. She wanted out. She had things to do, patients to help, goals to achieve. Each day that passed with her on her back in the hospital was one day closer to her forever falling behind in her clerkship.

I can do this she told herself. *I can catch up. I can graduate and get through a divorce.*

First, she called Mamma and told her not to come back to the hospital without her backpack full of books. Next she called Cecilia in Florida. Cecilia didn't answer, but Chiara left her a message anyway.

She cleared her throat. "Cici? Hi, it's Chiara. I…I just wanted to call and say I'm very sorry. I'm sorry for thinking you were behind the calls. I hope someday you can forgive me." Even if Cecilia chose not to forgive her, just saying it made Chiara feel better.

After she hung up, she called Dr. Roland and asked him if, as long as she got the okay from her neurologist, she could resume her clerkship. He told her she could. By the next night, she had reviewed every one of her patients' note cards, and visited them too, albeit at a snail's pace, with her tailbone shooting pain though her body with every step she took. She made up for her slow tempo by electing to stay in the hospital for a week, moonlighting. She'd at least save on travel time. Li stopped by every night before she went home and gave her photocopies of her class notes which she studied until she fell asleep. Two weeks later, although she was still suffering with headaches, she was caught up.

The next Sunday, she woke up in her own bed and walked her sore tailbone down to the stable to see Hemi. Her injuries would keep her from riding until her neurologist gave her clearance. Still, she couldn't stay away. She spent the whole day helping around the stable.

Around two o'clock, Julio hung some bridles in the tack room for her to clean. "You want a chair?" he asked.

"I'm all right," she said, zipping up her jacket and reaching for the saddle soap.

She heard someone ask for her in the aisle and she stepped out of the tack room to see who it was.

"Hello, Chiara," Father Vincent said.

"Father Vincent? Hi, how are you?" She was shocked to see him and barely recognized him in his Steelers jersey. She was relieved he was wearing it instead of his clerical collar.

"I hope you don't mind that I stopped by," he said. "I called first and your mother said it would be fine."

Chiara smiled, thinking how Mamma would never miss out an opportunity to convert her back to Catholicism. "Yes, yes, Father, it's fine."

"I see you're limping a little. Are you hurt?"

"I had a little riding accident, but I'm fine." Chiara looked at his jersey. "Steelers game today?"

Father Vincent smiled, rubbing his hands together in anticipation for game time. "Four o'clock sharp."

"Would you like to walk up to the house and have a cup of coffee?"

Father Vincent looked down at the ground, shaking his head. "No, thank you, dear. I just wanted to stop by and tell you I heard about what happened between you and Adrian. I'm sorry, Chiara. In some way I feel responsible. I failed to see through his lie; I shouldn't have married the two of you."

Chiara could tell he was truly agonizing over this. "Father Vincent," she said, "please don't feel that way. You failed at nothing. You married us in good faith." She offered him a smile. "Would you like to go sit in the garden?"

He nodded and she led him to a concrete bench in front of the fountain. It was late in November and it was a chilly afternoon in spite of the sun shining on them. The garden looked barren now. Autumn leaves lay dry and brown around the fountain's base and over the flower beds.

"I feel so deceived," he said as he sat down. "I can only imagine what you're going through. I'm a professional at marrying people, at listening to confessions. I should have been able to spare you this heartache."

Chiara winced and eased down next to him. "Please, don't feel bad, Father. He's a really good liar."

"I can see that. But I wanted some answers, so I called him."

Chiara braced herself for more disappointing news.

"I asked him why on earth he wanted to get married when he had another woman pregnant."

Chiara forced a smile. "I've wondered the very same thing. Did he tell you?"

"He did."

Chiara looked down at the flagstone walkway, waiting for the answer.

"He said he loved you, plain and simple."

She felt the stab of a fresh wound and she sighed away the urge to reminisce over what they once had. "I believe that," she said. "But not enough...not enough."

"He said he'd like to talk to you."

"In time I'll be able to, but I can't yet," she admitted.

She looked at the three-tiered fountain of two lovers entwined in each other's arms. She had spent far too long building more faith in her romantic notions and inclinations than in herself. "I think, right now, I need to work on having some faith in myself."

Father Vincent nodded. "I can understand that."

They sat for a minute without saying anything. Finally, Father Vincent said, "Chiara, before you got married, Adrian told me about someone else who hurt you. A priest."

Chiara was shocked that Adrian had shared the story with him.

Father Vincent offered her an apologetic smile. "I guess he's not very good at keeping secrets either," he said.

Chiara looked down at the ground again, embarrassed. "I guess not."

"I want you to know that I myself had issues with God and the Church when I was a young man." He leaned forward, placing his elbows on his knees, resting his head in his hands, staring off into the empty field beyond the garden. "When I was in high school, I lost my younger sister and my parents all in one day, in a car accident."

Sorrow pierced her heart. "That's terrible, Father. I didn't know that. I'm so sorry."

"It was terrible. My parents had driven my sister to her ballet class that day. I'd carpooled with my friend's parents to football practice."

Chiara shook her head. "How did you get through it?"

"It wasn't easy. For a very long time I was angry with God for taking them from me."

She wanted to tell him she had good reason to believe it wasn't so bad on the other side, that his family was doing just fine in spite of him missing them desperately. But she was still sorting out the business of heaven and not ready to talk about it yet.

"Eventually, I found healing in the Church," he said.

Chiara listened.

He sat up straight again and waved his arms in front of him as if he was calling some sort of football violation. "Now, I know it's not perfect. And I know people can pray how they want to, when they want to, and where they want to; I believe God hears everyone's prayers."

Chiara nodded, acknowledging this.

"The Church is supposed to teach morality, responsibility, gratitude, honesty and give people a place where all are welcome to share their love of God. As a parish priest at Saint Burt's I take this very seriously. Unfortunately, there are people who believe in our Lord and still choose to be bad people." His eyes softened as he looked at her. "People like Father Bob."

Chiara let out a heavy sigh, relaxed her shoulders.

"And for that I apologize too, Chiara. I apologize for the Church's sin against you. I apologize for the way the Roman Catholic Church has let you, your family, and many other people down."

Chiara didn't know why this simple apology from Father Victor was enough to ease the pain and sense of betrayal she'd been carrying within her for so long. But somehow it was. Perhaps she felt that she had been given a second chance at life and maybe this was a sign that her faith deserved one too. Whatever the reason, it felt good and she felt free on so many levels. She leaned over and hugged him. "Thank you, Father Vincent."

On the Saturday morning after Chiara graduated, she, Mamma, Sylvia, and Valerie threw an enormous sunflower planting party at Girasole. They wanted the entire twenty-acre field behind the gazebo and outdoor riding arena sowed before dinner. Chris brought equipment and manpower from his farm. Liam invited friends and family not only to help, but also so he could announce that Valerie was twelve weeks pregnant. Naturally. While Chris, Liam, and Julio organized the work force, Chiara walked out to the field by herself. She pulled two fistfuls of sunflower seeds out of her jean pockets and held them in the palms of her hands and admired them, remembering what they meant to Papà. She thought of the day when her family sowed its first garden so many years ago. It was a sunny spring day, much like today. She lowered her head and prayed, asking for God's forgiveness for having lost her way. She prayed for every lost soul in the world, and hoped, someday, they would find their way too. Then she recited Papà's sunflower poem: *Io sono il girasole, e tu il sole. Finche il girasole gira intorno al sole, Io giraró intorno a te.*

She kissed the seeds, thanking God for her life, and those last moments she shared with Papà. Then she tossed the seeds into the air, just like Papà had done so long ago, and let them fall where they pleased.

By nightfall, not only was the garden planted, but Enzo and one of his assistant chefs from Gian Carlo's had served up a feast fit for royalty under a massive candlelit tent in the backyard.

After dinner people stayed on, listening to music and drinking. Julio and Enzo had set up a makeshift bar at the stable entrance. Julio looked like he was having a great time pretending to be an experienced bartender; he'd always wanted to bartend for fun at Gian Carlo's. Chiara sat under the gazebo with her family and some friends, nursing a glass of merlot and talking to Valerie about her pregnancy and helping her think of baby names.

When Chiara glanced up and saw Chris at the bar with Julio, she told Valerie she'd be right back and got up and walked toward the bar.

"Will you make me another Stoli raz, soda lime?" Sylvia called after her.

"Sure, if I can remember all the ingredients."

Sylvia laughed. "You're a doctor, I think you can handle it."

At the bar, Chiara touched Chris on the shoulder and he turned around.

"Hey, Chiara," he said. "You've had me so busy planting sunflowers seeds all day that we've hardly had a chance to talk."

He smelled like freshly washed bed sheets, so inviting. He must have gone home and showered before dinner.

"I know, it seems like everyone's having a great time," she said. "Thanks again for all your help. It would've taken a whole heck of a lot longer without your equipment. Anything you need for your Saint Jude's event—or anything for that matter—consider it done." She looked down at the ground. Then back into his piercing blue eyes. "And thank you again for saving my life. I'll never be able to repay you for that."

He smiled, almost looked bashful. "You're welcome," he said.

They were standing close, face to face. Chris looked down at her empty glass. "What are you drinking?"

Chiara smiled and reached for a lime to make Sylvia's drink, avoiding his eyes. "I'm drinking merlot, but I'm going to attempt a Stoli raz lime something or other for Sylvia."

Julio glanced their way, plainly thrilled to see them talking. He took Sylvia's glass from her. "I will make it."

Chris grabbed a bottle of wine and filled Chiara's glass.

She gave him a playful, suspicious smile. "Are you trying to get me tipsy?"

"You're damn right I am," he said. "I've tried everything else over the years."

They both laughed.

"Would you like to come and sit under the gazebo with me and my family?" she asked. "Sylvia has it lit up like a Christmas tree, and she's pretty proud of her electrical engineering work."

He smiled widely, revealing his white teeth. "I'd love to."

Halfway back to the gazebo, Chiara stopped and turned to him. Above them the moon was full, glowing bright, glowing yellow, highlighting their features in the cool spring night.

"Chris, thank you, again. Your help not only meant a lot to me, but to my family too."

"It was my pleasure." He paused a moment. "Chiara—aside from the few times I've called to see how you were doing after the whole thing happened last year, I've tried not to complicate your life. I know you had a lot going on with the divorce and finishing up med school. But, I just want you to know that if you ever want to just go out to blow off some steam, a few of my buddies and I still get together at JR's on the weekends. You're welcome to join us anytime."

They both let out a nervous laugh, looking away, looking back, darting tentative looks at each other.

She hesitated a moment, gazing into his face, taking in his alluring dimple and his eyes sparkling like stars in the moonlight. "Thanks, Chris. I'd like that."

He leaned toward her then and kissed her slowly and tenderly on the lips and Chiara understood the wisdom in the old adage "Good things come to those who wait." *Wow.*

"Yee-haw!" someone yelled from somewhere near the gazebo. Chiara and Chris looked toward the gazebo where her friends and family were laughing and carrying on like kids. Chiara looked beyond them and the riding arena to the freshly sowed field. The full moon floated high in the clear night sky, illuminating the field like an enormous stage. In a few short months, the empty field would be crowded with gargantuan sunflowers, stretching their yellow heads toward the sky.

She smiled at Chris as they walked toward the gazebo. "It's going to be beautiful when it matures," she said. "Papà would be proud of it."

"He'd be proud of you," Chris said.

Chiara knew he was. She knew too now that in spite of her troubles, she was exactly where she was supposed to be in life. She got to peak through a window into heaven, make amends with Papà, keep her promise.

I used to think there was a perfect recipe one had to follow to be a person of faith. I now know this is untrue. Faith is a funny thing. It's a feeling. A feeling that sometimes questions, sometimes doubts, but in the end, always knows. Perhaps God exists exactly as we envision Him in our hearts or in our dreams. Perhaps He exists only in the synchronous events that shape us into who we are. Perhaps He simply exists in the circadian rhythm of the sun and the moon or in the heliotropism of the sunflower as it follows the sun from east to west. The point is, He exists.

He made man, math, nature, science, and spirit, a perfect amalgam. Perhaps Papà had been right. Perhaps the golden ratio and the Fibonacci pattern are the supreme link among them all.

Chris gave her a quizzical look. "You never liked the garden when we were kids. Why did you want to plant it again after all these years? And why so big? It's so much larger than the one your father used to plant."

She looked out toward the field again. "It's for Papà. Papà loved sunflowers. Papà loved yellow."